# The Mysteries and

CW01064590

# San Franci....

Showing up all the various characters and notabilities,

(both in high and low life) that have figured in San

Franciso since its settlement.

A Californian

Alpha Editions

This edition published in 2024

ISBN : 9789361474538

Design and Setting By
**Alpha Editions**
www.alphaedis.com
Email - info@alphaedis.com

# Contents

# CHAPTER I

## The Alarm—The Flames—The Ladder.

San Francisco, on the marge of the sea, with towering hills behind her, lay basking in the sun like a serpent by the side of a rock.

The dwellings of the more fortunate classes loomed pleasantly on the side of the large round hills in the distance, and might with the aid of a little fancy, have been metamorphosed into the castellated domains of the feudal barons whose reign succeeded that of absolute barbarism in Europe. Those quiet dwellings amid the solitude of nature, present a vivid contrast to the stirring scenes of the town below, and accordingly all who possess taste and the means of gratifying it, rear a building among the hills to which they can retire, after the fatigues of the day, and solace themselves with the comforts of domestic retiracy, and the grand simplicity of nature.

In giving a *coup d'œil* at the scene, from the city itself, one is struck by the pointed roof rising above a range of hills which lie to the south west of the noble harbor, and which crowns a dark pile that, on a nearer approach, seems to lean against the side of a mountain upon whose peak linger the last beams of the setting sun. This extensive edifice is the dwelling or homestead of the wealthy and far-famed Senor de Castro, an old resident of the country, and one of the proudest of the ancient lords of the soil. His horses are the best, his table the most sumptuous, and his servants the most numerous of any ranchero in the regions round about California.

It was early on one afternoon in June, 18—, that several young men, mostly Americans, were conversing around a table in one of the principle Cafes in the young city of San Francisco; a stout robust man nearly forty years of age, and dressed partly in the English style and partly in that of the country, with leggings and heavy blunt spurs, and a red sash about his middle, was discussing the merit of the auguadent sold in Santiago, a city of Chile, and having become very eloquent on this important topic, he set down his glass upon the table so violently as to shatter it to atoms.

'Give me your good old-fashioned horn tumbler,' cried he, with an oath, 'and leave these baby-toys to the women and children!'

'You like to take your liquor in a horn?' said a young American clerk to a provision dealer, 'now I prefer a glass, if it were only for the cleanliness of the thing,

Yes, by the mass!

Give me a glass

To toast a lass,

In horns should never be,

Remembered when

We married men

Quaff denty or chee chee.'

'You married men!' exclaimed the stouter disputant, laughing.

'A marriage extempore,' muttered a saturnine young American, with an enormous head of black hair. 'When are you going to send that little girl back to her mother?'

'Silence, Pothook!' cried the other, 'you know that you would have given all the old shoes in your locker to have got one smile from her, yourself—'

'Yes, envious Pothook,' cried another youth, whose accent betrayed the Cockney, 'if Cardwell has a notion to settle down in the calm of domestic life, and—'

'Settle! Ten thousand blunderbusses!' laughed the stout man, 'When did you ever know Cardwell to settle anything but his grog bills—them's the settlements he is most accustomed to.'

'But I mean,' added the Cockney; 'that he is not running around after every pretty face like—like some people, always excepting the present honorable company, as a matter of course.'

'Oh! of course!' said Pothook feelingly.

'Yet,' remarked a tall, pale young man, who seemed to have recovered from some dangerous illness—'Yet, let me tell you that Cardwell is not so innocent after all, as he seems to be. I saw him, the other day, stand for half an hour, looking up at a certain house in Clay street with all the eyes in his head, and meaning no offence to the gentleman, I don't by any manner of means dispute his taste.'

'Oh! the young villain!' cried the stout man, roaring with laughter.

In the midst of his jollity and noisy vociferations, a young fellow from 'the States' who had been silent until then, demurely asked—'Do any of you know what is good for rats?'

This made the stout man laugh still louder—'You had better inquire what is *bad* for rats,' said he at length; 'for to judge by their sleek hides and plump bellies, I should think they had already had enough that was good and wholesome—perdition catch the born devils! Last night, about an hour before morning—' the speaker stopped, as the sound of a bell rang violently, and the cry of 'fire' at once arose in the streets.

'Never mind, go on!' said the Cockney.

'Never mind the bell,' said Cardwell. 'We can't be disturbed in our pleasures by these domestic affairs.'

'Why, by the noise,' said the stout man, 'it would appear that there was a polite invitation given to all citizens that their presence might be required in the adjoining streets, and as the wind is coming up fresh—'

'There is no time to be lost, my good fellows!' cried a tall, elegantly formed youth, rushing into the apartment from an adjoining room. 'Half the city is in flames!'

So saying, the youth hastened away, followed by the revellers.

The whole town was in an uproar. As they gained the street, they were met by the strong sea breeze that filled the air with dust, and betokened no good to those whose property was at that moment encircled by the flames.

The Sansome Truck Company, with their hooks and ladders, were rushing by, their scarlet coats powdered with dust, and making the welkin ring with their shouts. The elegant youth of whom we have spoken was one of the first that reached the fire. Already was the house of Senor del Castro completely enveloped by sheets of flame, and from the windows of some of the adjoining buildings the streams of fire darted forth, and moved swiftly off toward the South on the wings of the gale.

Several persons, among whom were Cardwell, and the stout man of the cafe, busied themselves in tearing up the planks in the immediate vicinity of the conflagration, for the streets being laid down with plank, instead of stones, aid greatly in the spread of the flames. The firemen had brought streams of water to bear on the principal building, when suddenly there appeared at an upper window, a fair and youthful female form, evidently belonging to one of the higher classes of the country, whose dark hair fell in rich masses about her shoulders, and partly concealed a face in which the snow and the rose contended for mastery.

For an instant every one paused in astonishment, nor was her overmastering beauty unheeded in that moment of fearful excitement; for the cry that a woman was in the house now rose shrilly on the air, and was echoed in every street in the city. The ladders were hurried to the spot by men frantic in their haste to save so fair a specimen of mortality from a dreadful death, while the object of all this interest, the lovely cause of the wild confusion that pervaded the masses below, simply placed one little white hand to her eyes as if to shut out the sight of the surrounding horrors, and steadied herself with the other by placing it on the sill of the window.

In the moment that the ladder was placed against the side of the house, a shrill cry was heard in the rear of the firemen, and a stately form was seen forcing itself through the throng with giant strides, and thrusting aside everybody and everything which opposed its progress. One glance was sufficient to convince the spectators that the father of the imperilled girl was rushing to her rescue. His hat was gone, and his dark but silvered locks floated on the breeze, the sweat stood in beads upon his broad forehead, and his face, though bearded and mustachioed according to the custom of the country, was pale with anxiety and horror.

'Oh, for the love of God!' cried he, 'my daughter! my daughter!'

As he reached the front of the building, the flames gushing from the lower windows drove back the brave men who had charge of the ladder. The Senor del Castro clasped his hands, and uttering a cry of despair, would have rushed into the house, the lower part of which was completely filled with flames. The stout man of the cafe threw himself upon the distracted father, and by the timely aid of Cardwell and the Cockney, succeeded in dragging him out of the reach of danger. But the fire companies had not been idle while these events were transpiring. They had brought the ladder to the building at another place. They had placed it firmly against the side of the house, when a man, addressing an officer of the Fire Department, exclaimed in a tone of despair, 'Oh, my God! Charley, the ladder is too short. It don't reach anywhere near the window!'

Quicker than thought, Charley placed himself in front of the window at which the girl stood, and bade them place the feet of the ladder on his shoulders. In an instant, this was done, one foot of the ladder resting on each of his shoulders. The elegant youth of the cafe then sprang forward—

'That's right, Monteagle,' cried Charley, 'climb right up by me and then on the ladder; bring down the young lady or never live to tell of your failure.'

But before these words had been fairly uttered, the daring youth was half way up the ladder. All eyes were now fixed on the adventurer. For a moment all seemed silent except the hysteric wailings of the anguished father, and the awful roaring of the flames, as the wind swept through every aperture of the building, and added ten-fold to the fury of the conflagration.

Before Monteagle had reached the lower sill of the window, he was discovered to on fire; but at almost the same instant, a stream of water from the pipe of an engine drenched him to the skin. Then both the youth and the girl were entirely hidden from view by the rolling forth of a dense volume of smoke streaked with flame. One cry—one general cry of despair burst from the throng below, and the Senor, not doubting that both his daughter and her deliverer had perished, gave a deep groan and sunk senseless to the earth. But loud rose the voice of Charley upon the air at the awful crisis—'They are alive yet! Don't be frightened, man, I feel the weight of both of them on my shoulders, now—now—the ladder shakes! they are coming down!'

Several men with large *ponchos* were crowded around the bottom of the ladder to smother the flames, in case the young lady should be on fire, by wrapping her tightly in these ample garments, and they looked up on hearing the cheerful exclamations of Charley. The feet and legs of a man were discerned below the smoke that had enveloped the upper part of the ladder, then the bottom of a lady's robe, and finally the face of Monteagle begrimed and blistered looked down upon the trembling expectants. The head of the girl reclined on the shoulder of the gallant youth, her black hair flowing down his back, while her arms hung listless by his sides—she was in a state of insensibility.

As soon as Monteagle and his lovely burthen were within reach of the multitude a dozen hands grasped them, and while the friends of the youth bore him off on their shoulders to administer such healing remedies as his case required, for a part of his hair—his heavy brown locks—was burnt off, and a blister on his forehead showed too plainly that a moment longer would have consigned both the young lady and her deliverer to the realm from which no returning spirit has come back to describe the final parting of the soul from its material envelope.

The girl herself was carried to the arms of her father, who, just awaking from his swoon, cried in a gasping voice 'Inez! Inez! where is my Inez?' and plucking a sharp-pointed dagger from his breast, he was about to end his agony by thrusting it to the hilt in his heart. Quicker than lightning, the man who was called Charley grasped the wrist of the desperate man, and holding it like a vice in his stalwart grasp, pointed with the other hand to the girl, and said in his rough masculine voice:

'None of that! If I'd thought you would take it so hard that we had saved your daughter's life, but we would have—no, not that exactly, for she's worth saving on her own account!'

While Charley was delivering this speech, the cinders were raining down on his head, and he shook them off as a lion would have shaken great flies from his forehead, but others were not so insensible to a shower of fire-brands, and the Senor was dragged farther from the scene of ruin.

When the Senor perceived that his Inez was really by his side, he gave vent to the most extravagant exclamations of joy. Rushing to the Chief Engineer, whom he supposed to be the savior of his child, he clasped the sturdy fireman in his arms, called him every name that is flattering to the pride of man, emptied his pockets of all his gold, and tried to force into his hands a precious ring that he wore on his finger, and which was said to contain a diamond of great value. Charley said that his duty called him elsewhere, and we next saw him plunging into the thickest of the throng to bring up his forces to the principal point of attack, and to expedite the tearing up of the planks on the street, for they had become thoroughly ignited in some places, and the flames were marching through the slight wooden buildings of the town with the imperious step of a conqueror.

No sooner had the young lady recovered consciousness, than she raised herself to her feet, and looked anxiously on every side as if in search of some object which she could not find.

'Here comes your father,' said Cardwell, who had been the most officious in bearing off the girl to a place of safety, and applying cold water and other restoratives to her face and temples.

Inez took the hand of her father, but still her eyes wandered through the throng as if seeking another, and while she was led away by the old Senor, she walked listlessly and thoughtfully, as if something pressed heavily upon her mind.

By this time every gambling-house, every drinking shop, every pulperie, and every thieving den had poured out its crowds upon the streets of San Francisco, and a vast proportion of the inhabitants of the city were thronging around the scene of conflagration. Here was a gang of thieves, pretending to be very officious in removing the goods from a store-house that had just kindled, while the eager glancing of their eyes, and the half-shy, half-brazen way they shouted to each other, by way of encouragement to preserve and to hasten the work, sufficiently denoted that they had come to purloin whenever an opportunity offered, and that their zeal was merely intended to blind the eyes of others, and lull suspicion in regard to their ulterior purposes; and it would seem that no lack of opportunity was here, for such was the excitement, such was the confusion, the tumbling of men upon others, the running hither and thither, the cries of alarm and distress, the shriek of the wind, and the roaring of the flames as they went leaping, darting, and whirling from house to house, from corner to corner, and from street to street, that the cautious thief whose heart was marbled against human sufferings, and thought only of turning the disasters of others to his own advantage, might carry on his nefarious trade with almost as much impunity as that of the burrowing mole, who treasures his stolen grain under the earth while the plain above is rent by the tempest's fury.

Yet, even in the general whirl of reason and reflection attendant upon these rapid conflagrations, there sometimes chances to be an eye unengaged for a moment which may light upon the plunderer in the very nick of time, and when least expected by himself. Such was the case now, just as the flames had reached Montgomery street, and were reaching forth their long red tongues towards the pile of stores on Jackson street, the Cockney mentioned at the commencement of this narrative saw a fellow hugging to his bosom a little iron safe, and stealthily escaping under cover of the smoke, along the street towards the harbor.

He raised the cry of '*Stop thief! Picaroon! Coquin!*' and in as many other languages as he could bring to his aid, he gave the alarm to such individuals as were within the reach of his voice. The merchants themselves who were near the spot, joined in the chase, and in less than two minutes more than a hundred persons were at the heels of the man with the safe. He headed directly for the water, and had nearly reached it, when a couple of Chinamen in blue nankeens threw themselves across his path. The desperate wretch dashed the iron safe into the face of one of them, still retaining hold of it, however, and he fell covered with blood, and then, with one hand, the thief grasped the long cue of the other and jerked him to the ground. He then darted forward again, leaving the two disastered Fee-fo-fums sitting upright in the middle of the street, and uttering the most doleful lamentations. Amain the crowd came sweeping down to the water's edge, tumbling the two Chinamen over and over, who cried out most piteously while rolling in the dust under the feet of the pursuers. The thief perceiving no way of escape on the land, sprang into a skiff and pushed off from the shore. For a moment, his foes stood panting on the shore like baffled tigers, eyeing the man as with two small oars he ploughed through the waves and receded farther and farther from the strand. At length a loud hail was heard from a point farther down, some three hundred yards from the spot where the pursuers were clustered, and on turning their eyes in that direction, the crowd beheld a slender but well-formed youth tugging at a heavy boat, which lay partly on the shore and partly in the water, and vainly endeavoring to get it afloat.

With a yell that rang on the air like the onset cry of a troop of wild Indians, the whole body of pursuers ran towards the boat.

'Hah! Monteagle, is that you?' cried our Cockney, who arrived first at the spot—'It was I who gave the alarm! How much is there in the safe?' 'That is best known to my employers,' returned Monteagle evasively, 'enough, you may be sure, to warrant the most vigorous endeavors in getting it into our hands. Those who take the thief will be well rewarded.'

'Come then! heave O! heave, ahoi!' cried three or four lusty fellows who had now come up, and applied their shoulders to the boat in good earnest. It began to move, and as it finally slid roaring into the waves, Monteagle, and a dozen others leaped on board. A few strokes of their long oars cleared them from the beach and gave free play to their motions as they sunk the blades of their oars deep into the brine, and threw themselves far back at every stroke; a movement which to the practised eye of the mariner at once announced that whatever experience they might previously have had in this line, was not in the service of the nation, but had been acquired in the pursuit of that marvellous fish which swallowed Jonah.

The winds were unusually violent that afternoon, and the water was very rough. This circumstance was much in favor of the large boat, and although the robber was a powerful man, and exerted his utmost, yet his pursuers continually gained upon him. He was obliged to stop a few moments to bail out his skiff, using one of his boots for that purpose; and this fact at once convinced Monteagle and his men that he labored under great disadvantages in a sharp, combing sea such as was then driving into the harbor before the screaming gale. The thief himself seemed to give up all hope of escape and relaxed his efforts, no doubt husbanding his strength for exertions of a different character.

'Now, my brave fellows,' cried Monteagle, 'lay back and give it to her! do your prettiest and you can make the old barge hum, and we'll soon come up with that picaroon yonder; and understand that I am authorized to promise a high reward.'

'Oh, never mind the reward,' interrupted a stout Irishman, magnanimously. 'It's for the pure honor of the thing that we are working, sure, and to support the laws.'

'Yes, to support the laws!' cried a short, stout, red-faced fellow, of such equivocal appearance, that one might have taken him for a beardless youth or a man of sixty years, for a native or a foreigner, a cunning knave or a natural fool. He carried an enormous head on his broad round shoulders, upon which were only a few scattering hemp-like hairs, but his cheeks were fat and smooth, and his eyes always seemed ready to roll out of their sockets.

'Yes, to support the laws!' said the strange being, in a smothered tone that seemed to proceed from the bottom of the abdomen, while his heavy goggle eyes seemed to be thinking of something altogether foreign from the subject, and the continual working of his enormous mouth led Monteagle to say to himself that the fellow was 'chewing the cud of sweet and bitter fancy.'

But now they were within two oars' length of the villain in the skiff, when the latter ceased rowing, and starting upon his feet, brandished one of his oars in the air as if it had been the mace of an ancient knight, and shrieked out in a tone of fury, that he 'would dash in the skull of any man that laid a flipper on him!'

As Monteagle stood up in the head of the boat, this threat might be considered a matter more directly appertaining to himself than to any other person present. Yet, every one uttered a shout of defiance, and half a dozen strokes brought the barge up to the skiff. The head of the large boat struck the skiff a-midships, square off and on, and for an instant it seemed as if the latter would have turned bottom up. The thief, however, balanced his boat well, at the same instant that he struck a terrible blow with his oar at the head of Monteagle. The youth evaded the falling oar, by jumping dexterously aside and, at the same moment, drew a pistol from his breast. Before he could fire, he was surprised by a powerful blow on the side of his head which came from behind. Turning his head, he saw the big Irishman who had so gallantly disclaimed all interested motives, with both fists double and ready to repeat the blow which had nearly deprived him of recollection. This, however, lasted but an instant, for all was confusion now. The Irishman was choked down by an English cooper; the man with the big head and wide mouth came to the aid of the Irishman, while the robber in the skiff dashed his oar into the faces and brought it down lustily on the heads and backs of his adversaries in the barge.

The diversion which had been made in favor of the robber, plainly announced that the Irishman and the big head were accomplices of the former, and had entered the barge and joined the pursuit in order to render him efficient aid in time of need.

The fight became general. Big Head and the Irishman fully engaged the attention of Monteagle and two men of the barge's crew, while the robber, determined not to be taken alive, fought with a desperation not to be imagined by any who have never seen a man resolved upon death or escape.

'Blast me!' cried the Cockney, 'but these Sydney ducks are hatched out in the wrong nest,' as he received a kick in the face from Big Head while the latter was struggling under a thwart and using both hands and feet to defend himself against the loyal portion of the barge's crew. This melee had lasted some time, during which the pistol of Monteagle had passed into the hands of the big Irishman, who falling a second time from the effects of a chance blow dealt by his accomplice in the skiff, pointed the weapon at Monteagle as he fell, and pulled the trigger. The charge took effect on the youth; everything grew suddenly dark around him, and he fell senseless into the bottom of the boat. The battle, however, was still waged with relentless fury on both sides. The robber, cheered by the hope of final victory, now sprang from his skiff into the barge, and stamping on the head of Monteagle as he lay insensible under the thwarts, he used his oar, now broken into a convenient shape and size, about the heads of his enemies. To say that blood flowed, would be nothing new, as there was scarcely a man in the boat who had not received a wound already; but now heads and arms were broken; sometimes Big Head and the Irishman were both down at a time, and then victory seemed certain to the loyal party; then the former would be up again and fighting desperately. But three men against eight or nine could not hold out forever, and the big Irishman, at length, reeled and sank, overcome by fatigue and loss of blood. Big Head was then silenced by a rap on the skull with a tiller, and after a most desperate resistance, the robber himself was bound hand and foot.

The crew then sat down to take breath, and next proceeded to wash the blood from their faces. On their way to the shore they were met by another boat that had put off to their assistance, and in her was recognized Mr. Vandewater, one of the firm that had been robbed.

'Where's Monteagle?' was the first inquiry of this gentleman as the two boats met.

The boat's crew started and looked about them, discovered the youth lying senseless in the bottom of the boat. Smarting under their own wounds, and hot with the late contest, they had entirely forgotten the lad who led the charge. 'Oh!' said the Cockney, binding a handkerchief about his scarred head, 'I had like to have forgotten him, sir. It was he that first got hold of the barge—I was the one that saw the thief take the safe—I gave the first alarm, sir.'

Mr. Vandewater by this time held the head of young Monteagle on his knee, and was examining into his condition, but, looking up a moment, he replied to the Cockney,

'And the safe, where is it?'

'There, now,' ejaculated the robber as he wiped the bloody foam from his mouth against his shoulder, 'what a fool I was that I didn't cast the d— thing into the drink, God! they'll get it.'

Mr. Vandewater assisted in removing Monteagle to the other boat, and telling the men in the barge to call in the morning at his house, he told the rowers in his own yawl to pull for the skiff. The little bark was soon reached, and the safe was found in its bottom. Mr. Vandewater took possession of his property, and returned speedily to the shore with Monteagle, whose situation, if he were indeed alive, required immediate attention.

When the barge reached the landing, there was no lack of welcomers on the beach, for the latter part of the battle in the boat had been observed by many spectators. The robber, who had escaped injury better than could have been expected, was handed out of the barge amid the shouts of the populace, and taken possession of by the police; but, strange as it may seem, the Irishman and Big Head were suffered to go among their friends; perhaps it was judged by their appearance that they had suffered punishment enough already.

The devastations of the fire had been wide and fearful. In an incredible short time, a large portion of the city had been laid in ruins.—Houses and streets had suffered alike, the planking of the thoroughfares rendering them equally combustible with the buildings.

On the day succeeding these events, a pale youth, with a bandage about his temples, lay in a darkened room some two miles from the town of San Francisco, seeming to be asleep; and yet the almost marble whiteness of the features might have led a casual spectator to suppose that the coroner was required in his case, rather than the surgeon. The bed upon which he lay, as well as the chaste elegance of the furniture about the apartment, betokened that the master of the mansion had eminently been successful in the general struggle for wealth, and also that he possessed a liberal taste which enabled him to employ his means for the embellishment as well as for the support of life. The windows of the chamber looked out upon an extensive garden, nicely arranged and kept, and romantically varied with rocks and underwood of natural growth. The house itself was an elegant edifice standing on a hillside, and commanding a fine view of the surrounding country.

# CHAPTER II

## The Breaking Heart—A Scene of Tenderness and Despair.

The pale slumberer lay perfectly still, and a close observer could scarcely have perceived that he breathed. Thus had he lain a few moments, when a side door slowly opened, and a fair feminine countenance, a perfect blonde, surmounted with a profusion of flaxen ringlets, was thrust gently into the apartment. Then the door opened wider, and the symmetrical form of a young girl of seventeen years stood in the aperture. She listened a moment, and then advanced one tiny foot into the chamber; then the other; and finally she stood within the apartment, but with the door left open behind her. There stood the beautiful sylph trembling and pale, and sometimes looking back, as if hesitating whether to proceed or return. At length she stept lightly forward and fixed her eyes upon the countenance of the slumberer. She instantly clasped her hands across her bosom, raised her large blue eyes to heaven, and an expression of deep agony rested on those sunny features, like a heavy thunder cloud passing over a beauteous landscape in midsummer.

Her timidity seemed to have fled with the first glance that she had bestowed upon the invalid. Turning her back towards him, she even murmured aloud, 'And all this he has suffered for the preservation of my uncle's property. Oh! why could he not have delegated that duty to others more fitted for such rude work? Already had he performed a deed sufficient to gild his name with perpetual glory—in saving an accomplished—an—an—in saving human life; for it matters not who she was. To save a life is enough, and at the risk of his own.'

She turned and looked once more at the sleeping youth; again she pressed her hands against her heart, and, this time, she sighed deeply. A footstep was heard in the passage way, approaching the door that opened into the hall, and gliding through the one at which she had entered, the young girl had retired, just as two other individuals entered the sick chamber. One of those who now approached the couch of the invalid was a tall, slender, middle-aged man, elegantly attired, and yet with a sort of graceful negligence which drew the attention of the observer rather to the manners and bearing of the gentleman himself, than to the garb in which he was arrayed.

The other gentleman wore a plain suit of black, was of middling height, with light hair and eyes, and probably thirty years of age.

'Yes, doctor,' said the latter gentleman, as they entered the room. 'It is as I tell you.'

'But, sir,' returned the other, 'recollect the acquaintantship—female timidity and the gentleness of the sex's nature. To see one whom she had so long known dangerously wounded, brought suddenly into the house, with a mind unprepared; remember all the attendant circumstances, Mr. Vandewater, and you will not be astonished that the poor girl exhibited symptoms of agitation.'

'Oh, yes, yes, my dear sir. Otherwise she would not be woman,' replied the merchant. 'Agitation, sympathy, pity, all these were to be expected. But, sir, she would have been frank in the expression of her sympathy if all had been well. Instead of that, she strove to hide her concern. She became as pale as chalk—as white as milk, sir; and moved off without uttering a syllable, or making the least inquiry, and if my wife had not followed her and supported her to her chamber, she would have fell lifeless to the floor.'

'His pulse is better,' said the doctor, whose thoughts now ran in the line of his profession, and who had taken the youth by the wrist. 'He will escape a fever—it was that I dreaded.'

'And then her aunt has remarked her deportment while in the presence of the young man.'

'A fine constitution, sir. You must not throw him away—don't give him up yet. I think he will be restored to you, after all.'

'She is the daughter of a beloved brother, whose death, some ten years ago, occasioned me the most poignant distress, and I shall take care of her as if she was my own child.'

'You must not let him be disturbed, sir, and I will leave something to be administered to him as soon as he wakes.'

'I don't think you heard my last observation, sir.'

'Oh, yes—I heard, sir. You remarked that she was the daughter of your esteemed brother: but, pray, sir, if the young people love one another?—'

'You don't understand me, sir,' was the quick *coup de parole* of the merchant. 'I did not say that the young people loved each other.'

'Ah! now I understand,' said the surgeon, looking really concerned. 'I see—you wish to preserve your niece's happiness, not to prevent it!'

'Exactly, sir. There is not a man in the world to whom I would sooner marry my niece, than to him who lies before you. Of unquestioned integrity, candid, honorable, devoted to my interests, of elegant manners, without being effeminate, humane as he is brave, well educated, and of respectable parentage. I find no fault in Lorenzo Monteagle—none at all, sir. But my niece shall be forced upon no man, sir. The king's son is not good enough for her, when it comes to that.'

'But will he not, in time, admire Miss Julia, sir. It appears to me, that if I were a bachelor—'

'You shouldn't have her if you were, sir—'interrupted Vandewater with a burst of laughter that made the wounded man start in his sleep, 'would I have a son-in-law or a nephew-in-law, think you, that carries about with him such awful weapons—those horrible saws, gimlets, I know not what you call them, I should never feel sure of my legs and arms one moment, while he was in the house—ha! ha! ha!'

'However that may be,' said the other, 'if I were a young swain like your paragon here, I should deem my self but too happy to try to win a smile from that fair niece of yours, and if you are really willing that the match should take place—'

'It will never be,' returned the merchant, gravely interrupting the surgeon— 'Monteagle is very fastidious, even in his friendship. He is a singular young man. It must be a particular woman that strikes his fancy, possessed of decided qualities; none of your pretty faces and piano songs will steal away his heart. Of that I am too well assured. More than one young lady has tried her utmost skill—'

'But has the man no heart?'

'So decidedly one that it must have a decided choice,' cried the merchant, 'before it can consent to own itself the property of another. He likes the society of ladies; but he does not prefer one to another. I am persuaded that he has never seen the woman he can love. He has known Julia more than two years, and has never treated her differently from other women. But it matters not. So you think the young man is fairly out of danger?'

'It might be going too far to say so, sir—but I think he will recover. I would not be afraid to stake a hundred ounces on the event.'

'Glad to hear that. I don't doubt your skill, Doctor, so let us walk below and finish that old Madeira before it gets any sourer.'

After another brief examination of his patient, the surgeon followed Mr. Vandewater down stairs; and in half an hour afterwards might have been seen mounting his horse and winding over the hills and through the valleys towards the town of San Francisco.

Several days had passed since the occurrence of the events mentioned above, when on a fair morning, a pale youth sat in a recess at the bottom of the merchant's garden. A staff stood by his side, an evidence that he was not yet able to walk without support, and his white attenuated hands were pressed together in his lap, while his large blue eyes, which looked nearly black when contrasted with his white brow, were fixed upon some object in the distance.

His gaze rested on the dwelling place of Senor del Castro; but what were his reflections, we cannot pretend to divine; nor was he long permitted to indulge them without interruption.

From behind a cluster of bushes near, sailed out a figure in a white dress, which floating gently towards the invalid, placed one hand upon his arm, and caused him to turn suddenly towards her.

'Mr. Monteagle, I'm glad to see you abroad once more. Oh! it looks so much more natural to see you up and stirring, that it really reminds me of old times.'

With a smile slightly sarcastic, the youth replied—'I am but too happy to be the cause of reviving pleasant reminiscences in the mind of Miss Vandewater.'

A deep blush passed over the cheek and brow of the fair girl as she replied: 'You are very severe, sir. I will say then, in downright English, since I must, that I am rejoiced to see you improved in health, with a fair chance of recovery. Now, Mr. Critic, are you satisfied?'

'Oh! no doubt I ought to be, since Miss Vandewater has used the commonly approved phrase which custom has made necessary for all like occasions.'

'Nay, then I will send Inez del Castro to you: no doubt she will do the honors of the occasion better—at least her mode will be more *original* than mine.'

Miss Vandewater uttered the latter part of the sentence in a quick, hurried manner, and in spite of herself, delivered the word 'original' in a tone of considerable bitterness. The tears rose to her eyes, and she blushed deeper than ever. It was plain that she would have given much to recall her words and manner; but it was too late. The youth looked down and sighed.

The young lady heard that sigh, and it seemed to restore her to all her dignity. She lifted her head and shook back the flaxen curls from her snowy brow. 'I know that you are not acquainted with Inez, though she—fainted in your arms! It was very romantic.'

Monteagle had great self-possession; but he was obliged to turn his face partly aside to conceal an expression of surprise and sorrow at the broad raillery into which the young lady suffered herself to be betrayed by feelings too palpable to be mistaken. The many instances in which she had evinced jealousy of any attention showed by Monteagle to other ladies, had long since let him into the secret—if secret it could be called.

'Miss Vandewater,' said he, at length, 'I have seen the daughter of Senor del Castro but twice in my life, and have spoken to her, but on one occasion. When I stood at the top of the ladder enveloped in flame, I asked her to trust herself in my arms, and without betraying any affected delicacy, yet with great feminine dignity she placed her foot on the ladder and reclined upon my shoulder.'

'And did she say nothing?'

"She said, 'thanks, thanks, generous American—my father will bless your name at the altar of his God!' It was all she said, and the next moment the smoke stifled her, and she became insensible on my bosom."

'And, oh! Monteagle!' cried Miss Vandewater, clasping her hands and looking upwards, 'we heard that you were nearly perishing in the flames!'

As she uttered these words, the tears gushed from her eyes, and throwing herself upon a rock near the feet of the invalid, she covered her face with her hands and wept aloud at the recollection of that bitter moment.

'Ungrateful wretch that I am, how unworthy of this more than sisterly interest which she takes in my welfare!' said Monteagle to himself, and placing one of his hands upon the head of the unhappy girl, he said—'Oh! it was not so bad as that a stream of water soon removed all inconveniences, and a very trifling burn was all that I suffered.'

The girl looked up, seized the hand that had been extended to her, kissed it vehemently, and fled, blushing, to the house of her uncle.

'If the sacrifice of my life could make her happy!' ejaculated Monteagle, brushing the tears from his eyes which he could no longer restrain.

# CHAPTER III

## The Dance House—The Bella Union—The Last Stake!

The night was dark in San Francisco—that city far away on the confines of the Pacific. And far other scenes and other deeds are witnessed there than it ever entered into the imagination of the dwellers on the Atlantic sea-board to conceive of. Description is at fault; words cannot paint the mingled web, and fancy has no colors sufficiently vivid to depict the peculiar state of society in the newly-risen metropolis of California. Naturalists describe the state of the world long before man became a dweller upon the earth, and the fossils which they procure tell of strange animals that once existed here unlike anything which the world now presents.

In Pacific street—named after the ocean that rolls her floods to the very doors of the Californian traders—there are several houses in which congregate the lower class of ruffians and pleasure-seekers, where the tamborene and fiddle are seldom allowed to rest, where the merry dance is kept up the live-long night by men of all nations, all complexions, and all professions. Here may be seen the Lascar, the Mulatto, the Chilean, the Brazilian negro, the Nantucket whaleman, the escaped convict from Botany Bay, the red-faced Englishman, the native of the soil, the Mexican; and every other class and nation is here represented. Men of standing, wealthy people here flock promiscuously with the lowest classes of all countries.

It was in one of these dance halls, where the usual throng was engaged in beating the floor with their feet to the tune of the most simple instruments of music. Now a tall smooth fellow of jet blackness asked a light-haired Yankee to touch glasses with him, while a little infirm man in a blue nankeen jacket, who had once been the mate of a ship, could find nothing better than to explain to a Chinese sailor, in one corner, the way in which a Turk's head-knot was made upon a rope. But for the most part, boisterous mirth prevailed, some danced as if they had been bitten by a tarantula, while others roared out snatches from such songs as ears polite are not often saluted with.

Whatever was done was thoroughly done, done with a vengeance, without restraint and without fear of disturbing the neighbors.

On the night which we have mentioned, the noise and confusion was unusually great, the throng was more numerous than common from the fact that one watch was on shore from a whaleship in the harbor, and they had all blundered into this hall to drink and be merry.

'Keep it up!' cried one long-legged, broad-shouldered fellow, throwing up one of his feet to the very wall and then dancing with a violence that threatened to bring down the roof about his ears.

'He's a boatsteerer,' said one of the ship boys—'he's great at striking a whale,' and he gazed with admiration on this specimen of Nantucket enterprise.

'Keep it up!' shouted the boatsteerer making his long legs fly about the room as if he was under the influence of a galvanic battery.

'Keep it up!' screamed he again, as he caught a short Englishman by the arm and tried to inspire him with a portion of his own enthusiasm.

'Yes, yes,' said the Englishman, biting off the end of a tobacco plug, and walking off to the other side of the room to get out of the wind of those formidable legs.

'Keep it up!' bawled the boatsteerer to a couple of Irishmen who happened to enter at the moment; and so it appeared that the sum and substance of all that was in this man's cranium could be expressed in those simple words 'Keep it up,' a phrase that he continued to utter periodically throughout the entire evening.

But neither the Englishman nor the two Irishmen obeyed the summons on this occasion. They had 'kept it up' too often and too long to be peculiarly enthusiastic at the sound of a fiddle. The two latter especially seemed to have other matter in hand, and seating themselves upon one corner of a bench near the door, they thus exchanged thoughts in a sotto voice which, in the uproar that prevailed, was completely inaudible to any but themselves.

'Have you aver seed him since then?' was the question propounded by the shorter of the two.

'Faith! and only once, and then I drawed a trigger on him from behind the bush, Patrick, but a lump of a gal com'd out and stood in the way, or I'd kilt him at wunst; but there was no use of getting up a yell from the gal that wud have brought all the payple in the house about my ears.'

'An' I b'lieve you are right, Jamie, for them Vigilance Committees is kaping a bright look-out, now, for the like o'that; and I seed one of 'em up in the Boomerang jist when I was cooming down—'

'Ay, faith, Patrick, and it's on account of Montgomery that they're shying around this way, I'm thinking; but they will look a great while before they—'

'Ah! hush jist now! don't name it, for yees don't know what ears is open, if you was only to spake of the sand hills—'

'Hush, noo, Patrick! would ye be after revaling it all, and we sworn on the howly 'vangellers too?'

'But as for the Monteagle there, Jamie, there must something be done, for Montgomery swears he'll have his life, for the taking the safe from him, the bloody robber!'

'Faith, boy, make yourself parfectly easy, then, for there's another way to kill a cat besides the putting of a slug into her countenance, sure,' and Jamie winked sagaciously. 'You'll know then that Mister Blodget is going to undertake for him.'

'Och, thin, don't you belave the bit of it—one of these gintlemen will never shoot another. Wolf won't ate wolf—'

'Niver fear that, boy. It's not the shooting I'm coming at; but Mr. Blodget is one of ourself, the same as you and I, only it is in a more dacenter way, and didn't he promise to get him into wosser trouble up at the Bella Union—'

'Arrah, but when will he cotch him there, think you, and Montgomery all the time perishing, the poor boy, for want of his revinge! And the loss of the safe too that weighs heavy upon his sperrits like a leaden sinker all the time— Och, the bloody robber!'

'Och! the murtherer,' cried the other, 'and didn't I see the pistol in his hand when he stood up in the barge, and in a minnit Montgomery would have been come to his nat'ril end by foul means, but I jist chucked him under the ear a bit and he lighted down in the bottom of the boat like a breaker full of water.'

'Bad luck to the likes of him, Jamie, the unspakable murthering scoundrel! It's the like of him that spoils the counthry entirely, and a poor man like you and me is scragged for trying to get a dacent living in our own way.'

'Och, botheration! don't spake to me Patrick, for I'm as mad as my skin can hold now, when I think that I didn't put the could lead into his bowels, but it was all on account of the slip of a gal that would have given the ala-r-m if I had shot him, jist.'

'You shot him once, Jamie, and if—'

'Ah, boy, if I had took a fair aim in the boat, but my head was lower than my heels, as I was tumbling over like a duck wid one wing, and the ball jist touched him in the ribs, like—but no matter, Patrick, Montgomery will come to his revenge through Master Blodget who pretends to be a gentleman like hisself, though he's one of us sacret like, for the benefit of the society, jist.'

Here the two amiable interlocutors were interrupted by a squabble that had grown up between the long boat steerer and some Chilean new comers whom he had desired to 'keep it up,' and not satisfied with applying 'moral suasion' to the case, he had taken the liberty to drag one or two of them into the middle of the floor by their long ear locks. Not caring to dance on compulsion, they struck long-legs with their fists, and he gave them battle. He kept them at a distance a few moments with his long arms, but they made up for this by drawing their *cochillars*. Brandishing their knives they rushed upon him with great fury. The other whalemen interfered in behalf of their shipmate, while all the *cholars* present took sides with their countrymen. The battle threatened to be serious, and blood had already begun to flow, when the door opened and a stout, broad-shouldered man entered the apartment.

'Charley, is that you?' shouted the master of the house.

'Yes, what is the muss?' cried the new-comer, whom the reader will recognize as the hero of the fire who took the ladder on his shoulders—'Hullo! here! knives out! daggers drawn! Down, you rascals!'

Charley then seized two of the most forward of the combatants in his Herculean grasp, and hurled them against the wall, while the rest, recognizing the famous engineer, fell back, breathing heavily and eyeing their adversaries with murderous spite.

Patrick and Jamie, who had thus far taken no part in the affray, felt themselves aggrieved by the presence of an official whom they had no particular reasons for admiring, and whose presence had more than once been a check upon their professional labors. They first began to grumble together in a low voice, and finding that they could do this with impunity, they felt emboldened to proceed still farther.

'The boys has got to be very civil in these times,' said Patrick.

'Oh! it was nothing but a little spree like, they was having—no harm at all, at all, in a free country, just for a lark like,' returned Jamie carelessly.

'But the laws is very strict for all that,' said Patrick, nodding graciously.

'Oh, murder, yes,' returned Jamie, 'its English laws they are like more than like what it used to be, before their—'

'You mane the Vigilance Committee, Jamie; oh! bad luck to 'em, they is no lawful powers any how. There's niver been any good in the place since they began to meddle with the payple.'

Several of the company drew near the two Irishmen and seemed to be interested in their discourse, while Charley, in conversation with the keeper of the den, eyed them at a distance.

In the mean time, the two orators, believing they were at the head of a considerable party, got on their feet, and began to swagger about the hall and swing their fists in close proximity to such persons present as they supposed to be unfavorable to their views. Jamie was particularly violent until he happened to graze the shoulder of Charley who, shooting out a fist that would have startled an ox, struck the big Irishman under the ear and felled him to the floor.

What would have been the result of this demonstration, if the door had not opened at the moment, we cannot say, but all eyes were turned upon the individual who now made his appearance. This was a man of youthful appearance, some thirty-five years of age, rather tall and well made, with red whiskers and moustaches and a very good set of teeth. He was a little pock-marked though not enough to injure his chance with the ladies, and his manner was both brisk and ostentatious. He was dressed in the extreme of fashion, with a profusion of rings on his fingers, and his entrance filled the dingy apartment with the scent of musk.—Taking out a blue silk handkerchief with which he made as if he would have wiped his face, and which he then flourished about the room a moment, he thrust out a leg as if to exhibit a boot of patent leather, and planting his heel jauntily on the floor, he put the question—

'Well, boys, has Monteagle called here for me, to-night?'

Without waiting for an answer he clapped his hands familiarly on the shoulder of Charley, saying—'How about that prisoner of yours? all safe, eh?'

'Montgomery, do you mean?' asked Charley in his deep base voice.

'Ah! that *was* his name I believe. He'll be triced up, I take it—scragged, as the Botany boys call it. Ha! ha! ha!'

'You must have heard that he has escaped, Mr. Blodget?'

'Escaped! Ah!' cried Blodget, with a start of real or pretended surprise—'the devil! Got loose, eh? No man is safe while such fellows are abroad,' and he placed his hand on the guard of his gold watch—'but how did it happen, Charley? Come, boy, how did he get away, the villian?'

'If you haven't heard,' returned Charley, looking circumspectly at his interrogator, 'I'll enlighten you on that subject.'

'Do, do, I'm all impatience.'

'So I *per*-ceive,' announced the Engineer. 'You must know that Montgomery, the thief, was placed in the room of the Vigilance Committee, and Peter was set over him as a guard: that is, the door was locked and Peter was on the outside.'

'Yes, yes, I understand; and so he jumped out the window.'

'No, not that exactly, for the windows were barred and fastened; but he made a hole through the plastering above, and getting on a table and some other lumber he climbed up into the room above and so he got clear.'

'Oh! the villain!' roared Blodget, at the same time rubbing his hands very unlike a man who was indignant at the escape of a felon.

Charley observed the strange inconsistency of Blodget's conduct, and when, a moment afterwards, Monteagle thrust his head into the open window and hailed Blodget by name, the Engineer cast a rapid glance first at the latter and then at the former while a cloud came over his brow as if he was sorry to see the youth in such company.

With an almost imperceptible wink to the two Irishmen, Jamie and Patrick, the gay young man rushed out the door and confronted 'his friend' Monteagle.—'Upon my word you look vastly improved,' said Blodget as he drew Monteagle towards Kearney street, and pressed his arm cordially. 'I was afraid it was all day with you, one while, and I can assure you that Mr. Vandewater was deeply concerned about you. That man holds you in high esteem, Monteagle; you may depend upon that. He fairly lost flesh when you were considered dubious.'

'I believe, sir, that my employers place entire confidence in me,' returned Monteagle, 'and that is all that I expect of them. But, pray, where are you bound to-night? After my long confinement, I should like to see a little pleasure. I feel a great inclination to wander on the sea shore, or go on a little boating excursion.'

'Done, sir. I will go with you on Sunday, or whenever you please; but, for the present, suppose we just drop in here at the Belle Union and see some of these enterprising gents lose a few slugs, and the wry faces that they make.'

'I've heard sad stories of that place,' returned the youth, but suffering himself to be led in the direction of the gambling house. 'I have heard that more money has been lost there than ever changed hands in the hells of Baden, at the saloons of the Palais Royal, or at Crockford's. I have a strong dislike to every species of gambling.'

'So have I. Thunder and Mars: I think it no better than highway robbery,' cried Blodget with a great show of virtuous indignation—'that is—except you know—where for mere amusement one takes a cue with a friend. By the bye, are you good at shoving a ball, Monteagle?'

'Billiards you are speaking of. Oh, I like that game well enough, for exercise. I cannot call myself a proficient, though I can once in a while put something in a pocket.'

'But you don't believe in putting something into your own pocket—ha, ha. Nor in taking something out of your neighbor's. Well it is robbery. It makes me so mad sometimes to see how these things are done: but here we are at the Bella; let's just in and overlook the game.'

They entered a very large apartment where all the conveniences and implements for gambling were found arrayed according to the most approved style. Nothing was wanted to render this establishment equal to its 'illustrious predecessors' in the old world and in the Atlantic cities.

Here were refreshments offered to all comers free of cost. Wines were freely poured out and segars presented, so that 'good old-fashioned hospitality' was never displayed in these degenerate days so bountifully as Monteagle saw it exhibited at the famous Bella Union.

A large table devoted to the game of Rouge et Noir invited the attention of our two friends. A Californian of swart countenance and sinister aspect, here deals Monte for the benefit of the greenhorns who throng around the golden piles in momentary expectation of seeing them flit into their own pockets, but though riches have wings, they do not fly in that direction. In lieu of that the few acres which the 'Squatteroez' have left them, go rapidly out of their possession. Then the Faro players were thronging around the table, certain of a change of luck *next time*, and verifying the poet's declaration that 'man never *is*, but always *to be* blest.' Each sagacious adventurer fancies himself a perfect La Place or Newton in calculation, and believes that he has, at last, mastered the complex elaboration of chances, and shall eventually 'bust the bank.' Unmitigated ass! Even though your power of calculation surpassed that of Zerah Colburn, you would be sure to lose, even admitting that the game was fairly played.

But watch with the eyes of an Argus, and think with the profundity of a Fourier, and that placid, smooth-tongued arbiter of Fortune, will look you in the eyes and cheat you out of every farthing you have got.

On all the tables except the last which we have described, piles of yellow *oro*, like veritable offerings upon these altars of Mammon, make the heart of avarice ache, ay, and infect those who are not very greedy of lucre with a touch of the *yellow fever*. Gold in dollars, gold in five dollar pieces, gold in ten dollar coins, gold in twenty dollar pieces, gold in slugs, gold in lumps, gold in bars, gold in dust—gold in every and any shape meets the dazzled eyes of visitors, look where you will; and those bland gentlemen who cry 'Make de game, gentlemens—No moe, the game is made,' and who so liberally furnish the sparkling wine gratis, stand ready to hand over to you any or all of those glittering piles *as soon as you win them*!

During all this time, bursts of delicious music float through the apartment, the harmonies of Bellini and Mendelsohn contrasting strangely with the hoarse oaths of some loser not yet grown sufficiently hardened to stifle his emotions as he thinks of his poor wife and little children whom he has robbed of their support by his last venture.

Monteagle looked with a shudder at the scene presented to his eyes, as he entered this spacious apartment devoted to the goddess of Ruin, and glittering with gilded baits to serve the purposes of those who, in the worst sense of the terms might be called 'fishers of men.'

An impression far from agreeable was made upon the mind of the youth when he noticed that Blodget who had been recommended to his attention by the junior member of the firm in whose service he was—not only evinced no emotion at the fearful scenes enacted before him, but that he also replied to the familiar addresses of the practical gamblers like one who had long been on terms of intimacy with them. But the impression gradually wore off under the influence of the music, to the soothing effects of which Monteagle was peculiarly susceptible, and a glass of excellent wine tendered him by an attendant contributed to fortify his spirits and prepare him for at least, enduring the strange events that were taking place around him.

One very genteel middle-aged man, apparently a Mexican, passed by them with a smile upon his countenance, on his way to the door. Pride was evidently struggling with despair, for he had just lost his all, and that smile sat upon his cadaverous features like a sunbeam upon a charnel house. Nevertheless, he walked erect, and maintained a certain air of dignity, till he passed the portal, as some men have done while going to the scaffold.

That sight would have been sufficient of itself to have inspired Monteagle with a horror of gambling; but he was destined to see other sights than this. The working of the countenances which fell under his eye, the sudden flush of hope, the blood receding from the features and leaving them white as death—all these things the youth saw, and inly cursed the wretches whose bland smiles and tempting wines were leading on the hardworking laborer to deposit the last grain of gold dust in their greedy coffers.

There were some poor gold-diggers, who longed for even a more sudden shower of wealth than the mines afforded them; men from the States who, while losing their gettings at faro as fast as they won them from the soil, were writing home to their wives, that gold was hard to get on account of the drought—more rain was required. Alas! if it had rained gold slugs, they would only have gathered the treasure to dissipate it all in games of chance.—But even of these all were not equally reckless. One unfortunate creature had, by long and arduous labor, secured about five thousand dollars worth of gold dust. He had written to his family in the State of Vermont, in high spirits, assuring them that he should be at home in a short time; should buy some land and stock it, and that their days of poverty were over. But coming to San Francisco in order to embark for home he had been beguiled into the belief that he could double his money at the Bella Union. He was playing when Monteagle entered, and although ignorant of his history, the youth's attention was, at once, drawn to him by the emotion of his manner, and the intense anxiety which he betrayed as heap after heap of his treasure departed from him. Having lost part of his gold, he seemed desperately bent upon winning it back or losing the whole. He bent over the cards with blood-shot eyes, he scarcely breathed, except when some one spoke to him, and then with a short hysteric laugh and words half uttered, he replied as if not doubting of ultimate success, while his manner and tone gave the lie to his pretended confidence. But his last venture had been made, and with eyes fixed and glassy, he watched the process which ended by rendering him penniless and a beggar. He fell back, gasped for breath, and in the next moment, he lay upon the floor a corpse!

Monteagle flew to the spot, but he stood there alone, as nobody seemed to think the event worthy of their attention. Finally, however, the body was removed. But who shall describe the patient watching and waiting of that poor wife, the anxious inquiries of the little children when their father's promised coming was delayed week after week, and month after month—or the anguish of the bereaved family when at length they learned the truth, and instead of moving to a snug little farm, in the enjoyment of a comfortable independence, they were carted off to the Alms House friendless and despised?

Blodget was evidently troubled by these practical illustrations of the evils of gambling, which occurred at a very unfortunate time for his purposes. He, however, contrived to make Monteagle swallow several glasses of liquor which was not without its effects, and served in a great measure to deaden his sensibilities. The music, too, floated through the apartment, like a syren beckoning with her white and jewelled hand the thoughtless to their doom.

It was midnight—Monteagle, reclined on a settee, which overlooked the table of rouge et noir, and feeling the soothing effect of music and wine, said to Blodget—

'After all, Blodget, there is a certain amount of evil in this world, and I do not know that one can make it less. It is like filling up part of a lake—the waters only retire to another part.'

'Yes,' interrupted the other carelessly—as he adjusted his cravat—'and the ministers have been preaching for eighteen centuries, and what have they accomplished? They have only changed the character of sins, occasionally, while the same *amount* remains.'

'True,' said Monteagle, who was in a condition to be pleased with a congenial mind—'the Puritans, for instance, were too pure to eat mince pies or kiss a child on Sunday; so they made up for that by murdering Quakers and witches.'

'And what are speculators of all kinds but gamblers?' continued the tempter; 'forestalling markets, laying up grain, and other necessaries of life to increase the price and wring the last cent from the hard hands of the laboring poor.'

There was so much truth in all this that Monteagle began to entertain a higher opinion than ever of his companion, without reflecting that the man who spoke thus would not scruple to do these very things himself, and much worse.

'It is as you say,' returned Monteagle quite warmly—'your views coincide with mine exactly. It is singular, but I had supposed you to be a man of less reflection and philosophy. I now perceive that you are a man of thought— a—'

'Oh! I have my views as well as others, that's all. You must know that I was intended for a minister, and went to Andover. But come, just for amusement let's try our luck a little here. You can stop when you please, you know.'

The proposition was rather sudden; Blodget saw the flush that shot into Monteagle's cheek, and quickly added—'To be a man of the world it is absolutely necessary to know a little about playing, even if you don't practice. All the natives play, and let me tell you that a spirited *Margaritta* regards a young man as a milk-sop who never lost or won a slug.'

Something struck the mind of Monteagle at that moment, and he remained for a couple of minutes in a brown study, and seemed wholly unconscious of the presence of Blodget. The latter turned his face aside and smiled. It was a self-satisfied smile.

At length said Monteagle, looking up, 'How long have you known Mr. Brown, the partner of Vandewater?'

'Oh, these dozen years. He and I have met here often.'

'What! does Mr. Brown play?'

'He! Bless your soul—'suddenly checking himself—'he plays the same as you and I might, just a little for sport.—That's all: he's not a heavy player; or, I might say it is more for amusement than anything else that he occasionally— very seldom, though—lays down a slug.'

There are two classes of people who are quick at detecting villainy, the accomplished rogue and the honest, simple-hearted man. The sight of the latter is the more clear of the two as far as it goes, while the former measures more correctly the *extent* of the intended deception. But Monteagle was, at this moment, disposed to interpret every thing in the most favorable manner, and fancied that he saw in Blodget's hesitation a generous endeavor to conceal the picadilloes of Mr. Brown, his employer. He felt convinced that Blodget knew more than he was willing to tell, and there rushed upon his recollection several little circumstances of a somewhat equivocal character connected with the conduct of Mr. Vandewater's partner.

Just then, a stout, rude, and hairy man, nearly as broad as he was long, with large goggle eyes, and a low, retreating forehead, came swaggering up to Blodget, followed by a large and very savage-looking dog.

'Good night—good night—my old boy,' cried he in a rough and loud tone. 'Ha! ha! glad to see you.'

Blodget stared at the fellow as if he had some trouble in recognizing him.

'No savez, eh! No savez!' cried the man. 'Oh, well, any other time will do. I understand—a pigeon there—don't want to be known, ha! ha! I'm just from Sacramento, old boy. Plenty of dust—'

At this moment, the dog, who had been smelling about Monteagle, braced himself opposite the youth and gave a horrible growl, during which he showed his fangs. The youth, believing that the animal was about to spring upon him, drew a small revolver, and prepared to defend himself.

'Eh—youngster!' bellowed the brutal owner of the dog. 'Love me, love my dog, you know. Don't hurt that dog, sir.'

'Certainly not, unless he attempts to hurt me,' returned Monteagle.

'Afraid of a dog, eh? Ha, ha!'

'No, not afraid of a dog,' returned Monteagle, highly incensed, 'for you may observe that I don't act as if I was afraid of *you*, do I?'

'Seize him, Boatswain!' shouted the scoundrel, and the dog, nothing loth sprang at the young man, and before he could place himself on his guard, had fastened his teeth in his vest. At the same instant, Monteagle, sparing the brute, aimed his pistol at the owner and snapped the trigger. The ball just grazed one of the fat cheeks of the rascal, who, thereupon, threw himself upon the youth and begun to pummel him with his fists. It must be remembered that Monteagle had not yet recovered from his wound. Nevertheless, he defended himself bravely. But Blodget, as soon as he saw the conduct of the wretch, gave him a blow on the side of his head that felled him like an ox. At the same time, the dog left Monteagle and seized Blodget. Monteagle threw his pistol at the dog, and hit him in the side without doing him much damage; but Blodget turned quickly and drove a short, sharp dagger to the hilt in the animal's breast. That finished the business for the dog. But his savage owner was about stabbing Blodget in the back with a long, two-edged knife when Monteagle gave him a sudden push, which sent him reeling to the distance of several paces. Blodget and his enemy then encountered each other face to face, and as both were armed with deadly instruments, the issue would have been bloody had not several of the crowd, which had by this time clustered around the combatants, plucked them asunder. The stout man swore and threatened vengeance, and as he struggled hard to get away from those who held him, he was finally thrust out of doors with some violence. He was heard, for some time, prowling outside and threatening all manner of vengeance against Monteagle and Blodget, especially the latter whom he charged with all manner of crimes, and who, he said, would long since have been hanged if half his offences were known to the public.

All this passed for the ravings of baffled rage; and although it seemed to excite anger of Blodget, nobody else seemed to deem it worthy of the least notice.

The gallant manner in which Blodget had espoused his cause, completely won the confidence of Monteagle, and when he said to the youth, 'Come, now that rascal of a Sintown has been turned out, we will just amuse ourselves here, if you have no objection.'

'Sintown, is his name? it seems to me that I have heard that name. Was he not once arrested for robbing a Mexican?'

'Something of that sort, I believe,' returned Blodget, glancing stealthily at the youth, 'but there was no proof of his guilt.'

'Proof—there is proof enough in the scoundrel's eye and, indeed, in all the rest of his features, to hang a dozen men.'

Blodget smiled pensively and drew Monteagle to the table. After playing a little while, Monteagle lost a couple of slugs, when Blodget took his arm and said, 'Come, my good fellow, the luck goes against you to-night. You must wait till Madame Fortune, who, according to Bonaparte, always favors the young, is in a better mood.'

Monteagle had already become fascinated by the game, but he did not care to evince greater devotion to the gambling table than his companion; therefore he announced his readiness to depart.

They had scarcely gone a dozen paces from the door, when a man stepped lightly up to Blodget, and clapping his hand on his shoulder, said, 'You are my prisoner, sir.'

Monteagle started; but Blodget very coolly turned his face towards the man and let the segar-smoke stream from his mouth directly into the eyes of the officer.

'You will go with me,' cried the officer angrily.

'Will I? In—deed. Something of a prophet too—'

At this the officer began to tug at the coat-collar of his prisoner.

'Now, Oates, ain't you ashamed of yourself?' asked Blodget, loosening the hand of the other from his collar.

'Why should I be ashamed?' asked Oates, looking about him, as if to summon aid.

'Simply, to impose upon my good nature in this way. Don't you know that with one blow of my fist I could send you reeling, to say nothing of my friend here.'

'Your friend. What? You threaten me with a rescue, young man?' to Monteagle.

'I have said nothing,' replied the youth.

'But I don't like your looks, sir,' said the officer, trying to put himself in a towering passion.

'Bah!' cried Monteagle, 'Come along, Blodget, before you frighten this poor gentleman to death. You see that he is ready to drop with fear now.'

'Very well. This is pretty conduct—pretty talk to a police officer,' was the reply of Oates, 'but I'll report you to your betters. I know you both and I'll report you.'

'Take something along with you first, or you'll have nothing to tell,' cried Blodget, seizing the official by the back of the neck, as he was about to make a hasty retreat, and giving him three or four vigorous kicks.

'Murder! help!' cried the police officer. 'Oh, don't murder me, and I'll tell you all about it. It was Sintown who made the complaint. He said that you was—'

Before he could finish the sentence, which, for reasons of his own, Blodget did not care to hear at that moment, he was thrust into the middle of the street, and having picked himself up, the valorous officer ran around the first corner as if a legion of imps were at his heels.

'Now,' said Blodget to Monteagle, as they resumed their walk, 'if the fellow had showed any pluck, I would have given him enough to keep him drunk for a week, in order to have the appearance of buying myself off. As it is, he feels so much disappointment at having received 'more kicks than coppers' that he will go home to his masters with a horrible story of an attempt at assassination, of being attacked by forty thieves at once, and the whole town will be at our heels in less than ten minutes. Therefore, here we part. Do you drop in at your friend's in Montgomery-street, which is but a few steps from this spot, while I will shift for myself as I best may.'

The wisdom of this proposal was evident to Monteagle, who walked straight to a house where he had sometimes lodged when in town, and gaining an entrance after some little trouble, he felt himself safe from pursuit.

Meanwhile Blodget, directing his steps towards the sand hills, was very soon out of sight.

Shortly after the town was in an uproar. The quick tramp of feet was heard in the streets, cries and shouts resounded through the air, and many people threw up their windows to see what was the matter. Finally, nobody could get at the secret; the noise died away, and San Francisco lay silent and dark on the shores of its glorious Bay.

# CHAPTER IV

## The Footsteps of the Tempter.

He stood in the Plaza, Lorenzo Monteagle, head clerk to the house of Vandewater & Brown. Down into the sparkling waters of the Western main, the king of day was slowly sinking, like the glorious Constantine submitting to Christian baptism at the moment he was bidding the world adieu. Monteagle surveyed the throng that was passing hither and thither on the different streets bordering the neglected public square on which he stood. They were all personable, able-bodied men, who walked and spoke as if there was no enterprise of which they were not capable, no adventure too daring for their powers. The absence of children and the scarcity of women gives a singular aspect to the city of San Francisco, and this was realized by Monteagle, as he now stood gazing upon the hardy representatives of every country on the globe, as they moved before him on the great public square of the city.

As the evening shades began to gather around the black rigging of the vessels in the bay, and gloom upon the distant waters, the youth looked about him as if seeking for some individual whom he expected to meet on that spot. A man passed near him, nearer in the opinion of Monteagle than there was any occasion for. He grazed the youth's elbow as he went by, and appeared to do it on purpose.

Monteagle turned to look at the man, and the latter turning also, clapped his hands on his hips, and with a swaggering air, looked the former saucily in the face. Monteagle thought he had seen the fellow before; he was dressed much as an ordinary laborer, large in size, with big coarse features that glowed with the effect of frequent potations.

Monteagle was about to turn away from the man in disgust, when he said— 'I think yees will know me when yees sees me again.'

'Why so?'

'Bekase yees trying to look off the countenance of me, I believe.'

'I shall look where I please, and as long as I please,' returned Monteagle.

'That's unfortunit agin,' said the Irishman, 'for yees will see nothing but a jintleman, and that's what yees not used to seeing inside of the looking-glass.'

'What is the object of these insults, you scoundrel?' cried Monteagle, still in the belief that he had fallen in with the fellow before, but where he could not recollect.

'Oh—no object at all, at all. But if I is a scoundrel, there's more than one on the Plaza jist, and he's not beyond the raitch of my fist, nythur.'

This was rather too much for Monteagle's patience, and accordingly he rushed upon the intruder and saluted him with a violent blow in the face. The Irishman staggered backwards a few feet and then recovering himself approached the youth in a boiling rage. As they met and exchanged blows, the people came crowding to the spot, apparently bent only upon seeing the fight, as no one attempted to interfere. Monteagle was a pupil of Frank Wheeler's and the science he had acquired from the teachings of that accomplished gymnast enabled him to bother his bulky antagonist a good deal. This rendered the latter exceedingly angry, and a cry was raised by the by-standers, as they saw a Spanish knife in the hand of the Irishman, which he had dexterously drawn from some part of his dress, and with which he rushed upon the youth with the evident design of finishing him and the battle together. At that moment, and just as the youth had caught a glimpse of the steel flashing before his eyes, a powerful hand was laid upon the shoulder of the Irishman, and he was drawn violently backwards. Some of the crowd began to murmur, but the Irishman looked into the countenance of the intruder, and both he and Monteagle pronounced the word 'Blodget!'

'How now, sir. What are you doing with that knife?' cried Blodget in a peremptory tone.

'You see it's the thafe himself, the bloody robber!' said the Irishman, passionately, though evidently cowering under the gaze of Blodget.

'Who told you he was a thief? Begone, sir!' cried Blodget, 'Mr. Monteagle, I find you in bad company. Is that an acquaintance of yours?' continued Blodget, with a gay laugh, as he turned to our youth, and pointed at the retreating form of the Irishman.

'Not of *mine*, exactly,' said the youth placing considerable emphasis on the word.

'Oh—yes—a-hem. I have known the rascal some two or three months. We had his services in cleaning out a cellar and on several other occasions. Devil take the fellow—did he hurt you much?'

'Better ask if I hurt *him*,' returned the youth, 'for I think he would have carried away a piece of malleable metal with him, but for your opportune deliverance.'

'If he had not been too quick for you—he's dexterous in the use of the knife.'

'Is he, indeed?'

'You wonder how I found out that fact. I have heard of his encounters with the natives. His name is James, commonly called Jamie, and there are many stories extant as to his prowess.'

'Strange he should have taken so much pains to insult *me*,' said Monteagle.

'He seemed to have something against you,' answered Blodget. 'Cannot you remember of ever seeing him before?'

Blodget watched the countenance of Monteagle narrowly, as the youth replied, 'I have some faint recollection of the fellow's face. His nose, that seems to have been knocked out of its proper shape, struck me like an old acquaintance, but where, and under what circumstances I have seen it before, I am unable to determine. But let him go. You and me are met now for another purpose.'

'Let us walk along towards Dupont street,' said the other, musing.

'Well, on then. But what engages your thoughts at this moment?'

'As for that, Monteagle, what would you give to know?'

'It's not very important, I'll be sworn. Some love affair doubtless.'

'You are a wizard,' replied Blodget. 'It is a love affair, but one that interests you much more than me.'

'Interest *me*?' said the youth, much surprised.

'It is a great secret, sir,' and Blodget squeezed the arm of his companion.

'If it is a secret you are bound to keep it close. Is it not so?'

'Not exactly. But come into this shantee with me, and I will explain matters to your full satisfaction.'

Monteagle followed his friend into the wine shop, nothing loth; for though he assumed an indifferent air, he could not feel altogether uninterested in an affair of this kind. Besides, like all young men on such occasions, his curiosity was powerfully excited.

Blodget sat down in one corner and beckoned to the host to set on a bottle of champagne. He then pressed Monteagle to drink who, at first, refused, but being in haste to hear the news, he finally tossed off a glass in order to hurry on the recital which Blodget had in store for him.

'It is a strange story,' said Blodget, smacking his lips—'good wine—'

'But this queer business—the love story—some Mexican squaw, I suppose, has—'

'No—no. You are a lucky dog, Monteagle.'

'Very likely.'

Here Blodget poured out another glass and nodded to his companion—'Take another, and then to business.'

Monteagle drank to save time, and said; 'Go on with this wonderful story.'

'Well,' said the other, 'I think your chance is good. The firm hold you in high estimation—'

'Fudge! no more of that—'

'But I must tell the story in my own way. I say that you are a lucky dog, Monteagle. Come, one more glass and then to business.'

Monteagle drank, and motioned impatiently to Blodget.

'My friend, if you work your cards right, there is a fortune in reserve for you.'

A thought struck Monteagle, and for a moment he was agitated. He drank to hide his emotion.

'Good wine, is it not, Monteagle?'

'Yes, indeed, but we are coming to the end of the bottle before we get to the beginning of the story.'

'Oh, but I've told you the most important part—that is the *fortune*. Now with regard to the young lady, she is a perfect angel.'

'Of course—all angels till after marriage.'

'No, but you've seen her.'

'Have I, indeed?'

'The old man is rich—counts his money by tens of thousands. You have seen him, too. Landlord, another bottle.'

'I've seen him, too!' and the youth swallowed another glass, for his heart throbbed violently.

'The girl is beauty personified—accomplished—lovely as a seraph—eyes of the—the—'

'The blackest jet, of course.'

'Well, I'm not so certain of that.—But they are—'

'Oh, deuce take the description, now to the point.'

'Well, Monteagle, she loves you, loves you to distraction.'

Monteagle started to his feet.

'Sit down, friend of mine, and let us finish this bottle.'

'Certainly. But who told you this?—My God! who told you that she loves me?'

'Her own eyes ought to have told you that long ago.'

'Her own eyes!'

'Yes, ha! ha! ha!' roared Blodget, 'why, man alive, did you never hear of the tell-tale eyes which reveal what passes in the heart?'

'But who told you?'

'It is a secret, you know; you will not betray me.'

'Honor bright, of course.'

'I'll trust you. Brown told me.'

'What Mr. Brown, our partner?'

'Yes, indeed.'

'But how could Mr. Brown know anything of this affair, eh! You astonish me.'

'Not at all; easy enough. Vandewater told the doctor, and the doctor told Brown; so now I have betrayed all the three. You see it is authentic. The girl has confessed her love to Vandewater himself.'

'To Vandewater?'

'Yes, why not?'

'She must be in earnest, then. She loves me beyond a doubt.'

'She has loved you many months, now Monteagle is a chance—'

'She loved me many months! But—'

'Fact, sir, fact? She confessed it to Vandewater, who tried to persuade her to conquer her passion.'

The youth started to his feet.

'I'm much obliged to him. *He* try to—*he* interfere in a case of this kind.—But that exceeds his authority.'

'Tut! tut! work your cards right and the girl is yours, and then Vandewater's fortune, you know—'

'What have I to do with Vandewater's fortune?' cried the youth surprised.

'What has *she* to do with his fortune? what is hers is yours, you know, if you come together.'

Monteagle looked mystified.

'You know,' continued Blodget, 'that Julia is—'

'Julia?'

'Yes, Mr. Vandewater's niece—'

'What have you been talking about?' cried Monteagle.

'She loves you! Fact! Don't stare at me so incredulously. See, my boy—' clapping him on the shoulder—'the game's in your own hands if you only play your cards right.'

Monteagle sank back in his chair looking listlessly upon his half-emptied glass, while Blodget went on for a considerable time descanting on the merits of Julia Vandewater, and the brilliant prospects that would open upon Monteagle if he married her.

'No matter,' said our youth, carelessly. 'That doctor must be a regular gossip, and deserves to be called out for publishing family secrets with which he has been entrusted.'

Blodget gazed at Monteagle in amazement. He wondered that the young man who had been so anxious to hear the disclosures which he had to make, should seem so little affected at a fact which would have occasioned no small triumph to himself. But the reader is already informed that this marvellous secret was no news to Monteagle; who, so far from triumphing in the conquest which he had made of Julia's heart, was deeply grieved that he could not return her affection. But Monteagle had taken more wine than usual, and Blodget seemed to be perfectly satisfied with that circumstance at least. Monteagle followed him out mechanically, and suffered himself to be led wherever Blodget might choose to convey him.

# CHAPTER V

## Our Hero Treads Forbidden Ground—The Mansion in Dupont Street.

They walked but a short distance before they reach a splendid house in Dupont street. Monteagle had heard the character of this building, but had paid but little attention to it. He was now in a condition to enter almost any house where amusement was to be obtained, for in addition to the champagne which he had taken, he had experienced no small disappointment upon learning the whole extent of Blodget's wonderful *secret.* As they entered this elegant mansion it began to grow dark. The interior was far more imposing than the outside. They passed through a wide hall lighted by an elegant chandelier, which hung in golden chains from the ceiling. Other furniture betokened abundance of wealth.

Blodget opened a door that led to a large apartment, carpeted in the most fashionable style—fashionable in a land where ostentatious wealth may be deemed excusable. Rich sideboards, tables, chandeliers and ornaments of the most elegant form and costly materials here greeted Monteagle on every side.

On a sumptuous sofa of the richest Genoese velvet, sat two young ladies, whose costly dresses were admirably fitted to their forms, and so arranged as to betray their charms to the most casual observer. One of them, to whom Blodget addressed himself on entering, was not tall in stature but of exquisite symmetry. Her complexion, though that of a brunette, was so transparent, and the rose on her cheeks was so brilliant, that one would scarcely have noticed that she was darker than her companion. A pair of lustrous large black eyes beamed from beneath a profusion of raven tresses, and the clearly defined, arched eye-brows appeared to have been drawn by the pencil of a skilful painter. The upper moiety of two well rounded globes was displayed by the low dress, while the little foot and beautiful ankle were not covered by the long drapery in vogue with the daughters of a more northern clime.— Whether her mouth was made for speaking or kissing, might have been a question with naturalists and men of *vertu*; but most men would have decided practically in favor of the latter view. It was, indeed, a mouth that spoke eloquently while silent, like one of those sea shells which one sometimes finds in the Orient, ruddy and of voluptuous form.

'Mr. Blodget is come again. Very welcome Mr. Blodget,' said the fair creature. 'I wait much for see you, and never see you no more.'

But while addressing Blodget, she fixed her speaking eyes on Monteagle and surveyed his features and fine form with evident admiration.

The other girl was taller and fairer, with a majestic neck, blue eyes, and brown hair, the ringlets bursting from her head dress and showering over her well-turned shoulders. She smiled and showed pearls, she walked and exhibited grace and voluptuous proportions. She spoke and music fell from her lips.

Monteagle, aided by the champagne that he had drank, made himself agreeable very soon—sooner than propriety would have required had not his fair friends been accustomed to impromptu friends and acquaintances.

The sound of voices and occasional laughter in a neighboring apartment gave evidence that there were more of the fair consolers in the house, and that other men, beside Blodget and Monteagle, were regaling their eyes with feminine loveliness.

A few moments conversation sufficed to show that the dark eyed girl was a native of South America, while the other had been born and brought up in the land of Johnny Bull, though her accent betrayed that her earlier days had been spent in the 'North Countrie.' She was one of Burns' beauties, and how so fair a flower, who, even now seemed to have retained some portion of her modesty, should ever have found her way to a house of this description on the distant shores of California, was a problem which Monteagle found difficult to solve.

Throwing himself on a sofa and putting his arm around her slender waist, Monteagle said—'Were not you and I acquainted in the old country?'

Although this was merely common place nonsense, the girl slightly blushed before she replied—'Nae doubt, sir, they be all frae Scotland that speaks to me, sir.'

'You did not know that I was descended from the noble house of—'

'Douglas?'

'No, but of—of—'

'Oh! the Bruce it must be—'

'No—stop—the—house of Monteith.'

'*Monteith?*' cried she, removing herself farther from, and affecting horror at the name.

'Yes, that noble ancestry I claim, and you shall be my bonny bride, and we will return together to Scotia's shores, and live near the Highland cot in which you were born and reared.'

'With a *Monteith!* with a Monteith, think you?' and she stared curiously at the youth—'take off your shoes, sir, did I ever think I should ever set my twa een upon one of that family? Tak off your boot and let us see if ye have not a cloven foot, at least?'

Blodget had sent for wine, which was procured at twenty dollars the bottle—an excellent article, however; and now conversation, raillery, repartee, and compliments flowed freely. The two girls were entirely unlike those whom we find in houses of resort in the Atlantic cities. They had evidently received a good education, more especially the dark-eyed one, and their conversation was conducted in a style more usually heard in a fashionable drawing-room than in an establishment sacred to the Paphian Goddess.

This way the evening was spent, and the hour had become late. Other girls of various degrees of beauty were in the apartment. Music of a high order—added to the charm of the occasion. The men at this house were generally of the higher classes, or those who assumed to be so; and the utmost harmony prevailed. The wines sparkled—wit flew from mouth to mouth—and few things were said or done which might not have passed in the saloons of Mr. Vandewater himself.

Blodget had the air of a blase, and after having talked a little, in a tone of listless indifference, with the Spanish girl, he turned to another. At the close of the evening, Monteagle found himself in conversation with the lively and intelligent Spanish maid, who told him that she came from Santiago, a city of Chile, and where, from some words that accidentally dropped from her, he was made to believe that she had moved in a circle differing, in many respects, from that with which he now found her. He became more and more interested in Maria, as she was called. With all her liveliness there was a certain delicacy about her which enchanted him; and as she moved about to different parts of the room, her rounded form and voluptuous limbs could not escape his watchful regards. His imagination exalted by rich wines and fascinated by the beauty and the manners of Maria, Monteagle was in a condition to overlook the demand of prudence, and the whisperings of conscience. Blodget certainly exhibited no regret at observing this.

The saloon was full of visitors, and young ladies, and some of the latter knew the young clerk well by reputation. They became much interested in the flirtation that was going forward between Maria and Monteagle, and although they were too well bred to betray their interest, they saw and heeded all that passed between them. Some were much surprised, and others thought it very natural, while some few, no doubt, rejoiced in the opportunity for scandal, which would enable them to 'entertain company,' by the hour or the subject of youthful proclivities, and the danger of placing too much confidence in these 'promising young men.'

This was a moment of danger for Monteagle, and yet hundreds of other youths were in the nightly and even daily habit of visiting gambling-houses and places of debauchery, upon whose conduct no remark was made. The reason of this may have occurred to the reader. Monteagle was highly esteemed by his employers, and an opinion had got about that he was something better than common. All men are said to respect virtue, and consequently the aberration of Monteagle was very comforting to such as had previously regarded him with a sentiment approaching to envy. We may as well say, also, in this place, that the love of Julia Vandewater had been won as much by the unusual sobriety and decorum of Monteagle's conduct as by his personal and intellectual endowments. She regarded him as a very *uncommon* young man; and it may be perceived by the importance which Blodget attached to his 'secret,' that Julia was regarded as a great prize, and one not to be aspired to by every young fellow in San Francisco. Julia Vandewater could have commanded the admiration of any bachelor in California, whatever might have been his talents and acquirements, with the one exception of Lorenzo Monteagle, who, while he regarded her with the affection of a brother, had lived under the same roof with the young lady long enough to know that he could never feel toward her as he ought to feel towards the woman whom he made his partner for life. But this conclusion had not been formed upon any improprieties in the conduct or conversation of the young lady. Had Monteagle a brother who was enamored of Julia, he would have rejoiced to have seen a union take place between them: but there was the important point—it was necessary to be enamored first, for without that he believed that respect and friendship could not insure a happy marriage. On her part Julia loved sincerely, and for nothing more than for the virtuous and circumspect deportment of Monteagle.

I have said that our youth had been fascinated with Maria. He was in high spirits; he was pleased with the idea of having gained so pretty and genteel a mistress, for she had in the tenderest manner, consented to be exclusively his as long as he might feel disposed to keep her. Patting him on his bump of benevolence with her taper finger, she had said, 'Pretty American lad, I love you much. I love your face. I love your figure, and your voice. I shall be much please with you to-day and to-morrow all the same. Oh, you is one pretty. Come up to my room and you shall see how I love you, mine friend.'

Monteagle obeyed this tender request. From such lips and enforced with a voice ringing like a silver-bell, it was impossible for him to disobey the command. Blodget saw and heard it all; and when the enamored couple shut the door behind them, he placed his jewelled finger on one side of his nose, and winked to the Scottish-girl who appeared to fully understand it.

For the last half hour that Monteagle had remained in the saloon, he had overheard a lively conversation between three pretty French girls, carried on in their vernacular, which had for its object a lady apparently from Lima, as she was dressed in their peculiar attire. Her dress was dark, fitted to the form in a peculiar manner, so as to show the swell of the hips, without being wide and flowing like the dress of our ladies. Her form was entirely hidden, except that a small aperture permitted her to look abroad with one eye. This dress is singular, and yet it is worn by all fashionable ladies in certain parts of South America.

This lady had spoken little since her entrance, while she seemed to be an attentive observer of all that passed. The French girls were wondering who she was. Their observations were piquant and full of wit; and as Monteagle was a perfect master of the French language, he was not a little entertained by their funny remarks. To him, however, the presence of the strange lady was a matter of very little interest. As her face was invisible, she might be a perfect fright for all that he knew to the contrary, and in the few half-understood words that fell from her lips, he discovered no more than the most common-place observations. He did, however, observe that the mistress of the establishment—a very beautiful and accomplished woman herself—treated the incognito with marks of the highest respect.

Scarcely had Monteagle placed his foot on the stairs to follow Maria to an upper apartment, when the unknown appeared in the hall, and having thrust a billet into the hand of the girl, turned and left the house immediately.

Maria laughed slightly.

'What is this?' said she, in her broken English. 'One letter to read! Oh! very good; I shall read you a letter, mine friend. So much the better. I shall see.'

Pausing a moment, Maria opened the note, and read it by the light of the chandelier. The paper dropped from her hand, and she stood a moment as if transfixed with astonishment.

'She! Oh! She! the holy and devoted one!' cried Maria, at last, clasping her hands. 'She, here—she come to this place—and all for me—for me—'

'Come, come,' cried the impatient youth. 'Come, my beautiful one, and let us enjoy—'

'Enjoy nothing. Not to-night; some other time. I can do nothing to-night. So she has remembered me. She has not forgotten those days of innocence. Ah, me—they are gone *now*!'

These words were spoken in Spanish; but Monteagle found no difficulty in understanding them, and they partially restored him to a sense of his present plight. But who was this 'holy and devoted one?' Some nun, no doubt, who had stepped between him and his enjoyments.

Monteagle, whose passions were much excited, stood looking at the fine form and swelling graces of the Spanish girl; her tapering limbs, her little feet, her large dark eyes, and lovely mouth.

'Surely,' said he, 'you will not be so unkind—'

'Hush!' cried Maria, clapping her hand on his mouth. 'I am nothing this evening. *Her* hand has written this, and I cannot see you to-night,' and here the girl sat down upon the stairs, and fell into a deep reverie.

'What shall I do?' thought Monteagle, 'If I speak to another girl, every eye will be upon me; all sorts of surmises. No, no, I have it. I will consult Blodget.'

He then slipped a slug into the hand of Maria, who seemed to be almost unconscious of the act, and stepping to the door of the saloon, he opened it, and called to his companion.

Blodget was lazily conversing with the mistress of the house upon some topic of general interest, and though surrounded on all sides by the most fascinating beauties of almost every civilized country—who threw out their lures to entrap him, he appeared as unconscious as a pair of tongs in a china shop. When he heard Monteagle pronounce his name, he looked up surprised: he fairly started, and seizing his hat, quickly came out to him. They passed into the street together.

'What have you done with Maria?' said Blodget.

'She has received a note from somebody, and has retired alone to ponder upon its contents,' answered the youth.

'Oh! I know—I think, at least, that the lady who followed you out—the lady in the mask—ha! ha! ha! I think that she must have brought the note. But did she not make you acquainted with its contents?'

'No. But whatever its contents were, they made a deep impression upon her.'

'Ah,' exclaimed Blodget, stopping as if to think. 'I have heard something of this. I think I understand something of it. You must know that Maria received her education at a convent in Santiago, about a hundred miles from Valparaiso, an old-fashioned city where religion flourishes. This is a *religieuse* who came to the house enveloped in the costume of that city; and I think I have learned that Maria was the bosom friend of a young lady of fine promise, and very devout habits, before she *took to the road.*'

'The road?'

'Yes that broad road that we read of.'

'These are singular girls,' said Monteagle. 'Instead of mere hacknied mercenaries they seem to be women of sentiment and feeling.'

'Well, I can show you a few such—'

A heavy sigh breathed by some person near them caused Monteagle to turn around.

The lady incognito was near them, and the sigh must have come from her; but whether it had any relation to their conversation or not they were unable to determine. She did not look towards them, as she passed. Perhaps that the sigh had some connection with the unfortunate Maria. Still as her dark form receded from view, Monteagle could not but remember that it was immediately after Blodget's proposition to show him other females, when this sigh was breathed.

# CHAPTER VI

## The Ruined Wife—The Banker's Marriage.

They walked forward amid the darkness till they came to a house in Sacramento street, where instead of the sound of merry voices which they had expected, their ears were saluted by the most violent oaths and denunciations.

'How is this?' said Monteagle, 'is it a ring fight to which you are conveying me?'

'You may well ask that,' replied Blodget, stopping to listen; 'these are unusual sounds to proceed from this house. Here seems to be more of Mars than Venus.'

As they came to the door it was violently thrown open, and several females ran screaming into the street.

'Go in there!' cried one of the girls, recognizing Blodget; 'for God's sake go in, or there will be murder done.'

Blodget and Monteagle hastened to the apartment from which the noise proceeded, and there they beheld a table overturned and China ware scattered about the floor, while a stout, middle-aged man, with every appearance of a gentleman, lay on the floor, and another, equally respectable in appearance, was kneeling on his breast, with a revolver in his hand, and aimed at the throat of the prostrate man.

'What! gentlemen!' exclaimed Monteagle, 'forbear!' and he was proceeding to the relief of the fallen man when Blodget caught him by the arm, and whispered, 'Let them alone. It is all right. I know them both!'

'You know them?' cried Monteagle, struggling to throw off his friend's firm grasp, 'but is that any reason that they should murder each other?'

'That fellow seduced his wife!' cried Blodget.

'Promise, villain! promise!' roared the man with a pistol. 'Promise, or I finish you on the spot.'

'Help, I say,' cried the undermost man, frothing with rage and pale with terror—'Release me from this madman.'

'Madman!' cried he with the pistol. 'Is it mad that I am when I claim that you shall marry the woman whom you have stolen away from home and happiness. Gentlemen, you see here a villain—a banker of this city—who bloated with pride, and presuming on his wealth, seduced my wife and brought her to this city. I procured a divorce in such a manner that my ruined wife can marry again. I followed her and her paramour to this city, and here I find him rioting in a house of ill fame, while the woman that he has blasted—my late wife—pines in solitude at home, where she is scarcely allowed the necessaries of life. Now, you villain, see if these gentlemen will aid you.'

'No,' said Monteagle. 'We cannot interfere here; but pray don't shoot the villain in cold blood.'

'His life is safe, if he promises to marry the woman,' cried the wronged husband; 'Otherwise he dies! Promise!' and he thrust the muzzle of the pistol against the seducer's forehead.

'Murder—help!' cried the man, struggling desperately to regain his feet.

'Promise, rascal, promise to marry the woman, and I release you.'

Perhaps with the hope of making his escape if he consented, the banker at length said, 'Let me up, and I will marry the—'

'Call no names for she is your wife.' cried the other, suffering the banker to regain his feet, but no sooner was he up than he made a rush for the door— the outraged husband levelled a pistol at his head, and in order to save his life, Monteagle and Blodget seized the seducer, and in spite of his struggles, held him fast. The divorced husband then begged our two friends to lead the banker forward. Being concerned for his life, and thinking their presence necessary to his safety, Monteagle and Blodget led the man down the street, the husband leading the way, pistol in hand. In an obscure street, they entered a low-roofed building, where they found the unfaithful wife attended by a clergyman.

The banker started, as this vision met his gaze, and he would fain have retreated; but he was held by his two conductors as in a vice.

'Here,' said the injured husband to the seducer—'here is the woman whom you are to marry. I have procured a divorce from her, and left her free. You took her from me—from a good home—you have had her as long as it suited your convenience, but have now almost entirely cast her off in a strange land.—You shall marry her.'

The clergyman and all the others present said that it was no more than justice. Finding there was no other way, the banker yielded and married the woman whom he had seduced.

After witnessing the ceremony, and receiving the hearty thanks of the late husband, Blodget and Monteagle withdrew.

'What do you think of this scene?' said Blodget to Monteagle, as soon as they were alone together in the street.

'I think it is a hard case in every view of it,' returned the youth. 'The man has lost his wife—the seducer has married one whom he cannot love, and the new wife will doubtless have a hard time of it with the fellow.'

'The husband was bent on revenge,' said Blodget, 'and in riveting the two criminals together, I think he has punished both. It is not likely the wife will ever live to inherit the banker's wealth. He will either dot her or kill her with unkindness.'

'But shall we not go back to the house?' inquired Monteagle.

Blodget perceived that the young clerk's feelings had been too highly wrought up by the contemplation of female beauty to admit of his returning peaceably home without first becoming better acquainted with one of the inmates of the house which they had last visited. He was not averse to returning to the temple of pleasure, and accordingly he replied in the affirmative.

But on returning to the house, they found the light out, and the parties retired for the night, for the dawn of day was not far off.

It was enough for Blodget that he had inducted Monteagle into the downward path. He did not doubt that, hereafter the young man would take rapid strides towards the point whither he was so desirous of directing his steps.

Monteagle separated from his companion and returned home, where he was soon in the land of dreams.

He awoke late in the morning and felt a little confused after his night's career; for while he was not really intoxicated, he had been a little merry, and even that was a rare thing for Lorenzo Monteagle. His employers were not Puritans, and consequently they observed nothing peculiar in his manner or appearance. Mr. Brown, however, was very sociable with Monteagle on that day, and the latter imagined that he knew the cause. He supposed that the young man was in a fair way to marry Julia, and accordingly the former rose in his estimation. Brown was one of those worthies who worship the rising sun. He as well as Blodget thought that Monteagle was 'a lucky dog.' Indeed, he would have been glad to be in his place. Monteagle saw into all this, but did not act as if he perceived it.

In his hours of calm reflection, after dinner, Monteagle thought upon the events of the preceding night, how he had twice been prevented from associating with one of the seductive young girls at the houses of pleasure to which Blodget had conveyed him. In the first instance, a nun or something of the kind, had come to snatch Maria from his arms,—at the second house, the affray occurred between the banker and the injured husband. But he had also had a singular dream during the night, which he had scarcely had time to think of during business. It now came up vividly to his recollection. The details were as follows: He seemed to be sitting with Julia Vandewater, in her father's garden, in pleasant conversation, when suddenly the heavens became overcast and the thunder rolled heavily over his head. Julia started up and bestowing upon him a contemptuous frown, exclaimed, 'I love you no longer. I will tell my uncle of you and get you discharged from his service.' She then abruptly left him, while he was much revolted and displeased by the revengeful and unladylike look that she cast back at him as she retired. Still the lightning flashed and the thunder rolled, till, immediately after a tremendous crash, he observed that the mansion of Mr. Vandewater was on fire. It had been struck by lightning. For a time all was confusion in his mind, till he seemed to be again ascending the ladder to rescue a young lady from the flames. Again he heard the shouts of the intrepid firemen below him, and the roaring of the flames as he approached the window where, as he supposed, Julia Vandewater was standing. But no sooner had he reached her than she proved to be the nun who had given the note to Maria at the house of assignation. He seized her around the waist, and then the stifling smoke seemed to smother him. His mind was again confused till he found himself in a wilderness, fainting with heat, and seeking for a refuge from the burning sun. No shade was near, and he was about to lie down and surrender himself up to death, when *Inez Castro*, riding on an elephant, came that way, attended by a large number of very black slaves. On seeing him, Inez immediately descended to the ground, and commanding a huge basin to be brought, bathed his temples with a cooling and refreshing liquid, which restored all his powers and filled him with unspeakable pleasure. Soft music floated around him, the atmosphere was filled with the most delightful odors, and he finally sank into a sweet slumber upon the rounded bosom of the beautiful maid.

Such was his dream, and he now pondered upon it deeply, for it seemed to be fraught with meaning, as if it was something more than the effects of his night's adventures.

But the more he reflected, the more he became puzzled, for there seemed to be no rational interpretation to a dream so fraught with contradictions, and split up into separate portions, which seemed to have no agreement with each other. 'It is one of those jumbled visions caused by excitement and champagne,' said he—'late hours caused it; but I must give up late hours and be more steady—' he paused, for he knew in the secret of his heart that he should hail the appearance of Blodget with pleasure, and that he had more than once looked at the sun declining in the West. Once, at least, he must solace himself with beauty.

The hour had nearly arrived for leaving off all business, and shutting up store, when Mr. Brown, who had been absent a couple of hours, thrust a note into Monteagle's hand. He opened it and read—

'Friend M,—Unexpected business will prevent me from waiting on you this evening, as was agreed upon. To-morrow night I shall be free to attend you.

*Ever yours, BLODGET.'*

'The deuce!' cried the youth, 'then I will go alone.' He paused, and smiled as he remembered the good resolution he had been on the point of forming when he had no doubt of Blodget's coming. The feeling of disappointment which he experienced convinced him that it would be no easy matter to put his good resolution in practice.

He slowly crawled over the hill toward the house of Mr. Vandewater. When he sat down to supper with the family, he observed that Julia was in much better spirits than usual. Instead of regarding him with that heavy, mournful look that had been habitual to her for some months past, he caught her in glancing covertly towards him several times, with sparkling eyes and something like a glow of excitement on her cheeks.

'Mr. Brown called this afternoon, I understand,' remarked Vandewater in the course of conversation.

'Yes, sir,' returned his lady; 'he made himself very agreeable to your hopeful young lady here.'

'Now aunt, you are provoking,' said Julia, with an ill-concealed smile of pleasure. 'I was thinking if he was a jug what a fine handle his huge Roman nose would make.'

Vandewater roared as usual on such occasions. Monteagle smiled. A thought, however, had instantly struck him. He knew that Brown was a great talker, and like many great talkers, often said those things to his listeners which he thought would interest them rather than those things which were founded in fact. He imagined that in the glances which Julia had given him, at the supper table, there was a look of triumph as well as pleasure. Could it be that Brown, knowing Julia's secret, had made up a story about himself—had told her that Monteagle was truly in love with her, but only played shy for fear of the uncle? Was it not quite possible that Brown had misunderstood the doctor; and that he believed Vandewater was opposed to the match, and had advised his niece to conquer her passion on *that* account, instead of doing it because her passion was hopeless?

Nothing seemed more likely to Monteagle than this, especially as Blodget had so understood the matter, and Blodget had received his information from Brown. Besides, might not Brown have seen Blodget that day, and as the youth had become suddenly silent when the 'great secret' was told him, had not Blodget interpreted this silence as despair of success and consequently melancholy, and so reported it to Brown?

All that evening, Julia was extremely lively, and sometimes her aunt regarded her with surprise if not disapprobation, so piquant were her sallies and so pointed was her ridicule. Monteagle was more than usually grave; not only from his want of sleep on the preceding night, but because he thought he had detected the source of Julia's gaiety, and the mistake under which she labored.

At length, when Monteagle rose to retire, Julia contrived to place herself near the door, and as he went out, half asleep, and feeling very dull, she softly whispered the one word 'Hope!'

Monteagle started as if struck by an arrow at this confirmation of his fears. The poor girl had mistaken his gravity and dullness for that despair which Brown had taught her to believe he was laboring under, and had ventured to tell him that he might hope!

As Monteagle hurried off to his chamber, he knew not whether to laugh or cry.

There was something very comic in this mistake. The blundering Brown, with his big nose, getting hold of his story at the wrong end, and hurrying off to banter Julia about her conquest was ridiculous enough: but then the unfortunate girl who had suffered herself to be so readily deluded into the belief that her love was returned, and undertaking to cheer his supposed melancholy by a kind word, called forth his sincerest sympathy.

In the morning early, Monteagle met Julia in the garden.

'You are an early riser, sir,' said she, 'as well as myself. I think the morning is the best part of the day.'

'I am of your mind,' returned Monteagle, 'and so are many others, who rise early to get their morning bitters.'

'So I have been told,' said Julia, with a gay laugh. 'Am I to understand that Mr. Monteagle—'

'Oh, no. I am not one of them,' replied the youth. 'Instead of bitters, I fall in with *sweets*, it seems.'

'Yes, the flowers are fragrant,' said Julia, looking about her, and evading the compliment with the pleased and rather triumphant air of one who, *now*, felt secure of the affections of him who offered it.

Monteagle observed all this and condemned himself for having inadvertently helped along the deception; yet it seemed too cruel to dash her new-fledged hopes to the ground, as he might have done by a single word. Candor would have dictated an immediate explanation,—but the youth gave heed to the more tender pleadings of mercy, and even said to himself—'Time may cure her partiality for me; and another lover may supplant me in her affections; so I will let her rest in happy ignorance. I have no prospect of marrying at present, and why should I dispel a vision which, although baseless, pleases the poor, deluded girl?'

At the breakfast table, the liveliness of Julia, and her merry laugh, drew the attention of Mr. Vandewater, who looked first at his niece and then at Monteagle, as if he supposed an explanation had taken place between the young people, and that all was as Julia desired it to be.

On reaching the store, Monteagle was surprised to see a crowd of people about the door. Officers were there asking questions and noting down the replies.—Mr. Brown was flying about among the spectators, making himself so very busy that the youth almost suspected he had lost his wits.

'Oh, Monteagle, is that you? Where's Mr. Vandewater?'

'I left him conversing with Julia in the breakfast parlor.'

'Ah, yes—yes—fine girl that!' cried Mr. Brown, tapping the youth jocosely on the shoulder. 'But do you know what's happened?'

'Heavens! No!'

'Robbed!'

'The store been robbed, do you say?'

'Yes,' replied Brown, 'it was robbed early this morning.'

'At what time?'

'Why, at about four—at what time do you ask? Well, to judge of the exact time in which the store was broken open, you must, I think, inquire of those who were here. Ha! ha! ha!'

'They cannot have taken much,' said Monteagle, 'or you could not be so— that is, you could not speak so lightly on the occasion.'

'That safe's gone!'

'What! the little safe that we rescued the other day?'

'The same which was taken from the skiff by Vandewater himself.'

'Why, Mr. Brown, that's a serious loss. There was money in that safe—'

'Or the thieves would not have carried it off, to be sure, ha! ha! ha!'

'But how did he get in?'

'That's the puzzle,' said Charley, coming up and joining in the conversation. 'Nothing is broken. The rascals must have had false keys.'

'Rather *true* keys, than false ones,' replied Monteagle, while Brown gave a sudden start and slightly colored.

'Ha! ha! Yes, true ones, or they would not have answered the purpose,' said the latter.

'Yet it is strange,' continued Monteagle, 'for the doors were otherwise secured, as you know, Mr. Brown, by certain secret fastenings which must have been broken before any one could have got in from the outside, unless he was well acquainted with the premises.'

'Oh, the Sydney ducks make themselves well acquainted with all these matters,' cried Charley. 'All we have to do now is to trace out the villains—'

'And begin by searching the police,' said Brown. 'Half the thefts and robberies are committed by them.'

Mr. Vandewater arrived soon after, and was also surprised to find his store robbed without the rupture of a single fastening. He advised an immediate search of the premises, as the robbers might have left something behind them that would have led to their detection. Some persons who had gone into the loft to search, soon came running down with the intelligence that a man was up stairs, fast asleep. All ran up at once, and there Monteagle discovered, between two bales, the bulky form of the Irishman, Jamie. He was snoring melodiously, and seemed to have no idea that the sun was already up.

Mr. Vandewater uttered an exclamation of joy and surprise, for he thought discovery of the whole affair was now certain.

Monteagle shook the sleeping man with his foot. Jamie slowly opened his eyes, and on perceiving there were persons present, said hastily—'How— what—is time, Mr. Brown? Is it time?'

As Mr. Brown was not present, the by-standers were puzzled by these singular words.

'What do you want with Mr. Brown?' said Vandewater sternly.

The Irishman rubbed his eyes, and perceiving in whose presence he stood, answered, 'Why, Jim Brown, to be sure, the eating-house man, he was to call me up in time to go down the Bay.'

'Indeed! and so you slept here, did you?' said Mr. Vandewater sternly. 'But how did you get in?'

'How did I get in, is it? Och, and wasn't I working for Jim all day, and took a little of the mountain dew, and comed in here in the afternoon—and where is it, sure, that I am? Can you tell me at all, at all?'

'Who is this Jim Brown?' said Vandewater turning to Charley. 'Can you lead me to him?' asked Vandewater, quickly.

'Och, faith, and it's I can do that, same,' put in Jamie. 'I'll take you to him, right off, jist, if you'll show the way out of this—what do yees call it? A church is it?'

The Irishman affected such blind stupidity that Vandewater was inclined to believe that his being in the store on the night of the robbery was altogether accidental—that he had blundered in while drunk and got asleep. Nevertheless, he said to Monteagle, 'Keep that fellow in custody till I return.'

As Mr. Vandewater went out with Charley, he descried Mr. Brown, his partner, examining the fastenings, and he observed that the face of the latter was very pale.

'Poor fellow,' thought Vandewater to himself, 'he takes this matter hard.'

On arriving at the shop of Jim Brown, that worthy was found at home, although he had just returned from some expedition, and was covered with dust.

Charley introduced Mr. Vandewater.

Jim hung down his head a moment as if brushing the dirt from his leggings.

'I want to ask you, Mr. Brown, if you have contemplated an excursion lately?'

'Sir?' said Jim with a stare.

'He don't savez—give me leave, sir,' put in Charley. 'Jim, we want to know if you have had any business out of town, lately?'

Jim looked first at one and then the other. He was a little short man, with squint eyes, and looked as if he had not shaved in a month.

'I goes sometimes to see my folks that I trade with. I was at a rancho yesterday.'

'How late did you stay, Jim?'

'I am but just got home.'

'What time did you start to go away?' 'I didn't look at the clock,' replied Jim, in a surly manner.

'Come as near as you can, Jim, and give us a true answer as you value the safety of your bacon,' said Charley sternly.

Jim looked up rather fiercely, but he saw that Charley was in earnest, and replied, 'Well, I don't know what time it was. It may be 'twas eleven o'clock and may be it was only ten.'

'And you have just returned?'

'I told you so once before.'

'So you did. When have you seen Irish Jamie, last?'

Jim looked keenly at his interrogators before he replied, 'Well, I can't rightly tell. Not in a fortnight, I should say p'raps, three weeks.'

'It's all a cock and a bull story, that of Jamie,' said Charley. 'You see there's no truth in it. He must be arrested.'

Jim Brown turned away his face and his manner was suspicious upon hearing these words.

As Vandewater and Charley walked back to the store, the latter said. 'We must see the keeper of the rancho and find out from him if Jim Brown has been there.'

'Why do you suspect this Brown of having been engaged in the robbery?'

'It is strange,' said Charley, 'that the Irishman, before he had time to think, should have addressed Brown as one that had agreed to call him at a certain hour. We must make sure that Brown was at the rancho; and if he was, a Philadelphia lawyer would be puzzled to account for Jamie's exclamation when starting out of a sound sleep, and expecting to find Brown at his side.'

'True,' said Vandewater.

'Leave it to me,' continued Charley. 'I will find out what ranch Jim Brown visited yesterday. I will call there, and learn when he arrived, and when he left, if the fellow was there at all.'

On returning to the store, they found Jamie standing outside the door, and surrounded by Monteagle, Mr. Brown and several of the neighboring dealers.

'So, sirrah,' said Vandewater, 'that Brown you spoke of, says that he hasn't seen you for a fortnight, and he has just returned from visiting a friend out of the town.'

'Och, the lying villain,' exclaimed Jamie, in a tone of virtuous indignation. 'Och, the lying, thaving, murthering scoundrel, and wasn't it his own silf that tould me to go into the store and take a nap till mornin', and—'

He was interrupted by the appearance of Jim Brown himself, who rushed into the crowd, and confronting Jamie, cried 'How's this? What have you been telling about me?'

'About *you*, is it?' cried Jamie, with all the assurance imaginable, 'and is it you, you thafe o' the w-o-r-r-l-d, that's come to lie me down, and try to hang his friend widout judge or jury, and widout binifit of clargy, too. Och, you thunderin' wilyun! didn't you tell me to go in here, and slape a bit, just till the morning, when you was to call me up, sure?'

'Sir,' said Jim Brown, addressing Vandewater, 'When you called at my shop, I didn't understand your object, and as your questions seemed very odd, I wasn't well pleased with them; but I've been told since that this man pretends I had an engagement with him. It is a lie. I've no intercourse with the man when I can help it.'

'Hear the lying thafe,' cried Jamie, in a towering passion, and before he could be prevented, he had slipped a long knife out of his sleeve, with which he rushed upon Jim Brown and stabbed him to the heart.

Brown fell dead at the feet of Monteagle. The murder was committed so quick and unexpectedly that it was some minutes before the people collected there were apprized of what had happened! No sooner had the sad tale been told than the inhabitants came running in from all directions; a large mob was collected, a rope procured, and it was with great difficulty that Charley and his aids could prevent the populace from hanging up Jamie on the spot.

Mr. Brown also tried hard to rescue Jamie from the fangs of the incensed and vindictive crowd.

'Let the law take its proper course!' vociferated he, while Jamie kept crying, 'Och now, be aisy, you spalpeens—for there's more nor me you'll have to hang, when yees once begins that game, and some that's your betters, too, and as good as—'

'Let the law take its course!' roared Mr. Brown, so loudly as to drown the voice of the Irishman. 'Take him away, Charley, as soon as possible. See what a crowd is collecting around here. I'm afraid of a riot.'

Jamie was finally carried down the street, in the centre of a tumultuous mob, some pushing one way, and some another, with fierce hootings, yells, and hisses, that were fairly deafening.

A singular impression was left upon the mind of Monteagle by these proceedings, and he commenced the business of the day with a determination to watch closely every thing which was transpiring near him, and to propose to Mr. Vandewater that, in future, some person should sleep in the store every night.

Jamie, who had at length, completed the circle of crime by the committing of murder, was lodged in prison, and Monteagle felt somewhat relieved on account of it, as he believed that the man was for some reason, his deadly enemy. He had not yet recognized this man as the one who shot him down in the barge.

On that evening, Blodget called upon Monteagle, and appeared to be more affable than ever, talked with him about the robbery and made very minute inquiries about Jamie, whom he thought innocent of any intent to rob.

'It is not possible that a man bent on robbery should lie down and get to sleep in the store, or that he should be left by his accomplices,' said Blodget; 'and with regard to his stupid lie about Brown, the man whom he killed, it was probably told because he did not know anything else to say.'

'But,' replied Monteagle, 'in that case why did he address somebody as Brown when first starting from his sleep, and before he had time for premeditation?'

'There is something in *that*,' said Blodget, fixing his eyes very keenly upon those of Monteagle. 'It would seem as if he expected to be called at a certain hour by this Brown.'

'And why should he have been worked up to such a pitch of madness as to murder this Brown, if he did not feel that he was playing him false—'

'No—no—Monteagle. You are reasoning for civilized people now. You don't know these wild, unscrupulous fellows, who like Jamie had prowled about in the wilderness where no moral or religious instruction can reach them. I tell you that a man left wild, a prey to passions, is more to be feared than the tiger or the catamount.'

'You seem to think very hard of this Irishman,' said Monteagle.

'Is he not a murderer?'

The youth was silent. Many things rushed upon his remembrance, and all through there was running a thread of mystery which induced him to say to himself, 'How little do you know of what is going on in the world.'

# CHAPTER VII

## The Ruined Nun—The Mysterious Note.

That evening Monteagle accompanied Blodget to one of those gay houses in Dupont street, already mentioned.

Wit, wine, and beauty sparkled on every side, and again was the imagination of Monteagle bewildered by the transcendent loveliness of Italian, English, North American and South American beauties, who, although accounted frail daughters of Eve, were a much more intellectual, sentimental, and educated class than is to be found in the halls of pleasure in any of the older cities.

While Blodget and Monteagle were thus spending the evening in converse with the nymphs of the town, the latter several times observed Blodget to pause a moment, and sit with lips apart and absent eye, as if listening for some sound in the street.

He was under the impression that Blodget looked for the arrival of some other person. At length a confused murmur was heard as of a crowd at a distance. The sound approached nearer, and at length, in full cry, burst upon the air, such exclamations as 'Stop him! stop thief! Broke away! There he goes! Knock him down,' and this was followed by the discharge of fire-arms, and then came the trampling of many feet, and a confused roar as of a mighty concourse in motion.

Every one in the house flew to the windows and doors; but nothing was to be seen except a crowd of people hurrying along with loud outcries.

'What is the matter?' inquired Monteagle of a person whom he knew, and who just then paused opposite the window.

'Oh, nothing much, sir,' was the careless reply. 'A fellow confined for murder has broken loose; but that we shall always have while such a police exists.'

'There's next to no law in San Francisco,' observed Blodget, 'but do you think, my good man, that the Irishman,—that the prisoner—will get clear?'

'I don't know,' said the other, moving on, while Monteagle quickly said, 'So, you think it's Jamie?'

'Who else can it be?' said Blodget, 'he is the man who has been arrested for murder.'

'Of course,' returned the youth, and yet he thought it strange that Blodget had hesitated when he first mentioned the Irishman, and he connected it with the fact that Blodget had seemed to be listening all the evening as if in anticipation of some such occurrence.

These reflections were, however, soon swallowed up by the gay conversation that succeeded, and the pleasures of wine, music, and an interchange of sentiments with beings who, if virtuous, would have graced any drawing-room in the country. Still Monteagle was occasionally drawn to the contemplation of his friend who seemed quite restless and listened to every noise in the street.

Monteagle had attached himself to an Italian girl, who might be nineteen years of age. Round and plump—with black amorous eyes and good teeth, she seemed to be all alive, and wholly made up of kindness and affection.

Her history was somewhat romantic, as Monteagle learned it from another of the inmates of the house. She was called Loretto, but whether a real or a feigned name was not known. She had taken the vows of a nun from the purest and most sincere motives, but after being two years in the convent, she found it impossible to fulfil her vows. She was naturally formed for love, and could no longer endure to exist without yielding to the demands of an ardent nature, inflamed by a continual contemplation of imaginary love scenes, which always presented themselves to her mind when she would ponder upon more sacred matters.

She made her escape from the convent and returned to her father's house; but found no rest under the paternal roof.—Her parents upbraided her, and were proceeding to have her returned to the convent, when she pretended to go to her chamber for repose. She escaped by the window, and as she fled through the garden she met a handsome young Englishman to whom she at once told her story. He took her under his protection, without the least hesitation, and they lived together, in a retired part of the country several weeks. This young man was of a warm temperament, and here comes the strangest part of the story. He was so smitten by her charms that they upset his reason, and he went raving mad. Though she was actually at his disposal, he imagined that she was some great princess whose love he had sought in vain, and under this strange belief, he, one day threw himself from a cliff into a bed of rocks on the sea-shore and was killed.—She took possession of his mangled body and his effects, found out his friends and delivered them into their hands.

She mourned long and bitterly for the loss of her lover; but her passionate nature again prevailed, and she accepted the offers of a native Count, who was soon killed in a quarrel.

Believing that a fatality attended her in her own land, and learning that spies had been placed upon her actions by her relatives, she came to Brazil, and from thence, soon afterwards, to San Francisco. Such was Loretto, the Italian maid, whose fervid passions were kindled by the manly graces of Monteagle.

She appeared to be all life and soul, and she made a lively impression upon our youth.

As the evening waned, and while he sat conversing with Loretto, Monteagle heard three distinct, though very low taps, on the outer door. At the same time, he saw Blodget raise his head and listen. Then he conducted himself as if nothing had happened, and conversed carelessly with the woman to whom he had attached himself. But in a very few moments, he arose and whispering in the ear of Monteagle, said—'I must quit you for a little while. I have forgotten something: but I will return before long.'

Blodget then departed and soon afterwards, Monteagle withdrew with Loretto. He saw no more of Blodget on that night. In the morning, he learned that Jamie, the murderer, had made good his escape in a somewhat mysterious manner. He had disappeared behind the sand-hills although surrounded by several hundred men.

'The earth must have opened and swallowed him up,' said Mr. Brown, the junior partner.

'I think that he was not the robber of our store,' said Mr. Vandewater, thoughtfully, 'for he would scarcely have remained here all night, if he had shared in the booty.'

'What could have been his errand?' said Brown.

'The fellow might have blundered in here, in a fit of intoxication and gone to sleep,' said Monteagle.

'But why did he kill that tripeman?' inquired Mr. Vandewater.

'Oh, the fellow would kill anybody,' said Monteagle.

Mr. Brown looked very mysterious, and finally seeming to muster up courage, he pulled a note from his pocket, and said to Monteagle—'Perhaps you can tell why this note addressed to *you* was picked up on the very spot where the murderer was sleeping.'

'How!' cried Vandewater. 'What's in the note?'

'I have not taken the liberty to break the seal,' returned Brown. 'Its contents will be known to Mr. Monteagle whenever he chooses to do so.'

Brown handed the note to Monteagle. It was written on fine, gilt-edged paper, and directed to "Mr. Lorenzo Monteagle, Montgomery street."

The astonished youth broke the seal, and opened the note. On the top was marked "*Strictly Private.*" It read thus:

'Dear Sir: You may think it strange that you and I were separated so suddenly on that evening in Dupont street; but a particular friend of mine was the cause, as you saw. If you are at liberty this evening call without fail to see me, but not at that house. You know the cliff near which lies the English barque St. George. I will be under that cliff, on the sea-shore at 8 o'clock precisely. This is very private. Let no one see it. It is sent by a man who will hand it to you, privately if he has an opportunity. Come if you can.

MARIA.'

'Ah—it is too late!' said Monteagle aloud, and putting the note into his pocket.

'It would seem that we are not to be edified by the contents of your note,' said Mr. Brown, looking at Vandewater.

'What shall I do?' said the youth to himself. 'This is something important, without doubt.'

'Private is it not?' inquired Vandewater.

'Sir!' said Monteagle, rather surprised at the question.

'You must know that this is a peculiar occasion,' said Mr. Brown, rightly interpreting Monteagle's surprise. 'At any other time, it would be highly improper to express any curiosity with regard to the purport of that note.'

'This note is nothing,' said the youth. 'It is strictly confidential and has no relation to the robbery whatever.'

Vandewater looked at Mr. Brown, and the latter raised his eye-brows and slowly shook his head. The grimace was not observed by Monteagle, whose thoughts were with the young lady beneath the cliff.

'You will observe, Mr. Monteagle,' said Brown, in a very gentle and yet distinct tone, 'that a heavy robbery has been committed. An atrocious malefactor is found asleep in the store that has been robbed; a letter, evidently dropped by him bears your address upon its back. If he is taken and brought to trial, of course that letter will be needed.'

'So far I can satisfy your curiosity,' said Monteagle. 'It appears that Jamie was employed as messenger to bring me this letter. It is probable that he came here drunk and fell asleep.'

'That seems to account fully for the man's presence. It is as I thought, that he is guiltless of the robbery,' said Vandewater.

Brown compressed his lips, partly nodded, partly shook his head, raised his eye-brows, and turned away, like a man who is only half convinced, and who has made some discovery that he hesitates to unfold.

At supper that evening, Julia Vandewater was as gracious as usual; but when he arose to go abroad, she said to him as he passed the door, 'You keep very late hours, Sir Lorenzo; I must take you in charge, myself.'

Although this was said in a tone of raillery, yet there was the slightest possible air of reproof in it, enough to make Monteagle feel that the deluded girl considered herself entitled to express an opinion upon his conduct.

As he travelled over the hills towards the town, the youth said to himself— 'Would it be more cruel to break this bubble at once, or suffer it to collapse of itself in due time? Surely a flame that is never fed won't burn long, and I have given Julia not the least reason to suppose that I regarded her with partiality.'

He had arrived at a thick clump of bushes, at a considerable distance from any house though a small rancho was in plain sight, when he heard something stir among the leaves and branches. He drew out his revolver.

'Will you shoot me?' inquired a silver voice, and in another moment, Maria stood before him.

'Ah! Good night. I wanted to see you,' said Monteagle. 'I received your note—'

'When?'

'Not till to day,' replied the youth, 'although it must have been written two or three days ago.'

'He's longer than that,' replied Maria, 'I waited for you nearly all night.'

'At the place you designated—under the cliff?'

'Yes.'

'Then your business must be important. I am sorry that I did not get the note in time.'

Maria remained silent some moments. At length, she began—'My errand is no great things. I wanted to see you.'

The youth laid his hand on her shoulder kindly.

'No—'said she—'You don't understand. All you, gentlemens, think girls love you always. Nothing to do but love man, when man laugh at her,' and she shook her locks independently.

'But I am glad to see you at any rate,' said Monteagle.

'Oh, yes, you are very glad to see me—some—but you are more glad to see—'

'Whom?'

'You know best.'

Monteagle thought of Loretto, whose witching graces and rich personal charms had, indeed, wrought powerfully upon his imagination.

'Come tell me where she lives,' said he.

'You have just come from there,' returned Maria.

'No, upon my honor, I have not been there since last night.'

Maria started, and her eyes shone brilliantly as she gazed into his face.

'Not been home to-day?' cried she.

'Ah, yes, I have just come from the house of Mr. Vandewater.'

'And who lives *there*?' inquired she, fixing her eyes keenly on the face of the youth.

'Mr. and Mrs. Vandewater, their niece and the servants,' replied he.

'The niece! the niece!' cried Maria. 'What of *her*?'

'A very fine young lady, I believe.'

'Very fine? Yes, very fine—you find her so? Very fine.'

'Maria,' said he, in a decisive tone, 'if you have been told that I love Julia Vandewater, or that I have ever given her the least reason to suspect so, you have been told a downright falsehood.'

'You not love Julia? No? Not a little bit?' and she seized his hand and gazed into his face earnestly.

'No, Maria, I do not love her.'

Maria was silent, and looked much puzzled. She trotted her foot; she looked at Monteagle, and then she fixed her gaze upon the ground for several minutes.

Suddenly lifting her head, she said to Monteagle in a brisk tone, 'You tell me one very big lie!'

'No, upon my honor.'

After a moment's silence, she said, 'Where you have been last night?'

'I can't tell you that, Maria.'

'Ah! I find you out. You love one pretty lady: you see her last night, and you say I not tell you where I go last night.'

'No, Maria, I have answered one of your questions; but cannot answer the other.'

Maria looked down, and breathed a deep sigh.

Monteagle's pride was a little touched. He said, 'I do not know that I shall ever marry, Maria. But if I happened to fall in with a congenial spirit—a *virtuous*, *chaste*, respectable girl, I don't know what might happen.'

Maria threw back her head, shook her raven tresses fiercely, and her nostrils dilated as she answered—'What thing is men! they think of nobody but himself. Woman got soul for somebody besides herself,' and she struck her breast forcibly, so much so that Monteagle heard a dagger rattle in its scabbard.

'Oh, yes, Maria, I have feeling for others,' returned Monteagle. 'I have feeling for you, and although I may not wish to marry you—'

The girl whirled completely round on one foot, and interrupted Monteagle by a shout of laughter that might have roused the inmates of the distant ranch.

He looked at her surprised. Scarcely deigning him a glance, she began again, and laughed till her breath failed her.

'Man is so fool!' said she at length. 'Here,' she continued, taking a string of costly pearls from some place where they had been concealed about her person, and laying them on his hand. 'You think that poor Maria give you these? You think I buy?'

Monteagle examined the precious gift by the twilight, and perceived that it was, indeed, too magnificent to have come from the poor nymph, and that it must be a gift from some unknown individual.

He perceived the drift of Maria's questionings. He believed that this was the gift of some wealthy lady who was kindly disposed towards him; and that Maria had been commissioned to sound him on the subject of his reported attachment to Julia.

Here was an adventure, indeed, and his imagination was at once set on fire.

'Tell me, Maria, the name of the lady?'

'What lady?'

'The lady who sent me these pearls.'

'A Lady—ha! ha! ha! It was not a lady. It was one big gentleman.'

Monteagle's vanity fell ninety degrees, at hearing these words.

'Who was the gentleman?' inquired he, impatiently.

'Who is your lady that you saw last night?' questioned the wilful girl.

'Oh, nobody—nothing at all. Nobody that I shall ever fall in love with, I promise you that.'

'Not fall in love? Where you go to-night?'

Monteagle smiled at this close question, for he felt a little caught. He was bound to Loretto when he met Maria.

The girl turned and began to leave him.

'Stop, Maria, tell me more about these pearls. Who is the gentleman who sent them to me?'

'Who is the lady you see last night and go to see to-night too?' demanded she retreating.

Monteagle pursued, when she quickened her pace and finally fled with the fleetness of a fawn. Not caring to be seen chasing a woman by several travellers, whom he had observed coming that way, Monteagle slackened his pace. Maria was soon out of sight, and Monteagle was besieged by a thousand ideas at once.

'She tells me that this valuable gift came from a man—a wealthy nabob—and yet she inquires as closely into the state of my heart as if she was the agent of one of her own sex who had an interest in knowing whether I was in love with Julia Vandewater or not. At any rate, she has gone off in the belief that I have a lady in view—That I am in love with her, with whom I spent last night and to whom I am now going!—Perhaps—yes, perhaps, after all, this is a present from a lady, and that Maria was charged not to tell that fact unless she should discover that my heart was disengaged, and that believing it to be otherwise, she feigned that these pearls came from a rich old fellow who had nothing to do with his wealth but to send it about the country by the hands of ladies of pleasure begging young men to accept of it! No, no, that won't do. This gift has come from a lady.'

He thought of the veiled female, supposed to be a nun, who brought Maria the note. 'Might not she be the giver?'

'But no, her errand was to the girl, not me.'

A moment's reflection taught him, that it would be improper to go with his valuable prize to the house whither he was bound, as Loretto might suppose, in case she discovered it that it was intended as a gift to her, and would experience a disappointment when informed that such was not its destiny.

He turned on his steps to return to the house, and a moment afterwards heard quick footsteps behind him. He turned, at the same time placing his hand on his revolver; but the two men who now approached him seemed to be peaceably inclined.

'A fine night, sir,' said one of the strangers.

'It is indeed,' replied Monteagle.

'Have you seen anything of a large brown goat, hereabouts, sir,' continued the man who had first spoken.

'I have not,' was the reply, and Monteagle, bidding them 'good evening,' turned to take his way to the city. At this moment his arms were firmly pinioned to his sides by one of the men, while the other quickly and adroitly drew his revolver from his pocket, and passed a strong cord several times tightly round his arms. The man who had heretofore held him in his iron gripe, in spite of his determined struggles, suddenly tripped up his heels, and he fell heavily upon the hard beach.

The sudden shock for a few seconds deprived him of his senses, and when recollection returned he found himself still lying on the wet shore, from which the tide had but just receded. His arms were tightly lashed behind his back, and his eyes closely bandaged.

For a few moments no sound was heard but the low murmuring of the small waves as they rolled upon the beach, and his own heavy breathing, for he had violently resisted the ruffians in their attempt to bind him; but the assault had been too sudden and unexpected for his efforts to be of any avail.

He now attempted to unbind his arms, but all his attempts were perfectly futile.

'I hope you're having a good time of it, casting off them stoppers. Nothing'll open them lashings but a sharp knife, and if you get one at all it will be through your blasted ribs, if I had my way about it.'

'Who are you, sir; and what means this rascally violence?'

'Take it coolly, my young game-cock, and bless your stars you haven't a brace of bullets through your bloody heart,' said another voice, which he recognized as that of the person who had questioned him about the goat.

Monteagle revolved in his mind all the occurrences which had transpired in the last few days, in order to account for this strange outrage. At first he thought robbery might be their object; but this idea was put to flight when he remembered that while he lay senseless no attempts had been made to deprive him of the little gold he had about him.

Another person now joined the party, and he heard the three in low and apparently earnest consultation. Soon they ceased talking, and approached him.—Two of them raised him to his feet, and one of them said in a rough, brutal tone, 'Now, stir your stumps, and walk where we lead you.'

'But how if I refuse to walk?' said Monteagle.

'Then we'll take you by the neck and drag you over the beach, if the sharp stones scrape the flesh from your cursed bones.'

'Release me; or my cries shall bring assistance,' said Monteagle, resolutely.

'Speak one loud word, and the contents of this crash through your scull,' said the last comer, in a firm calm voice, and our hero felt the cold muzzle of a revolver pressed against his temple, and at the same instant the sharp click announced it was at full cock.

Monteagle had as brave a heart as ever beat in mortal bosom; but here was a dilemma that would have made even Jack Hays pause for reflection.

But little time was given Monteagle for thought.

'D—n,' cried one of his captors, impatiently, 'let's be moving. We've got a long road, and a heavy night's work before us yet.'

'By —, you're right, old hoss,' said one of them, 'there's been fooling enough already.'

So saying, he seized Monteagle by the collar with no gentle grasp.

The latter seeing that resistance would only lead to his being dragged along by main force, if not to his instant death, told them to unbind him, and he would walk peaceably along with them.

'That's right, youngster, you'll save us the price of a couple of bullets, and the trouble of reloading,' said the fellow with the revolver.

After proceeding alongside the beach for some hundred yards, they clambered up the almost perpendicular face of the cliff, by the assistance of the dwarf trees and jutting rocks. Monteagle being aided by two of the men, who each held one of his arms.

Before gaining the summit of the cliff, one of the party gave a low, peculiar whistle, somewhat like the cry of a curlew. It was immediately responded to and they set out in the direction from whence proceeded what was evidently the pre-concerted signal.

'All right, Jimmy,' said one of Monteagle's captors.

'The divil a bit of noise I hear, I heard only the barking of them cursed lane wolfs that the uncivilized graysers call key-ots. And the d—d half starved things made me feel a bit afeard, for they sounded like a dog howling, and you know when a dog howls it's sure some one that hears him is soon going under the sod.'

'Shut up your Murphy-trap, Jim, or just open it, and take a swallow of this: I got it at the Sazerac as I passed, thinking you might need a little Dutch courage, and that brandy would put pluck into even John Chinaman's chicken heart.'

'Come, come, let's mount and be off.' This order was given by a voice which Monteagle recognized as that of the man who placed the pistol at his head, and who appeared to be the leader of the gang.

Monteagle was placed upon a horse, and with a mounted man on each side of him, one of whom held the lariat of his steed. The word was given to proceed, and they all started at a brisk trot.

'What way?' said Jimmy.

'Right straight for the hut!' was the response.

Monteagle and his assailants had just disappeared in a deep hollow, when a man suddenly emerged from the thick shrubbery that enclosed the spot from which the party had departed. He was a short, powerfully built man. Even in the moonlight one could see that there were more white than black hairs in the abundant locks that fell upon his variously colored blanket; but his eye-brows were coal-black, and bent over eyes as bright and keen as the point of a dagger.

'Holy Barbara!' ejaculated he in Spanish, while his hands almost mechanically made the sign of the Cross. 'What in the name of *San* Diabolo are they going to do with that youth? But I must be off, or it will be too late to save him. No wonder our dear mistress Donna Inez loves him. I owe him a good turn, too, for he certainly saved my life when them two 'Pike' hombres were going to give me 'hell,' as they called it, because I was sober on the Fourth of July.' Thus soliloquizing, the Californian, for such he was, withdrew once more into the thicket, and in a second returned, followed by a noble looking steed, black as midnight.

'You shall have a good run now, my handsome Cid,' said the old Californian, as he patted the mane upon the forehead of the noble animal, as gently as a father would the curls that clustered on the brow of a favorite daughter.

Without touching foot to stirrups, he vaulted lightly into the saddle, shook the reins, and the next instant Cid was bearing his rider through the hollows and over the hills that lay between them and the Mission, near which was the rancho inhabited by the father of Donna Inez.

Sanchez, for such was the name of the horseman, never drew rein until he stopped abruptly at the gate of his mistress' domicile. Here he alighted, entered the house, and sought an interview with the beautiful daughter of Signor Castro.

# CHAPTER XVIII

## The Lone Hut—The Torture!

Return we now to Monteagle. The ruthless gang of fellows who had made him prisoner rode on in almost total silence over the vast treeless, shrubless, sand bank which lies between the bluff headlands and the little laguna, where the pig-eyed votaries of Confucius perform the scrubbing, dipping and pounding of linen, dignified with the misnomer of *washing*. As if anything immersed in that chocolate-hued fluid could emerge purer than it entered. Skirting the shore of the laguna, the party soon reached a tolerably good road. This they followed for about half a mile. One of the party riding some distance in advance in order to give notice of the approach of any unwelcome intruder. No person appeared, however, to interfere with their plans and they soon struck off into the sand hills, where their persons were hidden from view by the scrub oaks and wild lilac bushes that covered these lonely spots, since dotted with neat little cottages and smiling gardens. Heaven grant that they may ever be the abode of prosperity and happiness, as they have always been of open-hearted hospitality.

Half an hour's more riding brought them to the place of their destination. It was a rude hut or cabin, such as 'squatters' put up when taking possession— peaceably if they can, forcibly if they must. This hut was erected at the bottom of a deep dell, surrounded on all sides by hills so abrupt that they were forced to leave the horses tied above, while they made the descent on foot.

Both externally and internally this looked like the ordinary abode of a new settler. But no sooner had the gang entered with their prisoner, than a light was procured, and one of the party, moving a mattress, lifted a trap door that gave entrance to a subterraneous apartment of some extent. It was probably a natural cavern, the entrance to which had been accidentally discovered by these desperadoes. Its isolated situation suggested its usefulness to them as a secret place of rendezvous, and a receptacle for plunder. One of them had accordingly squatted on the place and put up the hut.

Monteagle was handed down into this apartment, his eyes still blindfolded— but the close, damp air informed his senses that he was in an underground apartment of some kind. The more he reflected the more he became mystified in his endeavors to ascertain the motives that had prompted these ruffians to take him prisoner in this most unaccountable manner. He had recognized the voice of the man called 'Jimmy' as that of the villian found asleep in Vandewater's store, and who had been arrested for murder, and afterwards escaped from justice. But this discovery did not explain why he had been thus kidnapped. His suspense was, however, soon ended, as shall presently be shown.

The cavern was of large dimensions, yet was more than half filled with silks, broadcloths, laces, and velvets of the costliest descriptions piled promiscuously together. Upon these heaps lay goblets, salvers and ladles of gold and silver ware, some showing signs of use, but most appearing bright and untarnished as when they glittered on the jeweller's shelves. These things were evidently the result of successful robberies and explained why the neighboring city had been swept by so many conflagrations.

In one corner of the cavern a small, thin, sharp-visaged man bent over a large crucible, the flickering flames beneath which shed a red glow upon his swarthy, anxious countenance. At the first glance this individual might have been mistaken for one of those alchemists who, in the dark ages, sought to transmute the baser metals into gold, or discover an elixir that would give to mortal man eternal vigor and immortal youth. He of the crucible was engaged in no such visionary employment. Beside him stood dies and other mechanical contrivances for the manufacture of coin, while a large box full of glittering 'octagons' showed that he was busy 'augmenting the currency,' by fabricating spurious 'slugs.'

Monteagle now once more demanded the cause of his detention.

'Your employer, Vandewater, lately sold a vessel on account of a New York merchant, for thirty thousand dollars, which sum he received in gold. That money was placed in your safe—'

'Then you are the robbers!'

'Silence, and listen! When we opened the safe, it only held a few thousands belonging to the firm. You know where the thirty thousand is placed. Inform us, and you shall be liberated, and if we obtain the money, you shall have five thousand dollars for your share.'

'I'll die first,' indignantly cried Monteagle.

'No—you'll confess first, and maybe die soon after,' said a voice which Monteagle to his surprise and joy recognized as that of Blodget.

'What, Blodget, my friend, you here? Then this is all a joke. But it has been carried much too far,' said Monteagle, his cheek flushing as he thought of the violence he had been subjected to.

'If it's a joke, youngster, you'll think its a d—d poor one before we get through with it. But enough of this fooling! Tell where the money's to be found, or by h-ll we'll make you!'

'Never—so help me heaven!' said Monteagle, determinedly.

'Just hand me that little vice,' said Blodget, in a cool, business-like, tone.

'Is it this?' said Jimmy, bringing over a small, portable iron vice, from among the tools by the furnace.

'That's right,' said Blodget. 'Now, lads, hold him fast.' Monteagle was suddenly prostrated upon the damp floor, and firmly held there by the ruffians, although he put forth lion-like strength in his struggles to shake off his enemies. 'Now, then, we'll try his nerves,' said Blodget, and immediately proceeded to adjust the vice on one of Monteagle's thumbs. 'Will you tell where the money can be found?' said Blodget.

Monteagle made no reply.

Blodget gave the vice a couple of turns but Monteagle gave no signs of feeling except an involuntary shudder and a heavy sigh.

Again his heartless tormentor gave the vice a turn. Still the brave youth remained silent, although the pain was fearful, and he could feel the hot blood gushing from under his nail.

'Knock out the stubborn divil's brains,' cried Jimmy, waxing impatient at the delay.

'Keep cool, Jimmy,' said Blodget. 'It is money we want, not brains.'

Another turn of the vice—but Monteagle, save by a low, involuntary groan, gave no token of the agony he suffered.

'Curse the fellow, it's as hard to extract gold from him as to crush it out of quartz rocks. He's so devilish stubborn, I see he will die, as he says, before he'll tell where the gold is placed. Now, boys, what's to be done?' continued Blodget, looking around inquiringly into the villainous faces of his companions.

They were all silent, for some seconds. At length the man that we have described as being employed over the furnace, broke silence, saying, 'Let me manage him, and I'll promise to make him tell, not only where we may find this gold, but reveal far weightier secrets, if such he knows.'

'Go a-head! Signor Maretzo,' said Blodget, 'but remember that we have no racks and wheels, or any of those other ingenious contrivances so common in your precious country.'

'My country is what tyrants and priests have made it;' returned the Italian. 'Even the accursed act I am now about to practice I learned in the dungeons of the *holy* inquisition. There my heart was turned to marble, and every drop of pity congealed forever.'

'Let the blessid church alone, or you and me'll have a row, old black-beard,' said Jimmy, quite fiercely.

'That 'Sazerac' brandy has awakened Jimmy's religious feelings. But, come, come—there's been too much of this fooling. Maretzo, if you can make this stubborn devil talk, do so at once!'

Maretzo made some arrangements about his furnace, and joined the party gathered around Monteagle—who still lay, bound and blind-folded, upon the dungeon floor.

The Italian then took up a piece of linen from one of the piles of dry goods, and placed it smoothly and tightly over Monteagle's lips and nostrils. He then took a glass of water, and poured a few drops upon the linen. The poor youth could draw breath with difficulty through the dry linen, but when its threads became swollen by absorbing the water his respiration was almost entirely prevented. His breast heaved by involuntary muscular expansion—great drops of sweat started from every pore, while the veins of his neck and forehead grew swollen and purple. It required the united force of all the scoundrels that surrounded him to retain his writhing body on the earth.

Poor Monteagle's convulsive and spasmodic efforts, however, soon subsided, and it appeared as if his tormentors had gone too far, and that death had stepped in and snatched their helpless victim from further cruelties.

Maretzo removed the cloth, and after a few heavy and painful attempts at breathing, Monteagle's low groans and sighs told how dreadful had been his sufferings.

'Now, G—d d—n your stubborn soul will you tell us where to find the money,' said Blodget.

Heavy, deep-drawn sighs, were the poor youth's sole reply.

'Give him another dose,' said one of the heartless ruffians, 'he likes the medicine so well.'

At this instant the trap door was lifted, and one of the gang, who had been stationed on the neighboring hill as a look-out, cried:

'I see a party of horsemen making right for the hut, at full gallop. We must have been followed. Let's be off, at once, or we're sure to be taken!'

'Sure an' let's have a brush wid 'em,' said Jimmy.

'Never fight till you're obliged to,' said Blodget.

'Lay hold of this fellow,' said Maretzo, 'and carry him to a horse, then let's all start down towards the Heads. I know of a cave there, that has never had any dwellers except seals. There we can keep this youth, and wring the secret from him, or, failing that, put him where he'll tell no tales.'

No more words were wasted; this striking the whole party as the best plan they could pursue under the circumstances. Accordingly, a couple of men seized hold of Monteagle, and bore him up the stairs, through the hut, and then to the summit of the acclivity where the horses were tethered. The rest of the party followed, bearing with them all the most valuable and portable articles they could get hold of in their haste.

By the time the whole gang were in the saddle and ready for a start, the approaching party of riders had got to within a quarter of a mile of the hut. They were coming from the direction of the Mission.

# CHAPTER IX

## The Maid—the Robber—the Race.

The reader will remember that we left Sanchez at the house of Signor Castro, whither he had ridden with speed, upon hearing the directions given to convey Monteagle to the solitary hut, with the whereabouts of which he was well acquainted.

Leaping from his horse, Sanchez merely cast the reins upon his neck, and the well trained animal stood almost motionless awaiting the return of his rider.

Upon entering the house the first inquire of Sanchez was for his young mistress, Donna Inez. She had gone to the Mission Church, to attend the vesper services, and had not yet returned.

Again Sanchez was in the saddle, and in a few moments reached the square fronting the rude antique edifice in which many generations of Californians have been christened, wedded and buried. Here he again dismounted, entered the church, and catching the eye of his mistress, motioned her to follow him, and then withdrew from the church. No sooner had they passed from beneath the sacred roof, than Sanchez related to her all that he had witnessed on the beach, when Monteagle was seized.

The youthful maiden's lovely cheek now paled till it was white as alabaster, then crimsoned till its flush rivalled the ruddiest rose, as she listened to the rude but graphic description given by Sanchez of the violent seizure of the gallant youth who had bravely rushed into the flames and saved her from a dreadful death.

Donna Inez directed Sanchez to go to a small hotel, on a road that leads into the Mission Plaza, and inquire for one Joaquin. If he saw him, he was to say the lady desired to meet him instantly, at her father's residence.

Sanchez did the bidding of his young mistress with due diligence. He found Joaquin busy at a game of billiards; but no sooner did he receive the message than throwing down his cue he rushed to the door, and leaped into the saddle of a splendid looking horse, which was quietly standing untied at the door. Bidding Sanchez to follow, Joaquin struck the spurs deep into the flanks of his fiery steed, and proceeded at a gallop towards the dwelling of Signor Castro.

When Joaquin arrived in front of the mansion, he found the young and lovely lady standing in the portico. She was attired in the rich garb of a Mexican cavalier. But neither the large topped boots, nor the ample poncho could disguise the matchless symmetry of that perfect form: rich in every grace that renders woman resistless. Her rounded bosom heaved wildly beneath the folds of her poncho as Joaquin lifted his hat before her, at the same moment reining in his foaming steed with such a sudden and powerful effort, that the spirited animal was forced down almost on his haunches.

'*Buenos noches*, Donna Inez,' said the robber, for such he was, respectfully.

'Thank you—thank you, Joaquin, for your promptness. You are indeed grateful,' said Donna Inez.

'My dear lady,' replied Joaquin, 'give me I beg of you, an opportunity to prove my gratitude in some more difficult shape than in riding a short distance on a fine evening.'

'I will Joaquin. I desire this night, to have your aid in an enterprise full of difficulty; nay, of absolute danger,' said Inez.

'Danger!' cried the robber, and his bright black eyes dilated and sparkled like those of a war-horse when the clangor of trumpets smites his ear. 'Let the enterprise be full of danger and I will execute it for the danger's sake—much more willingly however, if I also serve you, my dear, my noble young lady. Oh, never can be effaced from my heart your kindness to my poor, darling Carmencitto, after those fiends had—' the robber paused, his swarthy visage became of ashy hue, and his strong frame trembled with some violent emotion. 'Enough of this—I live but for two purposes—gratitude to you, and revenge on them hell-born villains—then welcome death in any shape; for what have I more to do in this world, when my poor Carmencitto lies in her cold grave?'

Inez, who knew how cruelly this man had been treated, waited ere she again addressed him. When he became somewhat calmer, she said:

'Joaquin, some villains have seized the brave young man who saved my life, and carried him to the lone hut over among the sand-hills. I am determined to rescue him, and need your aid, and that of some of your friends.'

'Most willingly,' replied Joaquin, and placing a small silver bugle to his lips he blew two notes, so sharp and loud that their echoes could be heard reverberating from the distant hills. But awakening the echoes were not the only effect. In a few moments, coming from different directions, nearly a dozen horsemen could be seen drawing towards the spot where the sounds proceeded.

Meanwhile, Sanchez, in obedience to the directions of his mistress had saddled her favorite horse, and led him to the front of the house; when Inez, declining assistance, vaulted lightly into the richly mounted saddle *en cavalier*, and as the fiery animal bounded and curvetted, her full but exquisitely moulded limbs yielded gracefully to each movement of the animal she bestrode, while she tried to check his impatience by patting his coal black neck with her little hand, whiter than the pearls that zoned her taper fingers, and speaking to him in those soft endearing expressions of which the Spanish is so full.

No sooner had the horsemen, summoned by the bugle of Joaquin, all assembled, than they started at a brisk pace, led by Sanchez, through the bridle-path that led in the direction of the hut.

It was the approach of this party which induced the gang who had captured Monteagle, to leave the hut in such haste.

Monteagle was so exceeding weak when he reached the spot where the horses of the thieves were tied, that, even had he wished to do so, he could not have retained his seat, in the saddle a moment. So, after placing him astride a horse, they lashed him in his seat with one of those ever-present and ever-useful lariats.

No sooner was this done than away they started in the direction of the Presidio Road, the pursuing foe, being less then a third of a mile behind them.

'Who the deuce can they be?' said Blodget, who rode on one side of Monteagle, to Jimmy, who rode on the other side.

'It's more nor I can conceive,' replied Jimmy.

'They can't be police, nor even the vigilance committee, or why come from the Mission instead of the city?' said Blodget.

'They surely can't be a pleasure party,' replied Jimmy. 'For the huntsman of Howth, that followed a hare to h—l, wouldn't gallop over those sand-hills for fun.'

'And most certainly not at such an hour,' said Blodget. ''Tis very, very strange. They still follow us,' he continued, as he turned in the saddle, and looked back at the approaching party.

By this time they had gained the road that—running almost parallel with the shore of the Bay—passed the Presidio, and went on toward the rugged promontory which forms one side of the famous Golden Gate.

For a few moments they proceeded on in silence; occasionally glancing back to see if the party that so alarmed them, continued the pursuit. What they had thus far feared was soon turned to certainty, for they saw the whole party, numbering nearly a dozen, emerge from the shrubbery, turn into the road, and follow after them at a good round pace.

'As long as we keep this distance from them, don't force your horses, and we may yet contrive to escape them. Their nags must be pretty well blown, as they had a long ride before they reached the hut; and ours started fresh, after a good long rest,' said Blodget to his companions.

Leaving the gang of thieves to pursue their way, let us return to Inez and the party accompanying her.

'They have all left the hut,' said Sanchez, as they drew near it, 'and I think that is the young American, between the two that ride in advance of the party.'

'Oh, for heaven's sake, let us spur on, and save him. Who knows what bloody purpose is in their cruel hearts!' cried Inez.

'We must spare our horses over this uneven ground, if we hope to catch the villains,' replied Joaquin.

'Be it as you say,' rejoined the maiden, reluctantly checking her eager steed who seemed impatient to leap forward.

While these conversations were proceeding, both parties had reached a fine piece of level ground that stretched away before them in the direction of the Presidio.

'Now,' cried Joaquin, 'urge your horses to the utmost!' and suiting the action to the words, his long spurs were buried into the side of his charger, who bounded forward like lightning.

Keeping leap for leap with his fleet steed was the gallant animal that bore Inez on his back, while the rest of the party were but a few rods in the rear. The vigilant Blodget soon observed that the pursuers had increased their speed, and were fast lessening the distance between them.

'Let your horses do their d——est!' cried the profane fellow, as he struck the rowels deep into the already bleeding sides of his courser.

His followers quickly obeyed his commands, and the pursuers and the pursued were soon scouring over the plain, at the very utmost speed of their respective horses.

# CHAPTER X

## The Chase Continued.

Inez and Joaquin had now arrived almost within pistol-shot of the gang, which had concentrated around Monteagle.

'They'll catch us sure, if we don't cast this fellow adrift,' said one of the party.

'He'll never live to see one of us hung, at any rate,' said Jimmy, drawing a revolver, and raising it towards Monteagle's head.

'Liar!' shouted Joaquin, as he raised himself in his stirrups, and cast his lasso, which had been for some seconds whirling round his head.

Before Jimmy had time to touch the trigger the unerring noose was fast around his neck. Joaquin's horse halted suddenly, bringing Jimmy to the earth with such violence, as to break his neck.

'Don't mind, Jimmy, but spur for your lives,' cried Blodget, as he urged on his own steed, and that to which Monteagle was lashed. Maretzo instantly taking the place just before occupied by Jimmy.

The lassoing of Jimmy necessarily caused some delay to the pursuing party, which the pursued made good use of to increase the distance between them.

Joaquin sprang from his horse to disengage his lasso from the neck of the fallen man, and in turning the body for that purpose, brought the face of the villain into the full light of the moon.

'Holy Virgin. Thanks, thanks. A golden candlestick shall grace your shrine,' and his eye sparkled, and a gleam of joy shot over his swarthy visage.

'Gracious Heavens!' exclaimed Inez. 'Why Joaquin, though the holy saints know how thankful I am that your skilful arm saved the life of my dear preserver, still I cannot conceive why you can take such pleasure in looking upon such an awful sight as the face of that wretched man,' and Inez turned her face aside sickened to the very heart.

'My gracious young donna,' replied the robber, 'too seldom have I prayed to the holy saints, and to the still holier ones. But of late I have thrown myself before every crucifix I saw and with tears begged that the ravishers of Carmencitto should fall by this hand, and this hand only. And the holy saints have heard my prayers.' As he spoke, he drew a long sharp blade from its sheath, and plunged it to the hilt in the still warm breast of his prostrate foe. 'And now, fair lady,' he exclaimed, 'once again I am at your service.'

'Let us ride like the wind, Joaquin,' said Inez impatiently.

Joaquin was in his saddle, and his horse at full speed in an instant.

But the few moments that had elapsed had sufficed for Blodget and his troop to be almost out of sight.

'They will surely escape us,' cried the maiden.

'No donna,' said Sanchez respectfully. 'They have turned down to the beach, and before they ride a quarter of a mile they will reach a rock that runs out into the sea, round which they cannot pass but at low tide, and even then with great risk.'

While Sanchez was speaking, Blodget and his comrades had reached the point alluded to.

'By G—d,' cried Blodget, 'here we are, brought up, all standing,' as he reined his horse, and gazed angrily upon the white breakers that dashed against the base of the high and jagged rock.

'This that you fear will ruin us, will prove our safety,' said Maretzo. 'I know this spot well. Though close at the foot of the cliff the water is deep, a little way farther out, it is comparatively shoal, and the blue water will hardly reach our horses' girths, though the foam and spray of the breakers may dash over our heads. Follow me closely, deviate not a single inch right or left, and my life for it, I'll bring you safely through.'

So speaking, Maretzo, taking the horse of Monteagle by the bridle, rode fearlessly into the seething and foaming cauldron that roared around the projecting rocks.

He was followed by Blodget and the rest of the party, and though the stoutest of them quailed when the tumbling waves reached their knees, and the cold spray dashed blindingly in their eyes, yet they continued on, seeing that the steeds of Maretzo and Monteagle kept their footing in the yeasty waves.

When Inez and her friends reached the point around which Monteagle had disappeared with his capturers, their first impulse was to follow, but Joaquin commanded his party to halt, till he first attempted the dangerous passage. Inez, however, refusing to let him risk the attempt alone, spurred her steed and dashed boldly into the roaring and foaming waters with him.

They naturally kept as close to the face of the cliff as possible, supposing they would there find the shoalest water, but before they had proceeded many paces the horse rode by Inez began to plunge and rear frantically, frightened by the noise and dash of the waves. The maiden lost all control of the terrified animal, when Joaquin, seeing her peril seized the rein of her steed, and by a sudden and powerful jerk turned his head in the direction of the shore they had just left, where he quickly regained sure footing.

'Donna Inez,' said the robber, 'to pass here is impossible. Either those fellows know some secret ford around this rock, or else the tide has risen unusually fast since they passed. At all events we cannot follow them. The tide is rising and it will be many hours before it will be possible to pass here. Before that time they will be beyond our reach.'

'Cannot we ascend these cliffs, and thus cut them off,' said Inez.

'No, donna,' replied Sanchez, 'we must go back for a long distance before we meet with a place which even a rabbit could get up.'

Reluctantly Inez admitted the force of these remarks, and slowly turned her horse's head in the direction of the city.

'They have some motive, beside murder, in going to all this trouble, else had they killed him when they first met him.'

'What motive could they have?' asked Inez.

'Perhaps, to keep him concealed, until they could obtain a heavy ransom for his release.'

'But from whom could they expect such a ransom; for the youth is neither rich himself nor has he rich relatives, at least not in this country.'

'May not some of the desperadoes with which the city abounds, have heard of the gallant manner in which the youth rescued you from the flames, and trust to obtain from the generosity of your father a round sum for the ransom of the savior of his daughter.'

Inez admitted the plausibility of this supposition, and inwardly resolving that all her own and her father's wealth should be expended, if necessary, to release Monteagle, she silently rode towards home.

When Maretzo, leading the horse of Monteagle, and his comrades, had safely passed around the cliff, they found themselves on a clear, crescent-shaped beach of some extent, the opposite end of which was bounded by a rocky headland, similar somewhat to the one they had just rounded, but still farther overhanging the flood that dashed into foam against the huge fragments strewed at its base.

'We are now safe from pursuit,' said Maretzo. 'Even I, would not venture to retrace our steps, now that the tide has risen so much.'

'Well, old fellow, we had a d—d tight squeeze of it, that's a fact. I thought at one time we were all going to a place where you wouldn't have to spend much for fuel for your furnace, eh, Maretzo?'

The Italian merely made some stale joke about the improbability of Blodget's ever dying by water while there was any rope in the world.

'How far yet to this cavern?' inquired Blodget.

'It's under yonder head,' was the reply of the Italian, as the party moved forward.

'But, deuce take it,' said Blodget, 'we shall perish of cold and hunger before morning. I've got a touch of the 'chills' already.'

'As to the cold, the beach is strewn with drift wood, and we can soon have a fire,' said Maretzo.

'But is the beach strewn with provisions?' asked Blodget.

'I have provisions for a month in the cave,' said Maretzo.

'Come, come, old hoss,—none of that Robinson Crusoe gammon. It's bad fooling with a hungry man.'

'I'll explain to you. During the last great fire, I happened to be near the end of Long Wharf. A lighter full of goods had just been made fast. All the hands rushed up the wharf, probably to assist in putting out the fire. They hadn't stopped even to lower the sail of their boat. The temptation was too strong. I leaped on board, set the sail, and was flying before a stiff breeze right for this cove, where I beached her. Her cargo, instead of rich goods, as I had hoped, proved to be provisions of different kinds, packed in tins. These I carried to the cave. That night it blew hard, and the lighter went to pieces. But, here we are at our journey's end.' So saying, Maretzo, again taking the lead, went boldly in among the breakers.—Blodget followed, leading the horse of the young man, and the remainder of the party brought up the rear. For a few moments, they proceeded on; now turning to the right hand, now to the left, to avoid some vast rock that blocked their way, or to escape falling into some hole in the bottom. The water meanwhile was at times so deep that the horses barely kept their footing, and their riders found great difficulty in making them proceed amid the dashing breakers and the horrid din.

Maretzo, at length, turned sharply to the left, and the next moment the whole party were in utter darkness, in a vast cave, through which they could hear the wind soughing and the roar of the sea reverberating.

'Stand fast, where you are, till I get a light,' said Maretzo, and dismounting, he groped about until his hand rested upon a box of candles, part of the cargo of the lighter. Half a dozen of them were soon burning, and by their glimmer the party fastened their jaded horses.

Monteagle was released from his Mazeppa-like bonds, and placed on the floor of the cave, more dead than alive from the cruel way in which he had been tortured and afterwards lashed to the horse.

A roaring fire was soon kindled, and by its lurid flames the party could see the vast size of the cavern. Maretzo pointed out where the provisions were stowed, and each man bountifully helped himself, and then they all assembled around the blazing fire.

One of the gang less unfeeling than the others, gave Monteagle a biscuit, and a drink out of his flask, which tended to relieve him somewhat.

'What think you, Maretzo,' said Blodget, drawing the Italian aside, after they had recovered from their fatigue, 'is there any more use wasting our time with this chap?'

'I fear not,' replied Maretzo. 'He is now so weak that he would probably faint under any fresh torture, and insensibility would baffle us.'

'Then we must be off. Brown was to try to find out, by some other means, where the money was placed, and if he has succeeded, we must be on hand before daylight to get hold of it. For the absence of Monteagle may excite suspicion, and our sport be spoiled.'

'What shall we do with our prisoner? Knock him on the head, and give the crabs a feast?'

'No. Brown has some old scores to settle with him. You had better stay here to-night with him, and in the morning I'll ride out here and report progress.'

'Be it as you say. I shall not be sorry to have a few hours rest,' said Maretzo.

'But how are we to get out of this trap?'

'You can easily get out of here on the side opposite to that by which we entered. By following the beach awhile you will strike a road that leads over the hills to the City. By that road return in the morning. I'll be on the look out for you!'

'Pick up, boys,' cried Blodget, and in short time they had departed, piloted by Maretzo, leaving Monteagle alone in the cavern.

While taking him from the horse the bandage had been partially removed from his eyes, and he had been a witness of all that went on.

No sooner had they all quitted the place than he at once determined to make a desperate attempt to escape before their return, as he felt that that was his only chance.

Approaching the fire, he seized a piece of wood with his teeth and applied the blazing end to the cords that bound his arms. For some seconds it resisted the action of the fire, but at length it blazed, and was soon so weakened that with the energy of despair the youth snapped it, and had his hands again at liberty. He next looked around for some weapon, and luckily found a hatchet which Maretzo had used to open the cases. Thus armed, he stationed himself at the entrance of the cavern with the determination to fell the ruffians to the earth as they attempted to enter, and then endeavor to make his escape. In a few moments Maretzo appeared and received a blow that sent him reeling and senseless to the ground. Monteagle waited a few moments, but no one else appearing he stepped out of the cavern, and fortunately took the direction in which the gang had just proceeded. At times the waves reached his arm-pits but by moving forward cautiously he at length reached the beach safely.

# CHAPTER XI

## *The Robbery.*

It was about two o'clock of the morning following the night in which so many events were crowded. The moon had gone down, and great masses of black clouds completely hid the stars. The wind blew violently from seawards, and the waves dashed furiously against the massive piers which the enterprise of the San Franciscans have carried far into the bosom of their glorious Bay.

'Well, if this ain't a hell of a night, I'm d—d,' said a powerfully built man, who might have been recognized as Montgomery had it not been so dark that a negro could not have been discerned from an albino.

'By Vere in 'ell is Blodget a keepin' hisself,' said his companion, whose unmerciful treatment of the v's and w's announced him to be a genuine Cockney, and such he was; but previous to visiting California, he had paid Botany Bay a flying visit, his wrists graced with these bracelets, so much more useful than ornamental.

These two men were in a large yawl, under a wharf near Davis street.

'Boat a-hoy!' cried Blodget, on the wharf.

'All right!' responded Montgomery from beneath it.

'Vere've you been this jolly long vile,' said the cockney, as he opened the slide of a dark lantern, while Montgomery drew the boat along to a place where an opening in the planking admitted Blodget's dropping into the boat.

'Hold her steady,' said Blodget, as he leaped square into the centre of the boat.

'Who else is vith ye?' said Jobson, the Londoner.

'Step down here, Belcher,' said Blodget.

As he spoke a man leaped lightly into the boat. To the casual observer there was nothing in the appearance of this individual to attract particular attention, but one accustomed to gauge men's figures by the eye, could not have failed to be struck by the broad shoulders, the full rounded chest, the muscular limbs, and the easy grace of every movement. Pity that a form so full of manliness should hold so black a heart.

'Pull straight for the big wooden store, at the foot of Sacramento street. Old Vandewater, thinking he was d—d sharp, had the kegs of specie, packed in barrels of mackerel by Monteagle and put in the old store, thinking some of us might hear of the sale of the steamer, and break into his store. Brown, to-day, accidentally overheard the carman speak of moving some mackerel, and as it tallied with the day the money was moved, guessed the rest. We can easily get into the store,' continued Blodget.

'Give way!' said the man we have called Belcher, and at the same moment he dipped the blades of a pair of oars into the water and the yawl flew forward.

Few words were spoken, although there was small chance of their being overheard, so loudly howled the gale.

When they reached the wharf upon which stood the store, they proceeded between the piles until all chance of their light being observed was destroyed. An auger was now produced, a hole bored in the planking, then a sharp well greased key-hole saw was introduced and in less than a quarter of an hour a hole sufficiently large to admit a man, was made.

Belcher Kay easily raised himself by his muscular arms into the store; he then assisted Blodget up. The others remained in the boat.

A very few moments sufficed for Blodget and his companion to saw the hoops of the mackerel barrels, and thus get possession of the boxes of gold.

They were quickly lowered into the boat, and the thieves got safely off with their booty.

'Vell if old Wandevater don't svear in the morning, I hopes I may never see old Hingland again,' cried the patriotic Briton as he saw the Golden ballast stowed in the bottom of the boat.

'Pull for Mission creek,' said Blodget, 'they'll give Sydney Valley an awful searching to-morrow.'

The robbers made good their escape, with the thirty thousand dollars in specie, that had been so ingeniously hidden as Mr. Vandewater supposed.

Great was the surprise of the worthy merchant, when summoned, early in the morning, by the storekeeper and informed that the store had been entered.—'But,' said his informant, 'they gained nothing by all their trouble, and out of spite destroyed the few barrels of mackerel that were brought to the store the other day.'

'Then they have got all the money.—Where's Monteagle?' cried Mr. Vandewater.

'I tried to find him at his lodgings,' said the man, 'but he had not been at home all night, I was told.'

At this moment Brown, Mr. V's partner, entered, and expressed great surprise at the fact of the money being in the store of which he had not been informed. ''Tis very remarkable that Monteagle should be out all night, the very time of the robbery. Was Monteagle aware of it being concealed in the barrels, and placed in the store?' continued Brown interrogatively, to Vandewater.

'He is the only person to whom I entrusted the matter. As it was funds with which the firm had nothing to do, I did not deem it necessary to trouble you about the affair. Indeed, it was Monteagle that suggested the mode and place of concealing the money,' said Mr. Vandewater.

'Why this is the most remarkable set of coincidences I ever heard of. A letter addressed to him, evidently brought by that fellow who afterwards stabbed a man—he proposes a way and place of hiding the money—the money is stolen, and on the very night of its being taken, he, Monteagle, is absent all night. Yet, he *may* clear himself,' said Brown.

'It is too clear,' said Mr. Vandewater sorrowfully. 'I would have trusted that youth with my life, and feel at this moment far less regret for the loss of the money than losing all faith in the integrity of my fellow-men.'

'We have both, I fear, been greatly deceived in Monteagle. Within the last few days I have heard that he gambled heavily, and was in the constant habit of visiting houses of ill-fame,' remarked Brown.

'Well, what steps had we best take in regard to this unfortunate affair,' said the merchant.

'There are suspicious circumstances sufficient to warrant the arrest of Monteagle,' replied Brown.

'No—no—I cannot think of that.—He has been misled by others, and though I never wish to employ, or even see him again, I would not wish him to be arrested. So justly indignant are the citizens at the numerous robberies and fires that have lately taken place, that his conviction would be closely followed by his execution. The respectability of his position would be no bar to this, for the Vigilance Committee have determined to make an example of the first man that is fairly proven guilty.'

'Be it as you will, sir,' said Brown, inwardly congratulating himself that in this manner all inquiry would be stopped with respect to the robbery.

'Let nothing more be said about this unfortunate affair, Mr. Brown. Let the store-keepers version pass as the true one—that thieves finding no booty in the store, departed after destroying some of the goods which were of too little value for them to remove.'

Leaving Mr. Vandewater to make arrangements for replacing the stolen money, let us return to Monteagle, who, the reader will recollect, we left safe on the beach after his escape from the cavern of the robbers.

It was with the greatest difficulty, that he continued to drag his wearied limbs along over the hills and through the valleys that lay between him and the city, and it was late in the morning before he appeared at the counting house of his employer, who was conversing with his partner at the moment.

'And this you think is Monteagle's cap,' said Vandewater.

'I know it to be his, and saw it on his head last evening, as he passed up Pacific street,' responded Brown.

'Ah, yes—yes. Too true—too true! Here are his initials, under the lining, in his own writing. This destroys my last hope of his innocence. And you say it was found close by the hole by which the robbers effected an entrance to the store.'

'Yes; it was handed me by the storekeeper. It was evidently dropped in the hurry and forgotten when too late. But here is the young gentleman himself,' said Brown, not a little surprised and alarmed at the appearance of Monteagle, whom he had supposed safely secured in the cavern.

'Mr. Monteagle,' said Vandewater, in a stern voice, slightly tremulous, however, with regret, 'Your services are no longer needed in this establishment, nor do I ever wish you to tread upon the threshold of my house again. Great God! what an escape poor Julia has had. It was to this man I wished to entrust the keeping of your happiness!'

Before Monteagle could recover from his surprise, Brown broke in: 'But perhaps, after all, Mr. Monteagle will explain from whom he received the note the other day, and what was the nature of the appointment it made.'

Monteagle blushed, hesitated, stammered but knew not how to reply.—'This, then,' thought he, 'is the cause of my dismissal. Mr. Vandewater has learned of my associating with wantons, and justly dismisses me from his confidence.'

Meanwhile, Mr. Vandewater who had been closely watching him, and with sorrow saw what he supposed were convincing evidences of Monteagle's complicity in the robbery. Not giving the youth time to recover from his confusion, he waved him out of his office with a cool, haughty gesture, which roused Monteagle's pride, as he thought that he was not worse than thousands of other young men. And this feeling of hurt pride was greatly increased as he reflected upon the manner in which he had suffered, the previous evening, all but death sooner than divulge the secret of this man who now treated him so ungenerously. Turning upon his heel he slowly withdrew from the office, and wended his way to his lodging.

# CHAPTER XI

## How Joaquin became a Robber.

It was one of the loveliest mornings of the loveliest of seasons in California—early summer—when two equestrians might have been seen cantering over a level plain not far from San Jose.

'Surely, Joaquin, this is the sweetest country upon earth, and we the happiest people in it,' said one of the riders, a young girl of some seventeen summers. As she spoke the glance of her dark lustrous eyes rested lovingly upon the face of the noble-looking man that rode beside her, and whose passionate gaze of admiration told how ardently he loved, nay, worshipped his beautiful companion.—And worthy, right worthy was she of all the love of his passionate nature; for seldom has a more bewitching form graced the earth with its presence, than that of Carmencitto; who had but a few days before become the wife of the youth.

Joaquin was the proprietor of a small ranch, a portion of which they were now riding over. He was gifted by nature with a muscular form, and was reputed to be the most daring rider, and the most skilful herdsman in the country. Carmencitto was the daughter of a wealthy Californian, and had been engaged to Joaquin from childhood.

'You say truly, dearest,' replied the horseman. 'Ours is a goodly land, and it needed not that its rivers should roll over sands of gold to make us love it.'

They were just passing a clump of dense shrubbery as he spoke, and hardly had the last word left his lips ere his spirited steed reared, and had he not been a matchless rider, he must have been hurled headlong from the saddle. As it was, before he fully recovered his seat, a lariat was thrown over his head, and his arms firmly secured to his side. While two men, armed with revolvers, held his horse firmly by the reins—their weapons pointed at his breast.

'Make a single attempt to escape, and we'll riddle your carcase with bullets,' shouted one of his assailants.

'Shoot the d—d greaser, at once't,' cried a low-browed, villainous looking fellow.

'Curse the yellar skinned devil, I believe he's glued to the saddle,' said the first speaker as he tried in vain to pull Joaquin from his seat, the latter meanwhile urging his horse forward but in vain, so firmly was he held by the man who had seized his horse by the head.

The assault had been so unexpected that for a brief instant the young Californian had forgotten Carmencitto, but now a wild piercing shriek recalled her to his mind, and turning round he beheld her dragged from her horse to the earth. His arms were bound, but his feet were at liberty, and he dashed his heavy boots into the face of the men who held his steed. But the same moment a brace of bullets whizzed through the air, and after a few convulsive clutches the young man fell heavily to the earth.

Leaving him, where he had fallen, the men rushed to the assistance of the fellow who had dragged the lady from her steed.

'For God's sake, gentlemen, don't kill Joaquin. He has never injured you.'

'Don't fret, honey, 'tisn't Joe Quin we're after. 'Tis your own elegant self,' said one of the ruffians.

'So, you d—d stuck-up thing, you wouldn't dance with me at your outlandish fandango, the other night. Now, my lady, you shall dance to other music;' and as he spoke he seized her brutally, and inflicted several fierce kisses upon her reluctant lips. Fired by her charms and her resistance, the villain was proceeding to further outrage, when, all her woman's nature flashing from her indignant eyes, she drew a small thin-bladed stiletto, and sent its bright blade straight to the heart of the ravisher. For a moment, and but for a moment, the villains were appalled at this prompt and terrible retribution. But even the thought of their guilty comrade hurried out of the world in the very act of perpetrating the most heinous offence, could not make them pause in their infernal intentions, for seizing the hapless woman, now become insensible, they bore her into a clump of bushes from which they had sprung upon Joaquin and his bride.

Hours after, when Joaquin returned to consciousness, he found himself bound hand and foot, with strips of green hide. His horse and that of Carmencitto both gone.

Joaquin's first impulse was to call aloud upon the name of his young wife. But all was silent. 'Holy Virgin!' he exclaimed, as recollection began fully to return to him. 'Where art thou, Carmencitto?' he shouted. A low, faint moaning was heard in the neighboring shrubbery. Again, and again, the wretched youth called loudly on Carmencitto. But the only replies he received were the faint moanings, which his foreboding heart, rather than his ear, told him came from the lips of Carmencitto. His suspense became insupportable. He would—he must—learn all. Even though that all confirmed a horrid suspicion that chilled the blood to his very heart.

With the fierceness of a starving coyote he gnawed the green hide that confined his arms, and they once released he soon entirely disengaged himself. He sprang to his feet, and rushed in the direction from whence the sounds of distress proceeded. Better had he been smitten with eternal blindness than ever have gazed upon that sad, sad spectacle.

Carmencitto lay almost senseless upon the grass. Her modest garments torn to shreds, exposed her fair young bosom, slowly heaving, as if with the latest sobs of expiring life. Her cheeks were colorless. Her lips white as chalk, except where they were dabbled with the crimson blood, that was slowly oozing at every respiration of her heaving breast! In one of her little pale hands she clutched a small gold crucifix, which the villains had overlooked in their lust or haste.

As Joaquin burst through the thicket and stood before her, the closed lids of her black eyes slowly opened, and she cast one look full of love and sorrow upon her heart-broken husband.

Tearing his black locks he flung himself on his knees by her side, and tenderly raising her, he pressed her to his heart and while he wiped the blood from her lips, his tears fell thick and fast upon her upturned face.

'Speak to me, oh! speak to me, Carmencitto. My life! My love! Speak! Oh, God, what have I done to deserve this? Speak, dearest Carmencitto,' and he pressed the form of his young wife again and again close to his heart. But no reply came from those dear lips.

Near at hand ran a babbling rivulet. To this Joaquin rushed, and scooping out some water in the hollow of his joined hands, laved with it the face of Carmencitto. But all in vain. Life had forever left that darling form, dearer to him than all the gold that strews the placers of his native land.

When Joaquin became certain that she was indeed dead, his grief at first found vent in the most pathetic lamentations; but suddenly pausing, he dashed the teardrops from his eyes, and drawing a dagger from its sheath, he swore upon its cross-hilt eternal vengeance on the ravishers and murderers of his Carmencitto.

Then decently arranging her disordered garments, he lifted her sacred form in his arms, and bore it to his home—henceforth forever desolate.

From the hour in which he saw the rude tomb raised over the ashes of his murdered wife, Joaquin left forever the home that promised to be such a happy one, and went forth an altered man. The crucifix of poor Carmencitto *on* his heart—revenge rankling in it.

From that time strange rumors began to circulate through California of daring robberies and frequent murders, and although no proofs of the guilty party could be obtained; yet when men spoke of them their pale lips almost involuntarily muttered '*Joaquin!*'

When Inez returned to her father's residence at the Mission, her first resolve was to acquaint her parent with the circumstances, but she found that he had been hastily summoned to a place at some distance, in consequence of a dispute between one of his tenants and a squatter.

Joaquin, whose advice she asked, recommended that she should wait the coming of morning, when if Monteagle was not liberated, the authorities should be informed of the matter, and by their interference his liberation would no doubt easily be effected. But Joaquin had his own private reasons for not visiting the city.

In the morning Inez accordingly rode to the city, and almost the first person she passed was Monteagle, who was just then repairing to the store of Mr. Vandewater. Of course there was no occasion for Inez to interfere farther in the matter. Her first impulse was to ride up to him and congratulate him on his escape, but maidenly pride checked her, and she proceeded on, leaving Monteagle in entire ignorance of the deep interest she felt in his fortunes, and of the efforts she had made to rescue him the previous evening.

Monteagle, meanwhile, sought his home to take a few hours rest, for both mind and body were terribly racked by the sufferings he had undergone.

The day after the robbery of Mr. Vandewater's store, a group of some half-dozen men were assembled around a fine fire kindled on the ground, in the midst of a dense thicket, at the foot of the mountains, on the Contra Costa side of the Bay of San Francisco.

'He's a daring young devil, and with pluck, quickness, and a little science, I'm d—d if I don't think he could whip any thing of his weight in the world.'

This remark was made by Belcher Kay to Blodget, as Maretzo, who was one of the party, finished narration of Monteagle's assault upon him, and his consequent escape.

'Curse his pluck, and your science Belcher. If ever I draw trigger on either of you all your science wouldn't save you from a quick trip to 'kingdom come.' But, the deuce take it, I dare not show my face in the city; for Monteagle will surely denounce me to that devilish Vigilance Committee, and then my fun's up,' said Blodget.

'Well, old fellow,' said Kay, 'I'll see that you're well supplied with everything needful, till this thing blows over. You stay out here and make yourself comfortable. If we could only get this Monteagle out of the way, all would go right. For from what Maretzo learned in the city, none of us are suspected except you, and you only because you kept Monteagle's company. Well, if that ain't a good 'un, I'm blowed,' continued Belcher Kay, laughing heartily at the idea of Monteagle's leading Blodget astray.

'I am this Monteagle's debtor for that blow he gave me,' said Maretzo, and his dark eyes flashed with vindictive hate. 'I'll get him out of the way.'

'Have a care, Maretzo, that knife of yours will bring us all into trouble some of those days,' said Blodget.

'This time it will not be the knife, but something even surer still,' and as he spoke, he exhibited a small bottle. 'A drop from this vial, and his tongue will never harm us again.'

'Well,' said Kay. 'We'll think over this matter. But just now let's split the swag.'

And forthwith the thieves proceeded to apportion out the thirty thousand dollars equitably between them, not forgetting a share for some who were absent but who belonged to the gang, and were entitled by their rules to a share of the plunder obtained in the course of their marauding expeditions.

For some days after Monteagle's dismissal he was too unwell to leave the house, but when he was sufficiently recovered to walk the street, he was surprised to find that all his former friends and associates either passed him with a slight nod of recognition, or gave him the cut direct. He was entirely at a loss to account for their conduct. Being out of a situation was not such an unusual thing in San Francisco, as to make a man's friends shun him. Nor could it be the fear that he might be transformed from a lender to a borrower, for no where are men more ready to assist a friend or even a stranger than in this country. Monteagle was not aware that from certain vague hints which Brown contrived to set afloat respecting the robbery that Monteagle's name was in some manner mixed up in the affair. The very indefiniteness of the rumor being the reason of its never reaching Monteagle's ear.

So that he who was most deeply interested in it, was almost the only one in the whole city who had not heard of the accusation. Of course his sudden dismissal from Mr. Vandewater's employ gave an appearance of truth to the story, which was more strongly confirmed by Vandewater's declining to assign any cause for Monteagle's dismissal when questioned on the subject.

Monteagle, whose generous disposition but little fitted him for hoarding money, was now by his sudden and unexpected loss of employment thrown entirely destitute on the world.

At first he resolved to depart immediately for the mines. Reflection however made him abandon this purpose. As he was hourly in expectation of a letter of credit from his home in the Atlantic States, which would place him in possession of ample funds, with which it had been his intention to buy a share of Mr. Vandewater's business.

There was another and far more powerful motive, however, that prevailed upon the young man to refrain from leaving San Francisco. In the hurry of business as in the allurements of pleasure one form was ever present with him. Need we say it was that of the lovely maiden whom he had borne in his arms from the devouring flames.

Although he avoided meeting Inez Castro, and her father, it was not that he did not ardently wish to meet with her; but his delicacy shrank from seeming to take advantage of the fact that he had conferred so great an obligation on them, and he feared that gratitude would induce Inez to betray a preference for him which he would fain owe to love alone.

One evening soon after Monteagle's discharge from employment, and after all attempts to procure a situation had proved futile, he wandered about the streets in that sad, dejected mood which comes over one, when friendless and moneyless in a great city.

Following a large crowd, he found himself in an extensive bookstore adjoining the Post Office. This was the general rendezvous of merchants, and others, while awaiting the tardy operations of Uncle Sam's officials. Huge stacks of daily, weekly, and 'California edition' papers were rapidly disappearing in supplying the clamorous demands of the eager throng anxious to hear from 'the old folks at home.'

Monteagle moved among them like a perfect stranger. He felt as though a brand was upon him; but the reason was to him a perfect mystery. Every eye, however open and direct its glance for others, became cold and averted when it met his.

He was about turning to leave the store, his sad feeling legibly expressed on his fine features, when he felt a hand upon his shoulder and turning quickly he confronted Mr. G—, one of the proprietors.

'Ah, good night, Monteagle. Here's your Herald, and the rest of your papers.'

'Thank you, Mr. G—, but,' and Monteagle lowered his tone, while his cheek was flushed, 'I'll come in again—in fact—I'm penniless.'

'Never mind that,' replied the bookseller. 'Here take the papers,' and as he spoke, he slipped a twenty dollar piece into his hand.

'Thank you—thank you,' cried the grateful youth. 'I expect a remittance from home to-morrow, and then I will repay you.'

But had Monteagle seen the expression of the bookseller's manly face, he would have known that he was repaid already. His own noble heart approved the generous, and with him by no means unusual act.

On the morning succeeding, Monteagle had early taken his place in the Post Office line, (as extensive as that of Banquo's issue which flitted before the eyes of the Scottish regicide,) awaiting the delivery of their letters.

This line is one of the most singular sights in the world, composed not only of representatives from every section of our own country, but from almost every nation on the face of the globe.

Monteagle was disappointed. There was no letter for him.

Only those who have been thousands and thousands of miles away from home, can understand the full effect of this crushing disappointment. Instantly the mind conjures up many dismal reasons as the cause of the non-arrival of the expected letters. What can be the matter?—Have our friends forgotten us, has sickness wasted the hand that used to seize the pen with such avidity to tell us all the warm feelings the writers entertained for us? Or has death forever stilled the beatings of those hearts we dearly loved?

Months we know must elapse ere these questions can have a response, and in the meanwhile we must experience all the bitterness of hope deferred.

Monteagle left the Office almost envying the lucky ones who were tearing the envelopes from the missives they had received and with eager eyes scanning the lines. But could Monteagle have narrowly watched the different readers, he would have seen that in the majority of instances the letters brought news that had better never reached the recipients. Here a splendid looking fellow, the very embodiment of manly beauty, read a letter that informed him that the girl, in hopes of wedding whom he had left home to win a fortune in California, had been married to a man with no other recommendation than a hundred thousand dollars. There might be seen a stalwart man, his rough cheek blanched and the tears gushing from his eyes, as he read that his only daughter—the cherished idol of his affections, had gone to the narrow house, appointed for all the living. But we need not pursue the theme, any one who has noticed attentively the 'line' we speak of has seen matter for much and melancholy meditation, even if he has been fortunate enough to experience none of those bitter disappointments himself.

Belcher Kay and his fellow-rogues soon expended the money they obtained by the robbery of Vandewater's store in riotous living. So a new crime was determined on.

But it was necessary that he should be quick in his plans, for his means were daily becoming more limited, and he was well aware that success depended in a great measure upon promptitude. But what was he to do when his pecuniary resources were entirely exhausted.

This was a troublesome thought, and one which he was unable for some time to answer satisfactorily in his own mind. Money he must have by some means or another, or he would not have it in his power to carry on his nefarious projects with any chance of success, and the bare idea of being reduced to poverty, after the life of indolence, luxury, and extravagance he had led, made the villain shrink with dread. No—no—such a fate must not be his, and he determined to avoid it, even if the means he should have to adopt in doing so, he should have been compelled to adopt the most desperate and dangerous schemes.

From any crime, however revolting, it might be, it has been very clearly shewn to the reader that Kay would not shrink; and, after deliberating for a short time within himself what was next to be done, he at last came to the determination of going for a few nights on the highway, and thus trying his fortune. If in adopting this guilty resolution, the villain should have to perpetrate murder, he would not have foreborne to do it, sooner than he would have been disappointed of his object.

Accordingly, on the following night, after he had come to this resolution, Kay, well armed, secretly quitted the hotel where he was lodging, and took his way to a lonely road, that led to the Mission, which was, notwithstanding, much frequented. Here he secreted himself, and eagerly watched the approach of some traveller who might possess the means about him of satisfying his wants.

Belcher had taken good care to strengthen his determination by drinking deeply, before he started on his guilty purpose, and he now felt fully prepared for whatever might happen. Money he had made up his mind he would have at all hazards, and therefore it was not a trifle that was at all likely to move him from his purpose.

The place which Kay had chosen to conceal himself, was just at the entrance of a dark and dismal lane, which branched off the road, and was a very convenient place for the perpetration of a deed like that he contemplated.

Here then he seated himself upon the ground, where he could have a distinct view of the road for some distance, and every person that approached.

It was a very fine night; the moon shone brightly in the heavenly arch, and countless myriads of stars added their twinkling lustre to her radiant beams.

Kay sat there for some time in a state of apathy, his thoughts wandered to no particular objects, but still his mind intent upon the desperate crime he had resolved to perpetrate if the opportunity should be afforded him.

At last, however, becoming impatient, and feeling rather cold, for the night air was keen, he arose, and walked for some distance along the road, taking care to keep close to the bushes, that separated it from the adjoining fields, and where he was less likely to be observed.

In the course of a conversation which Belcher had overheard between the landlord of the hotel and his wife after they had retired to bed, (for they slept in the next chamber to him, and the rooms only being parted by a very slight partition of canvas, he could hear every word they uttered,) he had learnt that a drover, who invariably called at their house, and who usually had a large sum of money about him, was expected there that day, and he was also enabled to ascertain that this was the road he always came; but he could not think of making an attempt to commit a robbery in the open daylight, and when his detection would be almost certain to follow, and thus his nefarious wishes would be foiled. But then, as he understood that the drover usually slept at the hotel, the villain thought there might still be a chance left of his being enabled to rob him in the night.

This, however, would be attended with considerable danger, for suspicion would, in all probability, light upon him, and should he abandon the place, it would, undoubtedly, be a direct confirmation of his guilt, and would put him to great inconvenience in having to quit the neighborhood.

Reflecting therefore, in this manner, Kay was constrained to give up all thoughts of plundering the drover, although it was with much reluctance that he did so, for he had no doubt but that he should from him have been sure to have got a very rich booty.

The day which succeeded the night on which Kay had overheard the conversation we have spoken of, was passed by him in a state of great agitation and uncertainty, and at one time he would determine upon some daring scheme, which the next moment would make him abandon all idea of.

The drover, however, did not come to the house that day, but Kay gathered from the conversation of his host, that he would sure to be there that night, so that he might be in time for the market on the following morning. Kay caught at this information, and his hopes once more revived; he resolved to lay wait for him, and make a desperate attempt to rob him as he had at first designed.

Kay was no coward, as that which has been already related, will fully prove, and he was, therefore, prepared for any resistance which his marked victim might make, and he had made up his mind not to be defeated easily. But from what he could learn, the drover was an old man, and one who was not very likely to offer much resistance, especially when he saw that the individual who attacked him was well armed, and a determined man, and, therefore, Kay calculated that his success was almost certain.

He had taken the precaution to provide himself with a mask and poncho, so that he might be fully enabled to disguise himself, and these were the more indispensable for the villain's safety, as he intended to return to the hotel after the perpetration of the robbery.

Impatient and gloomy, Kay continued to traverse the road for some time, but still he saw no signs of the traveller or of any other person, and he began to despair. The place was sufficiently quiet and lonely to inspire no very pleasant reflections in the mind of Kay, and so rapidly did they crowd upon his brain, that he had not strength to endure them, and he almost made up his mind to abandon his villainous project, and return to the hotel to seek that society which might alone banish such fearful thoughts.

At length the solemn booming of the Mission bell vibrated on the air, tolling the hour of ten, and Kay, whose patience was now quite tired out, and whose disappointment could only be equalled by chagrin, resolved to wait no longer but to return to the hotel.

He had just turned round for that purpose, when the low trampling of horses' hoofs, at a distance, arrested his purpose and rekindled his hopes.

The sounds proceeded from behind him, and looking eagerly along the road as far as his eyes could penetrate, at first he could not perceive anything, but at length he beheld a horse trotting slowly along the road, in the direction of the place where he was standing, and bearing on his back a person who he was unable at present, to observe, distinctly.

'It must be him!' muttered Kay to himself, and hope once more elated and nerved him. His mind was fully made up; he would have all the money the grazier had about him, even, if to obtain it he had to embrue his hands in his blood.

Quickly the miscreant glided cautiously along the darkest and most overshadowed part of the road, and he once more reached the entrance to the lane which the traveller must pass; and which appeared to him to be the most convenient spot for the perpetration of the deed.

'But—but—'muttered Kay, 'I will not harm him—no—no—I will not harm him, if I can avoid it! I do not want his blood, but his money, it will be his own fault should he lose his life.'

Nearer and nearer the rider approached, and at length he had got to within a very short distance of the place where Kay was concealed, and by the bright light of the moon, he was enabled to have a distinct view of his person.

He was a thickset man, about sixty, and carried with him a short whip with a very heavy handle. He was whistling merrily along the road, apparently, quite happy and unsuspicious of any danger, and what Kay could perceive of his features, he looked like a man who was not likely to be easily intimidated. Again he muttered to himself,—

'I hope he will resign his money easily; I hope he will not make any resistance; I would not have his blood upon my conscience, but his money *I will* have.'

The man had now got to within a very short distance of the lane, and Kay had no doubt from the description which had been given of him, that this was the grazier.

He clenched his fist nervously, and involuntarily placed his other hand on one of the pistols which he carried with him.

'I will let him pass me,' thought Kay, 'I will let him pass me before I pounce out upon him, and then I shall take him more by surprise, and he will be less likely to offer any resistance.'

The traveller had now left off whistling, and had broke into a negro melody, which he sang in self-satisfied tones, but which were anything but harmonious.

'Your money or your life!' cried Kay in a disguised voice, rushing up to the traveller, from his place of concealment, and laying hold of the horse's bridle.

The old man, was of course, rather startled, but he collected himself in a moment, and with the utmost coolness, said:—

'I tells thee what it is, young man, you're on a bad errand, and I advise you let go the bridle, and go about your business, before harm come to you.'

'There, there, no nonsense,' replied Kay, in an impatient tone; 'I am a desperate man and must have money.'

'D—n you, you are a daring rascal,' cried the traveller, 'let go of the bridle, or it may not be long ere I make you repent thy job. Leave go of the bridle, I again tell you! You won't, then, d—n me, if I don't soon make you, and that's all about it.'

With these words the traveller flourished his heavy whip, and aimed a blow at the head of Kay with the butt-end of it, which if he had not stepped quickly aside and avoided would, in all probability have deprived him immediately of farther power.

'Old idiot!' cried the enraged ruffian, 'you will urge me to that which I would rather avoid; will you deliver up your money, I say, once more?'

'No,' promptly replied the old man; 'I'll see you d—d first, and all such scoundrels.'

'Then, by h—ll! you will have to pay for your obstinacy with your life!' cried Kay, hastily groping about beneath his poncho to get out one of the pistols.

The old man immediately guessed at what he was about, and sprang from his horse's back with the agility of a youth, and the moment that Kay got out his pistol, and before he could cock it, he closed with him, and being a strong, powerful man, the struggle threatened to be a determined one.

Kay, however, was wound up to a pitch of desperation, for it was a moment of life or death, and he was taken somewhat by surprise, as, from the age of the traveller, he had not expected such an antagonist.

Kay was a very muscular man, and had youth on his side, and he, of course, mustered up all his strength for this occasion, and endeavoured to get his hands at liberty; but the old man had pinned them with such an iron grip, that all his efforts were ineffectual, and maledictions the most terrible escaped his lips, as the danger of his situation became every instant greater; for, as his strength decreased, so did that of the traveller appear to increase, and he expected nothing less that he must be overpowered.

The struggle lasted several minutes, the traveller having pinched the hands of Kay so tightly, that he was compelled to drop the pistol to the ground, and which the former was afraid to secure, for fear that, in resigning his hold of the robber, he should lose the advantage he had gained. But at length the foot of Kay caught in something on the ground, and he fell, dragging the old man with him.

Fortunately, the traveller did not fall upon him, or his weight would have quickly decided the combat, and Kay would have been defeated, but he fell by his side, and consequently was obliged to leave go his hold; and Kay, seeing the moment of advantage, and probably the only opportunity of saving his life, jumped to his feet with the speed of lightning, and snatching the pistol from his bosom, he sprang upon the old man, knelt upon his chest,—he pressed the fingers of his other hand tightly in his throat until the old man was nearly strangled, he presented the pistol at his head as he exclaimed—

'You deserve to lose your life for your infernal obstinacy, and it is at this moment in my power; but I do not wish to harm you if I can help it. Now, then, your money.'

The old man who was quite overpowered by the pressure on his chest, and the violence with which Kay pressed his knuckles into his throat, he tried to speak, but could only make a sign to his coat-pocket, which Kay understanding, released the old man from the hold which he had taken of his throat; and, putting his hand into his pocket, to which he had directed his attention, he drew forth a canvas bag apparently well loaded, and depositing it carefully in his bosom, he secured both the pistols, and, rising from the ground, he said to the still prostrate traveller—

'Beware! you see that I have all the power of your life or death in my hands; if you move a step to pursue me, until I am out of sight, that instant you die!'

The old man did not make any reply, for he had not yet recovered from the effects of the combat, and was unable to utter a word; and Kay, having satisfied himself that he had secured all the money in his possession, hastily retreated from the spot, and springing into the fields, threw away the poncho, and made the best of his way towards the hotel, which he reached in an almost inconceivable short space of time, and, without betraying any emotion, entered the bar, as was his usual custom, and taking his seat called for a mug of ale.

He had not been there long, when he heard a loud shouting and hallooing outside the house, and he immediately recognized the tones.

'Why,' said the landlord, laying down his pipe, 'that certainly is the voice of a friend; what the deuce can be the matter with him?'

Kay felt a little alarmed; but he concealed his agitation, and continued with apparent unconcern, to smoke his pipe, and to be completely absorbed in the enjoyment of that and his ale. He would have been glad to have retired to his chamber, so that he might have escaped all observation, but he was fearful that he might, by so doing, probably excite suspicion, and he therefore kept his seat and pretended to take no notice of what was passing.

The landlord having hastened to the door of the house to meet his guest, and to inquire what was the matter with him was quickly heard returning accompanied by the old man, who was grumbling, and swearing all the way.

On entering the bar, the drover gazed round upon the different persons there assembled, but appeared to take little notice of Kay, whose assumed color, no doubt, removed every idea of his being the robber from his mind.

'He was a most desperate scoundrel, whoever he is,' said the drover, 'and I feel the effects of his d—d knuckles on my throat, now. I wish I could only meet with the fellow, and I warrant me he'd not escape from my clutches again, very easily.'

'This is a bad job, a terrible bad job,' said the landlord.

'Aye, it is indeed a bad job,' said the drover, 'two thousand dollars is no small sum to lose as times go.'

# CHAPTER XII

## The Ride—the Midnight Fright—the Corpse—The Secret Burial.

Kay took no part in the conversation which followed, the staple of which consisted of denunciations of the scoundrels who infested the city of San Francisco and its vicinity, perpetrating with impunity the most daring robberies and even more atrocious offences.

Kay was slightly known to several of the 'crowd' who had been drawn to the bar by rumors respecting the robbery, and as Kay sauntered out of the room one of these persons whispered a few words to the drover, who turned and closely scrutinized the robber's person. Kay bore his fixed gaze apparently unmoved. But he inwardly determined that the drover should never bear witness against him!

A few evenings after this robbery, Inez had taken a long ride, and on her return was overtaken by a sudden and violent storm. She immediately put her horse to the run. Inez was too much accustomed to heavy rains and violent storms of wind to be much alarmed, as she knew her fleet steed would soon bear her home in safety. But scarcely had our heroine proceeded a couple of hundred varas when her horse fell heavily. Fortunately, however, Inez was but little injured. Her horse she soon discovered was unable to rise. Of course no alternative was left her but to proceed homewards on foot.

Notwithstanding, however, she sought all that was in her power to strengthen this idea, many doubts, fears, misgivings, and apprehensions would steal into her bosom, and every blast of wind which howled around her seemed to come fraught with the moanings of despair. She had travelled about three miles from the place at which she had lost her horse, and was upon a dreary waste, where there was nothing to protect her from the fury of the blast and the fast falling rain which drifted around her. It was a most awful spot, and in spite of her resistance to fear, she felt the most indescribable sensation of horror creeping through her veins.

'Holy Mary!' she exclaimed, 'my weary and benumbed limbs will not support me much further, and yet, if I pause, nothing but death stares me in the face. How awful is the darkness around, and here am I placed alone, and fated to endure all this toil and wretchedness. Could I but hear the sound even of a human voice, methinks it would be transport to my soul. This silence is appalling. Whenever I have had occasion to cross this wild spot, I always felt the most irresistible terror; it is, indeed, a fit place for the perpetration of the bloody crimes which report says have been committed here, and I do not wonder that people should shun it after nightfall in dread, my God! do not desert me in this dreadful moment. Oh! I remember there is an old house not far from this spot; could I but reach that, it would afford me shelter until my recruited strength will enable me to proceed. The storm increases; what will become of me? The rain falls faster than ever; I must proceed. Protect me, heaven!'

Trembling in every limb, and her knees smiting each other, Inez forced her way as well she was able, in the direction of the old house, which she at length perceived at no great distance from her, and so completely exhausted was she, that had she had to have proceeded many yards further she must have sunk to the earth. It was an old building, broken in many parts.

An old story gave the place a kind of fearful interest; and there was one period when Inez would not have ventured within its precincts, but now she thought nothing about it; she thought only of her weary and exhausted state. She reached the wretched place, and found no obstruction to her entrance, the door having long since been torn off its hinges, and she, therefore, staggered into the place, and threw herself, exhausted and breathless, upon a heap of rubbish in one corner, to rest herself for a few minutes, ere she could see what was best to be done for her accommodation for the night. The house was divided into two compartments, and one of these was in much better condition than the other. There, then, Inez determined to remain till daybreak; and gathering together some pieces of old boarding which had fallen from different parts of the building, and a heap of straw, which she found in one corner, she retired into it, contrived to make herself up some kind of a rude pallet, piled all the old rubbish she could find against the door which opened into this division of the house, and then imploring the protection of Heaven, she wrapped herself closely in her cloak, and laid down.

Completely wearied out, it was not long ere she was about to sink off to sleep, when she was suddenly alarmed and astonished by hearing a noise outside the building, and soon after, a light glimmered between the crevices, and the horror and amazement of Inez may be easily conjectured when she caught a glimpse of the shadow of two men, bearing something which seemed to be very heavy between them. They moved stealthily and cautiously round by the side of the building towards the entrance, and Inez had not the least doubt but that they were coming there; in another second her conjectures were confirmed, and she heard them deposit their burthen in the adjoining shed to that in which she was.

How shall we attempt to portray the terror of Inez at this circumstance? She did not venture to breathe scarcely, and screwed herself into the smallest possible compass in the corner, for fear that the men should discover her there; but, from a small hole in the boards, she could perceive what was passing.

'My God!' she thought, 'what can be the purpose of these men? Certainly no good, at such an hour.'

Inez placed her eye to the hole in the boarding, and perceived that they were two powerful men, dressed in ponchos, and as the rays of the light fell upon their countenances, she shuddered at their aspects.

They had placed the sack upon the floor, and began digging up the earth with a couple of spades which they had brought with them. A deadly chill fell upon the heart of Inez when she beheld this, and she could scarcely repress a scream, as a dreadful idea shot through her brain.

'Horror! horror!' she reflected, 'the wretches have surely been committing murder, and have come hither to bury their unfortunate victim.'

'There, we shall soon be able to make a snug lodging for him,' said one of the villains, taking up a spade and preparing to begin to dig, 'and no one will ever know what has become of him. How nicely we gammoned the old fool to take up his lodging with us.'

'You're right,' said the other, 'it was very well done, and I must give you the credit of doing the best part towards it. If the friends of the old drover look for his return home, how woefully deceived they will be.'

'Ha! ha! ha!' laughed the first villain, 'indeed they will. Well, we have got a very tidy booty for this job.'

'Yes, it will pay us for the trouble we have been at,' was the answer; 'but I'll warrant that we shall circulate the blunt a little more freely than the old fellow would have done. We must not be in the city many days.'

'As soon as the job's over we will quit the spot,' returned his companion, 'and it will be many a long day ere we shall revisit this neighborhood again. We couldn't have fixed a much better place than this to deposit the old fellow's remains in; but, I say, there is a door yonder, which seems to lead to another part of the house; suppose we examine that, and see whether it will serve better to conceal the body of the murdered man in than this.'

'Great God!' thought Inez, 'I am lost; they will discover and murder me. By what horrible fatality were my footsteps guided to this place?'

'Psha! what's the use of talking in that manner, Kay?' said the other ruffian, to whom this proposition was addressed; 'we have no time to spare; besides, we have half dug the grave here, and I dare say the old chap will lie as contented here as he would a foot or two off. Come, come, let's finish the business and begone, for I am almost tired of it, and if we remain here much longer, there's no knowing but that we might be discovered.'

'Oh, very well,' said Kay, as the other man had called him, 'it matters very little, so let's go to work, and get done as quick as possible.'

'I think we have given him depth enough,' remarked the other wretch, 'and he'll not pop up again in a hurry by himself. Come, out with him, and let's finish the job at once.'

This, as may be imagined, was a moment of unutterable horror to our heroine, who had watched the proceedings, and listened to the conversation of the assassins with the most breathless attention; and a shuddering seized upon her frame which she found it impossible to resist.—It would, however, be useless to attempt to describe the relief she felt when she heard the observations of the first ruffian, by which he was persuaded from entering the place in which she was concealed; but every moment that they prolonged their stay increased her terror and anxiety, for fear that her infant should awake, and, crying loud, betray her.

After having untied the mouth of the sack, they drew it nearer to the edge of the grave they had been digging, and turned out the body of a stout but aged man, whose long grey locks were matted together with large clots of blood that had issued from several deep wounds in the skull.

Horror enchained all the faculties of Inez, and with distended eyelids, she fixed her straining eyeballs upon the dreadful spectacle.

Her blood seemed turned to ice, and her heart seemed almost to cease its pulsation. Should the wretches find out that she was there concealed, and had been watching them, and overheard the acknowledgement of their dreadful crime, the death of herself would be certain to follow.

These reflections passed rapidly in the mind of Inez, as she watched, in a state of the most breathless suspense, the actions of the murderers, as they, in the most callous manner, tossed the body of their wretched victim into the grave they had dug for its reception, and commenced filling it up, occupying the interval during the disgusting scene, with the most ribald conversation, which smote the heart of our heroine with horror, as she listened to it.

'There,' exclaimed Kay, as he placed the last spade-full of earth on the grave of their murdered victim, 'that job's finished, and a long and sound rest to the old drover. The business has been performed throughout in a tradesman-like manner, and no suspicion can ever attach itself to us.'

'Suspicion,' reiterated the other with a laugh, 'oh no, we might almost as well imagine that somebody has been watching us all this time in this lonely place, as to suppose that even the shadow of an idea of we being the murderers of the old man could attach itself to us.'

'Ah!' exclaimed Kay, 'your observation have started an idea in my head, and, had you attended to my suggestion in the first instance, we should have been secured from any danger of the sort.'

'What mean you?'

'What mean I:—why, that door, which, as I before observed, no doubt, communicates with some other part of the house, and it is not at all unlikely that some weary traveller may have taken up his lodging there, or sought shelter from the storm, and been listening to our discourse all this time. Should such be the case, we shall not go far without falling into the hands of the Vigilance Committee, depend upon it. I'll examine the place.'

'Bah! why, you are growing worse than a child, Kay,' said the miscreant's companion, 'I never heard such improbable ideas to strike a fellow in all my life. Do you think any person could be within here all this time without betraying some signs of terror?'

'You may laugh at me as much as you like, Blodget,' returned Kay, 'but I am generally pretty correct in what I fancy, and I don't think I shall be far out in this instance. Here goes for to see.'

We must fail here to portray the feelings of our heroine, as the ruffian, Kay, approached the door, and tried it.

Such was the violence of her agitation, that cold drops of perspiration stood upon her forehead, and it was only by a complete miracle that she could prevent herself from screaming.

Kay tried hard to push the door open, and swore when he found the obstruction; and at that moment, when Inez had nearly given herself up for lost, some noise on the outside of the building, arrested the attention of both the villains, and Kay immediately quitted the door, much to the relief of our heroine.

'Hist?' muttered Blodget, in a cautious tone, 'did you not hear a noise outside, Belcher?'

'I fancied I did,' was the reply.

'Extinguish the light,' commanded the other, 'and I will reconnoitre.'

Kay immediately did as his companion directed him, and Blodget cautiously opened the door and looked out. As he did so, Inez could hear that the storm had increased in violence, and immediately afterwards she heard the voice of Blodget, observing,—

'Oh, the coast is quite clear, as far as I can see, and, therefore, it could only have been fancy; but, notwithstanding, Kay, I do not see the policy of remaining here. We had much better, on the contrary, make our escape as speedily as possible, while we have the opportunity; for, should we be discovered here, and the fresh earth upon the new made grave, we should be bowled out to a dead certainty. It's madness to suppose that anybody but ourselves have been here during the time we have been performing the funeral obsequies for the old man. Come, come, no more of this foolery, but travel's the word.—'

And 'travel' was not only the word, but the action of the wretches, much to the relief of our heroine, who had almost given her mind to despair; and after a short time had elapsed since they had quitted the place, and Inez, by attentive listening, had assured herself that they were not near the spot, first, with eyes brimful of tears, having returned her thanks to Providence for her deliverance from that death which she at one time imagined inevitable, she removed the rubbish which she had piled against the door, and left the place in which she had been concealed.

What an inexpressible feeling of terror smote her breast, when she passed the grave of the murdered man!—Her limbs trembled so violently that it is surprising how she was enabled to support herself, and she mentally offered up an involuntary prayer for the repose of his soul, and that his barbarous assassins might be brought to punishment for their inhuman violation of the laws. It was a second or two before she ventured to quit the place, but having listened at the door, which the ruffians had closed after them, and hearing no other sounds than those caused by the fury of the storm, she ventured to open it and look forth. The scene was awful enough, as a pitchy darkness obscured all around, save when, at intervals, the flashes of lightning succeeded the deafening thunder-peals. The rain also descended rapidly, and all around presented a scene of the most appalling horror. But, awful as it was, to Inez it presented not half the terrors of the old outhouse, which now contained the mangled remains of the poor old man, whom the monsters had buried.

Inez, trembling in every limb, left the place where she had witnessed such horrors, and with difficulty made her way in what she judged to be the direction of her father's house. This she would never have had strength to reach, had she not fortunately met with a party of her father's herdsmen, who had been sent out in quest of her. She was soon after joined by her father, and being placed on a horse, arrived safely at home, suffering greatly, however, in both body and mind from the anguish she had experienced, and the terrible scenes that had been enacted before her young eyes.

Leaving the maiden safely in the abode of her parent, we will now return to Monteagle. Day after day, he had called at the Post Office, but the same brief response ever met his inquiries,—'None, sir.' Disappointment was working a sad change in his appearances, and his broken fortunes were growing hourly more desperate.

As he was one day leaving the Post Office, and strolling down Clay street, he overheard a person addressing another, thus: 'Jake, you needn't go to the Post Office, up here, any more for letters. A couple of cartloads have just been found down under Long Wharf; which it seems, the Postmaster uses as a place of general delivery.'

Monteagle stayed to hear no more, but hastened to the place indicated.—A great crowd was assembled, every member of which was justly indignant at this infamous betrayal of trust in the Post Office officials, and while some talked of carrying their complaints to Washington; others suggested the rather less mild but somewhat more effective action of tying the Postmaster up in one of his mail bags, and dumping him where he had deposited their letters—in the Bay.

Monteagle sprang down beneath the wharf, the tide having fallen, and left the sand bare. Here he found a large number of letters, and newspapers: the directions of many being wholly or in part obliterated. But among all that number, he could find none addressed to him. While he was turning over the letters, he saw one addressed to a young lady, whom he recollected as having been pointed out to him by Blodget when visiting the house in Dupont street. She was called the 'English Girl,' and Monteagle remembered having been particularly struck by the lovely though pensive expression of her fair face. He took the letter and immediately proceeded to the house where she resided. As soon as the usual greetings were over, the young lady opened the letter, but had scarcely glanced at its contents before she fell heavily to the floor. Monteagle summoned assistance, and after some time she was sufficiently restored to converse with our hero; who deeply sympathised with her evident distress. The poor girl, in answer to Monteagle's inquiries, gave him the following account of her previous history:

'My father was a farmer, in comfortable circumstances, which he gained by his own industry and exemplary conduct. I will not attempt to describe him, for I should fail to do justice to his merits, eloquent, doubtless, as my affection for him would make me. Let it suffice that he was a man of superior education, having formerly moved in a different state of life, from which he had been driven by a long series of misfortunes, and his numerous virtues even by far exceeded his accomplishments. My mother was a complete counterpart of her husband, and never were two beings better formed to meet together. I was their only daughter, myself and a brother being the only offspring they ever had. Every indulgence that child could wish, or parent could think of, was bestowed on me;—my every thought seemed to be studied by them, and there was not a single happiness which they had it in their power to grant, which they seemed to think too great for me.'

'Our home was the happiest in the neighborhood, and it was the envy and admiration of all who knew it. Again, when I think upon it, and how different my situation is now, I cannot help giving vent to my feelings; indeed, it is to indulge them that I have sat down to record the events of my life, although, in all probability, no other eyes but mine may ever behold it. Home, sweet home; there cannot be a theme upon which the mind of sensibility pauses with more peculiar delight than this. It is the cradle of our infancy and our age.'

'The seaman, amidst storm and tempest, in fair weather and foul, thinks of his native village; the soldier that fights for kings; the merchant that dives for gain, are, alternately, stung with the thoughts of home; while the wanderer, who has followed pleasure, but found it a shade—that has bartered the humble content for splendid misery, thinks of home with a self-accusing regret, that renders even a return to its enjoyments full of bitterness and remorse. Sensibly do I feel the force of these observations, and, therefore, have I digressed from my simple narrative for the purpose of indulging in them.'

'I will pass over the early part of my life, which was passed in almost uninterrupted happiness, and come at once to that unfortunate circumstance which was the cause of my indiscretion, and occasioned me all that anguish I so severely felt afterwards.

'An accident brought Captain Darian and his friend, the Earl Mansville, to our house, from which the latter was unable to be removed for several weeks. Alas! it was a fatal day for me; the earl was young, handsome, insinuating, and the very first moment I beheld him, my heart felt a sensation it never before had experienced, and too soon I was compelled to acknowledge to myself that I had become deeply enamoured of him. Fatal attachment! had I not been unpardonably thoughtless, I should at once have seen the folly, the danger, the hopelessness of indulging, or encouraging a passion for one so far above me, and who would, probably, not feel for me a mutual sentiment, and have stifled it in its infancy. But it was not to be: I was to be taught reason by dear-bought experience. At length, the earl being restored to convalescence, quitted our house, but I felt convinced it was with reluctance, and I noticed the looks he fixed on me, with a sentiment of mingled delight and astonishment. The glances he bestowed on me, were those of admiration—of love! How my heart bounded at this idea, I need not tell; but, alas! it should have been its greatest cause of anguish, and my pleasure was greatly increased when I learned that Mansville having expressed his delight at the neighborhood, had taken up his abode in it for a short time; but Captain Darian had made his departure some days previous to another part of the country. I frequently saw the earl, and he seemed anxious to say something to me, but had not an opportunity, as I was mostly in the presence of my parents; but I needed no interpretation of his thoughts; my own sentiments fully elucidated them, and the warmth of the glances he bestowed upon me. If it required anything to strengthen the affection with which Mansville had inspired me, it was the amiable character he soon acquired in the neighborhood, his chief pleasure appearing to be the performing of acts of benevolence and philanthropy, and the blessings of the poor were amply lavished upon him. Rash, thoughtless, girl that I was. I should have made my parents acquainted with the real state of my feelings, and sought their advice upon the subject, but, for the first time in my life, I was anxious to conceal my thoughts from them, and continued to encourage and strengthen those passions which reason ought to have convinced me could never have been requited by the object who had inspired me with them.

It was about a month after the Earl Mansville had quitted our house, that I arose rather earlier one morning than was my usual custom, induced by the fineness of the weather. I descended from my chamber, and entered the garden, which was beautifully and tastefully arranged, and in which, as well as my father and brother, I took much pleasure. My attention, however, was particularly devoted to a rose tree, which I had frequently heard the earl express his admiration of it while he was remaining at our house. Could I but get him by any means to receive one how happy should I have been. This day I had resolved to make my father and mother a little present of some of these roses, which I knew they would receive with more delight than the most costly gift, coming as they did from me.

'How sweetly my roses have opened,' I soliloquized; 'they seem to know that they are destined to be gifts of affection, and to smile with the delight I shall feel in bestowing them on those I love so dearly. So this for my father, and this for my mother.'

I plucked two of the most beautiful, and had scarcely done so, when my father entered from the house, and greeted me with his usual affection.

'Ah, father,' I exclaimed, 'I have such a nice gift for you and my dear mother.'

'Indeed, my child,' returned my father, smiling fondly on me.

'Yes,' replied I, placing one of those roses which I had plucked in his hand, 'there,—is there a painting in any mansion in the country half so beautiful? What a name a painter would get who could only give a perfect copy of these roses, and, you see, I give you the originals for nothing.'

'Dear girl, dear girl!' ejaculated my father, his eyes glittering with fondness.

'And yet I do not give them to you for nothing, my dear father,' I added; 'for you give me in exchange those sweet smiles of affection, which are to me of more value than anything else in the world.'

'Darling child,' cried my father, raising his hand above his head, and invoking a blessing upon me; 'the look of affection will always reward innocence.'

'After having thus spoken he was about to depart, when I ran towards him, saying:

'What! leave us so soon, my dear father? Prithee stay till the air grows cooler.'

'My child,' answered my affectionate parent, 'these locks have withered in the hot sun. I have passed many years in toiling for others, and have never shrunk from its beams; and now, when it is partly for my darling girl I toil, the balm and comfort of my life, I cannot feel fatigue, and every drop that rolls down my weather-beaten forehead in such a cause, makes my old heart the lighter.'

I threw myself once more into his arms, and he embraced me fervently, after which he hastened away. As soon as he had gone, I was joined by my mother, who, hearing my voice in the garden, had come to summon me to the morning repast.'

'So, my dear,' she remarked, 'old Mrs. Weston is likely to be better off than ever; instead of being ruined by the burning of her cottage, the Earl of Mansville is going to rebuild it at his own expense, and has made her a handsome present into the bargain.'

At the mention of the earl's name I blushed, and a sensation filled my bosom which no other name could have excited.

'Indeed, my mother,' I observed, in reply to what she had stated; 'bless his kind heart! The whole village rings with his charities; and, whenever I see him, my heart beats so.'

'Ah, child,' said my mother, 'It is a very bad sign when a young girl's heart beats at the sight of a good-looking young man. When that happens, she ought at once to get out of his way.'

I felt uncommonly confused, and know I must have blushed deeply.

'Nay, my dear mother,' I at length answered, 'to me a warning is superfluous; your daughter's affections live in her home. Is it possible she will find elsewhere what home will yield her?'

As I afterwards learned, the earl and one of his attendants had watched the departure of my father, and at this moment the former descended from the bridge, and approached towards us. I started at his presence, and was much confused, especially as we had just before been talking about him; but, putting on one of his most affable smiles, he said:—

'Pray don't rise. Don't let me disconcert you. Is Mr. Heywood within?'

'He is but this moment gone into the fields yonder, my lord,' answered my mother.

'Indeed,' said the earl, with apparent disappointment, 'that is unfortunate, I have just now urgent occasion to speak with him.'

'Urgent occasion,' repeated my mother, aside to me; 'what can it be? My lord, then I'll hasten after him; pray have the goodness to wait one moment.'

'Nay,' said Mansville, 'I am ashamed to give you the trouble; but, being of importance—'

'I'll make the best speed, and bring him to you immediately,' returned my mother, hastening away, and leaving me and the earl alone.

Scarcely had my mother disappeared, when the earl, fixing upon me a look in which admiration and delight were blended, took my hand, and, in a voice of rapture, exclaimed:—

'Clara, beauteous Clara! behold before you one who loves you to distraction.'

Although my own feelings and observations had prepared me for this scene, I was so flurried and confused, that I could scarcely contain myself. My bosom heaved—my heart palpitated. Crimson blushes, I am certain, mantled my cheeks; but yet I was unable to withdraw my hand from his hold, which he pressed vehemently to his lips and then continued:—

'Lovely Clara, pardon this abruptness; often have I longed for this opportunity, but in vain; never before have I had it in my power to declare how the first glance of that enchanting face—'

'Oh, my lord,' I faltered out, in tremulous accents, 'I must not listen to this—leave me, I beseech you.'

'Leave you, angelic creature!' replied the earl, emphatically, and still retaining his hold of my hand; 'leave you! oh, there is madness in the bare thought! I cannot, I will not quit your presence till you have uttered some word of consolation—blessed me with some ray of hope!'

'I scarcely knew how to answer;—I could not behold the object of my love, kneeling at my feet, and soliciting my sanction to his vows unmoved; the cold dictates of prudence would have told me instantly to give him a decisive answer, and to force myself from his presence, but my heart pleaded against its rigid rules. The earl noticed my emotion, and doubtless saw his triumph, for he continued in more fervent and emboldened terms.

'But surely the gentle Clara cannot be so cruel as to bid one who is her devoted slave, despair? No—no—she will impart to him a hope—'

'Hope, my lord,' I interrupted, recollecting myself, and the remembrance of my mother's words, and my own assurance, rushing upon my mind; 'I am a poor girl, the daughter of an humble farmer, and have no right to listen to a man like you. Even were I no longer the mistress of my heart, I trust I am not yet so lost to principle, my lord, as to avow it where it might not be confessed with honor.'

The earl arose from his knee, relinquished my hand, and walked away a few paces in much apparent agitation; then suddenly returning, he said in tones of mingled regret and reproach:—

'Do you deem me capable of deception? Clara, it is to make you my wife, to give you rank and title, that I came. One word of yours can give splendor to the home you love, and make the heart that lives but in your kindness, happy!'

As he spoke thus, his manner became more energetic, and I felt my heart gradually yielding!—I trembled, and longed, yet dreaded the return of my parents; while the earl seeing the hesitation of my manner, urged his suit with redoubled determination.

'Clara,' he exclaimed, 'there is not a moment to be lost!—Can you doubt the sincerity of my protestations? Think you that I could be the base villain to deceive one in whom my very soul, my existence is wrapped up. Say but the blissful word; tell me that you will become my bride, the empress of my heart and fortune;—give me this sweet assurance, and—'

'Oh, my lord,' I interrupted, in a state of confusion, and agitation, I will not attempt to describe, 'spare me, I implore you!—I—I—' and unable to finish the sentence, I turned away my head, and burst into tears. The earl again seized my hand rapturously, and encouraged, by the emotion I evinced, his countenance became lighted up with an expression of delight, as he exclaimed—

'Oh, blessed moment! those tears convince me that I am not hated by her who hath taken possession of my whole affections. Blissful assurance! Ere another morn, my Clara, my loved, my adored Clara, will be my bride!—But time passes, we must away from this spot instantly.'

And the earl attempted to place his arm around my waist, but surprised at his words and demeanour, I recoiled from him, and looking upon him with astonishment, I demanded:—

'My lord, what mean you?—Leave this place!—Why, wherefore?'

'Nay, my dearest Clara,' returned Mansville, 'be not surprised, or alarmed; my proposals are honorable; reasons of rank require that we retire to my villa; our marriage must be secret and immediate or it may be prevented. Once mine, I will lead you back in triumph.'

'What,' I exclaimed, 'leave my parents in doubt, in misery?'

'Banish these childish scruples,' said the earl, 'your parents will applaud you when they know the truth. Come to a lover who adores you! Come to the altar which will pour forth blessings on those who love so dearly! Come, Clara, come!'

As the earl thus impatiently urged his suit, he attempted to lead me towards the bridge;—I felt my resolution getting weaker—I trembled—and could offer but a faint resistance.

'Urge me no more, my lord,' I cried, endeavouring to disengage myself from him;—'let me go—I dare not listen to you—farewell!'

'Still inflexible,' ejaculated the earl, turning away from me, with a look of the most inexpressible anguish and despair, 'then is my doom sealed. I cannot, will not live without you, and thus I—'

While thus speaking, he snatched a pistol from his bosom, and presented it towards his head! With a wild shriek of terror, I rushed into his arms, and arrested his fatal purpose. Some spell, some horrid spell came over me. I remember the last cloud of smoke curling over our ancient trees.—I—I've no further recollection. When my senses were restored, and reason was permitted again to resume its sway,—I found myself an inmate of the earl's villa, and far away from that home I had rendered wretched. Oh, God, how dreadful, how agonizing were the thoughts that first crossed my brain! I upbraided myself for a wretch unfit to live—as one who had disgraced herself and destroyed the peace of the most affectionate of parents for ever, and which ever way I turned, a curse seemed to pursue me.

Mansville tried all his eloquence could effect to console me; renewed his most tender asseverations, and repeated his promise to make me his bride. Strange infatuations!—I believed him;—I became tranquil—and if the thoughts of my parents and the name I had abandoned ever returned to my memory, they were quickly banished by the soothings, and fond protestations of the earl. Day after day passed away, and still he promised, but failed to keep his word. My humble dress was now exchanged for fashionable finery and Mansville visited me every day, repeating each time with greater energy the vows of love with which he had at first seduced from my home. Every luxury—every enjoyment that could be wished was at my command; but could they yield me real happiness? Oh, no. The splendour I was now placed in, was purchased with agony; and my own feelings constantly reproached me for that offence of which I had been guilty. Some fated spell must have been upon me, or I must have soon been convinced that St. Clair was not sincere in his promises, or he would not day after day evade the fulfilment of them. But it was my fate dearly to purchase experience of my own weakness and of the earl's treachery. Several weeks elapsed in this manner, and still did the earl neglect to fulfil the promises he had made me, while, at the same time, the ardor of his passion seemed to increase, and the excuses he made for delaying our nuptials, were so plausible, that I was deceived by them. Alas! the woman whose heart has been sincerely attached to any particular object, is made an easy dupe! Let me pass hastily over the time, until the anniversary of the day of my birth, at once the height of my misery, and the means of restoring me to reason and to peace. On that occasion, Mansville had made the most extensive preparations, for celebrating it in the most spirited manner. Numerous guests were invited to the villa, and the peasants in the neighborhood were also permitted to share in the rejoicings. Among other things, for my especial entertainment, the earl had engaged a troop of itinerant players, who were in the neighborhood, to perform a play in the grounds of the villa, which deserves particular mention, as it was the means of restoring me to reason, and saving me from that gulf of destruction, upon the brink of which I stood.

Seldom had I felt so melancholy as I did on that occasion; home and all its tranquil pleasures, came vividly to my recollection, and my heart was heavy. There was a song which was a great favorite in the village where I was born, and which described the pleasures of home in simple yet forcible language, and as it now came fresh upon my recollection, I could not help repeating the words. When I had concluded, I perceived that Celia, my waiting-maid, had entered the room, and had apparently been listening with much attention and admiration to me.

'Bless me, Miss,' said the loquacious girl, 'what a pretty song that was, and how prettily you sang it. Where might you have learnt it, Miss, if I might make so bold?'

'Where I learnt other lessons I ought never have forgotten,' replied I, with a deep sigh; 'it is the song of my native village—the hymn of the lowly heart which dwells upon every lip there, and, like a spell-word, brings back to its name affection which e'er has been betrayed to wander from it. It is the first music heard by infancy in its cradle; and the villagers blending it with their earliest and tenderest recollections, never cease to feel its magic power, till they cease to live.'

'How natural that is,' returned Celia; 'just like my nurse used to nurse me to sleep with a song, which I have never heard since without nodding.'

'Has the earl been inquiring for me, Celia?' I asked.

'He has been here this morning, and has only just gone,' replied the maid; 'but only see what lovely things he has left you, Miss!'

'And Celia displayed a costly dress, and several articles of jewellery, of which I expressed my admiration. But suddenly, gloomy thoughts again came over me, and while tears trembled in my eyes, I ejaculated:—

'But can these baubles make me happy? Ah! never! The heart that's ill at ease is made more wretched by the splendor which laughs in awful mockery, around its dreariness.'

'The presence of Celia embarrassed me; I wished to indulge in melancholy thought alone, but she seemed determined not to take my hints for her to leave me, and at last I only got rid of her by requesting that she would fetch me a book that I had been reading the day previously. When she had left the room, with much agitation, I unlocked my cabinet, and took out the plain village dress, I had worn when I quitted my home. The sight of this tortured my brain, and while deep sobs of anguish almost choked my voice, I thus soliloquized:—

'And shall I remain here, dazzled and betrayed by the splendor with which I am surrounded? Shall I still rack my parent's hearts, and—I—will escape! Escape! no, no—I can brave the shocks of fate, but not a father's eye: to expose myself to his wrath—no, no! my heart's not strong enough for that.'

'I was interrupted by the return of Celia with the book, who, on seeing the village dress in the chaise, expressed the utmost astonishment.'

'Lor' bless me, Miss!' ejaculated the girl, 'what's this dress doing here?— Whoever could have put such trumpery in the way?'

As she spoke, she snatched it up, and was going to throw it aside when I sprang forward emphatically, and hastily took it from her.

'Give it back!' I cried, 'that humble dress was mine;—I cast it off—the splendor that has replaced it, is the source of the most bitter misery!—Oh, my forsaken parents;—Come hither, Celia;—I have no one here of my own sex to talk to—no one to listen to my sorrows. I—'

'Pray speak freely to me, Miss,' observed Celia; 'though humble, you'll not find me insincere.'

'Celia,' I remarked, 'if you knew what a home, what parents I had left, you'd pity me.'

'I do pity you, Miss,' replied Celia, 'indeed I do. Better days will come; you'll be as happy as when you left them.'

I sighed, and shook my head with a look of despair, and then detailed to Celia the particulars of my flight from home, and the promises which the earl had made, but had hitherto failed to keep his word.

'Be of good cheer, Miss, I pray,' said Celia, 'he will keep it, depend upon it.'

Celia spoke this with such a tone of confidence, that it forcibly struck me, and eagerly I exclaimed:—

'Will he, Celia?—Now, don't trifle with me—tell me the worst at once!—Better is present death, than hope deferred; still lingering on, still doomed to be deceived.'

'My dearest young Mistress,' returned Celia, 'there is plenty of time before you think of dying; and, as a proof that the earl don't mean to deceive you, look here.'

And with these words, Celia presented me with a miniature of the earl, elegantly set round with diamonds, at the same time, adding:—

'On a chamber-maid's penetration, this nothing more or less than an earnest of the original.'

I took the miniature with transport, and my eyes became riveted upon it with admiration. Nothing could be more true than the delineation.

'Ah!' I observed, 'precious to the fond one, is the semblance of the object held most dear. 'Tis the enchanter's wand, which gathers around it in a magic circle, sweet recollections and feelings which make memory a paradise!—No, no!—treachery could never dwell in such a face!—I'll trust him still. He cannot mean me false.'

'Shall I put this away, Miss?' asked Celia, pointing to the village dress; 'I am sure the earl would be hurt to see it here.'

'Yes, take it away, Celia,' I replied, 'I would not, for the world, do anything to make him uneasy.'

Celia immediately obeyed, and she had not been gone many minutes, when St. Clair entered the room, and advanced joyfully to meet me.

'Ah, sir,' I ejaculated, 'why overwhelm me with gifts like these?—My humble habits shrink from such magnificence! This (pointing to the miniature,) is the only one I prize, the herald of a gift to follow, which shall restore me to my friends, my self-esteem;—my poor heart-broken parents.'

The earl turned away his head, doubtless to conceal the embarrassment which my words occasioned him, and then, in a tone which showed that he wished to change the subject, said:—

'This is your birth-day, Clara.'

That word tore my wounds open! Oh! what a joyous day was it when I was at home! The farm seemed to be one smile of joy;—the sacred halo of a parent's blessing descended on me with the morning sun; and even my birds, my flowers, my young companions,—all seemed to have a livelier look, and lift their heads rejoicing. These thoughts were too painful for my feelings, and I burst into tears.

'Nay, Clara,' observed the earl, 'cheer thee, love!—banish that woe; discard that dread; rely upon my promise.'

'Heaven's smile repay that word,' I exclaimed fervently; 'the weight which pressed me to the earth is removed, and all around me breathes ecstasy.'

'It delights me to hear thee say so, my dearest Clara,' replied the earl, 'go, sweetest, and put on your richest dress to celebrate this joyous day.'

'That day,' I added, with enthusiasm, 'that day which gives me back to honor. It shall be done, my lord.'

The earl kissed me affectionately, and left the room; and once more a cheering hope brought consolation to my heart, and assured me of future happiness and joy. Alas! how soon was I to be awakened to the greatest agony! To more misery than I had ever before experienced.

The festivities of the day passed off most brilliantly until the play commenced. The gardens in which it took place were brilliantly illuminated, and the temporary theatre was formed among the trees in the back. Just as the performances were about to commence, a servant entered and delivered to the earl a letter, upon perusing the contents of which, he excused himself to me and the numerous guests, it being necessary that he should be absent for a short time; but he begged that his absence might not interrupt their pleasure, as the village actors would amuse them with their humble efforts; and ere they had ended, he would return.

When the earl had gone, I beckoned Celia over to me, and the play immediately commenced; but what were my feelings of intense agony as it proceeded, when I perceived that the plot, and every incident of the piece, so corresponded with my own circumstances, that it seemed as if they had actually chosen me to sketch the heroine from. A nobleman wooed a peasant girl; he vowed the most unbounded affection for her;—promised her marriage, if she would but elope with him;—she was persuaded;—she sunk senseless in his arms, and was conveyed away.

During the time the piece was being played, my anguish was insupportable, and I was so worked upon by the power of each scene, that I could scarcely persuade myself but that it was reality.

'Fatal resemblance,' I ejaculated, at the passage where the seducer bears his victim away; 'has there before been such another deluded being?'

'Be calm, dear mistress, be calm,' said Celia, 'it is only a play.'

But my thoughts were too intently fixed upon the scene which followed, to pay any particular attention to her words. The parents of the betrayed one, as represented in the piece, upon hearing the screams of their daughter, rushed on to the stage, the father demanding of his wife the meaning of the alarm, and the cause of the cries he had heard. The mother looking round, and finding that her daughter was not there, exclaimed:—

'My child! my child!—A mere pretence—our darling—lost—escaped! Ah! there! there! behold the seducer bearing her away!'

'Ah!' cried the father, frantically, 'what fled? given up to shame?—Oh, art beyond belief! Have all your fond professions come to this? Oh, well-laid plan!—Lost! lost!—Oh, viper!—hypocrite!—I tear you from my bosom!—I sweep you from the home you have disgraced!—A father's curse—'

With a wild shriek, as the actor gave utterance to these words, I rushed upon the stage, and falling at his feet, I vociferated, in tones that made the place re-echo again:—

'Hold! hold!—curse her not! She is not lost! She is innocent!'

At this moment the earl entered, and the whole of the spectators seemed petrified to the spot with astonishment.

'Ah!' cried Mansville, 'what do I see?—What is the meaning of this?'

Celia raised me from the posture I had assumed, and by the commands of the earl, whose confusion and chagrin was evident, she led me to my own chamber, while the guests quickly dispersed, and the entertainments abruptly ceased.

After I had been taken to my own apartment for a few minutes, by the kind attention of Celia, I recovered myself, and addressing myself to her, said:—

'Thanks! thanks! a thousand thanks!—I grieve to have troubled you thus— 'tis over now; 'tis nothing.'

'The earl, Miss! the earl!' exclaimed Celia, and the next moment Mansville stood before me. There was an expression of sternness upon his brow which I had never seen before, and he seemed greatly agitated. I was alarmed, and advancing towards him, said:—

'Oh, my lord, how shall I apologize for—'

'No more of that,' he interrupted; ''tis past.'

'My lord,' ejaculated I, surprised.

'Leave us, Celia;' commanded the earl, and when the former had retired from the room, he turned to me, and the indignation of his looks seemed to increase.

'Oh, Mansville,' I observed, 'how have I deserved this indifference? Is it my fault that my feelings overcame me? Is it my fault that the scene revived my sense of duty? Oh, my lord, it is those fatal feelings that have made me what I am.'

'I am weary of this parade of sensibility,' replied the earl, impatiently; 'you have called up against me the laugh of my tenantry and domestics—let that content you.'

'What does the change portend? This freezing look—this language of reproach?' I inquired.

'For your own sake and mine press me no farther, Clara,' replied the earl; 'I would not have had the scene which has just past occur for millions. If you have placed yourself in unpleasant circumstances, common policy should at least teach you to shun the sneers of the world; but it is over and nothing can now be said which will not increase, instead of diminishing our mutual uneasiness.'

A burning pang shot through my brain as Mansville gave utterance to these words, and emphatically and hysterically I exclaimed—

'Am I deceived?'

'I cannot tell what childish hopes you may have indulged,' returned the earl, with the most freezing coldness, 'and I am only sorry that you should have been weak enough to deceive yourself.'

'Oh, no, my agitation has shaken my senses,' cried I deliriously, and clasping my temples; 'he could not—no, no, Mansville! in the name of all that you have professed, and I have believed, in the name of those vows that are registered on high, however man may slight them; and in that holiest name of all, the name of Him, whose bolt hangs o'er the hypocrite, dispel these doubts and this suspense; restore me at once to my parents, or at once name the hour for that ceremony to pass, when, before the world, you acknowledge me as your wife!'

'Clara,' replied the earl, 'since you will force me to be explicit, is it not strange that a mind so intelligent should fancy for a moment that it was possible for one in my rank to marry a girl in yours?'

'The oath!—the oath!' I cried, almost choking with emotion.

'My heart is ever yours,' returned he, 'but, of my hand, I have no power to dispose. Nay, you pass not hence.'

'Are there no pangs, that, like the dagger, kill the heart they pierce,' ejaculated I; 'I cast me at your feet in agony! 'Tis Clara kneels and supplicates! not for herself, but for the racked souls, and the gray hairs of age! For your honor and eternal peace, restore me to my parents.'

The earl seemed suffering the most acute mental agony, and for a moment averted his head.

'Clara,' he said, in faltering accents, 'believe my heart unchanged—my unceasing love—'

'Monster!' I interrupted in delirious tones; 'darest thou still profane that sacred word? No, my lord, the mask is torn away,—the attachment which was my pride is now my disgust; 'tis past! I know myself deceived, but, thank Heaven, I am not lost! To you, my lord, the bitter hour is not yet arrived; but, 'tis an hour that never fails to guilt. At some unexpected moment, the blandishment of pleasure will lose their force—the power of enjoyment will be palsied in your soul; it will awake only to remorse. In that hour of retribution think of these words of warning,—think of the hearts you've broken—think, my lord, and tremble.'

Without waiting to give utterance to another syllable, I rushed from the room, but the voice of the earl, tempted me to stop at the door and listen. He was apparently pacing the apartment in the most violent state of agitation, and thus soliloquizing:—

'The fatal truth curdles my blood like poison! I feel the hell in my bosom. Oh, what a heart I've lost? Why, splendid slavery of rank, must virtue be thy victim; why must affection be sacrificed to thee? The peasant mates him where his heart directs, and to his lowly bride brings happiness; his lord must fret, chained to some high-born fool; or either pine in vain for humble loveliness, or make its innocence a martyr to his choice. I was not born to be a betrayer. Wed! I cannot cease to love!'

The words recalled my scattered reason, and I was almost tempted to return to the apartment; but a feeling of pride restrained me, and bursting with anguish, I hurried away to my chamber, where I was soon afterwards joined by Celia, who was sent by the earl to watch me. I was at first insensible to her presence, and sat like a statue, with my eyes fixed upon the earth, and buried in deep and agonizing meditation. The poor girl spoke to me, but, overcome with my emotions, I burst into tears, and threw myself on the couch, and Celia, probably thinking that I should fall into a slumber, left. My mind being so dreadfully fatigued by the sufferings I had so recently undergone, I did gradually fall to sleep, from which I was aroused by hearing some person moving in the adjoining apartment. The door was partly open, and I perceived it was Celia. Anxious to ascertain for what purpose Celia was there, I still pretended to slumber, and shortly afterwards, she stole softly to the door which opened upon my chamber, and peeped in.

'Yes, she sleeps,' she said. 'Poor lady, my heart bleeds for her. Why, this strange, unlooked-for adventure has created a fine confusion among all of us; for see—if one wouldn't think, by the state this room is in, that it had turned the heads of the whole family. Scarcely a piece of furniture in its place, and my mistress's toilet, too. Here's confusion. But hold, Celia, that's your affair, so no complaining. I declare I'm almost worn out with this bustle. Heigh-ho! I'm ordered by the earl to watch my mistress here; but I'm sure I don't know what I shall do to keep awake, suppose I finish the new drawing the Lady Clara honored my humble talents by so much admiring—that's just the thing.'

Celia placed the drawing-stand before her, and sitting down, applied herself to her task; but it was evident, by her frequent nodding, that her words would soon be verified, and I was most anxious for it to happen so, as I had formed a resolution to make my escape from the villa that night by some means or other. She once more approached the couch, and having apparently satisfied herself that I still slept, she returned to the drawing.

'Oh, dear,' she exclaimed with excessive weariness, 'oh, dear, my eyelids are so very heavy, they stick together whenever I wink, and I can scarcely force them open again. My poor drawing will never get finished at this rate. However, I must try once more what it will do to keep me from sleeping at my post.'

She again endeavored to keep herself awake, but her efforts were all useless, she nodded, and nodded, until at length she fell back in her seat, fast asleep.

I now hastily arose, and attired myself in the village dress I had gazed at with such feelings of pain and regret in the morning. I approached Celia on tip-toe, and being certain she was really asleep, I soliloquized—

'Yes, she sleeps! Now is the only moment! I thought I could not brave a father's eyes; but there is courage in despair, which makes the weak frame wonder at itself. I have written this letter to the earl, and here are all his gifts—his diamonds, his detested wealth. Now, methinks, my heart feels lighter. Yes, like the prodigal, I will turn my steps where a child may always look with confidence. I have been imprudent, but am not guilty. Heaven receives the offering of the sincerely penitent, and can a parent's blessing be denied when Heaven forgives?'

The apartment upon which my chamber opened, and in which Celia was, was a magnificent one. On one side was a large French window, through which the distant country could be seen far beyond. Outside was a balcony overhanging the road. I undrew the curtains softly, and opened the window. It was a fine moonlight night, and the distant landscape could be seen as distinctly as at broad day. I took a scarf from the shoulders of Celia, which she wore, fastened one end of it to the balcony railing, then returned, made an appeal to Heaven for protection, and blew out the candles. With more firmness than might have been expected, I then began my perilous descent, and gradually letting myself down by the scarf, alighted in safety below. Fear of being re-taken lent speed to my feet, and I flew with the greatest rapidity across the country to which, however, I was complete stranger.

I scarcely abated my speed in the least for the distance of five miles or more, when I was obliged to pause, in order to rest myself. I looked fearfully around me to see whether or not I was pursued, and then reflected upon what course I should pursue. I feared to travel at that hour, and, indeed, it would have been most dangerous, to a young girl especially; I therefore resolved to proceed for some distance further, and then to seek shelter at some cottage till the morning. I then resumed my lonely journey in a state of fear and agitation, it is unnecessary for me to describe. After walking for above an hour longer, I arrived at a small and obscure hamlet, and by the light which I perceived in several of the cottage windows, I was satisfied that some of the inmates had not retired to rest.

Here, again I paused, for uncertain of the reception I might meet with, I almost feared to knock. At length, I approached the first one, and having first listened at the door, and hearing only the voice of an old woman, apparently in prayer, I became more confident, and having waited till she had ceased, I knocked, and shortly afterwards, the voice of the old woman demanded who was there, and what they wanted. I informed her, and begged that she would admit me. It was some time before she complied, and seemed to be consulting within herself the propriety or safety of doing so, but having put several more questions to me, as to whether I was alone, &c., she at last ventured to open the door, and eyed me narrowly from head to foot. She was a very clean, motherly-looking woman, whose appearance called the tears to my eyes, she was so much like the parent to whom I was returning.

'Good gracious, child,' she said, 'what causes you to be out at this time of the night and from whence do you come?'

'I am a stranger in this part of the world, my good dame,' I replied; 'I have recently made my escape from villainy, and crave a shelter in your cottage till the morning. I have sufficient to reward you for your trouble.'

'As for reward,' returned the old woman, 'I require none; and if your story is true, you are heartily welcome to the humble bed I have to offer you.'

I thanked the poor woman most sincerely for her kindness, and entered the clean little parlor, where the remains of her humble repast she had been partaking of, was still upon the table, and of which she requested me to eat, but I declined. Judging from her manners and appearance that she was one in whom I could confide, I gave her a brief account of my situation, and upon what purpose I was bent. She listened to me with evident commiseration, and applauding the resolution I had formed, after some conversation, she conducted me to the room in which she was able to accommodate me, and after bidding me good night left me to myself. Fatigued with the events of the day, it was not long ere I fell asleep, and I did not awake until the old woman aroused me late in the morning.

Having been prevailed upon by her to partake of her humble meal, and offered her some remuneration for her kindness which she persisted in declining, I took leave of her, and made my way to the coach office, to which she had directed me. I met with no interruption on the road, and succeeded in obtaining a place in one of the coaches just starting for my native village. I alighted from the coach a short distance from my place of destination, having made up my mind to walk the rest of the way.

I cannot adequately portray the nature of my feelings as I approached the home where I had never known anything but happiness until my meeting with Mansville; alternate hopes and fears racked my bosom. It was a beautiful morning; the sun shone forth in fall meridian splendor, and all nature seemed to wear a smile of gladness. When I came within sight of the village, my heart felt ready to burst, and suddenly the sound of pipes and tabors vibrated on my ears. Presently afterwards, a bridal procession approached towards the spot where I was, and stopped before the doors of one of my female companions, Ellen Greenley, and George Ashburne, who had long been her acknowledged lover.

George Ashburne having thanked his friends for their kindness, the father of Ellen joined them.

'Good morning to you, my dear child,' said Mr. Greenley, kissing his daughter affectionately, and smiling upon his son-in-law elect, kindly; 'may this prove a blessed day to you both. Go, lads and lasses, and gather the flowers to celebrate the ceremony.'

The villagers departed, and Mr. Greenley continued—

'I'll try if I can't prevail upon Mr. Heywood, the unfortunate father of Clara, to come to your wedding; poor fellow! he may be compared to the ruined wing of the crazy old mansion-house he was converted into a farm, that looks down in gloomy silence upon the bright and smiling landscape which everywhere surrounds it. Ah! that sad girl! the flowers they go to gather are less frail than she has proved. My children be virtuous if you would be happy.'

Thus saying, the old man re-entered the cottage, but his words had been so many daggers to my heart.

'Clara's father,' observed Ellen, when her father had left them, 'ah! if our poor Clara herself were only here now, how her heart would rejoice in our happiness.'

'Don't name her, Ellen,' said George, 'don't name her; a virtuous girl's lips ought not to be sullied by the mention of her name.'

'Ah! George,' replied Ellen, 'pity becomes the virtuous, and the more she has fallen, the more she deserves to be pitied.'

'Psha!' cried George, 'can't you talk about something else?'

'A sad day it was when she went away,' continued Ellen, 'everybody was downcast, as if some great affliction had befallen the village.'

'More fools they,' was George's abrupt retort; 'if you or I had gone, indeed, it might have afflicted them; now, Ellen, you shall not talk any more about her. Come, come, let us be going.'

Suddenly accumulating all my fortitude, I emerged from the place where I had concealed myself, and called upon Ellen by name. Both her and her lover started, and the former exclaimed in a tone of astonishment and alarm:—

'Bless us! what's that?'

'As I live,' said her lover, 'it is Clara Heywood, or her ghost!'

'Do not be alarmed, Ellen,' I said, 'but one word with you.'

'No, it's she herself, as I'm alive,' ejaculated Ellen: 'but oh, how changed she is.'

'One word, dear Ellen,' I repeated.

'I am not satisfied upon this subject,' said the timid George, 'so, as you seem resolved to stay here, I shall be off.'

'Ellen,' I repeated, as soon as George had departed 'Have you forgotten me?'

'No, Clara, no,' answered the affectionate girl, 'nor never shall forget you. I was even talking about you, as you called. Ah! Clara, you're sadly altered; and so is everything since you went away. Such a day as it was, when you left us!—There wasn't a dry eye, nor a cheerful word spoke in the village. Your poor father—'

'Well—well!' I hurriedly interrupted.

'I see it grieves you,' said Ellen; 'I didn't mean to make you sad—you look as if you had suffered enough. This is my wedding-day, Clara.'

Ellen sighed, and for a moment averted her head.

'Yes, Ellen,' I resumed, 'I wish to see my mother, and to see her privately. She would not, perhaps, admit me to her presence, if she was not forewarned. You can oblige me greatly, if you will induce her to come to me, by saying that a stranger desires to speak with her, immediately.'

'That I will, with all my heart,' said Ellen, 'and may it turn to good. Oh, may all the realization of her hopes attend the returning wanderer. But where shall I find you?'

'I'll follow you,' I answered, 'go round to the front door; I'll take the opposite side, and meet you at the gate. And Heaven will help the heart, determined to retrace the paths of rectitude and honor,' I cried, as with a heart beating with hope and dread, I made my way towards the house of my beloved parents.

Oh, never shall I forget the feelings with which I entered at the gate.

'Here is my home!—my blessed, blessed home!' I reflected; 'a frowning form appears to guard the threshold, shrieking in my ear—'Hence! thou shalt not enter!' But can I linger here?—I seem to tread the earth like a criminal. I must, and I will approach! Now, now now!'

Having at last made a violent effort to conquer my emotions, I rushed down the steps into the yard, and then exclaimed triumphantly—

'Once more I am surrounded by all that is dear to me!—Father! mother!—your unhappy child, sorrowing, imploring, returns to you!—And hark! I hear the song of my childhood floating on the air. How acutely doth its accents strike upon my heart in such a scene as this, around whose every tree and flower some recollection of infancy's entwined.'

My heart rose in my mouth, as I ventured, seeing the coast clear, to approach the house, and even to peep into the parlor-window. I trembled; and an indescribable pang shot through my frame, as I noticed everything that well-known room contained, and which had not undergone any alteration since I last beheld it. But how shall I describe my feelings, when immediately afterwards, the door of the inner apartment was thrown open, and the next moment my mother appeared with the breakfast things. With what eager fondness did I gaze upon her revered countenance, and yearn again to be enfolded in her embrace; and most severely did I reproach myself when I noticed the heavy marks of care that were upon her brow. The casement was partially open, so that I could hear all that passed, and my mother, having placed the breakfast things on the table, sighed heavily and observed—

'There, there!—There's the breakfast ready for my poor husband, and now I wish he would return. He has been out since daylight with his gun; the only thing that seems to attract his attention. At home, all day he does nothing but sigh, or,—if he thinks he is not observed,—weep. Oh, Clara! unthinking girl you have too much to atone for. How long he stays.'

My heart was ready to burst as these words reached my ears, and it was with the greatest difficulty I could avoid betraying myself. My mother now came to the door and looked anxiously out, but a little thatched summer-house close at hand concealed me from observation. Again she entered the house, and I overheard her, in tones of the deepest anxiety, exclaim—

'No, I cannot catch even a glimpse of him, yet my mind is never easy in his absence; his despondency sometimes makes me fear that—ah! surely yonder I see him moving mournfully among the trees. Yes, 'tis he—he is just at the bridge;—he comes!'

'Never shall I forget the sensation with which I strained my eyes in the direction which the observation of my mother instructed me in, and I thought I should have sunk to the earth with mingled feelings of the most intense anguish and awe, when my eyes once more beheld my father. But oh, how altered was he! Care had deeply imprinted its furrows on his cheeks, and his form was bent and attenuated. He walked with a feeble step, and at least twenty winters seemed to have passed over his head since I had last beheld him.

'My God!' I mentally ejaculated, 'and are these the terrible consequences of my imprudence? Oh, my poor mother, truly did you say that I had much to atone for!—How can I ever make sufficient reparation for the misery I have occasioned.'

My father at length reached the house, and my mother ran affectionately to meet him.

'You were wrong to have wandered so far,' she said, 'you seem quite exhausted.'

'No,' replied my father, ''tis only exercise that can divert the mind from gloom; When the mind's disturbed, the body does not feel fatigued. I'm late, I hope you haven't waited breakfast for me.'

'I would not certainly breakfast without you,' returned my mother; 'but you are too much heated to sit in this parlor; the breeze is too keen for you; we will go into the inner apartment. Go, and I will take the breakfast things for you.'

'Well, well, as you please,' said my father, 'where is Edwin?'

'He has gone to make one of the wedding party of Ellen and George,' answered my mother.

'A wedding!' said my father, with a sigh, 'ah.'

My mother had by this time hastily gathered up the breakfast things, and left the parlor.

'Poor, bereaved mother,' sighed my father, looking after her with the most poignant sorrow, 'she struggles with her grief, and endeavors to impart a joy which neither can feel; which we neither can know again.—No! no! peace of mind fled with my guilty daughter—never to return! Why did I repair the ravages time had made in this old mansion? Why strive to give an air of comfort to my habitation?—Because I deemed it would be the abode of bliss. She—my child, hath made it the abode of despair!—But, no matter, a few years of neglect, desolation will spread around, and hearth, roof, and tree will be ruined, like my happiness, and broken as my heart!—My daughter!—my Clara! Oh! misery! misery! She is gone! she is lost forever!'

As he thus spoke he rushed from the room, and my agony was so great that I could not help groaning aloud.

'Oh! God!' I exclaimed; 'what will become of me?—I shall go mad!—Would that I had not ventured hither; I shall never be enabled to withstand the scene!—Never can I find resolution enough to meet his reproaches. Alas! he is too strongly prejudiced against me, ever to be persuaded that I am guiltless!—But where is Ellen?'

I had scarcely given utterance to the words, when the latter approached, and before I had time to speak to her, entered the house observing me, however, and motioning me to remain where I was, and to wait patiently. I cannot do justice to the anxiety of my feelings during the time I was waiting there. A thousand doubts, hopes and fears, flashed across my brain, and every moment seemed to be an hour. At length, I heard Ellen in joyful accents exclaim, as she came from the house,

'Joy, Clara, joy!'

I sprang forward with rapture to meet her.

'I have succeeded, my dear Clara, said the generous-hearted girl, exultingly; 'she'll come to you. Wait in the summer-house, and she'll be with you presently.'

'Thanks! thanks!' cried I, 'a thousand thanks, my dearest Ellen.'

'She's coming,' observed Ellen, eagerly; 'go, quick. I pray for your success from the bottom of my soul.'

Scarcely had I time to enter the summer-house, when my mother approached. Now was the moment of my trial at hand; a deadly sickness came over me, and it was with difficulty I could save myself from fainting. The next moment my mother entered the summer-house, and she no sooner beheld me, than she uttered a loud scream of astonishment, and became, as it were, paralyzed to the spot.

'Mother! mother!' I cried, in frantic tones, 'if I may still call you by that dear name;—oh, pardon your imprudent, but not guilty daughter!'

I could say no more, but sank at her feet. A pause of several moments ensued! my mother being too much overpowered by her emotions to speak; but at length, in a voice choked with agony, she exclaimed:—

'Wretched girl! dare you again to approach that home, those parents whose hearts you have rendered desolate? Guilty, miserable girl—'

'Oh, no, no,' I interrupted hastily, 'imprudent, cruel, I have been, dear mother, but your child returns to you as pure as when she left you. I appeal to heaven to attest my innocence. Oh, my mother, pardon the poor prodigal, who erred alone through youth and inexperience, and who is now ready to make all the atonement in her power.'

'Can this be true? Have you indeed not endeavored to deceive me?' ejaculated my mother, eagerly, and her eyes beaming, fixed with a penetrating glance upon my countenance, as though she would read all that was passing in my soul. 'But no, it is impossible. How can you be innocent, uncontaminated? did you not abandon your home, your parents, and throw yourself into the arms of a villain, who—'

'Oh, mother, believe it not,' I returned, with the tears at the same time streaming down my cheeks. 'I acknowledge that by the most base and subtle means, and in a moment of thoughtlessness and imprudence, Mansville got me into his power, and bore me far away from my home. But I thought that he meant to act honorably towards me. He told me he would make me his bride. I was too ready to believe him, and day after day he made some plausible excuse to postpone the fulfilment of his promise. Think not, however, that I suffered nothing. That you were ever absent from my thoughts, or that the fondly cherished recollections of my home, that home I had quitted, ceased to torture my mind. Bitter, indeed, were the pangs I endured. Ofttimes would I have fled the place and returned hither, but I dreaded to meet the reproaches of my parents. When, however, Mansville threw aside the mask, I overcame that dread, and your unhappy daughter has come back to solicit your forgiveness, with her virtue as unsullied as when she left you.'

During the time I was speaking, the agony evinced by my mother needs no description, and when I had ceased, in a paroxysm of delirious transport, she snatched me from the earth and enfolded me in her arms, exclaiming—

'My child—my long lost Clara! Yes, I do indeed believe you, and pardon you, Oh, this is a happiness that I never expected!'

'Mother, dear mother!' I cried, in a tone of gratitude and delight which I cannot adequately describe, 'to be suffered once more to speak to you in this place—to hear those blest words—to know myself pardoned. My heart is so full. Thus, thus only can I thank you.'

Again I threw my arms around her neck, and pressing vehemently to her bosom, she wept tears of joy.

'Unfortunate girl,' at length she said, gently withdrawing herself from my enthusiastic caresses, 'I believe you innocent; but a mother's heart is more indulgent than the world. And, ah! there is yet one to be appeased. Hark! I hear footsteps. It is your father. Softly—stand out of sight! He comes, but must not know you yet.'

Hastily throwing a veil over me, my mother urged me into the summer-house, and the next moment my father and the father of Ellen came from the house. They were in conversation, and by the words which I overheard, it seemed that the latter had been endeavoring to persuade my father to join the wedding party.

'But at any rate,' said he, 'for half an hour you might.'

'No,' returned my father mournfully, 'I should only mar the festal hour. I am the scathed tree of the heath that cannot drop. The bolt that struck off my branches has left my old trunk erect in wretched loneliness.'

''Tis a shame, neighbor,' observed his companion, 'it is a shame, I say, for a strong mind like yours to give itself up to sorrow in this way. You might as well put a pistol to your head at once, for you will be sure to kill yourself by it, sooner or later, and self-murder in one form is quite as criminal as in another.'

'When you have seen the being for whom you've lived,' retorted my father, 'the object of every solicitude—the child you've reared with unceasing watchfulness, wrenched from you by a villain's grasp, then come to me and talk of patience, and I'll listen.'

'Well, well, I'll not weary you any longer,' observed Mr. Greenly; 'from my soul I'm grieved to see you thus abandoned to fruitless sorrow. Farewell, my friend, and may days be at hand when we shall see you smile once more.'

Thus saying, and grasping the hand of my father most cordially, the father of Ellen retired through the gate.

'Smile,' soliloquized the former, as his friend left him; 'smile! Oh, happy father!—happy to see his daughter safe in her native innocence—safe from the bane of wealth. I once hoped that such a fate would beam on me; but fate was jealous. Lost, lost, wretched girl!'

While my unhappy father was thus speaking, my mother entered the summer-house, and leading me forth, she placed her finger on her lips to enjoin me to silence. We stood aside, and watched him, unobserved.

'As I gaze there,' he continued, 'methinks I see her in her days of innocence, when first her little steps began: laughing, she ran, with arms extended towards me; then I trembled lest her young feet should fail, and she should fall. But she passed through those fearful times unharmed. She escaped those thousand dangers. Now she falls—falls to the earth, never to rise! She's gone—she's lost! My Clara! Oh, my child!'

My heart was ready to burst, and I was almost choked with endeavouring to repress the heavy sobs that heaved my bosom. My father threw himself into a chair, and my mother advanced towards him, and touched him on the shoulder.

'A tear,' she observed, in gentle accents. 'Did I not hear our Clara's name too? Did not your lips utter the name of our child?'

'No, no,' he replied, hastily rising; 'let us, if possible, not think or speak of her again.'

'Well, well, dearest husband,' returned my mother, 'I will not urge it now; but here is a poor creature, the daughter of—'

'Away—away!' hastily and vehemently interrupted my unhappy parent. 'I have no daughter now.'

'No,' replied my mother; 'but this repentant child, the daughter of a neighbor, is on her way to ask forgiveness of her offended father. She faints with shame and grief, and dares not meet him. Do speak a word or two of comfort to her, and teach her in what words she should address him to gain his blessing, and to sooth his anguish.'

'None,' replied my father, hastily, and his eyes beaming wild, 'none. Let her not dare to look upon him. Let not her presence insult the home her infamy has disgraced. Perhaps, too, she had a mother, rich in every virtue. Let her shun that mother, for contamination is in her touch. Virtue can hold no intercourse with vice, though vice, with double baseness, kneels affecting reverence for virtue.'

I found it impossible to help groaning aloud, as I listened to my father's observations, and I threw myself into my mother's arms. He turned his eyes steadily upon me for a minute or so, and then resumed—

'Yet hold! I will not judge too harshly; for there are shades of guilt, and hers, perhaps, may not be of so deep a dye as to preclude forgiveness. Perhaps her father was not affectionate—Perhaps (poor child!) he was morose and frigid. Perhaps neglectful, cold, unindulgent.'

'Oh, no!' I sobbed, and sank on my knees before him with clasped and upraised hands, 'he was most kind, affectionate, and good.'

'What,' eagerly demanded my poor parent, 'did he love you better than all the world?—did he rear you in domestic tenderness, and train you in the paths of virtue?—did he clasp you to his doting heart, and in his foolish pride proclaim his child the paragon of earth?—and did you then blast all of his fond hopes, and clinging to another, leave him in his storm of grief?'

Again I groaned with the almost insupportable power of my anguish, and still remained on my knees before him.

'Dearest husband,' said my mother, 'do not aggravate the dear child's misery. She is repentant—she is the shorn lamb, temper the storm to her affliction, but do not add another wound to a heart already too much lacerated.'

'Well, well,' returned my father, 'be it so. I will forget my own, and try to sooth her sorrows. Young woman, rise.'

He raised me from the earth, and taking my hand tenderly, continued:—

'What your miseries are, I well can guess; but what your father's sufferings are I too well know. You fear to meet his eye; you dread to hear his curse. A father's curse is heavy; shall I paint this agonizing suffering to you, child! I can do so; for I have felt it. I have it now. I once had a daughter.'

'Oh, sir, do not name her!' I cried, with a feeling of agony, too powerful for utterance.

'Oh, how I doted on that daughter,' he continued, and his countenance betrayed the terrible mental agony he was enduring. 'How I adored her, words cannot tell; thoughts cannot measure! Yet—she sacrificed me to a villain,—her ingratitude has bleached this head,—her wickedness has broken this heart, and now my detestation is upon her! Oh, do not you resemble her,—remain not a moment longer from your father,—fly to him ere his heart give way, as mine does now—ere he curses you as I now curse—'

'Oh, no more!' I interrupted, darting forward in excessive agitation; 'in mercy, oh, no more.'

'Ha!' groaned my father, as he recognized me and retreated from me, 'away! away! away!'

In a wild delirium of agony, I followed him on my knees, exclaiming, in frantic accents,—

'Your vengeance cannot make you deaf to the agony of a despairing child; behold me on my knees; I bring the sacrifice of a broken spirit. I do not ask your love till you know I am worthy of being loved. I do not ask your confidence till you feel I can be trusted; but do not deny me the shelter of your paternal roof.'

'My father spurned me violently from him, and as he did so, he cried, in hoarse tones,—

'Hence! hence!—I know you not! My sight rejects you—spurns you! If you have wasted all the spoils of guilt, there—there's gold! Your idol, gold! for which you bartered all your hopes of bliss!'

He dashed a purse furiously to the earth as he spoke, and hastened towards my mother, fixing upon me looks of scorn and hatred. Oh, Heaven! how each glance penetrated to my soul! How every word burnt to my heart! It was wonderful that reason could retain her empire in that trying scene.

'Father! father!' I implored, with redoubled vehemence, 'hear me, I beseech you.'

'Husband, dearest husband!' supplicated my mother, 'hear her, she is innocent.'

'Innocent!' he reiterated, 'she innocent! No, no, impossible!—she left us; left her happy parents—her happy home—to follow a villain!'

'Father, dearest father!' I cried, 'temper mercy, I pray you, with your severity. I am not the poor, guilty, degraded being that you suppose me to be. Your child is still virtuous—still unpolluted; her only crime has been in loving one too fondly, who sought to betray her! In the name of Heaven, I assert my innocence, and if I speak not the truth, may its most awful vengeance descend upon my head! But you cannot, you will not, longer doubt me. I see you will not! Oh, bless you for this, father, father!'

I could say no more; but sobbing convulsively, I threw myself into his arms! He wept;—yes, I could feel his chest heave with the power of mental anguish, and the big round tear of sorrow fell from his eye upon my cheek; he pressed me with all the fervour he had ever been wont to do to his heart, and ere he pronounced it, I knew that I was forgiven.

'My child! my Clara!' he at last cried, 'is it possible that I again hold you innocent to my bosom? But no, the bliss is too great to be real! And yet it is her! yes, it is my child; it is her lips that have asserted her innocence and appealed to Heaven to attest it, and I can no longer doubt! Oh, happiness supreme! My long-lost, reclaimed child! Receive a parent's thanks.'

He could say no more for a minute or two, but again did he clasp me with ecstasy to his bosom, and weep tears of gratitude upon my cheek. Then he would, withdrawing himself from me, with an expression I find it impossible to describe, gazed in my countenance, and clasping his hands together, raised them towards Heaven, in humble thanksgiving for its goodness in restoring me, uncontaminated to his arms; while my poor mother's emotion was equal to his own, and she gazed on the scene with a sensation of the deepest gratitude and joy.

'But where is the villain who has been guilty of this outrage?' he at length demanded; 'let me hasten to him, and demand satisfaction for the wrongs he has done us; the many days and nights of bitter misery he has caused your unfortunate parents! Tell me to what insult, what anguish did he expose you? I am mad to hear the guilty tale!'

'Pray defer it, my dear husband, till your feelings are more composed;' said my mother.

'No, no, no,' hastily ejaculated my father, and with the greatest impatience depicted in his countenance. 'I will hear it now! I will no longer hesitate!'

In as few words as possible, I complied with my father's request, and related all the particulars of the earl's conduct to me during the time I was in his power. During the recital, the violent agitation of my father was plainly visible, and when I had concluded, he walked backwards and forwards for a short time, with disordered steps, and muttering incoherent sentences to himself.

At length he turned to me, and clasping me vehemently to his bosom, exclaimed:—

'My child!—my own one!—my still innocent Clara!—Can I longer doubt you? Oh, no! you are restored to my arms; guiltless as when in a moment of imprudence you were snatched away from your paternal roof! Oh! God! I thank you for this! The trial has been a heavy one! But my child has withstood the temptation, the artifices of the libertine, and the tempter, and I am again happy! Bless you, bless you, my Clara!—Oh, I was too severe to imagine for a moment that you could be the guilty being I supposed you to have become!—Bless you again!—Here in this fond embrace!—This kiss of fervent affection, let me at once seal your pardon for the indiscretion of which you were guilty. We will never again part, till death shall interpose between us.'

Thus saying he snatched me fervently to his heart, and imprinted warm kisses upon my cheeks, my lips, my temples! How shall I describe the feelings that rushed through my veins at that moment? Language is by far too weak to do justice to them. They must be left to the warm imagination of the susceptible reader!—I was unable to return any answer; emotion choked my utterance, and stifled the words of ecstasy that would otherwise have flowed from my lips. Again I felt the ardent embrace of that father whose forgiveness I had despaired of ever being able to obtain; once more I felt the glow of his kiss upon my lips, and heard him pronounce his forgiveness for the many, many hours of bitter agony, of doubt, of fear, I had caused him.—Surely an age of anguish would have been trifling to purchase such a few moments of bliss, of exquisite transport, as those I then experienced. Again and again he enfolded me to his heart, and wept: like a child did the poor old man weep tears of inexpressible joy and gratitude upon my bosom. My mother, too; what pen could sufficiently depict her emotions upon that occasion.—She joined my father in the embraces he bestowed upon me, and then we all three knelt, and with hearts of sincerity, poured forth our gratitude to that Omnipotent being who had thrown the Almighty shield of His protection around me in hours of such eminent peril, and restored me innocent to the home wherein I had passed so many days of virtue and happiness, and which the wily seducer had endeavored so artfully to make me disgrace for ever!

'But I will seek out the villain,' cried my father, in vehement tones, after the first ebullitions of our joy and gratitude were over;—'yes I will go to him and upbraid him for his base and brutal conduct, and demand of him all the satisfaction he can afford!—The feelings of affectionate parents are not to be racked and insulted with impunity!—No, by Heaven, he shall find, that in spite of his rank, he shall not escape the just indignation of those humble individuals whom he would have disgraced and rendered eternally wretched. To-morrow I will repair to the titled rake, and demand—'

'Oh; my dearest parent,' I interrupted, 'pray do not think of such a thing; rather leave him to his own conscience, which, depend upon it, will sooner or later, be a severe monitor to him, and amply punish him for his guilt. The journey is too long, at your time of life, and besides, the result of such an act, without affording any satisfaction, might be such as I dread even to think upon.'

'Clara!' observed my father, 'think you I can tamely brook the injuries I have received from the Earl Mansville? Oh, my child, did you but know, could you but form the least conjecture of the intense agony your disappearance, and the fears, the suspicions, that naturally resulted from it, caused both me and your poor mother, you could not thus advise.'

'Alas! my dear father,' I returned, 'you do me an injury to suppose that I have not keenly, severely, felt the misery yourself and my dear mother must have undergone; in the midst of the luxury and magnificence that were displayed to ensnare me, it would rise in such vivid colors to my imagination, that many a time it surprises me how I can have retained my senses. Then would suspicion of the truth of Mansville rush tumultuously upon my brain, and only that I had dreaded to meet your reproaches, long ere this I should have made my escape from him, and return to your fostering arms. Not able to form any conjectures of your suffering?—Oh, my father, the imagination constantly haunted me;—sleeping or waking, it was ever present to my mental vision; but the deceptive art of Mansville, of which he is so consummate a master, never failed to use all the powers of his eloquence to soothe me, and by specious promises, day and day to quiet my apprehension—I will own my weakness;—such was the powerful ascendancy he had obtained over my heart, that I was too ready to listen to him; too willing to believe that he spoke the truth—Oh, my beloved parents, do me not the injustice to suppose that I could for a moment learn to become insensible of the imprudence I had committed, or of the consequent anguish that I knew it would involve you in.'

'And do you not love Mansville now, my child?' demanded my father, looking earnestly in my face.

'Love him,' I repeated, and a blush of indignation mantled my cheek as he spoke;—'Oh, how degraded, how fallen I should be, could I now feel anything but the utmost disgust and abhorrence for one who has acted with such duplicity to me, and who would have destroyed the happiness of my parents for ever! No, my dear father, the youthful passions that are more powerfully excited in favor of any particular object, are more likely to become changed to those of hatred and scorn, when it is discovered that the being who has created them, has acted the part of a heartless traitor,—the vile deceiver,—It is thus with me, Mansville is torn from me forever; the place which his image occupied once, is now replaced by the deepest scorn and detestation.'

'Darling child!' cried my father, clasping me again in his arms. 'There is sincerity in every word you utter. Oh, how could I ever suspect that you'd yield to the temptations of the guilty, and abandon the paths of virtue, in which you were brought up? This—this indeed is a joyful day; such a one as I never expected to experience again.—Come, come, child, into the house; let the blissful news be conveyed to all our neighbors, that this day restores a daughter, imprudent once, but guiltless, to her doting parents' arms.'

'And let the past be forgotten in the happiness of the present,' said my mother, tears of ecstasy starting to her eyes:—'oh, Clara, you have returned at a time when joy predominates in the bosoms of those dear friends, with whom we have been so long associated. Little did Ellen expect such a happy occurrence on the day of her nuptials.'

Encircling my waist with their arms, my parents led me affectionately to the house, and in a short time I was seated at the breakfast table, and about to eat of the repast beneath the roof in which I had been reared, and from which I had been so near being discarded for ever.—How shall I describe my feelings on that occasion, or those, it was evident, were passing in the minds of my parents.—I could scarcely believe that I had undergone what I had;—that I had ever even for a moment quitted my parental roof. Everything seemed as it was on the eventful morning when I had been borne away, and the whole seemed like some vision to warn me from the imprudent step I had actually been guilty of. The change effected in my father and mother in so short a time was most astonishing. The heavy care, the anguish of my father seemed dissipated, and was succeeded by joy and gratitude; looks of love and intense feeling which he constantly beamed upon me; while my mother could scarcely control her happiness within bounds of reason.

It might be imagined that my heart was too full—but it was not so—on the contrary, I partook of the repast with a relish I never before enjoyed since I had quitted my paternal home. I was again at home! in the home of my childhood restored to the love of my parents; and never was the contrast of the comforts of a virtuous home, with the empty luxuries of wealth and magnificence, presented more powerful to my mind.

Never shall I forget the felicity I enjoyed on that day. In the course of an hour or two my brother returned to the farm. He embraced me affectionately, but his indignation against Mansville was equal to that of my father.

It appeared that both my father and brother, had been indefatigable in endeavoring to trace the earl, but without success.

The day passed away, and at night, for the first time in some months, I retired to my chamber with the blessings of my parents. What ecstatic feelings thrilled through my veins, when I entered the little room where for so many years I had slept, and gazed upon every well known object, which had undergone no perceptible change since I had before reposed in it. It seemed indeed, to have been unoccupied since the time I had been from home; and every article I looked upon, appeared not to have been disturbed. There was the same little clean bed, with its furniture arranged with such admirable care and precision—the humble toilet—and everything the same as when I had last used it. There was the prayer book, the one which had been presented to me by my father many years before, and in which was inscribed his name, with the leaf turned down at the particular prayer I remember to have used the night before my elopement. With a heart overflowing with gratitude, I knelt down, and fervently breathed that prayer, and to it added one of thanks to Heaven, for the manner in which I had been saved from the sorrow and disgrace with which I had been threatened, and invoked its blessings on the heads of my parents and my brother. Then, with a lighter heart than I had experienced for many a day, I retired to my couch, and soon fell off into a calm slumber. No painful vision haunted my imagination that night; my dreams were those of bliss. Of the joys of home, and the affection of adoring parents; and in the morning I awoke to a renewal of that happiness and content, which had ever been mine before I became acquainted with the Earl of Mansville.

But what were my sentiments now as regarded Mansville? Need I try to portray them? I am certain that I need not! They were fully embodied in the observations I had made use of to my father. The mask which the deceiver had thrown off, having shown me his character in its real light, I thought of him only with disgust and abhorrence, and had he even then offered to make all the reparation in his power, by bestowing upon me his hand, I felt confident that I should have rejected it with scorn. Great as had been my trial, and painful as had been the circumstances by which it had been attended, I felt I had no cause to regret it now, but, on the contrary, to feel, in a manner thankful that it did occur, as it had taught me a lesson I shall never forget, and had afforded me that experience in the deceptive practices resorted to by the wealthy and unprincipled of mankind, which would prevent me for the future from approaching the precipice of destruction, down which I was so near being plunged.

I arose the following morning at the early hour to which I had been accustomed, and found my father, mother, and brother, already assembled in the little parlor, and the morning's repast spread upon the table. I could perceive, as soon as I entered, that they had been discussing something particular, and it was not long ere I was made acquainted with it. I found that my father and my brother had come to the determination of going to the Earl Mansville, in spite of my entreaties, and the observations I had the previous day made use of, to induce them to abandon their design, and such was their eagerness to see Mansville, and demand an explanation of him, that they had resolved not to delay any longer than the following day.

'I fully appreciate your motives, my dear child,' said my father, 'but, after mature deliberation, I cannot consent to comply with your wishes. Were we to suffer the matter to rest where it is it would be yielding a cowardly submission to guilt, which my heart revolts from; and, moreover, would give the foul tongue of slander an opportunity of propagating surmises derogatory to your reputation. No, nothing will satisfy me, but a plain acknowledgment of his guilt, and your innocence from his own lips, and a sufficient apology to satisfy the world at large. Were I to seek reparation in a court of law, his wealth and high rank would be a sure protection for him.'

'It would,' coincided my brother, 'and I see no other means of obtaining any satisfaction than the course we are about to pursue.'

In this opinion, my mother coincided, and, much as I dreaded the consequences that might attend it, I was at a loss for arguments to combat their resolutions. This day passed away in the same manner as the previous one, and the following morning, after a most affectionate farewell, my father and brother took their departure by the coach, for the mansion of the Earl Mansville.

After my father and brother had left, my mind underwent several gloomy presages, and though I perfectly agreed with the propriety of the arguments my father had made use of, I could not but sincerely regret that they had not abandoned their design.

My mother endeavored to sooth me by all the arguments in her power; and said that, doubtless Mansville, for his own credit's sake, would be ready to make all the reparation that was in his power.

'Alas!' thought I, 'what recompense can he make me for the injury he has inflicted on my peace of mind? Nothing can make amends for the pain of discovering that the only object upon which we have placed all our young heart's warmest affections is base, treacherous, and unworthy of that passion; and I now as thoroughly despised Mansville as I had before loved him, for that he had thrown a blight upon my mind from which I could never thoroughly recover.'

We expected the return of my father and brother in about three or four days from the time they had left home, as they would have nothing to detain them after they had obtained the interview they sought with the Earl Mansville, as they were fully aware that if they protracted their presence, it would excite our utmost alarm. The fourth and fifth day, however, elapsed, and still they remained absent. Our apprehensions began to be excited in the utmost degree, and all the fearful forebodings that had before haunted my mind, returned with redoubled force.

In spite of all her efforts to appear to the contrary, the fears of my mother, were, if possible, more excited than my own, and conjecture was exhausted in vain, to endeavor to account for the procrastination of their return.

Another day elapsed in this manner, and yet we heard nothing of them, and then, indeed, our terrors were aroused to an almost insupportable pitch, and we no longer sought to disguise from each other the real state of our feelings upon the agonizing subject. I expressed to my mother all those forebodings

I had before indulged in, and she could not but admit the too great probability of them. Now did she join with me in deeply regretting that my father and brother had not yielded to my advice, or that she should have made one to urge the propriety of the course they had taken. What step to pursue we were at a loss to conceive.

'I cannot wait in this horrible state of suspense any longer,' my mother ejaculated, when the seventh day dawned, and we heard no tidings of them; 'I'll instantly take G——m, and learn at once the cause of this mysterious delay, and whether or not anything has happened to them. This dreadful state of doubt and suspicion is worse than the most terrible certainty.'

She had scarcely given utterance to these words when a knock was heard at the outer door, and a letter was presented to my mother, which she knew immediately to be in the hand-writing of her husband. Trembling violently with apprehension, she broke the seal, but had not read more than two lines when, with a piercing scream, she fell senseless to the floor. I flew to her, raised her in my arms, and then, taking up the fatal letter, began to read the contents. The commencement of it was enough to smite my heart with horror; and it is marvellous how, under such trying circumstances, I retained possession for an instant of my faculties. My unfortunate father and brother were in gaol, accused of murder—of the murder of my deceiver, the Earl Mansville!

My frantic cries soon brought the servants of my father to the room, who immediately conveyed my mother to her chamber, while I was reduced to such a state by the shock which my feelings had sustained, that it was found necessary to call in medical advice to me, as well as the former. I remained in a state of almost utter unconsciousness for several days, during which period I continually raved of the murdered Mansville, and the awful charge which I would fain have believed my unhappy parent and brother were innocent of; but which, under peculiar circumstances, seemed, alas! but too probable.

My mother had been restored to comparative composure much earlier than might have been anticipated from the violence of the shock her feelings had received; and when I regained my senses, I found that she had started, the day following the one on which she had received the fatal letter, for G——m, to seek an interview with her wretched husband and son, and to obtain an explanation of the horrible circumstances. The person who attended me had the utmost difficulty in persuading me not to follow her; and it was only by the determined tone in which the medical man spoke, stating that the consequences of such a journey, in my then state of mind, might be productive of the most fatal results, that I was prevented from putting my wishes into effect.

Too soon, alas! the horrible particulars reached my ears, which I will proceed to relate as they were afterwards detailed by my father.

It appeared that after my father and brother had left home, they immediately repaired to the coach-office, where they had booked their places the evening before, and took their departure for G——m, whither they arrived the evening without anything occurring worthy of being particularly noticed. As it was rather late, they resolved not to visit the earl till the morning, and accordingly took up their lodgings at an inn in the place. Not feeling disposed to go to rest for the present, they thought they would take a bit of a walk in the neighboring fields previous to supper, and accordingly they walked forth, and instinctively directed their footsteps towards the mansion of Mansville. They had proceeded across several fields, and had entered upon a dark and gloomy lane, which, they had been informed, led to his house, when suddenly they beheld, by the dim light of the moon, the shadows of two men before them, one of whom was a short way in advance of the other. They did not take particular notice of this at first, as there was nothing at all extraordinary in the circumstance; yet, when they perceived that one of them still kept in the rear of the other, and that he was evidently fearful of being seen, they determined to watch his actions more narrowly. They, therefore, kept as close to the hedge as possible, so that they might not be observed, and yet cautiously kept advancing towards the two men, and taking particular notice of their actions. The one in advance made a motion as though reflection was almost too dreadful for him would turn round, when the other immediately stepped aside so that he could not be seen; and it then became very clear that he was after no good purpose, or why appear so anxious for concealment? My poor father and brother, therefore, redoubled their speed, entertaining strong suspicions that the fellow was a highwayman, and that they might be the means of preventing, probably, robbery and murder.

They had not proceeded far when a turning in the lane hid them from observation, and directly afterwards the report of a pistol vibrated on their ears.

Fearful, from all they had observed, that murder had been committed, they now ran with all their speed in the direction which the two persons had taken; and having arrived at a dark and lonely spot, to which they were attracted by groans of agony, they beheld, by the faint light of the moon, whose rays now penetrated through the thick foliage above their heads, the form of a man elegantly attired, stretched upon the earth and weltering in his blood, while by his side lay the pistol with which the fatal and cruel deed had been committed, and which the assassin had left behind him.

My father raised the unfortunate man in his arms, and the moonlight streaming full upon his countenance, my brother suddenly exclaimed, in a voice of mingled astonishment and exultation—

'Ah! by Heaven, retribution has overtaken the guilty! It is the villain, the betrayer, Mansville!'

The fatal words had scarcely escaped my brother's lips when a party of men, who had also been attracted by the report of the pistol, rushed to the spot; and having overheard what he said, and seeing the wounded nobleman stretched upon the earth, and my father and brother standing over him—the latter with the weapon of death in his hand, believed them to be the perpetrators of the bloody deed; and accusing them accordingly, and seizing them, in spite of their remonstrances and solemn protestations of their innocence, they bore them away to the nearest prison, while the wounded Mansville was conveyed to his mansion.

My God! how my very soul trembles when I recall to my memory this dreadful event, and my blood freezes in my veins with the most indescribable sensation of horror. Alas! who shall say that my sufferings have not indeed been severe!—It is really wonderful how I have found strength of mind to endure them all; how one so young, and, until lately, a complete stranger to misery, should be able to bear up under such an almost unprecedented accumulation of horrors. But my troubles were far from being yet complete.

The unfortunate Mansville was mortally wounded, and breathed his last before morning, never having rallied from the first, and having been unable to speak after he was first discovered. And here must I pause to reflect upon the terrible fate of the Earl Mansville; as I do so, the remembrance of his faults, and his conduct towards me, are forgotten in the one strong and irresistible feeling of pity which inhabits my breast. His fate was marked by the most signal retribution of Heaven. The week following that of his assassination, he was to be united to a young, beautiful, and wealthy heiress, to whom he had been paying his devoirs, at the same time he was pleading the most powerful passion for me, and most solemnly protesting, from time to time, that he would make me his bride. Ill-fated, but guilty Mansville! Heaven pardon you for the deception of which you were guilty, as I now do.

My father and Edwin underwent several examinations before the justices, and evidences of their guilt appeared so numerous, that few, if any, attempted to defend them.

It was well known in what manner they were related to me, and the circumstances under which I had been placed with the murdered Mansville, and, therefore, what had brought my father and brother to G—m, but to seek revenge? Besides, it was proved by the landlord of the inn where they had taken lodgings, that they had left his house at a late hour in the evening together, and, that, previous to doing so, he had a conversation with them, in course of which they had asked several strange questions respecting the deceased Earl Mansville, which were quite sufficient to strengthen the suspicions that were already excited against them; and more particularly they had made several inquiries as to the nearest way to the murdered nobleman's mansion, and had been directed the exact way in which they had been discovered. An inquest was held upon the deceased, the jury upon which unhesitatingly returned a verdict of wilful murder against my father and brother; and ultimately they were committed to the assizes for trial.

This was precisely the state of the affair, when we received the letter which was from my father; need it, therefore, excite any astonishment that our feelings were almost maddening?—The circumstantial evidence against them was very strong, and alas! how many innocent persons had suffered under far less suspicious circumstances?—The idea was enough to freeze the blood with horror, and here again did I find cause most bitterly to reproach myself for one act of indiscretion which had thus been productive of this awful misery, and might be the occasion of bringing my father and brother to an awful and ignominious fate, for a crime of which they were entirely innocent.

The day after this, I received a letter from my mother, in which she described, in language I should fail to do adequate justice to, were I to try, the interview she had had with her husband and son at the gaol in which they were confined, but sought to inspire me with hope that something would take place to establish their innocence, and bring the real perpetrators of the horrid crime to justice. I tried to think so too. Never, I reflected will the Almighty suffer two innocent beings to suffer for the sanguinary crime of the real assassin! They will be saved, and the monster who has committed this atrocious crime brought to that punishment which his guilt merits.

These were but for a short time my reflections, then would the heavy weight of circumstantial evidence, which would be adduced against them on their trial, recur to my memory, and despair would again begin to settle upon my heart.

My mother mentioned in her letter that the assizes were expected to commence in about a fortnight, and that, until the result of this awful affair was known, she intended to reside near the gaol, so that she might be enabled to visit the unfortunate prisoners every day. She added, that, if I thought myself capable of the task, and able to support an interview, I might also repair to the spot, leaving the farm for the time we were absent to the care of Ellen and her husband. To remain where I was, alone, with no one but Ellen to offer me the least consolation or advice, I felt would be worse than death; and, therefore, having made a powerful effort to conquer my emotions, I arranged the business with Ellen and her husband, and with the prayers of my friends for the happy termination of the trial, I set forward upon my melancholy journey.

What tongue could give utterance to the intense agony of my feelings, when the coach arrived at G——m, the place which I had so lately quitted to seek the forgiveness of my parents. Alas! under what different, what horrible circumstances did I now return to it. He who had first tempted me to act wrong had met with an untimely fate, and my father and brother the inmates of a prison, accused of his assassination.

The day after my arrival at G——m, I had an interview with my unfortunate relatives, but I must pass over that deeply agonizing scene; I cannot recall it to my memory without harrowing up my feelings. They both, however, attempted to appear more composed than I might have expected them to have been, and endeavoured to inspire me and my mother with the most sanguine hopes as to the result of the trial. We, however, could see but very little to excite any such ideas, and although, for the sake of calming their feelings, we pretended to place some reliance in what they said, we were very far from actually entertaining any such feelings.

I will pass over the time which intervened previous to the trial, and come at length to the morning on which the fate of all my family, I might say, depended. The hall of justice was densely crowded, and the trial excited the most uncommon interest. Myself and my mother were accommodated with seats near the dock in which the accused were, and whenever, by chance, I happened to look up, I caught the eyes of the spectators fixed alternately upon me and my mother; but in the brief glance which I suffered myself to take, I beheld that the expression with which they contemplated us was more of pity than any other feeling.

I know not how it was, but I felt a degree of firmness on that awful occasion which I never thought it would be in my power to assume, and my mother was perfectly calm and resigned. As for the prisoners, their whole demeanour showed the dignified firmness of perfect innocence, and a firm reliance on the goodness of Providence for the issue.

The jury having been called over and sworn, the trial commenced, and the charge having been made, my father and brother both answered in a firm voice to the usual interrogatory put to them, as to whether they were guilty or not guilty—

'Not guilty!'

The trial then proceeded, which is quite unnecessary for me too recapitulate.

The jury retired to consider their verdict—and oh, God! what a moment of horrible suspense was that! All eyes were turned alternately upon me and my mother, and then the prisoners in the dock. But the latter were as firm as if they had only been spectators themselves, and frequently turned upon me and my poor mother glances that were meant to encourage us.

The jury were absent about twenty minutes, which seemed as many hours to those who were so deeply and painfully interested in this important trial, and at length they returned into the court.

The foreman of the same, in a deep voice said—

'GUILTY!'

An appalling shriek followed the pronunciation of the verdict; it proceeded from my mother, who sank insensible in my arms. It seemed at that time as if I were endowed with superhuman power; my faculties were all restored to me, and I was enabled to support with firmness that was most extraordinary. The verdict had fallen upon my ear, in a manner of speaking, with complete indifference, and it appeared as if a voice at that moment whispered to me hope instead of despair. But I feared to look at my father and his unhappy son. I was apprehensive that their bare glance of horror and despair would be sufficient to deprive me of my senses. The judge then proceeded to pass sentence of death, but ere he had uttered half-a-dozen words a gentleman suddenly arose from his seat, and with his whole frame convulsed with emotion, exclaimed—

'Hold my lord!—proceed not to sentence men who are entirely innocent of the charge.'

After the lapse of a minute or two for the court to recover themselves from the confusion into which this event had thrown them, the judge demanded of the gentleman the meaning of his interruption.

'In a few words, it is this,' said the gentleman, 'you behold before you an unhappy wretch, who ought to have been placed in the dock now occupied by those much injured, and wrongly accused men. Nay, you may well be surprised, and it will doubtless be increased, when I tell you that in me you behold the actual murderer of the Earl Mansville, and I, therefore demand that justice be done upon me!'

Nothing could now equal the extraordinary sensation which prevailed, and it was at first, no doubt, imagined by many that the gentleman's feelings who had thus denounced himself had been worked upon and excited by the circumstances of the trial, and that insanity had suddenly seized upon his brain; but they were soon convinced of the contrary, for the self-accused having paused awhile to suffer the excitement to subside, continued—

'It was this hand which perpetrated the hellish deed upon the unfortunate Mansville, the pistol which was found by the side of the deceased will be seen to have my initials engraven upon it.'

The pistol was here handed up to the judge, when the initials were found.

'The awful tale is soon told,' continued he.

'The late Earl Mansville and myself had been companions at college. Soon after our return from the university, I formed an attachment to a young lady, and was permitted to pay my addresses to her. This courtship went on for a period of two years, when it was suddenly broken off. In vain I sought an explanation. Nothing more relative to this affair transpired until about a month ago, when, judge my resentment and surprise, to learn that the late Earl Mansville, was the admitted lover of the lady, and that their nuptials were actually fixed to take place on a certain day. On ascertaining the truth of this, I demanded an explanation of such extraordinary conduct; but all that I obtained in return, was the most provoking raillery! I quitted the unfortunate nobleman vowing the most dreadful vengeance. On the evening that I committed the hellish crime, I quitted my own house, with the pistols now produced in my possession, fully bent to way-lay and murder my rival. Once he turned to look round, and then I jumped into a dry ditch, and concealed myself. He resumed his journey, and acting under the influence of a sudden impulse, I presented the fatal weapon at him, and fired, just as he prepared to walk on. What followed has already appeared in the evidence brought against those two men, most wrongfully accused. As the day of trial approached, so did my agony increase. Could I be guilty of a three-fold murder? I could not; so, this day, I resolved to be present, and confess. I admit, that my resolution failed me so much, that I was unable to put this into effect, until after the trial had proceeded to the present length; but I have now acquitted my conscience of that additional and heavy sin, and I feel content to abide by the consequences. I repeat that the men in the dock are entirely innocent, and that I only am the murderer of the late Earl Mansville. I demand that justice be done, and thus give myself up to this tribunal to be tried and punished by the laws of my offended country.'

A murmur of surprise, horror, and satisfaction ran through the court at this remarkable confession, and for a few moments, the business was entirely suspended. My mother had recovered, and overheard all that had passed. But suddenly, the court was aroused by all the judges rising, and declaring it as their unanimous opinion, that the two individuals who had been tried had been charged and convicted by the jury of the murder of the Earl Mansville, were now shewn to be clearly innocent, that the court, therefore, annul the verdict, and ordering them to be discharged out of custody, command

Richard Archibald Holland, to be placed at the bar and indicted, upon his own confession, for the wilful murder of the said Horatio, Earl Mansville.

My father and brother were immediately released from the dock, while, the real assassin was placed at the bar.

But misfortune and I had still got to be longer acquainted; and too soon her heavy afflictions came upon me with overwhelming force. The shock which my mother's feelings had undergone by the recent events had made fearful inroads on her constitution, and it soon became too alarmingly apparent, that she was sinking under a rapid decline. All the medical resources were of no avail, and she at length yielded to the fearful malady.

My father and all of us, were inconsolable for her loss.

Only three months after my poor mother's death, my brother was seized with a violent typhus fever, which my father quickly caught of him. A few short months only, consigned those two dear relatives to the grave also. Would that it had pleased the Almighty to take me also, then I should not have had to undergo the miseries, the degradations I have too much reason to fear it is yet my lot to suffer. Illness and incessant trouble had involved my father's affairs in difficulties, from which I found it impossible to extricate them. Let me draw my melancholy recital to a conclusion. Hard necessity drove me at last to seek the protection of relatives, whose jibes and cruelties drove me to the life I now lead, and the letter you brought me was from the clergyman of our parish, who having learnt of my whereabouts, addressed me an exhortation to repentance; recalling all the incidents of the bitter past. Here Clara burst into a fresh flood of tears, and owned her intention to quit her present shameful mode of life.

'And now, Mr. Monteagle,' continued Clara, 'to prove to you that I am really penitent; I will divulge to you a contemplated crime, which was planned in this very house, and this night it is to be carried into effect. Belcher Kay and Blodget one night killed a rich old drover, and buried him in an old adobe hut. They have since learned that Inez, the daughter of old de Castro, had taken shelter in the building from a storm and witnessed all their proceedings. The Vigilance Committee are already apprised of the facts, but in Miss de Castro's terror at the fearful scene, she forgot the names by which they addressed each other; but she is convinced that she will know their persons if ever she meets them. You know these villains will never consent to live in hourly fear of arrest and punishment. They have, therefore, determined to attack the mansion of de Castro, at the Mission, rob it, and I fear kill his daughter to prevent her appearing as a witness against them.'

# CHAPTER XII

## INEZ CARRIED OFF.

In a public room of a tavern in Pacific street, we shall find Belcher Kay. It is night, and through the thick haze of cigar smoke which filled the room the candles glimmer like distant lights seen through a fog. The close atmosphere of the dirty room is laden with the odor of the said tobacco smoke, and with the fumes of rum and whiskey, and through the hum of noisy conversation and over the occasional bursts of laughter may be distinguished the 'Hagel und donner' of the Dutchman, the 'sacre' of the Frenchman, and the imprecations which the Englishman invokes upon his visual organs and the crimson tide that circulates through his veins.

At one table sat half a dozen sailors, bronzed by the tropical sun of Java, and smoking long pipes with enormous bowls. At another table sat a group of English, French, American and Portuguese, similarly engaged, while two other tables were surrounded by Lascars and Malays, who being worshippers of the one race of Brahma, the other of Boodha, choose to sit and drink apart. Mingled with the men at each table were a number of Kanaka and Chilean women, dark-eyed, seductive creatures; all well formed, lithe, and graceful, and of all ages varying from twelve to eighteen years, for beneath the scorching sun of the tropics woman advances towards maturity as quickly as the rich fruits are ripened and the gorgeous flowers expanded into beauty. These lost and degraded creatures sat by the side or on the knees of their lovers of the hour, their long, shining black hair falling in plaits or ringlets upon their dusky shoulders, and their bosoms very much exposed, and many of them smoked cigars with their male companions.

Kay sat apart from the revellers, smoking a cigar, with his arms folded across his breast, a moody and sombre expression upon his countenance, and his eyes bent upon the dirty floor. He was thinking of the past—thinking, amid the riotous din of jests and oaths, laughter and song, of all that he had been, and of what he might have been, of time misspent, and golden opportunities lost, of talents misapplied and energies misdirected. It was a mournful retrospect for the man not wholly lost, his heart was not entirely corroded, nor all indurated by vice and profligacy, the powers of his mind had not become sapped by the vicious excesses in which he had indulged; he was capable of forming a sound judgement of human actions, both his own and those of others; and to look back excited for these reasons, feelings, sombre and mournful. The past of his life was a dreary waste to look back upon; he was fully conscious of the fact, he was able to discriminate between the right and the wrong, and to perceive his errors, and he felt at that moment all the dreariness, the moral void, of the vista upon which he turned his mental vision. True, the desert was not entirely without its oases; there were green spots breaking the gloomy monotony of its arid and cheerless aspect, but these only deepened by the contrast the impression made by the general barrenness.

He was roused from his reverie by the words of a song sung, or rather shouted by one his countrymen—an Englishman—a sailor belonging to a vessel then lying in the harbor. There was nothing to interest him in the words themselves, but they seemed familiar to him, like a voice heard in our youth and half forgotten, which we hear again after a long interval of time, and they struck upon his mind by the force of association. In his boyhood he had heard that song, which had been a favorite chant with a schoolfellow, and the words now called up a thousand recollections of the time when he had first heard them, just as the remembered sound of the church-bells of our native place will recall such memories when we hear them after long absence from the scenes of our early existence. To the mind of the robber, predisposed to reflection, the words of the song recalled the school-room and the play-ground, with many a reminiscence of merry companions and boyish games; and from these his heart wandered to the home of his childhood, to the little garden into which he had transplanted primroses and cowslips from the woods to the rippling brook upon which he had launched his tiny ships, to the darkly shaded seat under the old elm tree on which he had rested when weary, to the innocent and smiling faces of his fair-haired sisters.

It was not for the first time that Belcher Kay thought of these things—it was not the first time that they had drawn a sigh from his breast; but, now at that distance of space from the scenes which he visited in thought, the tide of memory rolled over his brain with redoubled volume and force. A melancholy pleasure might have been experienced in travelling over in thought the scenes of his youth, but for the reflection that between the past and the present rose darkly and frowningly one of those barriers of crime and folly, which such men build up with far more perseverance than they would exert to acquire a fame that would endure as long as truth and virtue command respect and admiration. Such a barrier had Belcher Kay raised with a diligence and energy which he had never displayed in aught worthy of praise, and from it he now looked back upon the Eden which he had abandoned, with such feelings as may be imagined.

He was still sitting in the position which has been described when Blodget entered the room, and, coming up to him, clapped his hand upon his shoulder. Kay started, but looking up, he was reassured by the recognition of his fellow criminal, and extended his hand, which Blodget grasped with friendly fervor.

'Come!' exclaimed Blodget. 'I have been seeking you everywhere. Let us get away from this.'

'I am ready,' responded Kay, rising.—'What's in the wind now, mate?'

Blodget made no reply, but led the way into the street, followed by Kay.

In a few minutes they had left the city behind them, and could hear the hoarse roar of the sea as its waves, after chasing one another over the wild expanse of the Pacific ocean, broke upon the shell strewn beach, and the sighing of the night wind among the bushes. The moon was sinking, and the shadows prevailed over the lights, but it was principally the land which lay in shade, while the ocean spread out like an illimitable sheet of silver.

After crossing the hills which surmount the city the two men gave a loud shrill whistle which in a few moments brought three more desperadoes to assist them in their scheme. This was no other than an attack upon the mansion of Senor de Castro with the intention of making themselves masters of the money and plate to be found on the premises, and for another purpose which will appear in the course of the narrative.

When the five robbers arrived in the vicinity of the house Blodget proceeded towards it, for the purpose of carrying their plot into execution, while the rest of the party lay closely concealed ready to hasten to the assistance of their associate the moment such service should be required.

'Yes, there is the window; I wonder, now, if she will look out to night?' said Blodget to himself as he cautiously drew near the house.

Blodget took a good look at the window and then slowly glided away under the shadow of a wall.

With great tact, Blodget as he did so glided along, kept the little window with the balcony in sight.

Now, the little window of the room in which Inez resided, was not very far from the ground.

That is to say, at all events, the lower portion of its balcony certainly was not above twelve feet from the green sward actually below it.

The idea struck Blodget, then, that through that window he must get, and through it again he must make his way out with his captive.

How he meant to overcome the very many difficulties that still stood in his way, it is impossible to conceive; but he had not come totally unprepared with the means of action.

Coiled up in the pockets of the clothes which he had worn all the latter part of the day, he had had a couple of ropes of silk, with a hook at the end of each of them.

He expected, and not without reason, too, that they would be to him of the very greatest possible assistance.

It took him some little consideration before he would venture to cross the bit of lawn that separated him yet from the house; and, strange to say, while he was so considering, another circumstance began to operate in his favor.

A soft, but rather thick and penetrating rain began to fall.

'Aha' he said, 'this is capital. This will clear the ground of all loiterers. This is providential.'

Letting the rain continue for some five minutes or so until he considered it had had all its effect, Blodget crossed the lawn, and stood beneath the balcony of the window.

Blodget was very acute in his sense of hearing, and he now bent that faculty to the very utmost to listen if any one were moving in the rooms above.

All was as still as the very grave.

'She has gone to bed,' thought Blodget. 'Well, I don't care. I must take her away, and take her I will.'

A very dim light was close to the window.

'I wonder,' thought Blodget, 'if she will scream before I can get a gag put into her mouth? If she does, I may have dangers to encounter; but I never yet abandoned an enterprise on that account, nor will I now.'

Truly dangerous was a climate in which such a man as Blodget lived.

He now looked carefully to the right and to the left of the place of which he was, so as to assure himself that no sentinel was close at hand, and then he boldly flung up the cords to which the hooks were attached, to the balcony.

It took him three or four efforts before he succeeded in getting the hooks to hold fast, and then he found that the cords easily suspended him.

This was rather a ticklish part of the business to climb up to the balcony now with the possibility, if not the probability, that some one might see him; but yet he meant either to do it or abandon the whole affair at once, so he set about it with a feeling that might be said to approach to recklessness.

He reached the top of the parapet of the balcony, and rather rolled over it than stepped over, so that he exposed himself to observation to as small an extent as, under the circumstances, it was at all possible so to do.

There he lay crouched up in the balcony, pretty well shaded by its stone work and parapet from any further observation from without.

He breathed in rather an agitated manner for a few moments, for he had undergone, to tell the truth, very great personal exertion.

Soon, however, he recovered sufficiently to assist him in going on in his enterprise; and accordingly, sidling along very carefully till he got quite close to the window, he cautiously tried if it were fast.

No. It yielded to a touch.

'More good fortune,' thought he.

Slowly, for it took a good five minutes to do, thinking that any noise now occasioned by precipitation would be fatal to him and his project, he got the window open about a couple of feet.

He put his hand into the room, and felt that there was a table close to the window.

By carefully moving his hand and arm horizontally from left to right and from right to left, he found there was nothing on the table but a glass of water, in which were some flowers.

In order to get it out of the way, he lifted the glass into the balcony, and placed it carefully in one corner out of the way.

Then it was that the audacious Blodget, like an oily snake, slid into the room through the partially open window, and was fairly within the apartment.

His next step was to remove the table from before the window, and to open the window itself very much wider—in fact, as wide as it would possibly go.

Then it was that he saw where the faint light had come from that was in the room.

A little oil night-light was on a bracket fixed to the wall of the room.

That light, although very small in itself, was yet sufficient to dissipate the darkness that was in the place, and by it Blodget with great satisfaction looked around him, and was quite convinced that he was in the suite of rooms in the occupation of Inez.

There was one circumstance that to him was quite convincing on that head, for on the chimney-piece was a small but finely painted miniature of Monteagle.

'Yes,' whispered Blodget, as he drew a long breath, 'I am on the right scent now.'

Immediately opposite to the window there was a door that seemed to lead to the next apartment. It was a very ticklish thing indeed to open that door.

Before he could at all make up his mind to do so, he tried to peep through the key-hole of it, but, unfortunately, there was on the other side a piece of pendant brass that blocked it up, so he saw nothing.

Delay, though, to him now was something worse than danger—it might be fatal; so with a feeling almost of desperation, he turned the handle of the door and opened it.

It led into a room that was, like the last one, dimly lighted by a night-lamp in a niche in the wall.

'She is fond of light,' thought Blodget.

There was a door in the side wall of this room, and that door was a little way open.

Through it Blodget could see the bed-curtain.

The room in which she was, constituted the dressing-room to the bed-room further on.

Blodget, with eyes like a hyena, cast a glance round the room. A silk dress was upon a couch, and on the dressing-table were various articles of female apparel and jewelry.

He approached, on tip-toe, the door of the bedchamber, and listened most intently.

The sound of one breathing rather heavily in sleep, came upon his ears.

'She sleeps,' muttered Blodget, 'and my task is consequently all the easier of performance. Yes, she sleeps, and soundly too.'

He now took from his pocket a gag made of cork and string, and so constructed that if once fixed in any one's mouth it would be out of the question for them to utter an articulate sound.

This, with a silk handkerchief, which he intended to fix around the head and face of his prisoner, were the implements with which he hoped to capture Inez, and by the aid of which so to terrify her that he might get away in safety with her.

'Now for it,' he said.

He took another step towards the door of the bedchamber, and then he hesitated.

'A good thought,' he muttered. 'I will put out both the lights, and then no curious eye will see me emerge from the window with my prize.'

He crept back and blew out each of the little oil lamps that were in the separate rooms.

All was darkness then; but it was evident there was another lamp in the actual bedchamber itself.

It was convenient for Blodget that there should be, at all events for a brief space, a light there.

'Now courage and impudence assist me,' he muttered.

As he spoke he on tiptoe glided into the bedchamber in which he would have wagered his life that Inez now slept.

The difficulty, though, he thought was really and truly at an end, when he, as he fancied, found himself so far successful as to be actually in the sleeping chamber of the young lady.

No wonder that even he, accustomed as he was to all sorts of escapades and strange eventful proceedings, felt a little affected at his own temerity when he set foot within the sacred precincts of that chamber.

The idea of what Monteagle would think and say when he heard of this evidence of unexampled audacity came across the mind of the unscrupulous villain, and for a moment he hesitated.

It struck him that, after all, such an outrage was of so diabolical and daring a character, that it would be difficult to say what might be the result of it.

But it was not for long that such a man as Blodget ever hesitated about the completion of an act of atrocity, or boldness or baseness.

'Let him take it how he may,' thought Blodget, 'I'll carry out my designs; and if danger should come to Inez in the carrying it out, that is her own fault.'

He listened intently.

The regular breathing of some one in a deep sleep still came upon his ears.

Now the chief difficulty was to get away with his captive without noise, and there was but one way of doing that. It was so to terrify Inez, that for her life's sake and that of her father she would obey the directions he might give her.

But, then, upon the first impulse of finding some one in the room, he considered that she might utter some cry that to him, would be full of danger; and to guard against that was the first step he took.

There came through the window of the sleeping chamber a faint light, which just enabled him, after a few minutes, when his eyes had got accustomed to it, to look about him, and see the outlines of one object from another.

To be sure, these outlines were but dim ones, but still they served to enable him to avoid encountering any piece of furniture, and so making noise enough to awaken his victim from the sound sleep she was in.

To tie a silk handkerchief in such a manner around her mouth, and then another over her head, so that the possibility of uttering anything but a faint sound would be out of the question, was Blodget's idea.

Indeed, he had prepared himself with the means, as will be recollected, of completely enveloping the head of his prisoner, so that if any attempted alarm was tried, the sound of it would not penetrate far enough to be successful in reaching the inmates of the house.

It was a very delicate and ticklish job, though, so suddenly to envelope the head and face of a sleeping person in a silken bandage as to prevent them from uttering a single cry until the operation was complete.

But that was just what had to be done, and so he did not shrink from it.

He only waited a few moments longer, in order that his eyes might be accustomed to the very dim light that found its way into the chamber.

During those few moments, too, he turned his head aside to listen if the whole attention of his faculty of hearing could detect the sound of any one stirring in the mansion; but all was as still and silent as the tomb.

'Now for it,' said he to himself.

In a half-crouching posture he approached the bed.

If what he was about to do was to be done at all, it was only by the very excess of boldness in the attempt to do it.

When he reached the side of the bed, he rose to his full height, and slipping adroitly his left arm right under the head of the sleeper, he in one moment lifted it from the pillow, and with his right hand he placed the silken envelope over the head and face, and drew it close round the neck.

'Utter one sound of alarm,' he said in a low, clear voice close to the ear of the bewildered occupant of the bed, 'and it is your last upon earth. Be quiet and submissive, and no sort of harm is intended you. On the contrary, everything possible will be done to render your situation as agreeable as possible, and you'll be treated with delicacy and with every consideration.'

A gasping sort of a sob was the only reply.

'Hush!' said Blodget. 'Your fate is in your own hands. I am compelled for my own sake to remove you from the mansion; but you will be treated with all the respect and all the consideration becoming your sex and rank, unless you by your own conduct, force an opposite condition of things.'

Some muffled sounds, that might be considered to mean anything, came from beneath the covering of silk.

'Am I to comprehend,' said Blodget, 'that your own good sense enables you to see the necessity of submitting to circumstances that are beyond your control entirely?'

A something was said; or attempted to be said.

'Let me assure you,' added he, 'that I am well aware of the love your father has for you, and that he will spare no means to liberate you from me. It would be quite an insult to your understanding to attempt to deceive you for one moment with regard to the object of thus making you a prisoner. It is simply in order to get money from him who loves you beyond all the world beside. Do you hear me?'

'Yes.'

The tone in which the yes was spoken was very consolatory to Blodget, for it let him think that Inez saw the inutility of attempting any resistance to him.

'You are reasonable, I feel,' he said, 'and I can assure you upon my word, lightly as you may think of that word, that where I am trusted I know how to behave myself with honor. The readiness with which you succumb to circumstances that now surround you will have the greatest effect in inducing me to make this as agreeable to you as possible. Do you comprehend me?'

'Yes.'

'Will you, then,' he said, 'quietly come with me to a place of safety away from here?'

'I will.'

'You will?'

'Yes.'

'Then I have to compliment you upon your conduct in this affair, and I know that by saying that for your sake I will not contrive aught against the life of him who loves you, I shall be bestowing upon you the greatest recompense that's in my power.'

'Yes.'

'Then we are equal. Allow me to hope that you will arise and follow me. Here are various articles of clothing about the room. You have the use of your hands, and if I hand the things to you, one by one, will you then put them on?'

'Yes.'

'I am very sorry to place you in such a position as this—very sorry indeed.'

Blodget was so pleased at the compliance of Inez with all his plans, that he really felt a kindness for her, and he was determined, therefore, to behave to her with all the delicacy that the transaction could possibly enable him to practice.

He caught up various articles of female apparel, and with his back towards the bed.

'Be as quick as you can,' he said, 'for the fact is that I am in danger here, though you are in none.'

'Yes, yes,' said the voice.

'Upon my life, she must be terribly frightened to give way to me in this manner.'

One by one he kept handing articles of clothing, and they were put on, till at last he said—

'I should think you are ready to leave the house now, along with me, are you not?'

'I am so.'

'Then follow me, if you please; but let me again assure you before I go that I am only going to make a kind of hostage of you, and that as soon as I have you in safety I will send to your father and let him know; and upon his promise not to molest me for the future, I will release you.'

'Yes.'

'You are quite content with that arrangement, then, may I hope?' said Blodget.

'Oh, yes, quite.'

'Then come on at once, if you please.'

Inez felt that resistance would be useless, and would probably put in peril the life of her father, without availing to save her. She, therefore, quietly yielded to circumstances, knowing that her father would cheerfully pay any ransom to rescue her.

As soon as Inez was dressed, Blodget led her to the window, and giving a low whistle was quickly joined by his confederates. By their aid Inez was swiftly and noiselessly conveyed from the house, carried into the adjacent shrubbery, and placed upon a horse, stolen, like those on which the robbers were now mounted, from a neighboring corral.

The whole party immediately dashed off at full speed, and never once halted until they arrived at a solitary rancho, some eight or nine miles distant from the home of Inez.

Monteagle, meanwhile, had started at full gallop for the Mission, in order to frustrate this villainous plot, but just as he was turning the sharp angle at the turnpike road, his horse stumbled, and Monteagle was violently thrown over the animal's head. He remained insensible in the road, just where he had fallen, until daylight, when he was discovered and hospitably cared for by the inmates of a neighboring cottage.

# CHAPTER XIII

## A DESPERATE BURGLARY.

Leaving Inez in charge of some of his trustiest confreres, Blodget hastened to the city, to disarm suspicion as well as to attend to an important robbery which he had already planned.

A previous arrangement with some of the principal members of the gang had assured Blodget that he should find plenty of aid in carrying out his views on that particular evening.

It was two o'clock as Blodget reached the door of the house that was connected with the gang, and a drizzly rain was beginning to fall which he saw and felt with pleasure, for he knew that it would materially aid him in his plans, as it would tend to clear the streets of stragglers, as well as to muffle any sounds that might otherwise betray the presence of himself and his companions.

'All is well,' he said. 'This is my old good luck. Who knows but I may yet do a good stroke of business.'

Blodget was soon in the old house along with some half dozen of the most desperate and knowing thieves in San Francisco.

A dim light burned in the place, which was only just sufficient to let them see each other's faces.

The falling of the rain upon one of the windows was the only sound that the night brought forth.

'All's right,' said one of them. 'Here's Blodget.'

'Yes,' said another, 'we shall now no doubt have a job to do.'

'Yes, my lads,' said Blodget, assuming an air of reckless jocularity, which he often thought proper to put on—'yes, my lads, you will have a little job to do, and it is one that you will like too.'

'Bravo!—bravo!'

'You know me, and that it is not likely I should send you on a profitless expedition; but there are a few little arrangements to make before we start.'

'Name them.'

'I will. They relate, in the first place, to who is to have the command of these little expeditions?'

'Oh, you, of course.'

'Is that then thoroughly understood and agreed?'

'Yes, yes.'

'Very well, then. The next point is as regards the division of the spoil.'

'Yes, that should be well understood.'

'It must be well understood or I am off to find some others to help me in the matter. I have thought over my terms, and I do not, I assure you, intend to flinch from them.'

'What are they?'

'Listen, then. Let all the plunder be fairly divided into two parts, I will then take one part to myself and my friend, Kay, and you can divide the other among you in equal shares.'

The thieves looked rather blank at this proposition, and Blodget seeing that, added—

'Well, if you don't like that you have but to say so, and our bargain is at an end; but if I get all the information, and put up a robbery in the safe and quiet way that I can do it, I think myself entitled to the share I speak of, and I will have it too.'

'Be it so, then,' said the spokesman of the party, 'I agree, and I'm sure I can say the same for my friends here. We all agree to it.'

The others seconded the words of their spokesman, so that Blodget found he had made a pretty good bargain with the thieves, and he set to work arranging the robbery with all the tact and all the ingenuity he could bring to bear upon such an enterprise.

When such an accomplished hand as Blodget took so much trouble, the result was all but certain.

'Meet me, all of you,' he said, 'in half an hour's time by the corner of Jackson- and Commercial-streets, and I will take you to the place. There will be no difficulty at all about it if you take care to comprehend what I wish each of you to do, and take care to do it as promptly as you possibly can.'

'Trust us for that,' said one. 'We know we can depend upon you, so you have only to say what you wish and you will soon see it accomplished.'

With this understanding, then, Blodget left them to proceed to a junk store which he knew was always open, to a particular knock, at any hour of the night.

There Blodget bought a complete set of skeleton keys, besides such other little implements used in the art or profession of housebreaking, and concerning which the people of the shop asked him no questions.

Thus provided, then, he took his way to the corner fixed on, there to wait the arrival of his confederates.

He had not to wait long.

In the course of two or three minutes the four men that he had deputed there to wait him were upon the spot.

'You are punctual,' said Blodget.

'We ought to be.'

'How it rains,' said one.

'Yes; but that is all the better for us, you know,' said Blodget.

'It is indeed.'

'I say,' said another, 'there is a watchman coming, and holding his hand before his lantern so as to get a good look at us.'

'Confound him!'

'Step aside,' said Blodget, 'I will confront him.'

A watchman who happened to be wakeful had chanced to see them all meet at the corner, and had hurried towards them, expecting that they were after no good.

'Hilloa—hilloa!' he said. 'Come now, what do here at this time of night?'

'What's that to you?' said Blodget.

'What's that to me?'

'Yes.'

'Why, don't you see who I am?'

'Yes, that's seen in a moment; you are a troublesome fool, but I don't know why I should be bothered with you.'

'Curse me, then, if I don't lock you up. Come along, will you? Don't resist, now. Come along.'

Blodget snatched the lantern from the hand of the watchman, and with one blow of it on the top of his head not only smashed the lantern but nearly stunned its owner, who lay sprawling on the ground, and calling out murder.

'Jump on him!' said Blodget.

'Take his lantern,' said one of the thieves, 'and his rattle.'

'Ah, his rattle,' said Blodget, as he suddenly stood upon the fallen watchman, and nearly squeezed the life out of him. 'I have it, and now come on. It seems to me as if he could not very well move now.'

This was the fact. The brutal assault that had been committed on the unfortunate watchman had really for a time deprived him of all power of speech or movement, and Blodget and his gang went on with perfect ease and composure.

'This way,' said Blodget, as he crossed the road to the back of some low stores. 'This way.'

'Hilloa!' said another watchman, 'did I hear a row?'

'Yes,' said Blodget, as he struck him such a blow in the face with the butt of a revolver he had in hand that he fell like a corpse.

'He's quieted,' said Blodget.

The four thieves really looked at each other with some alarm, and one of them said—

'You have a good kind of way of quieting people, Mr. Blodget, I rather think.'

'Yes. But don't call me Mr. Blodget; call me Captain, if you please; but if you use my name it may reach ears that it is not intended for.'

'That's right, Mr. —, Captain I mean. Are we near the place, though?'

'Yes, close to it.'

'Ah, what is that?'

The sharp whistle of a watchman broke upon the stillness of the night air.

'This way—this way,' said Blodget. 'Let us hide for a moment or two.'

The five got under a doorway, and there they hid and let no less than four watchmen run past them in the direction of the sound of the whistle.

No more of the guardians of the night seemed to be coming that way, so that Blodget came forth from the hiding place with his friends and went quietly on.

All was dark, the guests had departed, and the street in which the lady resided was restored to its usual equanimity for the night.

There was not the least appearance of any light in any of the windows in the front of the house; but Blodget hardly supposed that such a residence would be left entirely without light in any of the rooms, so he fully expected that some of the back windows would no doubt show symptoms of the apartments being in some degree illuminated.

'Halt! This is the house,' he said.

'All right, captain.'

'Now attend to me all of you, and you will know what you have to do—I will manage to open the door, and then you will remain just within it on the watch.'

'Yes, captain.'

'You will take charge of the pantry, which I will point out to you, and possess yourself of all the portable plate.'

'I'll do it, captain.'

'You, then, will ransack the rooms on the first floor.'

'All's right.'

'And you will follow me.'

'I'll do it, captain. Now we know what we have all got to do, and can do it well.'

'You can if you will; and remember that we all assemble here in the hall again as soon as possible, and that if the one who is to keep guard at the door sees proper to give an alarm, it shall be with a whistle such as no doubt in the night time will be distinctly heard by all of you.'

'I have a whistle in my pocket,' said the fellow, 'that I'll warrant you will all hear.'

'Then that is settled; so now let us go to work.'

Blodget himself commenced the attack upon the door, and he did so with amazing tact.

With one of the picklocks he had in his possession he easily turned the lock of the door, and then he found that he was impeded by a couple of bolts and a chain.

To most persons these would have been rather insurmountable obstructions, but to him they only required a little time and skill and perseverance to overcome them.

With a fine and exquisitely tempered saw, which was so thin that he got it between the door and the joist, he managed to saw them both in two in a very short space of time.

The door was now only fastened by the chain.

'Is it done now?' asked one of the thieves.

'Not yet.'

'Soon?'

'Yes. Why do you ask?' said Blodget.

'I think—I may be mistaken though—but I think some one looked out at one of the windows of the house opposite rather more earnestly than they ought to have done.'

'The devil they did.'

'Yes, I think so.'

'A man or a woman?'

'It is too dark to say.'

'Curses on them, be it whom it may!'

'Amen to that, captain.'

'But you are quite sure you saw some one, be it man or woman?'

'Yes, I am.'

'Then go over two of you to the door, and wait there for a few moments while I work at this chain.'

'And if any one comes out?'

'Well?'

'What shall we do?'

'Do you ask me what you shall do while you have the use of your hands? It won't do to make a noise, so I should say that the only thing open to you to do is to throttle any one who should appear.'

'Throttle!'

'Yes, and why not? Pray what business have the people opposite to interfere in my affairs, I should like to know?'

'Well, certainly—but—but—'

'Do you hesitate?'

'No—no. Don't be in a passion, captain. If it must be done, why, it is no use saying anything more about it, and it just will be done.'

'I should imagine so.'

The two men who had been thus ordered over the way by Blodget went upon their errand; and although it is true they had at first rather started at the idea of throttling somebody who might be so very interfering and imprudent as to come from the opposite house, it is yet difficult to say whether after all, this admonition of Blodget was not very greatly increased by the off-hand manner in which he proposed to get rid of obstacles to the progress of the particular little enterprise upon which he was.

'Curses on it,' muttered Blodget to himself, 'it seems as if I were fated to be thwarted to-night.'

He saw his two companions take up their station on the opposite door-step, and then he set to work upon the street-door chain.

It was rather a peculiar process by which he, Blodget, got rid of the obstacle to his progress.

Having sawed the bolts and opened the locks he could just get the street-door open as far as the slack of the chain would allow it to go, but although that was not above a couple of inches in all, yet it was sufficient for his purpose, as will be very quickly seen.

He took from his pocket a very peculiar shaped iron instrument, capable of very great extension as regarded length by other pieces fitting into it like the joints of a fishing-rod, only that the sockets were squared, so that they fitted quite tight and would not turn.

One end of this instrument he fixed in a link of the chain, and then he lengthened it about two feet, and fitted a cross piece on the end, so that he had a very good amount of leverage to work with.

Blodget gave this instrument about three rapid turns, and then the iron chain broke in two or three places and hung uselessly from the door in the passage of the house.

'It is done,' he said, 'Come in.'

The two thieves who were still with him now crept into the hall, and at that moment Blodget heard a noise opposite.

He who had seen a head project from an opposite window had not been deceived. A man at the house opposite had chanced to see the persons on the door-step, and being a very cunning sort of individual, instead of giving a noisy alarm at once, which would have had the effect of scaring the thieves off, he thought he would gently slip out, and run to the nearest policeman and tell what he had seen.

With this view he had hurriedly dressed himself and slipped down stairs. He opened the door with the utmost caution, and then made a dart into the arms of the men, who were there waiting for him so quietly and patiently.

This sudden capture of the man from the opposite house was the noise that Blodget had heard opposite just as he had succeeded in removing the last obstacle to getting an entrance to the hall of the house.

The attack upon the man was so sudden, and withal so totally unexpected by that individual, that, for the moment, he was too terrified to cry out.

That moment was precious to him, for before he could recover presence of mind sufficient to have the least idea of what best to do, one of the thieves had him by the throat with such a clutch that he began to get black in the face.

Blodget ran over from the other side of the way in another moment.

'Who is it?' he asked.

'Somebody going, no doubt, to give an alarm,' said the man who had hold of him.

'Now is that possible?' said Blodget.

'It is, captain.'

'Dear me, what interfering people there are in the world, to be sure. Has he a cravat on?'

'Yes, captain.'

'That will do.'

Blodget took the unfortunate man's cravat from his neck, and in another moment wound it round again so tightly and tied it in a knot behind, that his doing more than just slightly breathe was out of the question.

'Now,' he added, 'one slight tap on the head just to make him remember us, and all is well.'

The tap on the head that Blodget so facetiously called a slight remembrancer consisted in a severe blow with an iron jemmy, beneath which the victim fell to the ground as if he had been struck dead.

'Push him into his own passage,' said Blodget, 'and then close his door quietly. It will be quite a pity to disturb the, no doubt, highly respectable family to which he belongs.'

This was done, and with so little trouble, too, had the whole affair been accomplished that the man was disposed of, and Blodget was back again to the house before one would have thought it possible to do so much.'

'Now, come in all of you,' he said.

'Yes, captain.'

'You did that well, captain.'

'Hush, we will talk about that another time, when we have plenty of time to do so, for we have none now.'

'Yes, captain.'

'You know your separate directions now. Here we are in the house, and our grand object is, of course, to do our work here and then to get out of it as quickly as we can.'

'Yes—yes, that's it.'

'A light!'

One of the thieves—it was the one whose appointed duty it was to go up stairs with Blodget—lit a loco foco match, and then as it burned up they all started, for one of the first things they saw was a servant apparently fast asleep, but, in reality, dead drunk in a huge chair.

'Confound the rascal,' said Blodget, 'who now would have supposed he was so near to us?'

'He sleeps.'

'Are you sure of that? Is it a cat's sleep?'

'No, captain, that is a sound sleep.'

'It looks sound.'

'He is as drunk as blazes, captain, I can see. Ah, he has been at the decanters and bottles after the guests have gone.'

'No doubt about that,' said Blodget, with a smile; 'and I don't mind saying that it was a part of my calculation in this little affair, that the servants would be mostly drunk, and so in too deep a sleep to hear us, or to mind us if they did hear us.'

'Ah, captain, you know how to act about it, if any one in the world does.'

'What is to be done with this fellow?' said one of them.

'Nothing: let him be. Now furnish yourselves with lighted tapers, and let us set to work.'

Each of the thieves in the course of another moment had a little piece of lighted taper in his hand, and it had the advantage that it could be, by a little pressure of the finger and thumb, stuck on any convenient place in an instant.

'Now, quick, all of you,' added Blodget, 'and you follow me.'

He spoke to the one whose appointed duty it was to do so, and then at two steps at a time Blodget ascended a staircase.

When they got to the first floor landing, Blodget and the man who was with him both stopped, and sitting down on the stairs, they drew rapidly over their boots, each of them a pair of thick worsted socks, so that their footsteps were really quite inaudible after that.

Neither did they leave any signs of footmarks any where, which otherwise, coming out of the wet street, they might have done; and any attempt to trace them beyond the first floor, after they had put on the socks, would have been very difficult indeed.

'This a good dodge,' whispered the thief to Blodget.

'Yes, but still be as quiet as you can.'

'I will.'

'This way. This way.'

The thief was of rather a loquacious order of men. Perhaps, after all, he was a little terrified at the situation in which he found himself, but certainly he could not, or would not, obey Blodget's injunctions to silence.

Blodget would, under any other circumstances, have quarrelled with him for his contumacy, but just then he did not think proper to do so, as he could not tell what emergency might arise in which he might require the best services of his companion, with good will to render them; so did he answer him, although it was as shortly as he possibly could, to be at the same time at all consistent with civility.

They made their way up to the second floor of the house, on which the sleeping apartments were situated.

On a gilt bracket, fixed about twelve feet high in the wall of the sort of corridor which ran the whole length of the house, Blodget saw a night lamp burning, and by its aid he was able to distinguish the different doors of the sleeping portion of the house.

The man who was with him, and who was named Ben, saw Blodget looking about him.

'Don't you know the room?' he said.

'Yes—oh, yes; all's right.'

'Well, that's a comfort. Do you know, captain, that it ain't pleasant to be so far off in the street?'

'Why so?'

'Because, if there should be a row, how are we to get off?'

'Pshaw! I never contemplate anything of the sort.'

'Oh, you don't?'

'No; and if you will but be a little cautious and careful in what you say, we shall do well enough.'

'Trust me for that.'

'Curse you,' thought Blodget to himself, 'for a chattering parrot. It is the last time I will take you with me upon an expedition of this sort.'

Blodget carefully now laid hold of the handle of the bed-room door, and gave it a quick, sharp turn at once. He knew that that was the best way to prevent it from making any rattling or squeaking sound.

The door remained fast.

Blodget turned the handle again to its proper position, and stood quiet for a moment.

It was quite clear that the bed-room door was fast on the inside in some way, and if it was a night bolt, the difficulty of getting rid of such an obstruction was rather serious.

That is to say, it was serious as regarded time, for he was well prepared with any means for getting over such an obstacle, if he had but the time given him to do it in.

'Step this way,' he whispered to the man who was with him.

'Yes—yes.'

Blodget led him to the top of the staircase, and then added—

'You will stay here till I come to you again—keep your eyes and your ears open. There is a night-bolt to the room door, and I have the job of cutting my way to it. It will take me five minutes.'

'Yes—yes.'

'Be vigilant and quiet.'

'I will, Captain.'

'And don't stir from this spot.'

'Trust me for that. I will sit down on the top stair here.'

Not a sound came from whoever slept in that apartment, and Blodget congratulated himself upon having got so far without his giving the smallest possible alarm.

Passing his arm through the little hole in the door, now, he carefully lifted the night-bolt, and the door was, in a moment, open.

'It is done,' thought he.

As he now paused for a moment he took a half mask of black crape from his pocket and put it over his face, so that he was effectually disguised and then he stepped back to the stair head where he had left his assistant, Ben.

Ben was still sitting on the topmost stair, and leaning forward to catch any sounds that might come from the lower part of the mansion.

Blodget placed his hand upon Ben's shoulder, and whispered in his ear the one word—

'Now!'

Ben started, and turning his head, the first thing he saw was the black mask, and not expecting it he gave such a start of surprise and terror that he was on his feet in a moment.

No doubt he thought his infernal majesty had all of a sudden found him out.

'Murder!' he said. 'Oh, Lord; no!'

'Silence, idiot!' muttered Blodget, as he placed his hand over Ben's mouth and cautioned him to quietness.

The sudden consternation of Ben all evaporated before the sounds of Blodget's voice.

'You cursed fool,' said Blodget in his ear, 'what do you mean by uttering an exclamation of that sort?'

'I—I didn't know.'

'You didn't know?'

'No, captain; I think I was in a sort of a brown study, you see, and so I—'

'Silence!'

'Yes, captain.'

'Who is there?' said a voice from the room, 'who is there?'

'Hush,' said Blodget as he clutched the arm of Ben, and they both stood like statues.

Ben shook in every limb.

'Did you speak?' said the voice again.

'Be still,' said Blodget. 'Don't move, on your life, Ben.'

'I won't. Oh—oh! It's all—'

'What?'

'Up with us.'

'No, fool, it is not if you keep yourself quiet.'

'I will.'

Blodget ran back to the door in a moment, and he drew it close shut.

'I'm sure I heard a voice,' said the same person. 'Kitty—Kitty, I say. The wench is fast asleep. Kitty, I say.'

'Yes, madam,' said a sleepy voice, and a door opened from the lady's room into another smaller one that adjoined it, and a young girl, in her night dress, appeared.

'Did you hear anything?'

'Yes, ma'm.'

'What?'

'You call me, ma'm.'

'Tut—tut! I don't mean that; but did you hear anything else before I called you?'

'No, ma'm.'

'Well, I thought I did.'

'You was a dreaming, ma'm, I suppose.'

'I suppose I was. See if the night-bolt is all right, Kitty, before you go to bed again.'

'Yes, ma'm.'

'I feel so nervous to-night; I don't know why.'

Blodget felt there was danger now unless he could adroitly put the night-bolt in its place again. The difficulty to do so without being seen, and in a hurry, too, without making any noise, was very great, but if any man living could do that, that man was Blodget.

Kitty, fortunately for him, was half asleep, and she shuffled along the floor in such an odd, devious kind of way, with her eyes scarcely open enough to see at all where she was going, that she gave Blodget every chance.

It happened, too, that as she went she completely obstructed the lady's view of the door.

Blodget put his hand in the little orifice he had cut in the panel, and replaced the night-bolt.

He was only just in time.

'Is it all right?' said the lady.

'Oh, yes, ma'm.'

'You are sure?'

'Yes, ma'm.'

'Then it could not have been anything surely; I was dreaming. But it is no matter, you can go to bed again, Kitty. Dear me, what are you about now?'

Kitty had, in her half sleepy state, ran against the foot of the bed and shaken it well.

'Eh? Oh, ma'm, I beg your pardon, I think I am a little drowsy, you see, ma'm.'

'A little drowsy indeed! Plague take the girl, she is dead asleep. Go to bed directly.'

'Yes, ma'm.'

Kitty did manage to steer herself now clear of the various articles of furniture in her mistress's room, and to pass through the door that led to her own, and in another moment she was again fast asleep.

'Dear me,' said the lady, 'I do feel nervous to-night, to be sure, and I don't know why.'

Ting—ting—ting! went the little bell of her repeater watch as she pressed the spring of it.

'Three o'clock,' she said. 'Well, I'd better try to go to sleep, I suppose, while I can.'

She did not utter another word, and in a few moments the most deathlike silence was in the room again.

Blodget put his hand in the little circular hole in the door, and drew up the bolt once more.

'Curses upon all this delay,' he said to himself, 'we shall have the daylight upon us soon.'

This was indeed so, as another hour would without doubt bring the dawn, and then the situation of Blodget and his companions in iniquity would be rather perilous.

There were many other circumstances which rendered it desirable to be quick about the affair.

In the first place the collision with the watch had no doubt been, by that time, communicated, and no doubt the police were active.

Then again, as the man in the house over the way had after all only been stunned, there was no saying when he might sufficiently recover to give an alarm.

From all these reasons Blodget felt the necessity of bringing the job to a speedy end, and with such a determination he then crept very quietly into the lady's bed-room.

In the dim light of the bedchamber, he looked like some evil spirit as he stood casting a broad shadow on the bed and its occupant.

For a moment, he considered what to do, and then he stepped up to the bedside and said:—

'Give any alarm and you die—be still and you live! Be quiet—quite quiet, for your life's sake.'

The terrified woman opened her eyes and uttered a faint cry.

'Yes, ma'm,' said Kitty from the next room.

'Curse you!' cried Blodget.

He took a revolver from his pocket, and held it to her head, saying in a calm tone:—

'If you wish to save your life you will be quiet. It is your jewels, plate, and money I come for, not your life, but if you place it as an obstacle in the way, that obstacle must be removed. You understand me.'

'A robber?'

'Yes.'

'A house-breaker?'

'Just so.'

'Yes, ma'm,' said Kitty, blustering into the room with her eyes half shut as before. 'Did you call me?'

'Yes,' said he, stepping up to her, and placing his hand right over her mouth; and then in her ear he said—

'Kitty, if you speak one word or utter one scream, or make the least noise, I will cut your throat from ear to ear this moment.'

Kitty stopped short, and looked as if she had been suddenly turned to stone. Blodget placed her in a chair, and catching up a handkerchief, he tied it in her mouth, and round the back of her head, and so on to the back of her chair, like a bit.

'Now be quiet,' he said.

Kitty sat profoundly still; indeed, her faculties had received such a shock that it would be some time before she'd recover again.

The lady sat up in bed.

'You wretch! What on earth do you want?'

'Plate—jewels—money.'

'There is my purse on the dressing-table—the plate is in the pantry down stairs.'

'And in the little secret cupboard at the back of this bed, you know it is, madam.'

The lady uttered a groan.

'I will trouble you to get up.'

'Oh, no—no!'

'But I say, oh, yes—yes. Now if you please.'

Without any further ceremony, Blodget took her by the arms, lifted her out of the bed, and put her on the floor. He then went to the door and cried, in a low tone—

'Ben!'

'I'm coming,' said Ben, as he entered the room.

'Keep watch over this lady, Ben.'

'Oh, yes.'

'And if she tries to get away, or if she gives alarm, you will be so good as to cut her throat, Ben.'

'Oh, yes.'

'And don't make a bungling job of it while you are about it. If you have to do it all, do it with humanity—that is to say, do it at once and effectually.'

'Oh, yes; trust me for that, captain.'

The lady was now really alarmed.

Ben took from his pocket a large clasped knife, the blade of which he opened in a ferocious kind of way with his teeth, and with that in his hand, he kept an eye upon her.

Blodget now sprang upon the bed, and tearing down some of the hangings from the back part of it, he saw a small square door in the wall. It was not fastened.

No doubt the secrecy of the position of that receptacle for valuables was much more relied upon by the lady than any sort of lock or fastening.

The fact was, that when once it was found out that that was the hiding place for the valuable property that could be put in it, the security was gone.

No lock or bolt could for many moments have added to it in any shape or way.

Blodget saw at once when he pulled open the door that he had received correct information. Immediately within the little square door were some shelves built in the thickness of the wall, and upon them a heap of property of a valuable and portable nature.

Bracelets—rings—necklaces—watches—spoons—gold           quartz—and jewellery of all descriptions, met the gaze of the robber as he glanced upon the shelves.

'All right,' said he.

The lady was a bold woman, and she had kept her eye upon Blodget, and when she heard him say 'All right,' the thought that he had discovered all her most valuable property drove her to an act of defiance.

'Thieves!' she said, and she raised a loud scream.

'Kill her!' said Blodget.

Ben had sprung to his feet, and made for the door of the room, although he had his knife in his hand. The fact is, this fellow wanted the nerve to be a murderer when any one resisted at all. He might have been an assassin, but he had not the courage to engage in a struggle.

'Kill her, I say!' cried Blodget.

'No, no!' said the lady, and springing to her feet, she with a rush made her way into the servant's room; and slammed the door shut in Blodget's face.

'Curses on her! you have let her escape.'

'I could not help it,' said Ben.

'Here, there is no time to be lost now—she will rouse the neighborhood. Take this pillow-case, which I have filled with the swag. We must be content with it. I will see to her and be with you in a moment.'

'Yes—yes, I will go—'

'No further than the head of the stairs, though.'

'No—no.'

Blodget made a rush at the door of the room into which she had retreated; but it was too strong for him, and by great good fortune there had chanced to be some very effectual mode of fastening it on the inside. Blodget heard a lumbering noise in the room, that he could not make out.

He called aloud,—'No harm is intended you, and I will compromise the matter with you, if you will be quiet.'

Something rolled upon the floor, and then hit the door a great knock that shook it.

'Confound her,' said Blodget, 'I know what she is doing now. She is piling the furniture against the door, and that was the bedstead. I say!'

Blodget heard a window thrown open, and then a voice calling out,—

'Help!—help!—thieves!—thieves!—Murder!'

Blodget turned from the door. His eyes fell upon the young girl who was tied to the chair, and in a moment he rushed up to her and untied her head. Then shaking her to and fro, he said—

'Listen to me. Do you hear me?'

'Ye—e—es.'

'Go to that door and call to your mistress that I have gone.'

'Ye—e—es.'

'At once, or I will cut your throat.'

The girl tottered to the door of the inner room, and called out in a loud voice,—

'Mistress, they have gone now. They have gone now. Open the door. It is only me, Kitty.'

Kitty, in her fright, had done even more than Blodget had asked her. The dread of death had sharpened the wits of the girl, so that she had seen fully what was wanted of her, and she was willing at that moment to think that self-preservation was indeed the very first law of nature, even if it was taken in its most extended signification, and involved the destruction of another.

'That is right,' said Blodget, as the girl tapped upon the panel of the door of the inner room, and called to her mistress; 'call her again, or you die!'

'Mistress!'

'Who calls?'

'It's me, ma'm!'

'Kitty?'

'Yes, ma'm!'

'How came you free?'

'Oh, they have run away, ma'm!'

'Open the front window, then, and call out for the police at once, do you hear?'

'Yes, ma'm!'

'Tell her to open the door,' said Blodget, 'or mind your throat.'

'Open the door, ma'm!'

'No.'

'Implore her to do so. Say you are hurt.'

'Oh, I am hurt, ma'm! Do open the door.'

'Hurt?' said the lady, 'You don't mean that?'

Blodget heard from the voice that she must be just outside the door, or rather, we may say with more precision, just on the other side of it. Full of revengeful thoughts at the idea that she had endangered his safety by her obstinate, and what we would call heroic, resistance to be robbed, he determined on her destruction.

Placing a revolver within a couple of inches of the panel of the door, and close to the side of the face of Kitty, although at the moment the girl was too confused to see it, he fired.

The report was very stunning.

Kitty fell to the floor from fright with a loud scream.

'Hush!' said Blodget, as he held up his hands, in an attitude of listening. 'Hush!'

All was still.

A deep groan came from the inner room.

'Ha! ha!' cried Blodget. 'I have hit her!'

It was at that moment that a shrill whistle sounded through the house, and Blodget at once recognized it as the alarm that he had told the man whose duty it was to stay at the outer door of the house to give in case of danger.

'It is all over,' said Blodget, 'and it will be a close touch now as regards escape.'

He made his way to the door of the room, and was out in the corridor in a moment.

'Ben? Ben?'

'Here I am, captain. Oh, Lord!'

'What's the matter?'

'Nothing—only—only—'

'Only what, idiot?'

'I thought I heard somebody in trouble.'

'How so?'

'A pistol shot, captain, from your hands, I take it, is reason enough for that.'

'No, it is not. When you hear a pistol-shot from me again do not take it into your head that somebody is in trouble.'

'No?'

'Certainly not; but you may pretty safely conclude that somebody's troubles are over.'

'Oh, Lord!'

'Come away at once now—there is no time to lose. Take care of the bundle. Have you it?'

'All safe.'

'Follow me then.'

Blodget ran down stairs as quickly as he could, and by the time he got to the hall he found that the whole four of the thieves he had brought with him had assembled there, and were looking at each other by their little pieces of lighted taper with something like consternation.

'What is the matter?' said Blodget.

'Oh, captain, it's all up.'

'What is all up?'

'All up with us. There is a force in the street of police. They don't seem to know which house it is, but they are on the look-out about something being amiss at one or other of the houses on this side of the way.'

'Humph! What do you mean by a force?'

'About a dozen of them.'

Blodget bit his lips.

'Yes, and they are close outside too.'

'No!'

'Yes they are.'

'I will satisfy myself. If it be only the ordinary watch I don't think a couple of dozen of them ought to stop us from proceeding, and I will not permit them doing so either; but if they are some of these cursed Vigilance fellows, it is another affair.'

Blodget acted promptly. Nobody certainly could accuse him of want of courage or decision. He knew that the only way of discovering who were without was to take a good look himself; so, to the consternation and surprise of his comrades, he opened the street door and coolly looked out into the street.

A sudden rush was made at the door by a couple of men, and Blodget soon saw ten or twelve others not far off.

'Hold hard there, hoss,' said one of them. 'Don't shut that door again, my fine fellow, if you please.'

'Ah, indeed!' said Blodget, as he closed the door; but he was not quite quick enough, for a stick that one of the officers had with him had been pushed through the opening, and prevented the door from closing.

'Ha, ha! it won't do,' cried the officer.

Blodget laid hold of the stick and called upon the others to do so. By their united force they pulled it out of the officer's hand, half dislocating his wrist as he did so, for he had tied it with a strip of dry hide to his arm.

The door was closed in another minute, but it was only held by the lock, for Blodget had cut the bolts and had broken the chain, so that his situation with his four companions was anything but a very agreeable one.

'Oh!' said Ben, 'I do begin to think as we have all dropped in for it at last.'

'Not at all,' said Blodget.

'Not at all, captain? Why how the deuce are we to get out of this mess?'

'I don't call it a mess. There are two ways out of a house; one at the street door, and the other at the roof. Follow me.'

'What, upstairs again?'

'Yes, to be sure. Remember you are under my orders, and you may as well remember why, too.'

'Why?'

'Yes, why. Was it not because I knew more than you did, and could so take the command with more advantage to you as well as to myself? Come on; I will yet see you all safe out of this affair, you may depend upon it.'

They accordingly proceeded up stairs, where as Blodget anticipated, they found a scuttle affording an exit to the roof—through this they escaped, and scampering over the flat roofs of the adjacent houses, got safely off with their blood-bought booty.

# CHAPTER XIV

We must now retrace our steps in order to introduce a different phase of life in the Golden City.

Among the many hundreds of passengers who landed one drizzly day from one of the Panama steamers, was a young and very handsome female.

Her personal attractions had excited the attention and admiration of many of the male passengers, who would fain have improved the chance of becoming more intimate with her, had they not been kept aloof by the distant manners of a gentleman, under whose protection she appeared to be, and, perhaps, even more by the young girl's reserved ways and apparently sad expression of countenance.

Who this lady was will appear in the course of our tale. Her companion called her Fanny—but whether she was his wife or not, was unknown to the rest of the passengers.

About a fortnight after Fanny arrived in San Francisco she rose from her slumbers, broken by unquiet visions, with pale and gloomy looks, for she had not yet decided upon the course she would adopt in her present extremity, and her sombre countenance and spiritless manners attracted the notice of her landlady.

'Mr. Edwards has gone to Sacramento, I hear,' said she, as she placed the breakfast equipage upon the table.

'Yes.' replied Fanny, coldly.

'He did not say anything to me about the rent,' observed the woman, in a doubtful and hesitating tone. 'He engaged the apartments, you know; but if you pay the rent when it is due, of course it is all the same.'

'You have always received your rent from me, Mrs. Smith,' returned Fanny, somewhat haughtily, 'and as long as I occupy your apartments I shall continue to pay for them. I hope you do not doubt my ability to do so?'

'Oh, no,' said her landlady. 'Only as Mr. Edwards engaged the apartments, and has now left without saying anything about the matter, I did not know how matters might be; but I meant no offence, I am sure.'

Mrs. Smith whisked herself out of the room, and Fanny was again alone to contemplate the dread realities of her position. Still undecided, still reluctant to adopt either of the alternatives which she had canvassed over, but keenly alive to the necessity of a speedy decision, she yet sought to avert the crisis, if only for a few days; and having made a bundle of a silk dress and a handsome shawl which Edwards had given her, she left the house to obtain the means of liquidating the week's rent, that would be due on the ensuing day.

'Mrs. Edwards,' said a female voice behind her, as she stood before the window of a pawnbroker's shop, unable to summon courage to enter; and turning round she beheld a young girl, stylishly dressed and possessed of considerable pretensions to beauty, whom she instantly recognized as a fellow-lodger with whom she had once or twice exchanged civilities when they had met upon the stairs or in the passage.

'I have renounced that name forever, Miss Jessop,' said she 'and would forget all the associations belonging to it.'

'Ah, I heard that Mr. Edwards had gone to Sacramento,' observed Miss Jessop.

'You knew it, then, before I did,' returned Fanny, with a slight bitterness of accent.

'Indeed!' rejoined Miss Jessop. 'But do not think of going to the pawnbroker's, for I am sure that is where you are going.—'

'Who told you that I was going to the pawnbroker's?' inquired Fanny, coloring, and speaking in a tone of mingled vexation and surprise.

'Nay, do not be angry!' said Miss Jessop, whose manner was kind and conciliating. 'I was sure of it, as soon as I saw you, and you cannot deny it; but do not look vexed because I have penetrated your intentions. I see that you want a friend, and it was because I felt convinced that you were going into the shop that I accosted you.'

'I do indeed want a friend, Miss Jessop,' returned Fanny, sighing, 'I never felt the want of one so much as at this moment.'

'Then come home, if you have no where else to go to, and we will have a little chat together,' said Miss Jessop, in a very friendly tone. 'I am older than you in years, and still older in experience, for all that you now see dimly louring upon the horizon, I have long ago passed through.'

Fanny was in that frame of mind which prompts the seeker after guidance or consolation to be communicative and to give confidence wherever friendship is proffered, and she walked home with Miss Jessop, whom she invited into her own sitting-room.

'You are very comfortable here,' said the young lady, as she glanced round the apartment. 'I hope you do not think of leaving?'

'I have thought of many things, but as yet have been able to decide upon nothing,' returned Fanny, with a faint smile.

'And yet you were about to do the most foolish thing imaginable, if I had not prevented you,' observed Miss Jessop. 'For whatever course you decide upon, it would be foolish to make away with your best clothes, and the money you raised by so doing would only serve to avert for a few days the decision that you would have to come to at last. For instance, if you decide upon returning home to your friends, where would be the use of delaying your return until you had eat up all your clothes? Again if you determined upon receiving the visits of any other gentleman, would it not be foolish to delay accepting of his proposals until you were penniless? If you will take the advice of one who has been in the same position, you will do at once, whatever you decide upon doing, for, however desperate your position may be, procrastination will only make it worse.'

Fanny felt the force of her new friend's reasoning, and after reflecting upon it for a moment, frankly disclosed her position, signifying the repugnance which she felt to returning home.

'You see that I understand your position as well as if I had been acquainted with it,' said Miss Jessop, with a smile. 'If you will go out with me this evening I will introduce you to a banker who is sure to be delighted with you. He is very liberal, and I know he admires your dark style of beauty above all others.'

Fanny's curiosity and vanity were both excited by this flattering description, and as reflection had confirmed her in her determination not to return home, little persuasion was needed to induce her to assent to her new friend's proposition.

Night found Fanny and Miss Jessop seated in a temple dedicated equally to Venus and to Bacchus. The former was surprised by the scene which met her gaze, and the appearance of the females who promenaded the saloon, or were seated by the side or on the knees of gay gentlemen, enlightened her both as to the character of the place and that of her companions, if indeed there had been in her mind any doubt as to the latter, previous to her introduction to that flowery scene of vice.

'There!—that is the person of whom I spoke to you,' said Miss Jessop, in a whisper, as the banker entered the saloon, and as the roue caught the eye of Fanny's companion, and saw by her side a beautiful young female whom he had never seen before, he advanced towards the table at which they were seated, and sat down opposite to them.

'You look blooming to-night, Miss Jessop,' said he, eyeing Fanny as he spoke. 'Champagne, waiter. Who is your handsome young friend?'

Fanny blushed at the compliment, and her companion answered, with a smile, 'A young friend of mine whom I have promised to introduce to you, Mr. Edwards.'

Fanny and the banker were soon upon the most friendly terms. He invited the ladies to take wine with him. Fanny's reserve vanished by degrees under its influence, and the compliments of the banker appealed to her vanity. She was soon induced to accompany him to a house in the neighborhood. Fanny had committed herself to the tide of destiny, suffering it to bear her wither it would, and she entered into the house, of the character of which her inexperience allowed her to form no conception. But when they were conducted by an attendant into a bedchamber, she was recalled all at once to the nature of her position, and she blushed deeply; her companion, however, found means to remove her scruples, and she left the house, in company with Miss Jessop, richer indeed in purse, but bankrupt in honor.

It was near midnight,—some weeks after Fanny's fatal resolution—the gay votaries of pleasure were leaving the Jenny Lind Theatre, some few in equipages, but a greater number on foot; beyond the immediate neighborhood of the theatre, however, the bustle was little increased, for the bar-rooms, the Arcade, the El Dorado, the Lafayette, and the Bella Union, received the human tide almost as fast as its waves ebbed from the portico of the theatre.

One female form alone lingered under the portico!

She was a lovely dark-eyed girl, rather below the middle height of woman, and wore a silk dress, faded and stained, a mantle of the same material, creased and much worn, and a velvet bonnet modish in form, but worn and faded, and adorned with a black feather in the last stage of decay. Her complexion was dark, and dissipation and late hours had not yet banished the last tinge of rose from her cheeks; her bright eyes were shaded by long jetty lashes, and her black hair was glossy as the pinion of the raven; her lips seemed formed of coral by the art of the turner, and her form was symmetrical and attractive in the highest degree. A little while before those dark eyes had beamed with simulated passion, and those vermeil lips had been wreathed with the most winning and wanton smiles; but as the last hack drove away from the front of the theatre, the expression of the girl's countenance, which seemed to have been stamped there as with a searing iron, by the vivid consciousness of shame and degradation. The change was like the removal of the garland and veil from the skull of the skeleton guest at the banquet of the old Egyptians. A light rain was beginning to fall, the pavement was becoming wet and clammy, and the girl looked down with a sigh and a shudder at her thin shoes.

Then she stepped upon the pavement, shivered for a moment on the edge and crossed the slippery street, to where the large lamp over the door of a large cafe threw its yellow glare upon the wet sidewalk. A tall, well-shaped man came out of the tavern at the moment she approached the door, and between him and the young girl there passed glances of recognition.

'Blodget!' she exclaimed, in a low gasping tone.

'Ah! why it is little Fanny!' said he, in a tone between a recognition and surprise.

'Yes,' returned the young girl, with a look at once appealing and reproachful, 'It is Fanny—your victim.'

'Humph,' said Blodget, averting his countenance from the girl's earnest gaze, and biting his lip. 'Have you been looking for me?' he inquired, after a moment's pause, and still without looking upon the girl's wan countenance, as if he felt that her looks would reproach him, even though she uttered not a word.

'No,' returned Fanny. 'I knew not that you were in this city. I am glad, Mr. Blodget, to perceive that you have still so much virtue left, that you cannot look upon the face of the girl you have wronged and deceived, that you shrink from the contemplation of your work of evil.'

'Don't let us quarrel,' said Blodget, in a low voice, and with an evident uneasiness of manner. 'Come in, and we will go up stairs, and have a bottle of wine.'

'Never, with you, Blodget!' exclaimed Fanny, energetically.

'Your baseness has reduced me to a depth of degradation to which I would not at one time have believed possible for me to fall, but never will I sit down in a public room with the author of my ruin.'

'Well, where do you live?' said Blodget in a tone of vexation. 'I cannot stand talking to you in the street—besides, it rains.'

'Ah, you are ashamed of me?' returned Fanny in a tone of bitterness, though her voice trembled and her lips quivered as she spoke. 'Why were you not rather ashamed to become the destroyer of my happiness, my innocence, perhaps, my soul?'

'Pooh, nonsense, Fan,' returned Blodget, the glow of conscious guilt mantling upon his cheeks, in spite of his assumed nonchalance. 'You are in a melancholy mood to-night, and if you mean to stand here talking like that, I shall rush off. It is getting late, and you had better go home.'

'Home!' ejaculated Fanny, with a bitter intonation, and hot tears gathered in her dark eyes, and trembled on her black and silken lashes.

'Bill!' said Blodget, to a pale, shabby dissipated-looking young man, who came out of the bar-room at that moment—'bring a hack!'

In a few minutes the vehicle rolled up to the spot, and the driver jumped from his seat to open the door. Fanny allowed her seducer to hand her into the hack but her thoughts were wandering, and she felt a slight degree of surprise when Blodget got in, and seated himself by her side.

'Where to, sir,' said the driver, as he closed the door.

Blodget looked at Fanny, who mentioned the name of the street in which she lived, and in a few minutes the hack was dashing over the miry road. Fanny leaned back in silence, and when her companion passed his arm around her waist, she shrank from his touch, and he instantly removed it.

'What is the use of your being angry with me, Fanny?' said he, in a deprecating tone. 'What has passed can never be recalled, and had better be forgotten. Let us—'

'Forgotten?' exclaimed Fanny, raising her dark eyes sadly and reproachfully to his countenance, as he saw by the light of a lamp which the coach passed at the moment. 'Do you think that I can ever forget what I have been or what I am now? That I can forget there was a time when I was innocent and happy, and cease to contrast that time with the wretched present?'

'Why are you not happy now?' inquired the roué.

'Can you ask me why I am not happy now, Blodget?' returned Fanny, in a tone of deep and touching emphasis. 'Ah, do not affect what you do not feel. Do not make me think you so thoroughly heartless as such a question would imply. You know that I am not and cannot be happy.'

Blodget was silent, and in a few moments the hack stopped opposite the house that had for some weeks been the abode of the lost and degraded Fanny. Blodget sprang out, assisted Fanny to alight, and having discharged the hack, followed the young girl up the court and into the house in which she lodged. She ascended the stairs, permitting Blodget to follow her, and when they had entered a small bed-room of the most wretched appearance. She closed the door, set the light which she had received on entering the house, upon a pine table, and sinking upon a chair by the side of the bed, buried her countenance in the clothes.

'How long have you been in such a place as this?' inquired Blodget, as he threw a quick glance round the wretched chamber.

'I permitted you to come here, that you might form a faint idea of the depth to which you have plunged me,' said Fanny, raising her head from the bed.

'Reproaches are useless,' returned the man, gloomily: 'I am sorry for what has passed, Fanny, and now let us be friends again.'

'On what terms?' inquired Fanny.

'Oh, never mind the terms.' returned Blodget, sitting on the side of the bed, and taking the young girl's hand. 'Kiss me, Fan, and we will have a bottle of wine up here—no, not here,' he added, again casting his eyes around the miserable chamber. 'Come away with me to a house of accommodation.'

'And to-morrow?' said Fanny, doubtfully and inquiringly.

'To-morrow we shall be as good friends as ever we were.'

'Blodget,' said Fanny, in a deep and even solemn tone, while she raised her dark eyes to his countenance, with an expression of profound earnestness, 'I would rather die than continue to lead the life which I have lived since you so unkindly deserted me. Indeed, I know not why I have not long since sought death in preference to such a life of shame, and misery and conscious degradation. Tell me whether you mean to atone for all that you have made me suffer by making me your wife?'

'You cannot expect it,' returned Blodget, dropping her hands, and taking a hasty turn across the room. 'You have seen enough of life by this time, I should think, to see the foolishness of such an expectation.'

'My experience of life has been bitter enough, God knows,' said Fanny, heaving a deep sigh, while tears again gathered in her dark eyes. 'Why did you ever seek my love? Was it honorable to do so, and to win my heart, and then, when I had given you the tenderest proof of love that woman can bestow, to cast me from you as you might a flower that you had plucked for its beauty and fragrance, and when it had ceased to charm, you cast upon the footway to be trodden upon and to mingle with the mire? That is what you have done—that has been my fate.'

'Well, it cannot be helped now, Fan,' observed Blodget, some twitchings of remorse giving a slight degree of impatience to his tone. 'Will you come away from here and have a bottle of wine with me? Nay, if you like it better, for once I will stop here.'

'Never again, Blodget, will I press the same bed with you, unless as your wife,' exclaimed Fanny, with solemn earnestness. 'I would rather lay down in some secluded spot, and die of hunger; or seek a refuge from the shame and misery that are killing me, in the waters of the bay.'

'Good night, then,' returned the seducer. 'I am off! I will do the generous, though.'

The libertine's tone and manner were hurried and uneasy. He took a slug from his purse and laid it on the table, but Fanny rose immediately, her dark eyes flashing and her cheeks glowing, and taking up the coin, threw it at his feet.

'Not from you, sir!' she exclaimed vehemently. 'I will neither sell myself to you, nor have it thought that I have done so. You sought me, and you gained me, and I do not blush for what has passed; but my fond and trusting heart betrayed me, and not such a paltry bribe as that. Would you have me despise myself more than I do already?'

'Fanny,' said Blodget, in a tone which evinced considerable agitation, for the words, look, and tone of the poor girl had at length penetrated to his heart. 'Let us be friends, as we were before I left New-York. Forgive me for what you have suffered, and kiss me.'

'No! no!' returned Fanny, extending her hand to ward him as he approached her. 'I forgive you, and now leave me; but remember that there is One besides whose forgiveness you have to seek, and whose pardon is of more consequence than mine.'

'You will not kiss me, then—not even as a sign of your forgiveness?' said the libertine, who thought that if the young girl suffered him to hold her in his embrace he should be able to win her to a more agreeable termination to their interview than appeared likely otherwise.

'No,' replied Fanny, firmly. 'You have ceased to love me, and I should loathe myself were I to suffer any approach to a renewal of our former intimacy.' Blodget lingered a moment longer, glanced toward the slug which still lay on the floor, where the indignant girl had thrown it, and then quitted the room.

When the door had closed upon her seducer, Fanny threw herself upon the bed, and hiding her countenance in the clothes, burst into a flood of bitter and scalding tears. Oh, how agonizing were the reminiscence, how bitter the reflections, evoked by the accidental meeting with the man to whom she owed all the unhappiness she ever knew. The thought of her home, of the poor, but honest parents whom she could never look in the face again, of the companions of her childhood, in the village of her birth, and from these subjects of reflection her thoughts wandered to the beginnings of her ill-starred acquaintance with Blodget, and the sudden dissolving of the dream of happiness she had had, so bright and blissful, but, alas, so transient.

Her tears ceased to flow, without having brought her any relief, and seating herself by the bedside, she grew by degrees more calm, but it was an unnatural calmness, not the tranquility which speaks of peace within, but a mere lull in the tempest of human passions. She glanced at the glittering coin upon the floor, but she felt that to pick it up and appropriate it to her own use, would be to accept a money compensation for her wrongs, and though husbands in the upper classes of society are accustomed to accept such compensation from the seducers of their wives, yet the purer soul of that crushed violet of the pavement, revolted at the thought.

Yet must she have money; she was penniless, and for her there was no alternative between a life of infamy and degradation, and the unblessed grave of the suicide. Moreover she could not bear to be alone with her heart-crushing brain-searing, maddening thoughts: she felt that she must fly from them, or, madness or suicide would be the result. The thought of surrendering herself to the embraces of a stranger was less repugnant to her mind, in the mood which had come upon her, than that of selling to her seducer for money the favors which he had once enjoyed through her love; if she must sin, she resolved that it should not be with him, to those arms she had originally gone pure and chaste.

Leaving the money upon the floor, she went down stairs, darted past a stout red-faced old woman in a faded silk dress, whom she met in the passage, in order to avoid an explanation, and rushed through the miry court into the street. A misty rain was still falling, and there were few persons in the streets, but she knew there were yet plenty of loungers and revellers in the taverns about Commercial Street, and thitherward, she retraced her steps. She had nearly reached the crossing of Montgomery Street, when she saw a young man come out of the corner bar-room and walk down towards the wharf, with a reeling gait, as if under the influence of liquor. Thinking that he might be easily induced to accompany her home, she followed him, but before she could overtake him he entered another bar-room.

Fanny lingered for a moment on the clammy pavement, but the deserted appearance of the streets speedily decided her, and she turned into the house and entered.

The young man was sitting at one of the tables over which he was leaning, with his head leaning on his arms, and his countenance concealed: but no one else was in the room. A glass stood on the table. The man did not move when she entered, though she knew he could not be asleep, having only entered the house a moment before.

'What a disagreeable night,' Fanny ventured to observe, in the hope of attracting the young man's attention.

At the sound of her voice he started from his seat as if he had received a shock from a galvanic battery, and gazed with mingled wildness and earnestness at her. Fanny started also, and staggering backwards, sank upon a bench, and covered her face with her hands, for she had recognized Robert Jervis, her affianced lover, in the days of her virtuous happiness. Jervis was pale, and the unexpected meeting with one whom he had once loved so ardently had given to his countenance an expression of wildness and extreme agitation.

'Has Fanny sunk so low as this? and so soon, too,' said he, in a low voice, rendered hoarse by the agitation of his feelings. 'Has she who ran away from her home become in so short a time a midnight frequenter of overcharged, and the common associate of the vicious portion of a class, the reputable members of which she once looked down upon with disdain?'

'Spare me, Robert,' said Fanny, in a faint and broken voice, and without removing her hands from her countenance, 'You know not what I have suffered—what I am suffering now.'

'I can easily believe that,' returned Robert, surveying her with a look of mournful interest. 'You have made me suffer, too—more deeply than I can find words to express; but I will not reproach you. While you have a heart to feel, if vice does not harden it to the core, you will find reproaches there which I cannot spare you.'

'I do,' exclaimed Fanny, sobs choking her voice, and the pearly tears trickling down her hands. 'You cannot reproach me more severely than my own heart does at this moment. If you knew all that I have endured and am enduring you would pity me.'

'Pity you!' said Robert, who had become perfectly sober the moment he recognized the lost girl upon whom he was now gazing. 'I have never ceased to pity you since the moment of my return to reason after that hour of madness that ruined both myself and you.'

'It was all my fault,' sobbed Fanny, weeping as if her heart would break.

'It matters little now, whether the fault was wholly yours or partly mine,' said Robert, taking a hasty turn up and down the room. 'It was more the fault of that villain Blodget: may heaven's avenging lightnings scathe and blast him! May his own happiness and peace of mind be wrecked as ours have been!'

Fanny sobbed bitterly, and dared not raise her eyes to Robert's agitated countenance. The young man took two or three turns up and down the bar-room, and then he became a little calmer, and pausing near the table at which he had been sitting, threw a furtive glance towards the weeping Fanny.

'And you have really fallen so low as your presence here seems to imply?' said he, endeavoring to steady his voice, though it was low and tremulous, and his lips quivered as he spoke.

'Imagine the worse, and you will know all,' replied Fanny, in a broken and faltering voice. 'I have wished a hundred times that I were at the bottom of the bay, but I cannot do it. I pray for death, that I may be spared further misery and sin, and yet I live.'

'Heaven have mercy on us all, for we have need of mercy!' exclaimed Robert, in a tone which betrayed the emotion that he felt, and leaning with his elbows on the table, he buried his face in his hands.

He heard Fanny sobbing, but for some moments neither of them moved or spoke. Then he heard a slight rustling, and he removed his hands from his pale and agitated countenance, and slowly raised his head. Fanny was hurriedly leaving the room; it was her mantle brushing the door as she passed out, which he had heard. He sighed heavily, and then he dropped his head upon his hands again, and sat silent and motionless, until roused by the entrance of the bar-keeper who, thinking that he was asleep, shook him, and bawled that he was going to close the house. Then he arose, quitted the house, and walked slowly, and with an expression of misery and despair upon his pale countenance. The rain had now degenerated into a thick fog, through which the lamps twinkled dimly, and the pavement was covered with thin mire of the color and adhesive quality which distinguishes the mud of San Francisco, except where the broken condition of the pavement of the footway permitted the turbid water to lay in large puddles, dimly reflecting the street lamps. Regardless of the puddles, Robert walked on, now with his eyes fixed upon the miry pavement, and now looking forward with contracted brow and moving though silent lips; and when he reached a lane, he went straight on and entered a house. Thither we will not immediately follow him.

On leaving the bar-room, where she had encountered Robert Jervis, Fanny had hurried down to the wharf, where she began to walk more slowly, the terrible excitement which had until then impelled her onward, beginning to subside. But though she walked more slowly, she kept towards the bay, and still walked slowly onwards. About the hour of one, she advanced towards steps leading down to some water. It was not the first time since she had added herself to the thousands of unfortunate women who seek the wages of sin, that she sought the bay with suicidal purposes, but there was something so terrible and so awful to her mind in the thought of death, that she had never dared to attempt the execution of it.

'It must be done,' she murmured, as she approached the steps. 'I can endure this dreadful life no longer.'

She descended the steps hurriedly, but on the lowest that was uncovered by the water, she paused, and gazed upon the dark bosom of the flood that rolled with a hoarse dull murmur.

'Death! What is it?' murmured the miserable girl, clasping her small white hands, and looking down upon the water that rolled darkly at her feet. 'Awful mystery, which I wish, yet fear, to solve! Is it but the intermediate state which mortals pass through to free the soul from the grossness which clogs it during its sojourn on earth, and fit it for a higher and happier state of existence? or is it a long sleep—a night without dreams, and to which no morrow comes? Is it, as some say, the chrysalis state from which we emerge into new life, like the butterfly? Unfortunate analogy!—the repugnance to the soul's annihilation, this longing after immortality? Oh there must be something beyond the grave, though what I cannot say. It cannot be worse, whatever it may be than the life I am leading.'

She paused in her muttered soliloquy, thinking she heard soft and cautious footsteps behind her, but on casting a look up the steps, she saw no one; indeed the fog prevented her from seeing more than a couple of yards.

'It is nothing,' she muttered. 'Now to end a life of which I have long been weary! It is but a plunge—a splashing of the water—a circling ripple on the surface—and all will be over!'

As she murmured these words, the poor girl threw herself into the dark waters, adding to the long list of man's perfidy and inhumanity—'One more unfortunate victim.'

# CHAPTER XV

We must now return for a space to Inez and her captors. The unfortunate girl had but a very confused idea of where she was being conveyed. When the party reached the ranch she was taken from her horse, and carried rather than led, into the building.

She was taken down a narrow flight of steps into what appeared to her to be a subterranean apartment. And such, in fact it was, for the dwelling to which she had been taken had formerly been a portion of one of the old mission establishments, which are so numerous in California. The vaults beneath it, had doubtless been excavated as a place of retreat in case of attacks from hostile Indians, or as a depository for the sacred vessels of the church.

At length they reached the bottom of this subterranean flight of stairs, and then she was borne along a narrow passage of considerable length, the footsteps of her ruffianly abductor raising dismal and prolonged echoes. Her brain began to reel before the appalling idea that she was being carried into the bowels of the earth, perhaps to be immured for life in some dungeon, where the atmosphere would be close and damp—where moisture would trickle down the green and slimy walls—perhaps, to be deprived of life; or, maybe, and the thought made her shudder convulsively, subjected to the brutal lusts of some vile miscreant whose crimes had made him shrink into gloomy vaults from the light of day and the arm of retributive justice.

Her bearer seemed to be fatigued with her weight for he twice set her down and rested a few moments. At length the end of the journey appeared to be reached, and she was now laid down upon some blankets, and the gag removed from her mouth, and the covering from her head, and when she cast a glance of terrified apprehension around the place to which she had been brought she was alone and in profound and impenetrable darkness.

Almost frantically the unfortunate maiden gave vent to her long-suppressed emotions in a piercing shriek, and then sank into insensibility.

How long Inez lay in that state of insensibility which came upon her when she found herself alone and in utter darkness, in the place to which she had been borne, she had no means of ascertaining; but at length consciousness returned to the bewildered maiden by slow degrees. Back from the memory cells of her brain came the recollection of her retiring to bed the evening previous beneath her father's roof, then the midnight abduction, the long and fearful ride, and her falling insensible in the dark and gloomy chamber in which she now was.

'Where was she? Why was she brought there?'

She rose from the floor, and groping with her hands to avoid coming in contact with any projecting article of furniture, she made a few cautious steps in the direction of the door, by which she had been borne into the room by her abductor, but her hands encountered no tangible indication of an entrance.

The secret door, the darkness that seemed palpable, all must be parts of some infernal contrivance to shroud in secrecy and mystery some diabolical outrage, from the contemplation of the probable nature of which she shrank in horror. Through that concealed door which she could not discover, but which she yet knew to exist, the perpetrator would enter—those walls would shut in every sound, and deaden every shriek—that palpable darkness would veil the crime, and guard from the chance of future recognition the criminal! It was dreadful for one so innocent, so defenceless to stand there alone, enveloped in darkness, anticipating all that was horrible and revolting to her pure mind, and fearfully conscious of her utter powerlessness to evade her impending doom.

She clasped her hands, and though in darkness, her eyes wandered round the room, and could any one have seen her countenance at that moment, it would have been seen pale and impressed with an aspect of mingled wildness and despair. A new thought suddenly struck her, and partly stilled the tumult of her mind; she would pray—it was impossible, she thought, that God would forsake her, if she prayed to Him, for succor and deliverance. In obedience to this impulse, she knelt down upon the thick carpet, and prayed long and fervently that He whose name was Love, and whose attributes were Power, Wisdom, Justice and Mercy, would deliver her from the doom which was impending over her, whether that doom was a violent death, or dishonoring outrage, which she dreaded most. This act of devotion exercised a tranquillizing influence over her mind, and she rose from her knees considerably comforted and strengthened.

While Inez was still pondering upon her condition she heard a door open and close. The person who entered ignited a match and lit a lamp, and confronted the trembling girl. Judge of her horror when she recognized one of the villains whom she had seen engaged in burying the murdered man in the old adobe building. Although her knees trembled with fright she mustered courage enough to ask him, 'What means this outrage, sir.'

'It means this,' said Blodget, for it was that miscreant himself who stood before her. 'It means this,—that you take the oath which I shall administer, swearing in the most solemn terms never to reveal aught that has happened since you left the mission last evening. The second is, that you become my mistress.'

'Then I reject your conditions with scorn and abhorrence!' exclaimed Inez turning away.

'Reflect well, my charmer,' said the villain.

'Cease, sir!' exclaimed Inez. 'Say no more! I reject your offers with disdain.'

'I thought to find you more reasonable,' said Blodget after a pause. 'However, if you hold out a week, you will be the first who ever did. There are some slices of fowl and ham, and some bread, and a pint of wine, in the basket; and in the evening I shall visit you again.'

As he turned to leave the room, Inez bent her gaze steadily upon the door, in the hope of detecting the means by which it was opened, but it had only the appearance of a portion of the wall, revolving upon hinges, and undiscoverable on the inside when closed, from the uniform appearance which the entire wall then presented alike to the eye and the touch. The door again rolled noiselessly on its hinges, it closed with a click, and Inez was alone in the pitchy darkness of her prison.

Satisfied that there must be some means of acting upon the concealed mechanism connected with the door, she ran her hands over the inside, and pressed every square inch with her fingers, in the hope of touching something which would set in action the secret spring. This manipulation producing no result, she next treaded the floor near the door in the same manner, but still without making any discovery. It then occurred to her that the spring might be situated above her reach, and instantly mounting upon the wicker basket which Blodget had brought her, she felt over the upper part of the door, and the wall around and above it as far as she could reach.

An indescribable emotion of joy and hope thrilled through her bosom, as her fingers all at once encountered a small knob or button, about six feet from the floor, which yielded to the pressure, and acting on some concealed mechanism, caused the heavy door to revolve slowly and noiselessly upon its hinges. Stepping from the basket, she peered into the semi-obscurity of the lobby upon which the door opened, and discovering an ascending flight of stairs, she felt half inclined to venture up them; but on reflection, she thought such a step would be imprudent, and satisfied with possessing the means of opening the door at pleasure, she closed it to reflect, at leisure, upon the way in which she should make her discovery available for the purpose of escape.

The impression that the door which she had discovered was not the one by which she had been borne into the chamber by her abductor still lingering in her mind, she resolved to examine the opposite wall in the same manner; and, setting the basket against the wall, she stood upon it as before, and passed her hand over the wall in every direction. To her great joy she was not long in discovering a knob similar to that which communicated with the secret spring of the other door, and pressing upon it, a door opened like the one by which Blodget had entered, and the rush of cold air which fanned her cheek, and the continued darkness, called to her mind the recollection of the subterraneans through which she had been borne the preceding night.

She hesitated for a moment, and then she advanced her right foot cautiously, and found that she stood at the head of a flight of steps leading downward. She descended two or three, and then she returned to her chamber and closed the door, resolving to wait until night before venturing into the subterraneans, so fearful was she of having her evasion detected before her escape was complete, and of steps being taken to preclude the possibility of a second attempt. The cravings of her stomach now began to demand attention, and feeling that some degree of vigor would be required to enable her to complete her escape, she sat down, and taking the provisions from the basket, ate a portion of the bread and meat. She hesitated as she afterwards raised the wine to her lips, lest it should be drugged, but reflecting that such a step was little likely to be resorted to after the open violence to which she had been subjected on the preceding night, she took a small quantity, and then began to reflect upon the course which she should pursue.

By deferring her attempt to escape until night, as she had determined, she would be exposed, she now reflected, to a repetition of the outrage of the preceding night; and would likewise be less capable of ascertaining correctly the house in which she was a prisoner than she would be should she escape by daylight. She therefore opened the door by pressing upon the knob which communicated with the secret spring, and cautiously ascended the dark flight of stone stairs. She reached the top in safety, groped her way along a passage of considerable length, and at the end was involved in as pitchy a darkness as before.

At length she knocked her head against a flat stone which appeared to seal up the subterranean staircase, and almost reeled under the concussion; but recovering from the blow in a few moments, she endeavored to raise the stone by pressing upward with her hands and shoulders. The stone was heavy, but at length she succeeded in raising it on end, and when thus poised it was easily removed from the aperture, and she emerged into a large gloomy vault or cellar, which was little less dark than the stairs and passage which she had traversed, or the chamber from which she had escaped. The only light came from a rude doorway in one corner, where she could see the bottom of a flight of rough steps, towards which she hurried; but at the moment she put her foot upon the lowermost step she heard rough voices.

No sound from the underground chambers in which Inez was imprisoned could by any possibility reach the outside of the building, even had there been neighbors in the vicinity, but the place was far remote from any other human habitation. She had no means of marking the flight of time, and could not even distinguish between day and night. But her persecutor had told her that he should visit her again in the evening, and she resolved to be in readiness to fly the moment the first warning sound of his intrusion struck upon her listening ears. At length when she heard the click of the secret spring, she ascended with precipitation the stone stairs which led, as she thought, to liberty.

She had scarcely reached the top, when she heard hurried footsteps behind her, and, without casting a look backwards, she fled in terror along the subterranean passage. Her rapid footsteps were echoed by those of her pursuer. She had nearly reached the top of the stone stairs leading to the place in which she had found a lamp, and the means of lighting it, when she stumbled over a stone, or some other impediment, and fell prostrate upon the ground, a scream bursting from her lips, and the lamp falling from her hand.

By this untoward mischance, the lamp became extinguished, and before she could recover her feet, she heard the footsteps of her pursuer close at hand; and in another moment she felt herself clasped round the waist, and all her faculties succumbing to the force of terror, she became insensible.

It was Blodget who had pursued her, and he was greatly alarmed lest she should escape.

As he was bearing her insensible body into the chamber, a new cause of alarm presented itself. One of his accomplices in guilt rushed in to tell him that a party of horsemen, apparently Californians, had dismounted in a neighboring grove, and that two of their number were reconnoitering the ranch.

Blodget paused for a moment to think, and then speedily determined how to act.

The party of which the man spoke was composed of Monteagle, Joaquin, and a few Californians, who, after infinite pains, had discovered a clue to the course pursued by the capturers of Inez, and had traced them to the ranch in which she was a prisoner.—Joaquin and Blodget had approached the house in order to determine the best course to pursue in order to capture the villains and release Inez.

'Listen,' said Blodget to his accomplice. 'If they find me here, I may be recognized and arrested, if not for this, for other trifling affairs, which may end in neck-stretching. They can have no proof of our carrying off the girl, unless the wench is found. That is not possible, as no one can have any suspicion of the underground room.—They will search the house, and finding their search in vain, must leave the place. I will try to get off unobserved through the ravine at the back of the ranch, and catch the first horse I can find and make for the city. Let me hear from you as soon as they go, and we will concert future measures about the girl. I will be at our old place in Jackson street.'

As the villain concluded speaking, he drew and cocked his revolver, and noiselessly moved from the back of the house towards the ravine of which he had spoken.

Hardly had the ruffian entered the ravine ere he was descried by Monteagle, whose party had been placed so as almost to surround the ranch.

'Stop! or I fire,' cried Monteagle.

Blodget burst through the thicket, and Monteagle leaped his horse after him, but the fugitive turned sharply round the moment the horse's hoofs touched the turf, and discharged his revolver. The darkness and hurry in which he fired prevented him from taking aim, and Monteagle remained unscathed, but the bullet crashed through the head of the horse, and the animal reared up, and then fell upon its side and expired.

Blodget fled precipitately, and as soon as Monteagle could extricate himself from his dead horse, he rushed after him, calling loudly on his friends. Two of them followed him, but Blodget kept the advantage which he had gained by shooting the horse, and sped across the meadows with the swiftness of a hunted coyote. Beyond the ravine there was a high steep hill, thinly wooded, and on the farther side of the hill a thick and extensive wood. If he could gain this wood, he doubted not that he should be enabled to baffle his pursuers, and he made for the hill with the speed of a grayhound.

He threw a hurried look behind him as he reached the foot of the hill, and then dashed up the ascent, for he heard behind him the shouts of his pursuers and the voice of Monteagle urging the two men to come on faster. The hill was steep, and, except where a scanty vegetable soil had been formed during successive winters by the decay of moss and leaves, its rugged side was covered with smooth pebbles, in which the fugitive's feet sunk and slipped as he toiled upward. Until Monteagle reached the hill, therefore, Blodget lost ground, but when his pursuers commenced the fatiguing ascent they were again upon an equality.

The pursuers and pursued were unable to see each other, and could only discover their relative positions by pausing to listen, and then only by such sounds as the slipping of pebbles under the feet, the rolling down of some displaced stone, the rustling of brambles and brakes, or the snapping of boughs. The hill became steeper as the robber and his pursuers approached the summit, and they had to grasp the boughs of dwarf oaks to assist them in the ascent, and sometimes to drag themselves over the smooth faces of bare brown rocks, polished by atmospheric influences, clinging to roots of trees which appeared above the soil, and inserting their toes into crevices, or setting them upon projecting points.

Near the summit Blodget paused to rest, to listen, and to look behind him; below him he heard the voices of his panting pursuers, the rustling of bushes and brakes, and the grating sound of their footsteps in the loose pebbles. He wiped the sweat from his brow, and then he resumed his clambering progress, still hoping to find a refuge in the wood on the other side. The summit of the hill was sharp and bare, the brown rock coming to the surface uncovered by the scantiest layer of soil, and its bald crest passed, he had little fear of his ultimate escape. A glen, or ravine, the sides of which were clothed with breaks or ferns, led from the summit down to the wood, and the shortest way of gaining access to the glen from the side which he was ascending, was through a gap or cleft in the rocky crest of the hill. In the bottom of this gap laid a large fragment of rock, nearly flat on the upper side, and rounded at the edges by the abrading influence of rain and fog; probably it had originally been disruptured from the crags which arose on either side, and remained in that position for ages. It partly overhung the steep acclivity which Blodget was now clambering up, and by pausing a few moments to recruit his strength, and then clinging with his fingers to the fissures in the rock, he drew himself up until he reached its top in safety.

He felt the stone move as he crawled over its smooth flat top on his hands and knees, and as he paused for a moment in obedience to the instinct of self-preservation, he heard some stones in which the large rock was imbedded, roll down the hill, chinking against the pebbles, and bounding onwards, until arrested in their course by the boughs or roots of dwarf oaks and wild lilacs which grew upon its side. It was clear that the impulsion which his weight had given to the stone, had displaced these small fragments, chipped from itself or the crags which it laid between when it first fell there, and he hesitated in the fear that in quitting the stone he should cause it to topple over, and be crushed by its falling upon him.

In this dilemma he determined to leap from the middle of it, in order to avoid overbalancing it, and, standing upright for a moment, he measured the leap with his eye as well as the darkness of the night would permit, and bounded forward like a mountain goat. He cleared the edge of the stone, and alighted in safety below it, on the other side of the hill; but again some fragments of rock rolled down, and he sprang aside, lest the whole ponderous mass should slip from its position and hurl him before it down the hill. But the massive rock moved not, and he sped down the hill with the speed of a deer.

Monteagle had made slower progress than the robber up the steepest part of the hill, and his companions did not engage in the chase with equal vigor. Hence they allowed Monteagle to keep the lead; and, on coming near the summit of the hill, they diverged from the track which he was following in order to reach the glen on the other side without passing over the large stone which has been described. Monteagle had caught a glimpse of Blodget as the dark figure of the latter was for a moment dimly defined against the lighter darkness of the sky, when he stood upon the stone to leap into the glen, and shouting, 'There he is!' he strained up the steep acclivity direct for the gap in the hill's bare and rocky crest.

He was not aware until he reached it of the obstacle presented by the massive stone; but, as Blodget had passed over it, he thought he could do the same; and, clinging to it with both hands, drew himself up, and succeeded in reaching the flat top; but scarcely had he done so when there was a rustling fall of stones from beneath, the massive fragment of rock slid from its place, and a shriek of terror burst from the lips of Monteagle as he found himself falling backwards, and the stone with him.

His two friends heard the cry, and for a moment stood silent and motionless on the steep hill-side, with their hands still holding the boughs and roots which they had grasped to aid their ascent. They heard the great stone rush with a dull hoarse sound a few yards, and then bound down the hill, crashing through the dwarf oaks and clumps of lilac, snapping the tender trunks of the mountain trees, and grating over the loose pebbles which filled the channels made by the rapid descent of water during heavy rains; but that cry of horror and affright was not repeated, and in a few moments all was still upon the dark and lonely hill.

'It is the great stone!' said one with bated breath.

'Poor fellow,' ejaculated the other, with a shudder. 'If it has fallen on him, he is crushed!'

'Let us look for him,' said the first. 'Hush! I thought I heard a groan.'

They listened, but heard nothing, save the sighing of the night wind among the trees, and they went towards the spot from which Monteagle had fallen, and followed the track of the displaced stone, which was marked by broken boughs and torn herbage, down the hill. About fifty yards down they found our hero lying against a bush, which had arrested his further progress. The night was too dark for them to perceive the full extent of the injuries which he had received, but the inertness of the body when lifted from the ground, gave but faint hope that vitality remained. A rude litter was made of boughs, and the crushed body being placed upon it, was borne down the hill and across the meadows to a little ranch not far from the place.

# CHAPTER XVI

A rude chorus that was being sung, or rather shouted by several coarse and desperate-looking men, who were seated around a table in a back room of a very low cabaret, and which was never visited only by the most depraved persons who resided in, or resorted to the neighborhood. They were thieves, and if anything could be judged from their countenances, they were capable of doing the most desperate deeds. The table was covered with glasses containing gin, rum, and brandy, and of which they had all been evidently partaking very freely, and they were smoking as hard as they were able.

There was a large wood fire upon the hearth; and the red glare it cast upon their features, gave them almost a supernatural appearance, and altogether the scene was as effective as one of those that are often represented in a melodrama. Obscene jokes and songs had been freely indulged in, and it did not seem as if they were inclined to leave off for some time. It was night, and the wind blew boisterous without, but the ruffians were making such a riot, that they heeded it not; and they were evidently determined to enjoy themselves to the most unlimited extent.

'Drink away, my lads,' said one Mike, raising the glass to his lips as he spoke;—'drink away; we ought to be merry, for Fortune never smiled more brightly upon us than she has done for some time past.'

'Ay, you say right, Mike,' observed a tall, dark whiskered man, whom the thieves called Joe; 'but leave us alone for doing business, and for availing themselves of fortune's favors when they are to be obtained. Cap'n a toast!'

'Ay, a toast; a toast;' responded the others.

Mike raised a large glass, filled to the brim in his hand, and said;—

'Well, my lads, I will give you a toast, and that shall be, Success to our dare-devil gang!'

'Bravo! bravo!' shouted the thieves. 'Here's to the dare-devil gang!'

'A capital toast,' said Mike; 'and well responded to. With your leave, I will propose another.'

'Ay, ay, a toast from Mike,' shouted two or three of the thieves, amongst whom he was a particular favorite; 'a toast from Mike.'

'Fill your glasses then, my boys,' said Mike; 'bumpers! bumpers!'

The thieves needed no second invitation to do as Mike desired, and the glasses were very quickly replenished.

'Here's confusion to the Vigilance Committee!' was Mike's toast; and it was followed by loud shouts from every one in the room; the landlord of the house at that moment entering, and joining loudly in acclamation of it.

'Ah!' observed Joe,—'they have found us rather troublesome customers to deal with, and will again if they should venture to attack us.'

'I don't think that there is much fear of that,' returned Mike; 'for we keep too well out of their clutches, and have met with such a career of success, that we may set them at defiance!'

'Ay, ay,' answered Mike; 'and may we be always able to do so; and all those daring fellows, who will run the risk to live a free life.'

'But Jenkins,' asked Mike, 'do you not think that it was a very foolish thing for us to loose so much time in affecting the accomplishment of this plot of Blodget's?'

'Certainly not,' returned Jenkins; 'Blodget has well rewarded us, and it will ultimately pay us much better than a trip to the mines would have done.'

'How?' demanded Mike.

'Why, Blodget must continue to do the thing that's liberal, or else his game will be up,' replied Jenkins. 'The lady is in our power, and we must continue to keep her so; if Blodget does not come to our terms, why, Old de Castro, no doubt, will, and, therefore, we are sure of a reward one way or the other.'

'Yes, the gallows!' observed one of the thieves, who had been sitting apart from the rest, and smoking his cigar heartily, did not seem to feel any particular interest in what was passing.

'There's Ben at his croaking again,' said Mike; 'he seems to take a delight in—'

'Speaking the truth,' added Ben, in a quiet tone; 'it is very unpleasant to hear it sometimes.'

'Pshaw! don't make yourself a fool, Ben,' exclaimed Jenkins; 'any one would suppose, to hear you talk, that you had become tired of a thief's life. But what think ye of my determination, my lads?'

'It is a famous one,' answered Mike, 'and cannot fail to work us good.'

'It must add much to our coffers one way or another,' resumed Jenkins; 'and I take no small credit to myself for the thought; besides, you know that we have the fellow, Blodget, entirely in our power, that murder, which—'

'Right, right,' interrupted Mike; 'if that were known, it would not be long before Mr. Blodget would swing upon a gallows.'

'Indeed it would not,' returned Jenkins; 'and he knows that, and dreads us. The lady is a beautiful woman, and I almost envy him his prize; but something may yet happen to place her in my possession instead of his, and I do not know that I should be over nice about availing myself of such an opportunity.'

At this moment, between the pauses of the blast, they heard a loud knocking at the door, and they looked at each other suspiciously, and starting involuntarily to their feet, placed their hands upon their revolvers, and prepared for action in case they should be surprised.

'Who is there?' demanded the landlord.

'It is only I, Blodget,' was the answer, and being satisfied that it was his voice, the door was cautiously opened, and the villain entered. He greeted them all heartily, and then, by the invitation of Jenkins, having taken his seat at the table, the mirth of the gang was resumed, and carried on with increased spirit, Blodget joining in with as much freedom as if he had been one of the gang.

'Well, Mr. Blodget,' asked Jenkins, 'and don't you think I managed this business very well for you?'

'Aye, Jenkins,' answered Blodget; 'you did everything that I could wish; but think you she will be safe where she is?'

'Safe!' repeated Jenkins; 'as safe as when she was buried deep in the bowels of the earth. Gordon is just the man who will take care of her.'

'That is well,' replied Blodget; 'but it is not unlikely that I shall not have any occasion to trouble him long.'

'Why, you would never be such a fool as to attempt to remove her from a place of security?' demanded Jenkins.

'Circumstances may compel me so to do.'

'I understand you; but we must see about the best means of preventing all chance of that,' said Jenkins; 'you have been a lucky fellow, Blodget, to get the lady in your power and at your mercy; it is glorious revenge.'

'It is, it is!' answered Blodget; 'but not sufficient to gratify me.'

'No?'

'No!'

'What would you, then?'

'I would have the life of Monteagle.'

'Ah! would you, then, again commit murder?'

'Hold!' said Blodget; 'mention not my former crime; I cannot think of it without horror.'

'And yet you can contemplate another deed equally as sanguinary?'

'Yes, the death of the detested Monteagle I can contemplate, coolly contemplate; and I shall never rest satisfied until it is accomplished.'

'And would you dare to perpetrate it yourself?' asked Jenkins.

'I dare,' answered Blodget; 'were he to cross my path; but were I to follow him to the Mission, or wherever he may be, I should in all probability be discovered, and taken prisoner, and then all my schemes would at once be frustrated. If any one would undertake to commit the crime, I would not fail to reward them handsomely.'

'I see,' said Jenkins; 'you would have me or one of my men perpetrate the deed of blood!'

'I care not who it is, so that it is a man on whom I can depend.'

'And the reward?'

'A thousand dollars!'

'It shall be done.'

'Ah! say you so? when?'

'Come, come, you are in too much of a hurry; and there is never anything done well where so much precipitation is used. We must first ascertain where Monteagle is.'

'And that we may have some difficulty at present in finding out,' said Blodget, 'for, doubtless, he has gone in search of Inez. My heart throbs impatiently for the accomplishment of the deed, and I shall not rest until I am sure that Monteagle is no more.'

'On your promise of the reward you have mentioned, the deed shall, by some means or other, be despatched,' replied Jenkins; 'but you must wait with patience, and we will not lose any time or opportunity to discover where he is, and to put our plans into execution.'

'This assurance gratifies me, and I am satisfied that you will not deceive me!'

'You have had no reason to doubt me hitherto,' returned Jenkins; 'and, therefore, there is no occasion to do so now, I believe.'

'But have you any idea how to proceed?' asked Blodget.

'In the first place,' returned Jenkins—'It will be the best plan to send one of the gang to the Mission, in disguise. He may be able to learn the proceedings of Monteagle, and probably find out where he is.'

'I agree with your design,' said Blodget, in reply; 'and should it meet with success, I shall not be very particular in giving a few additional dollars to the sum already promised. But Inez, for whom I have run such a risk, still remains obstinate; and I do not think I shall be able to conquer her aversion in a hurry.'

'And of what consequence will that be as she is in your power, she must yield to your wishes, or you can gain your desires by force.'

'Force! but I would rather that persuasion would prevail; as notwithstanding my passion, I cannot bear the idea of violence.'

'Why, true, it would be much better if it were avoided,' observed Jenkins, 'but come, drink!'

'Here's success to all our undertakings,' said Blodget; and he quaffed off the contents of his glass.

'Success to all our undertakings,' responded the thieves and the toast was drank tumultuously.

'You have been a fortunate fellow, Blodget, throughout your whole career, and have, no doubt, accumulated some money.'

'Why,' returned Blodget, with a self-satisfied grin; 'I have not much cause to grumble. But then I have had to depend upon my own wit and ingenuity.'

'Well, certainly, Blodget, you are a most perfect villain.'

'I believe I may lay some slight claim to the character.'

'Not a very slight one either,' remarked Jenkins.

'You pay me a very high compliment.'

'Ha! ha! ha!'

'But who among your gang will undertake the murder?'

Jenkins looked round upon his fellows, but in not one of their countenances, reckless and determined as they were, did he notice any signs of a desire to undertake the sanguinary deed.

'Who among ye is willing to earn this reward?' he asked.

There was no answer. Blodget became impatient.

'What! are ye all silent?' asked Jenkins.

No one offered to speak.

'What say you Mike?'

'I like not the shedding of human blood when it can be avoided,' he answered; 'if, however, Jenkins, you order me to perpetrate this crime, although it is against my inclination, I will obey you: if I am permitted to use my own free will, I say I will not commit the crime. Will that answer suffice?'

'It will,' said Jenkins; 'but Joe, you will not refuse the thousand dollars?'

'I would not stain my hands with innocent blood for twenty times one thousand dollars, unless it was by your command,' was the answer.

'And Ben, what say you?'

'I am a robber, ready to defend myself and my comrades from an attack; but I am not a cold-blooded deliberate murderer,' replied Ben.

'Damnation!' cried Blodget, fiercely; and he arose from his seat and hastily traversed the room.

'Be patient,' said Jenkins; 'this matter will be arranged, quicker than you could possibly expect. You see, Blodget, although they are desperate men, they are not quite such atrocious monsters as they have been thought by many.'

'They are cowards if they shrink from the—'

Before he could finish the sentence, the thieves were all upon their feet, and by their menacing looks, threatened vengeance.

'Hold!' cried Blodget, and they all immediately resumed their seats, although it was very evident that the observations of Blodget had greatly enraged them, and there were many scowling brows, which convinced the villain that he had proceeded almost too far.

'Blodget,' continued Jenkins, after a pause; 'you should be cautious in what you say, my men are not used to hearing such terms applied to them, nor do they merit it.' If Jenkins thought he had a coward amongst his gang, he would hang him up to the first tree he came to.

'I was wrong; I was wrong;' hastily apologized Blodget; 'and I hope they will pardon me.'

'That is enough,' observed Jenkins; then turning again towards his men, he demanded—

'And, so you all refuse to do this deed?'

'We do;' was the answer from them all; 'we shed not human blood only in our own defence.'

'One amongst ye shall do the deed, since I have promised this man, and will not recall my word;' said Jenkins peremptorily.

There was a discontented murmuring arose from among the thieves.

'What means this murmuring?' demanded Jenkins, and his eyes glanced fiercely upon them; 'is there one among ye who would dare to disobey my commands?'

'I will answer for all my comrades, and say, no,' said Ben; 'but we would avoid an unnecessary deed of blood, and especially under the circumstances.'

'I have given my word, and it shall be kept;' said Jenkins firmly; 'you must cast lots!'

The thieves still looked dissatisfied at this determination, and glanced significantly at each other, but they did not say a word. They scowled upon Blodget, who, however, did not take much heed of them, certain as he was, that while the captain of the gang was on his side, he had nothing to fear from any act of violence they might otherwise contemplate towards him.

Reluctantly they were about to cast lots, when there was the well-known signal heard at the room door, which being opened, Gordon was admitted.

'Ah!' exclaimed Blodget, 'you have just come in time, Gordon; I have a proposition to make to you.'

'Name it,' answered the ruffian.

Jenkins repeated the question he had put to the others. Gordon appeared to catch at the idea, and the thieves eagerly awaited his reply, anxious to be released from the perpetration of a crime, from which they all revolted.

Gordon did not make any immediate answer, and he appeared to be meditating upon the proposal.

'Do you also hesitate, Gordon?' inquired the captain;—'you were not always so particular.'

'I do not hesitate, only for one reason;' returned the miscreant.

'Name it!' said Blodget.

'Let Blodget give two thousand dollars, and the deed shall be accomplished,' was the villain's answer.

'It shall be yours,' ejaculated Blodget.

'Enough!' said Gordon, 'I have your word that the money shall be paid, and Jenkins, no doubt, will be answerable that you do not fly from your agreement?'

'I will,' returned the captain.

'There is no occasion for it,' observed Blodget, 'if you do not deceive me, I will not deceive you.'

'You had better not,' said Gordon, with a sinister look.

'You have good security for my keeping my promise,' added Blodget; 'let the deed be done, and the money shall immediately be yours.'

'But if I should fail?'

'If you do not wilfully fail, then one half the money shall be your reward for your trouble,' said Blodget.

'Enough,' replied Gordon, 'then the bargain is sealed; I will undertake the hazardous deed.'

'Thanks, thanks!' said the blood-thirsty Blodget; 'perform your task well, and you will have my eternal gratitude.'

'Pshaw!' cried the ruffian, with a sardonic grin; 'of what use is gratitude to me? It is not a marketable commodity. But what about the care of Inez?'

'Blodget will reside in the house during your absence, and I will leave Joe to assist him in his charge,' replied the captain.

'That arrangement will do,' said Gordon, after a pause.

'When will you start on your expedition?' inquired Blodget.

'Immediately. There is no necessity for delay,' answered Gordon.

'Tis well,' observed Blodget; 'but you will go disguised?'

'Oh, leave me alone for that,' returned Gordon. 'I have more reasons than one not to wish to be known; or the first news that you heard of me would, in all probability be, that I was the inmate of a prison. I will so disguise myself that it must be a penetrating eye, indeed which could recognize me.'

'To-morrow, then?'

'I quit this place, and make my way for the Mission,' rejoined Gordon.

'True; and to meet with success, I trust.'

'It shall not be my fault, if I do not.'

'You will forward us intelligence when you arrive there; for I shall be all impatience till I hear from you;' said Blodget.

'I will,' replied Gordon, 'unless I see that there would be any danger in so doing.'

'Certainly.'

'And now that this business is settled,' observed Jenkins, 'let us proceed to enjoy ourselves—come, my lads, replenish your glasses.'

The thieves obeyed this order with hilarity, and the villain Blodget being satisfied with the inhuman design he had formed, and the atrocious wretch who had undertaken to accomplish it, joined heartily with them in their revelry, which they kept up for more than an hour afterwards, when Blodget, Gordon, and Joe returned to the house, and the captain and the rest of the thieves departed.

Blodget felt a savage sensation of delight fill his bosom, at the prospect of the full consummation of his most diabolical hatred and revenge against Monteagle; and he entertained the most sanguine anticipations of the success of his plot. Gordon was a deep, designing, and determined villain, and he had no doubt but that the reward which he had promised him, would induce him to exert himself to the uttermost.

'Yes,' he soliloquized, when he was alone in his chamber, after parting with Gordon and Joe for the night; 'I feel confident that Gordon will not fail, and, that ere many weeks have elapsed, my hated foe will be no more. Oh, this will be goodly revenge. Inez, too, will then be securely mine, and nothing will release her from my power!'

The wretch paced his chamber, as he thus spoke, and his eyes sparkled with exultation. He pictured to himself in imagination, the unbounded bliss that was in store for him in the gratification of his sensual and disgusting passions, and he determined that but a short time should elapse, ere he would have the full accomplishment of all his wishes. He slept but little that night, for thinking upon his villainous stratagems, and when he reflected that he was beneath the same roof with the unfortunate Inez, and had it in his power to force her to an immediate compliance with his wishes, he could with difficulty keep his ecstasy within the bounds of reason.

In the morning Gordon, after having so disguised himself that no person could by any possibility recognize him, and having received some fresh instructions and injunctions from Blodget, took his departure on his inhuman errand, and Blodget and Joe, with an old woman, were left alone in the house.

We need not inform the reader of the distracting hours of misery Inez had undergone since her incarceration in the house. Her sufferings were almost too powerful for human endurance, and it was wonderful how she could retain her senses. Her agonizing thoughts were divided between her own situation and that of her father, and her disordered imagination pictured them, if possible, more dreadful than they actually were.

'I shall never behold him again,' she sighed, and scalding tears chased each other down her pale cheeks; 'alas! I am torn from them forever. Or, if we should be again destined to meet, under what circumstances may it not be? Myself, perhaps, dishonored—heart-broken; my poor father a raving maniac. Oh, Heavens! the picture that arises upon my imagination is too horrible for contemplation.'

She wrung her hands, and traversed her gloomy chamber with a trembling step.

'To be beneath the same roof with a murderer, too,' she added, 'and that, too, a murderer of the blackest dye! Oh, God! have I not good reason to be distracted? That terrible night when I overheard the wretches conversing upon the monstrous crime of which they had been guilty—when I saw them inter the mangled body of the poor white-haired old man, their unfortunate victim, comes fresh upon my memory as if it had only been just enacted. My heart seems chilled to ice; oh, surely the misfortunes that have since attended me have been a curse upon me for not having given such information of the circumstance as might have led to the apprehension of the assassins. The unfortunate old man's bones moulder in unhallowed ground, and his blood calls to Heaven for retribution.'

She trembled violently, and almost imagined that she heard a melancholy sigh breathed close to her ear. She staggered to a chair and leant upon it for support, fearing to look around her, lest she should encounter the ghastly and blood-stained face of the murdered man.

All was profoundly still in the house, and the miscreants who inhabited it seemed to be locked in the arms of sleep. Sleep! how could wretches whose consciences were burthened with such a heavy weight of crime, sleep?

The light in the lamp burnt dim, and imparted a still more gloomy appearance to the chamber; and the wind howled dismally without, increasing the horrors of that solemn hour. Inez seated herself by the side of her bed, and, after a pause, did once more venture to look around the room, but nothing but of an ordinary description met her observation.

'What dreadful crimes may they not have perpetrated in this house! in this very chamber!' She once more reflected, and again her terrors arose to a pitch almost insupportable.

The light in her lamp, which had for some time only been faintly glimmering, now suddenly died away, and our heroine was left in utter darkness. How she longed for the morning, and that she had some female companion near her in that dismal place, if it was only the repulsive old woman; some one to whom she could speak; but silent and dreary was everything around her, it was like being confined in a tomb. She had kept the embers of the fire together as long as she could, but that had also become extinguished, and the room felt cold as it was dismal and cheerless.

At length she crept into the bed with her clothes on, and covered her head with the counterpane, filled with a sensation of terror, she found it utterly impossible to conquer. She endeavored to sleep; but her mind was too much distressed to suffer her to succeed, and she tossed to and fro in a state of agitation, which no one but those who have been placed in a similar situation, can form an adequate idea of. The interview she had had with Blodget, rushed upon her memory, and she recollected every word that he had spoken, and which had given her every reason to apprehend the worse consequences from his determination. Even the sight of that inhuman man inspired her with a feeling of horror no language can do justice to, and she dreaded a meeting with him as much as she would have done the most fearful calamity which could have befallen her.

'But I will be firm,' she reflected; 'I will muster up all my woman's fortitude, strong in the defence of her honor, to meet him, and oppose his importunities in a manner that shall deter him from proceeding to violence. Providence surely will not forsake me in this moment of bitter trial, but will throw its protecting shield over me, and defeat the brutal designs of the libertine and the miscreant! Yes, I will put my trust in Heaven, and prepare to meet my heavy trials with a firmness and resolution becoming of me!'

These thoughts somewhat composed her spirits, and after a short time spent in further rumination, she did at last sink into a disturbed slumber, in which she remained until the sun had risen in the eastern horizon.

She arose, not in the least refreshed, and had not been up many minutes when she heard the key turning in the lock, and soon afterwards the old woman entered with the breakfast.

She placed them on the table, and then fixed upon our heroine a scrutinizing look, and shook her head.

'Well,' said she, in her usual disagreeable tones;—'pale cheeks and red eyes; no sleep again, I suppose, it puzzles me how you young women can live without rest? when I was your age, nothing could ever prevent my sleeping.'

'When the mind is oppressed with such unprecedented and heavy sorrows as those that disturb mine,' answered Inez—'if it is not entirely insensible, sleep may be courted in vain.'

'Pho! how very melancholy and dismal you do look, to be sure,' answered the old woman; 'any one would imagine that you had experienced all the troubles in the world; but stop till you become my age, and then you may have cause to complain.'

'Some person's troubles,' returned Inez; 'are brought on them by themselves; by their own vices, and—'

'Ah!' interrupted the old woman, snappishly; 'no doubt you think that a very pointed and sarcastic observation, but, as the cap don't happen to fit me, I shall not wear it. Mr. Blodget will pay you a visit presently, and perhaps you may deem it prudent to behave a little more civil to him.'

Inez shuddered.

'Oh, tell me,' she said; 'is he in the house?'

'Oh, yes, to be sure he is,' answered the old woman; 'for he has taken up his quarters here altogether now, and therefore you will have plenty of his company.'

'Living in the same house,' muttered our heroine to herself, and she trembled more violently than before; 'alas! what will become of me?'

'Oh, no doubt he will take plenty of care of you, young lady,' answered the old woman, with a bitter sneer.

'He shall find,' said Inez, mustering up sudden firmness, and speaking in a tone that astonished and abashed the old woman, 'he shall find that I have both the spirit and the virtue to resist his importunities, and Heaven will aid me to defeat his design. The guilty wretch; surely for his many crimes a terrible retribution must be now pending o'er his head.'

'The spirit you boast of, young lady,' said the old woman, 'I have no doubt will be very quickly turned, or Mr. Blodget is not half so accomplished as I take him to be.'

Inez darted upon her a look of disgust and indignation, but she could not make her any reply, and after making two or three observations of a similar description, the old woman quitted the room.

We need not attempt to describe the feelings of our heroine when the old woman had gone: the disgusting observations of the old woman, and the fearful prospects which was before her, filled her bosom with the utmost consternation, and although she tried very hard to rally her spirits, and prepare to meet Blodget with fortitude, it was some considerable time before she had it in her power to succeed. To know that Blodget was an inmate of the same house with her, was sufficient of itself to excite the greatest agony in her bosom; and when she reflected that it was not probable that he would longer be able to restrain his wild, unbridled passions, and that any resistance on her part, would be completely futile, she became almost distracted.—Alas! she thought, how much more preferable would death have been to the state of agony in which she was thus constantly kept. It was only for the sake of

Monteagle and her father, whom she could not entirely despair of beholding again, that she clung to life, and had she not had them to occupy her thoughts, and her heart's warmest affections, she would have met death with fortitude, nay, even pleasure. What had been the last few days of her life, but of misery? All mankind had seemed arrayed in enmity against her, and few indeed were the real friends she had found. Her tears flowed fast at these thoughts, and they gave relief to her overcharged bosom.

At length she struggled with her emotions, and so far regained her composure, that she was enabled to partake of the repast which the old woman brought her, and to prepare to meet Blodget, whom she had no doubt, and indeed the old woman had said he would, visit her in a short time.

She had but just risen from her knees having implored the protection of the Holy Virgin, when she heard footsteps ascending the stairs, and directly afterwards, her room door was unlocked, and the object of her fears and detestation entered.

He stood in the doorway for a minute or two, and it was hard to perceive whether he was awed and abashed by the calm dignity and firmness of her demeanor, or lost in admiration of her superlative beauty—still most exquisite, although her once blooming cheeks were pale and wan with heavy care.

Inez had mustered up uncommon fortitude, and, as Blodget entered, she fixed upon him a look which was sufficient to penetrate the most insensible breast. It was one of the most cutting reproach, while resentment, and a firm reliance upon the strength of her own virtue, and the protection of heaven, shown predominant in the general expression of her resistance, and approaching her with a look of admiration which could create no other sentiment than one of hatred in her breast, he attempted to take her hand and press her lips, but she hastily withdrew it and, spurning him scornfully away from her, exclaimed—

'Begone, sir, your presence is disgusting to me. Dare not thus to insult the victim of your guilt.'

'Who's the master, now, fair Inez?' demanded the villain, and a look of exultation overspread his features; 'who triumphs now?'

'Oh, villain—heartless villain!' cried Inez, her bosom swelling with agony, 'can you stand there and talk to me thus? Are you not afraid that the vengeance of the Almighty will immediately descend upon your head, and render you powerless to do further harm?'

'I scorn it.'

Inez shuddered with horror at the words of the wretch; who, however, presently altered his tone, and once more endeavoring to take her hand, which she successfully resisted, he assumed an insinuating smile, and in a voice of gentle persuasion, said—

'Pray pardon me, beauteous Inez, if I have been led into the expression of words that have caused anguish to your feelings; but the injuries I have received from Monteagle—'

''Tis false!' scornfully replied our heroine, and her brilliant eyes appeared to flash fire; 'Monteagle never injured you, but you was ever the serpent in his bosom, waiting an opportunity to destroy his peace, and you have yourself acknowledged the same, and expressed your inhuman exultation at the misery which you have caused him.'

'Well,' returned Blodget, with the utmost coolness, and the boldness of his manner increasing, 'I will not deny it, because there is no necessity for my so doing, as the power is now mine. I have already had a terrible revenge, but still it is not complete, and never will I rest until it is wholly accomplished.'

'Oh, Blodget!' ejaculated Inez, her fortitude failing her when she saw the villain's recklessness and determination, and reflected that she was entirely in his power, and left solely to his mercy, or the interposition of Providence, 'will nothing induce you to relent in your cruelty?'

'Nothing,' answered Blodget, 'until I have gained the full gratification of my wishes, and the consummation of all my hopes. Then only shall I be satisfied.'

'What mean you?'

'You will behold Monteagle no more.'

'Oh, God!' ejaculated Inez, and her heart throbbed heavily against her side, her cheeks turned ashy pale, and her limbs trembled violently as a dread of something terrible about to take place, through the guilty machinations of the wretch who stood before her, darted upon her brain; 'cruel as you are, surely you would not seek his life?'

A grim and sardonic smile passed over the features of Blodget as she gave utterance to these words, but he returned no answer; his looks spoke more than words, and had a thunderbolt at that moment descended upon her head, Inez could not have felt more paralyzed and awe-struck than she did at that time. With distended eye-lids, she fixed upon him a look which was sufficient to have penetrated even the most obdurate heart, and to carry awe to the guilty soul; her features became stern and fixed; her lips parted but she uttered no sound, and, suddenly approaching the astonished Blodget, she grasped his arm vehemently, and looked full upon him. Blodget could not help, in spite of all his hardihood, shuddering beneath her gaze, and the singularity of her behavior, but he was not a minute before he completely recovered himself, and looking coolly and indifferently upon her, awaited what she had got to say without first offering any observation of his own.

'Blodget!' at length ejaculated our heroine, in a solemn tone of voice, and with her brilliant and expressive eyes still fixed with the same earnestness of expression upon his countenance; 'Blodget, in the name of that Almighty power who guides all our actions, and before whose dread tribunal you must some time or the other appear, however much at present you may despise His name—by all your hopes of forgiveness for the many and heinous crimes you have committed, I charge you tell me—solemnly tell me, what are your wicked designs?'

'Psha!' cried Blodget, and a fearful smile again overspread his countenance.

'Nay, I command you, in the name of the most High, to set my horrible fears at rest, and tell me,' demanded Inez, and her heart throbbed more violently than ever, and her whole soul seemed to be wrapped up in the answer which Blodget would return to her; and she appeared as if she would drag the secret from his heart with her eyes.

'Enough of this,' at last said Blodget, 'I came not here to talk upon a subject like this, and—'

'Heartless miscreant!' interrupted Inez, 'too well can I read in your dark and portentous looks the base design you have in contemplation. But Heaven will interpose to prevent the execution of your infamous intention, and to save Monteagle from your monstrous machinations.'

'We shall see,' returned Blodget, with the same consummate coolness he had before evinced; 'we shall see. But hear me, Inez—'

'I will not listen to you, until you have answered my question,' observed Inez 'your very words are as poison to my soul.'

'But you must and shall hear me,' exclaimed the other, with a determined air, and once more endeavoring to take our heroine's hand; 'you are securely in my power, and think you that I will be frightened from my purpose by an obstinate woman's heroics. I come to offer you my love; you reject it, but that shall not avail you, for force shall make you comply with my wishes. As for Monteagle, I tell you once again you will see him no more.'

The courage of Inez completely failed her, tears gushed to her eyes, and, sinking upon her knees, with clasped hands, she supplicated the ruffian's forbearance; but she pleaded to a heart callous to every sense of feeling: he gazed upon her emotion with indifference, and he exulted at the manner in which he had subdued her spirit, and flattered himself that, in time, she would be entirely conquered, and made to yield subserviently to his will. However, he endeavored to disguise his real feelings, and, assuming as mild an expression as he could, he raised Inez from the posture in which she had been kneeling, and affected to smile kindly upon her. For the moment she was deceived by his looks, and hope suddenly darted upon her mind.

'You will relent,' she ejaculated, 'that smile assures me that you will. You cannot, surely, be so cruel as to seek the life of Monteagle. Has not the anguish you have already caused him, and the miseries he is at present undergoing, all through you, been the means of sufficiently appeasing your vengeance? Oh, Blodget! repent ere it is too late, and restore me to my friends, and again I promise you that you shall receive my pardon and that of those who are dear to me, although the injury you have inflicted on them and me is almost irreparable. If there is one spark of humanity in your breast, if there is the smallest portion of that feeling remaining in your heart, towards that sex who claims protection from every man, I shall not supplicate in vain; you will accede to my request, and once more open to me the doors of liberty; and suffer me to fly once more to the arms of my father—my poor bereaved parent!'

'Beauteous Inez,' returned the wretch; 'this is madness, and a silly waste of time. Think you, then, that after all the trouble I have taken, the risks I have run, and the plans I have laid down to get you in my power, that I will now quietly resign you? Think you that I would place myself at the mercy of my enemies? No, no! you must give up all idea of such a thing, and, henceforth, look upon me in the same light as your husband, for you and I must not again easily separate! You must yield to my wishes, and that speedily; I would have you do so of your own free will; but if, after a given time you still remain foolishly obstinate, then must I, however much it may be against my wishes, use force. Resistance, you perceive, will be in vain, and therefore, I advise you to make up your mind to assent without it; then shall you receive every attention from me, and I will behave in a manner that shall leave you no cause to regret your separation from your father.'

'Fiend in human shape,' ejaculated Inez, 'leave me! My soul freezes with horror as I listen to you! But I will not entirely despair, although you have bid me to do so; Heaven will interpose to prevent the execution of your base threats.'

'Did Heaven interpose to prevent my getting you in my power?' inquired Blodget, with a sardonic grin. 'Once more I tell you, you shall be mine, and nothing shall save you!'

'Never, villain!' cried Inez.

'Be cautions what you say, lady, lest you exasperate me,' returned Blodget, with a threatening frown, which made our heroine tremble; 'you forget that

I could this day—this very moment—force you to a compliance with my wishes, and where is there one near at hand who could come to save you?'

'By Heavens I would die first!'

'Bah!' sneered Blodget; 'but I am tired of this useless contest of words; you know my determination, and rest assured that I will only await a very few days for your answer, and then, if you do not consent, you know the consequences.'

'Once more I pray your mercy,' said the distracted Inez, with clasped hands, and looks of earnest supplication; 'beware! oh, beware! ere you proceed to extremities.'

'You have it in your power to move me to pity and love, fair Inez,' returned Blodget; 'one smile from you, one word of affection from those ruby lips would act with the influence of magic upon me and make me quite a different man. Blodget would then live alone for love and you; and there should not be a pleasure which it should not be my constant endeavor to procure you.'

Inez turned from the villain with a look of the utmost disgust, and she groaned aloud in the intensity of her anguished feelings. Blodget advanced nearer to her, and sought to put his arms around her waist, but the action immediately aroused her, and retreating to the further end of the room, she fixed upon him such a look as awed him into immediate forbearance.

'Still madly obstinate!' he exclaimed; 'but time must alter this proud beauty, and you must yield to the desires of Blodget, however repugnant it may be to your feelings. At present I leave you, but shortly you will behold me again, and then I trust that you will see the policy of giving me a more favorable reception than you have done this morning.'

As he spoke, Blodget fixed one glance of expressive meaning, and then quitting the room, he securely fastened the door after him.

'The perverse woman,' he soliloquized, as he walked away; 'but she must be subdued;—she must be subdued; Blodget cannot much longer endure her resistance. Oh, did she but know the plot I have formed against the life of Monteagle—but I said quite enough to arouse her fears, although I now wish that I had not done so, as it would be sure not to promote my wishes. I wish not to have to use violence, or I could do so directly; no, my greater triumph would be to prevail upon her to give her own free consent, and that would add to the gratification of my revenge. Blodget, if you fail in this, it will be the first time that you have failed in any of your undertakings.'

The villain walked away, and after giving strict injunctions to Joe to keep safe watch over his charge, he bent his footsteps towards the cabaret, at which he and the thieves had been the night before carousing, and where, in a back room, he could commune with his own thoughts, without any fear of interruption.

---

# CHAPTER XVI

## The Critical Move—Attempted Escape.

When Blodget had retired from the room, our heroine gave vent to the painful feelings which her interview with him had excited in her bosom; and hope seemed to have faded entirely away from her mind; for if the villain remained obstinately resolved to put his diabolical threats into execution, what means had she of resisting him? None! Then again the hints he had given convinced her that he had some base design in his mind.

She was aroused from these reflections by the entrance of the old woman who had come to do something in her apartment, and whose disagreeable looks assured our heroine that she took a pleasure in tormenting her, and saying anything which she thought might excite her feelings, and Inez, therefore, determined to avoid conversing with her, as much as she possibly could. The old woman, however, appeared to be determined that she should not escape so easily; for the words she had so pointedly directed to her in the morning, remained in her memory; and after having eyed her with an insolent glance for a second or two, she ejaculated, in her usual harsh but querulous tones:—

'I hope your ladyship feels happier after the interview you have had with your lover, and that the observations he has addressed to you, have met your approbation. Oh, he is a very nice gentleman! He! he! he!'

And the disgusting old woman croaked forth a laugh, which could scarcely have been imagined to have been uttered by anything but a witch; and appeared to think that she had spoken very wittily and sarcastically. But Inez did not deign to condescend her any answer, and she averted her eyes, for there was something so remarkably disagreeable in the woman's face, that she could not bear to look upon it.

The old woman saw plain enough that her observations annoyed Inez, and although she felt rather vexed and disappointed that she did not answer her, she determined to follow them up.

'It seems that you have lost your tongue since your interview with Mr. Blodget,' she said; 'but that is of very little consequence, I can talk enough for you and I too, and as Gordon has left the house, you will, in all probability, have a little more of my company than you otherwise would have done.'

'Gordon left the house?' repeated our heroine eagerly; 'thank Heaven!'

'Indeed!' said the old woman; 'then, if his absence affords you pleasure, I can tell you that it will not be of long duration;—he is only gone some distance on a secret mission, for which he is to receive a handsome reward from Mr. Blodget!'

'Ah!' cried our heroine, turning very pale, and a feeling of horror coming over her; 'on a secret mission for Blodget? In what fresh plot of villainy is he engaged?'

'Oh, that I do not know; and if I did, it is not very likely that I should inform you. It is something of importance I dare say, or else Gordon would not have been employed; and no doubt concerns you.'

Inez felt her horror increase, and she trembled so that she could scarcely stand. The old hag observed her emotion with much satisfaction, and a savage grin overspread her features.

'Something that concerns me;' she exclaimed, and her terrible forebodings convinced her that the old woman did not make use of these observations without good reason.

'Oh, my dear friend!' she added, as she recalled to her memory the dark hints which Blodget had given utterance to, and covering her face with her hands, she sobbed hysterically. 'Oh, my unfortunate rescuer;' she continued, 'I tremble for you; surely this is some dark plot against you. Heaven protect you and avert the evil fate destined to you by your implacable enemy!'

'If Blodget only plays his cards successfully, as he has hitherto done, I do not think that there is much chance of your seeing your *poor unfortunate* lover again;' said the hag with a sneer, and a look which was perfectly hideous.

Poor Inez gazed upon the unnatural old beldame with a look of horror and disgust.

'Inhuman woman;' she ejaculated, 'thus to take a pleasure in tormenting one of your own sex, who has never offended you, and whose misfortunes and oppressions ought to excite your pity and sympathy.'

'Pity and sympathy,' repeated the woman, with bitter sarcasm; 'they are qualities that none but fools would retain possession of; I never experienced them from any person yet, and I have banished mine from my breast many years since.'

'I do believe you,' sighed Inez; 'but I can sincerely pity *you*, for there will be a time come when you will be brought to a terrible sense of your iniquities, and awful will then be the punishment you will have to undergo.'

'Hey day!' exclaimed the beldame; 'I declare you're quite an adept at preaching a sermon, but its beauties are entirely lost upon me; and I do not think that you will find Mr. Blodget any more ready to approve of them than I am.'

'Leave the room,' said Inez, in a tone of resentment, 'and let me alone to my reflections; your language is brutal, and I will not listen to it.'

'But I am afraid you will have to listen to it very frequently,' returned the old woman, 'as disagreeable as it may be. As for leaving the room, you will please to recollect that you are not mistress here, consequently I shall not attend to your orders until it pleases me.'

Inez walked away, and throwing herself into a chair, once more covered her face with her hands, determined not to pay any future attention to what the old harridan might say. The latter laughed sneeringly, and after muttering a few spiteful remarks that our heroine did not hear, she applied herself more assiduously to the task she had to perform in the room, and at the same time hummed, in discordant tones, snatches from different vulgar songs, which fell listlessly upon the ears of Inez, who was too deeply engaged by her own melancholy thoughts to pay any attention to them.

At length having, much to the satisfaction of our heroine, completed her domestic duties in the room, the woman fixed upon Inez a spiteful look, and then retired from the apartment. When she had gone, our heroine immediately sunk upon her knees, and, with upraised hands, she implored the mercy of the Supreme Being, and that He would protect her father and her lover from any danger by which they might be threatened. She arose more composed and confident, and endeavored to hope that, after all, the wicked designs of Blodget might be foiled, and that something would yet transpire to release her from her present incarceration, and the future persecution of the villain Blodget, for whom no punishment could be adequate to the different crimes he had been guilty of.

Frequently did her thoughts revert to home, and she could well imagine the grief experienced at her mysterious disappearance. The idea of the deplorable condition of Monteagle was maddening nay, perhaps he was no more, and she was not present to receive his last sigh, or to enfold him in a dying embrace.—The thought was almost past endurance; and it was a fortunate thing for our heroine that a torrent of tears came to the relief of her overcharged heart.

Three weeks elapsed without any material change taking place in the situation or prospects of Inez. Blodget visited her every day, and she was annoyed by his disgusting importunities; and frequently was he so worked up by the opposition which she offered to him, that he was half tempted to proceed to violence; but a secret power appeared to restrain him, and to watch over his unfortunate victim.

Blodget was in a state of considerable anxiety and suspense, for he had not yet heard anything from Gordon, and sometimes he was fearful that he had been detected and was in custody; but again he thought, if he had been so, he should see some account of it in the newspapers, and he, therefore, at last endeavored to conclude that Gordon thought it prudent not to write to him, and that he was in a fair way of being ultimately successful in his blood-thirsty designs.

The thieves had made several successful hauls, since the departure of Gordon, and they were not less anxious than Blodget was to know what had become of him, and whether he was safe, for Gordon was acquainted with many circumstances that might greatly endanger them, should he be tempted to divulge them. Such is the doubt and suspicions that ever exist between the guilty.

At length, however, after another fortnight, a message arrived at the ranch of Gordon, which came from him, and it may well be imagined with what eager haste Blodget broke the seal, and glanced his eyes over the contents. They afforded him the most unbounded satisfaction.

'Ah! by the infernal host! this is capital,' exclaimed Blodget, when he had concluded perusing the letter; 'my vengeance will soon be complete; and I have no doubt that Gordon will shortly be able to discover Monteagle, and to accomplish the deed for which my soul pants.'

He immediately sought out Jenkins, who was at his usual place of resort when he was not on his expeditions, and showed him the letter from Gordon. The robber captain perused it with satisfaction, and his apprehensions were now at rest.

'What think you of the suggestion which Gordon has made?' asked Blodget, when Jenkins had finished reading the letter.

'Why, that it is a very excellent one,' answered the captain.

'True,' coincided Blodget.

'You will avail yourself of it, then?'

'Why, think you not I should be foolish to miss such an opportunity?'

'I do.'

'Gordon deserves an extra reward for this.'

'He is a shrewd fellow.'

'And one who does not stand particular about trifles.'

'No, crime and he are familiar. But how would you accomplish this design?'

'I have not as yet had time to consider it properly,' answered Blodget; 'can you give me any advice, captain?'

'Gordon I do not think can do it without assistance.'

'Probably not.'

'If I and a crew run the risk of going in a boat to Mission Creek, and bring the fellow away, of course you will reward us?'

'Certainly; but that course will be attended with much danger, for should the real character of your boat be known—'

'Oh, I can manage it so that there will be no danger of a discovery taking place,' replied Jenkins.

'Ah, then, be it so, and we will not fall out about the reward.'

'Agreed,' answered the captain, 'an answer must, therefore, be despatched to the place where Gordon is staying, acquainting him with our intentions, so that he may make the necessary preparations for carrying our designs into execution.'

'It shall be done immediately. But think you that success is at all likely?'

'It is all but certain.'

'And had Monteagle better be brought to the house where Inez is confined?'

'That you can use your own pleasure in,' replied Jenkins.

Blodget reflected for a few moments.

'No,' he at last said, 'it shall not be so at present; I think it would be as well not to let Inez know anything about it for a short time.'

'Why so?'

'Why,' returned Blodget, 'in the first place, the sudden shock might be attended with fatal consequences to her; and in the next, I think it would be better to break it out to her by degrees, and make the circumstance subservient to my designs upon her.'

'That is my opinion,' remarked Jenkins, 'but you are a fool, Blodget, to delay the indulgence of your desires so long, when you have it in your power to gratify them immediately. If you wait until you prevail upon the lady to consent, I think you will be likely to tarry a long while.'

'That is your opinion?'

'It is.'

'Mine is a different one.'

'You must have a very high opinion of your powers of captivation, if that is really your belief,' returned Jenkins.

'Perhaps so,' said Blodget, 'but time will show; and now that I have the prospect of getting this fellow into my power, I am the more disposed to wait patiently and give my plans a fair trial.'

'And wait until de Castro or his friends discover the retreat of the lady, force her from your power, and bring you to punishment,' rejoined Jenkins.

'If Gordon is successful, there will be no fear of that.'

'Maybe so; but you remember the old proverb—"a bird in hand is worth two in the bush."'

'At any rate, I have made up my mind to run the chance of it.'

'Well, of course, you are at liberty to do as you think proper,' observed the captain; 'but if you succeed in getting this youngster in our power, where do you think of placing him?'

'Know you of any person that can be trusted with him?'

'I do.'

'And does he reside far from this place?'

'Close upon the spot.'

'Is the place obscure?'

'It is little frequented.'

'And who is he?'

'One of my gang; you may depend upon him.'

''Tis well; and you think he will accept of the charge?'

'I am certain of it; he would do it gladly.'

'Perhaps you will see him and make the proposal; it would come better from your lips than mine.'

'I will do so.'

'You have my thanks, captain.'

''Pshaw! I don't want them. But, mark now, he must be well paid for his trouble, and keeping the secret.'

'I have no objection to that.'

'This will be an expensive job for you.'

'Were it to cost me twenty times as much, I would not begrudge it to gratify my revenge.'

'You are a most implacable foe.'

'So my enemies have good reason to say.'

'But come, there is no necessity for delay; have the letter written and forwarded to Gordon as quickly as possible.'

'It shall be done.'

'In the meantime I will go down to Kitson, and make the proposal to him.'

'Ay, do; and do not be afraid to promise a most liberal remuneration.'

'I will do so, depend upon it.'

'And when do you propose starting on this expedition?'

'By the night after to-morrow, at the latest.'

'Your promptitude pleases me.'

'Delay is dangerous; that is always my motto.'

'And a very good one; I will adopt it on this occasion; farewell.'

'Good night; although I shall probably see you again.'

'Well do, if you can, for I shall be anxious to know whether or not this Kitson, as you call him, will undertake this charge.'

'Oh, there is very little doubt but that he will do so.'

Having arrived at the conclusion of this brief colloquy, the two worthies separated, and Blodget bent his way to the ranch, to write the letter to Gordon; elated at the prospect of the success of his diabolical stratagems, and determined at any expense or danger to prosecute them.

In the epistle he gave Gordon all the information he could require, and highly praised his indefatigability, at the same time encouraging him to further exertions, by the promise of rewarding him accordingly.

The letter was immediately forwarded to the proper quarter, and had not long done so, when Jenkins returned.

'Well, captain, how have you succeeded?' asked Blodget.

'As I anticipated.'

'Then the man is willing.'

'He is.'

'And think you we may depend upon his secrecy?'

'There is no fear of that!'

'Did you not bind him by an oath?'

'There was no necessity for that! Kitson's word is his bond.'

'And did you make him acquainted with the particulars?'

'I was compelled to, to enable him to be more upon his guard.'

'Ay, true! And you mentioned the reward?'

'It is not so much as I anticipated.'

'What is it?'

'He demands two hundred dollars.'

'It shall be his freely, immediately the fellow is placed in his care, one hundred more to that, if he well perform his task, and keeps the secret inviolable.'

'I tell you again, there is no fear of his not doing that.'

'Then all, so far is well,' observed Blodget.

'It shall be so; and now we will have a glass or two together, to drink success to this undertaking.'

'With all my heart,' replied the captain; and taking his seat, bottles were immediately placed upon the table, and they proceeded to drink with much alacrity, toast after toast following each other in rapid succession, while the deep potations which they quaffed, took but a trifling effect upon them, so accustomed were they to habits of intemperance.

'Perhaps,' said Blodget, after a pause, 'it would have been much more satisfactory had Gordon succeeded in despatching him.'

'I like not the unnecessary shedding of human blood.'

'Then you have never felt the sentiments that I do.'

'You know not that; but, villain as I am, and have been from a boy, I never yet shed the blood of my fellow man, unless it was in a fight and in self defence.'

'And yet you would have insisted up on one of your fellows committing murder, had not Gordon undertaken to do it.'

'Because I had pledged my word to you that it should be done, and nothing would have induced me to break it.'

'Ha! ha! ha!' laughed out Blodget; 'there's honor for you, in the captain of a desperate gang of robbers.'

'Ay you may mock me, if you think proper, but I have spoken the truth.'

Blodget made no further observation, but walked away, and Jenkins rejoined his companions at their rendezvous.

In the meantime Inez' situation was just as helpless as ever, and Blodget daily continued to annoy her with importunities, and hourly became more bold and confident in his manners towards her, and she noticed it, and could not help thinking that something had happened to occasion this alteration in his behavior, and at times her mind felt some severe misgivings, which she found it impossible to comprehend. Blodget had not, however, yet mentioned anything, and, therefore, she could not entertain any positive suspicion.

So well secured was every place, that our heroine had long ago given up all idea of escaping, and rested her only hope of deliverance upon her friends discovering her place of confinement; but a circumstance, a short time after this, happened, which gave her some reason to hope.

Notwithstanding the utter disgust which our heroine ever evinced in the company of the old woman, she persisted in obtruding her society upon her at every opportunity, and, as we have before stated, it was very evident that she felt a pleasure in making Inez miserable. Guilt is always envious of the virtues it never possessed, and feels a delight in evincing its hatred of its possessor in every possible way. This, however, she concealed from Blodget, well aware that he would not approve of it, and Inez considered it too contemptible to take any notice of it, and if she had, she would not have troubled herself to mention it to her persecutor, who might feel little disposed to trouble himself in the matter.

The woman would make any excuse to be in the same room with our heroine, and when she was tired of talking to her, Inez seldom condescending her a reply, she would sing portions of vulgar songs, in a manner which would have done honor to Sydney Valley in its darkest days. The mind of Inez, however, was so fully occupied with her own thoughts that she seldom paid any attention to her, and not unfrequently was she almost entirely unconscious of her presence.

It was one evening, a short time after the events which we have been recording had taken place, that the hag paid our heroine her accustomed and unwelcome visit, and, as soon as she entered the room, Inez could perceive that she had been drinking and was quite intoxicated. This circumstance rather alarmed her, for she was afraid that the old woman being thus excited, might be guilty of some excesses; but still she reflected, she had nothing to apprehend from her, as the persons who were in the ranch would be sure to come to her aid, and thus she was in safety. But to be alone, and in the power of wretches who cared not what crime they committed, was sufficient of itself to fill her mind with terror, and she had great difficulty in supporting her feelings.

The old woman staggered to a seat, for she could scarcely stand, and having dropped into it, she raised her blood-shot eyes towards the countenance of our heroine, and fixed upon her a look expressive of her usual malevolence. Inez averted her head, and, taking up a book, pretended to be reading; but the old woman was not to be diverted that way, and, after several ineffectual attempts to speak, she stammered out—

'They are all gone out but one man, and he has fallen asleep by the fire, and so I thought I would come up stairs and keep you company, you are fond of my company, I know.'

This speech was accompanied by sundry hiccups, and the disgusting old woman rolled about in the chair apparently in the most uncomfortable manner. Inez trembled, but she endeavored to conceal her fears as much as possible, and pretended to be continuing to read the book she held in her hand, and did not make any reply.

'Mr. Blodget is a very foolish man,' continued the old woman—'he is a very foolish man, or he would not stand shilly-shallying and dilly-dallying with you, my fine lady, in the manner he has. Such squeamish minxes, indeed; poh!'

We need not attempt to describe the feelings of our heroine, while the old woman was thus proceeding; she endeavored to close her ears to the words she was giving utterance to, but in vain, and the disgust which she felt was most unbounded.

'Why don't you answer me?' demanded the beldame in a surly tone; 'I suppose you think yourself above me, don't you? But I can tell you you are not. You are a prisoner, but I am not, and—'

A very long yawn stopped the old woman's tirade, and her head dropped upon the table. She muttered two or three incoherent words, and shortly afterwards her loud snoring convinced our heroine that the effects of the liquor she had been drinking had overpowered her, and that she had fallen off to sleep.

Inez laid down her book; a sudden thought darted across her mind, and her heart palpitated with emotion. She remembered what the woman had said about there being but one man in the house, and that he was asleep below.— The room door was open—the old woman slept soundly, and she was not likely to be awakened easily—a famous opportunity presented itself for her to attempt to make her escape. The chance was worth encountering any danger in making the effort, and she determined to avail herself of it.

Hastily putting on her shawl, Inez mentally invoked the assistance of Heaven, and then, with noiseless footsteps, approached the chair on which the old woman was sitting, to make sure that she was not assuming drunkenness and sleep, and she was soon convinced that she was not. She now lightly stepped on to the landing, and closing the door gently upon the unconscious old woman, locked it after her, and thus left her a secure prisoner. She then leant her head over the bannisters, and listened attentively, but hearing no noise below, she was in hope that all was right, and ventured to begin to descend the stairs.

Having passed down one flight, she once more paused and listened attentively, but all remained as still as death, and her hopes became more sanguine.

At length she reached the door of the parlor, which was closed, and Inez hesitated, and her heart beat so vehemently against her side that she could scarcely support herself.

'Courage, Courage!' she whispered to herself, 'this is the critical moment. Let me be firm, and I may escape.'

Her trembling and hesitation decreased as these thoughts crossed her mind, and she laid her hand on the handle of the door. It opened with a creaking noise, which again excited her fear, lest it should arouse the man; but her alarm was, fortunately groundless. A light was burning on the table, and the fire cast forth a cheerful blaze, and by their light our heroine beheld a ruffian seated in the chair, his arms folded across his chest, and fast asleep.

Inez's heart bounded, and hope was strengthened tenfold. The near prospect of liberty excited in her breast a feeling of extacy which may be conceived but cannot be described. The moon shone brightly in at the window, and its silvery beams seemed to smile encouragement upon her. Another moment, she reflected, and she might inhale the pure air, and be as free. The thought nerved her on; and knowing that every moment was fraught with danger, she determined to act with promptitude. But the sleeping ruffian was so seated that she could not gain the door without passing him closely, and then she must act with the greatest caution or she might arouse him. She advanced one step, but hastily retreated again, hearing him yawn, and he seemed as if he was about to awaken. She stood in trembling suspense, but it was not for long; the man having stretched out his arms, and yawned two or three times, sunk back on his chair again, and his loud snoring soon convinced her that he was again asleep.

She now once more commended herself to the protection of Heaven, and again advanced towards the door. She had passed the sleeping ruffian—the door was in her hand, and liberty was just before her; when there was a loud noise, like that of some heavy weight falling, from the room above; and Inez was so alarmed that she had not the power of moving one way or the other, but stood at the door trembling violently.

The noise immediately aroused the man, and, hastily starting to his feet, he rubbed his eyes, and stared eagerly around the room. They instantly rested on our unfortunate heroine, and, giving utterance to a dreadful oath, he rushed towards her, and seizing her fiercely by the arm, dragged her back. Inez sunk upon her knees, and in terrified accents exclaimed—

'Oh, mercy, mercy! spare me—save me, for the love of Heaven, save me!'

'Ah! you would escape?' exclaimed the ruffian; 'speak, answer me—how did you contrive to leave the apartment in which you have been confined?'

The ruffian looked ferociously upon her while he spoke, and Inez trembled more violently than before when she gazed upon the frightful features of the man. Her lips quivered, and in vain did she endeavor to articulate a syllable.

'Speak, I tell you again!' demanded the villain; 'how came you hither? By what means did you contrive to leave the room?'

'The door was left unfastened,' faltered out Inez; 'oh, do not harm me.'

'The door left unfastened?' repeated the man; 'who left it so?'

'The woman.'

'Ah! the old hag—if she has done this she shall answer for it. But where is she?'

'In the room I have just quitted, and asleep,' replied Inez.

'Ah! I see how it is; myself and her have been indulging ourselves rather too freely, and both are equally to blame; we must be more cautious for the future. Come, my girl, you must allow me to escort you to your old quarters, and depend upon it, you will not have such another opportunity as this. Come!'

'Oh,' supplicated our heroine, not thinking in the despair of the moment, of the uselessness of appealing to the flinty heart of the wretch, 'do not consign me, I beseech you, to that dismal apartment again, take pity upon me, a deeply injured woman as I am, and suffer me to escape. Believe me, you shall be amply rewarded for such an inestimable service.'

'Oh, no,' returned the ruffian and a malignant grin overspread his countenance; 'it won't do, I'm not to be caught in that way; I can very well understand what my reward would be, but they must catch me before they give it me. Ha! ha! ha! Come, come, you must come with me, or I must use force—that's all about it.'

Poor Inez clasped her hands in the intensity of her grief, and finding that it would be useless to entreat any further, with a despairing heart, she slowly retraced her footsteps to the chamber from which she had so recently escaped, followed by the wretch.

On opening the door they found the old woman stretched at full length upon the floor; and it was evident that it was from her that the noise had proceeded, which so unfortunately aroused the man, and prevented her escape, at the very moment when the chance was before her.

It was some time before the thief could arouse the old woman to sensibility, and when she did so, he commanded her sternly to follow him.

'Hey day!' cried the hag, rubbing her eyes, and looking with stupified amazement at our heroine, who had sunk despairingly in a chair, and leaning her elbow upon the table, and her head upon her hand, was weeping bitterly; 'what's the matter now?'

'What's the matter!' reiterated the man, 'why, that through your infernal stupidity, the bird had nearly flown.'

'Ah—what, do you mean to say that she had nearly escaped?' croaked forth the old woman, and she looked more savage than ever at Inez.

'Yes, I mean to say that she would have escaped,' replied he, 'and a pretty scrape we should then both have got into.'
'Why, where was I at the time?'
'Fast asleep, and a safe prisoner in this room, locked in.'
'Locked in!' ejaculated the beldame, 'oh, I see it all now, that confounded gin got the better of me, and you too, I think, and, therefore, one is as much to blame as the other. We ought to thank our lucky stars that it has turned out as it has. But the artful jade, to lock me in, to—to—'
'There, that's enough,' interrupted the fellow, 'you would stand talking here all night. We will leave the lady to her own reflections, which, doubtless, will not be very pleasant. Blodget will be home shortly, I expect, and, should he find us together, he might suspect something wrong. Good night, my lady, and when you next try to escape, you had better use a little more expedition with your caution. Come, we must see and arrange this business somehow or another.'

The old woman fixed upon Inez one more malicious look, and appeared to exult in the agony she was undergoing at having been thwarted in her attempt, and then following the wretch, they both quitted the room, and secured the door after them.

They both congratulated themselves when they had got below, that Inez had not been successful, and were determined to be more cautious in future. Another moment, and our heroine would have been at liberty, and they trembled when they reflected upon the consequences that would have been certain to follow her escape. They both, however, considered that it would be better for them not to mention anything about it to Blodget or the others, as it would only excite his suspicions that all was not right, and probably deprive them of his confidence and friendship, which, as he was very liberal, was not to be treated lightly. Thus the affair was amicably arranged between the two worthies, and the old spitfire determined to annoy our unfortunate heroine more than ever, for the 'audacious' (as she termed it) attempt she had made to escape, and moreover, for her unparalleled presumption and atrocity, in having actually made her a prisoner in the very place where she had been herself confined.

As for poor Inez, she was completely overwhelmed with the intensity of her anguish and disappointment, and for some time after the man and the old woman had left her, she remained in almost a state of unconsciousness.

'Alas,' she at last ejaculated, beating her breast, 'fate has conspired against me, and I am doomed to perpetual misery. Am I never to escape from the power of these wretches? Has the Omnipotent Being entirely forsaken me? Oh, God! let me die rather than live to endure this succession of miseries and disappointments.'

She clasped her burning temples, and arising from her chair, traversed the room in the greatest possible agony. If Blodget should become acquainted with the circumstance, she could not help thinking that he would be induced to adopt even more stringent measures towards her; but then she consoled herself with the reflection that it was not likely that the man or the old woman would let him know anything about it, as they would be blamed for neglect, and Blodget would deem it prudent to remove her to some other place of confinement. She passed two or three hours in the greatest state of agitation, and could not venture to retire to rest, but listened to the slightest sound which proceeded from below, fearing to hear the villain Blodget return home.

At length all was still in the house, and tired out with thinking, Inez committed herself to the care of Providence, and undressing herself, hastened into bed, and, in spite of the state of her mind, after the painful event which we have been detailing, she was so weary, that it was not long ere she sunk to sleep.

# CHAPTER XVII

## The Seducer Resisted.

We left our heroine in a calm slumber, into which she had sunk after the fatigue of thinking and the anguish of her mind. She continued in it until a storm arose, which awoke her, and jumping up in the bed, she scarcely knew where she was. Confused thoughts darted across her perturbed imagination, and she had in an instant a foreboding, a presentiment, that something particular was about to occur to her. She heard no one but the old woman moving below, and recollecting that she had seen Blodget quit the house at an early hour in the morning, she thought it was probable that he had not yet returned, and she became rather more composed. Then, however, she remembered some dark hints which the hateful old woman had thrown out to her in the morning, and again were her utmost apprehensions of some fresh misery excited. Sometime she continued in this manner, when she heard a confusion of voices from below, among which she distinguished that of a female and Blodget's, but she could not understand a single word that they gave utterance to.

She now endeavored to calm her feelings, and prepare for the meeting which she had no doubt would take place between her and Blodget; who she resolved to meet with all the fortitude she could possibly muster. She knelt down, and supplicated the aid of the Almighty; and implored that He would frustrate the designs of the wicked, and not suffer her to fall a victim to the diabolical stratagems of the miscreant who at present held her in his power.

As it ever is the case, when the sincere heart breathes its prayers to Heaven, our heroine felt almost immediately more tranquil and prepared to meet her oppressor, and she arose from her knees with a determination to support herself with an air of fortitude, which should abash rather than encourage the villain's nefarious hopes.

She had not long come to this resolution, when she heard a footstep ascending the stairs, and shortly afterwards the door of her apartment was unbolted, and the door was opened, and the object of her hatred and her fears presented himself before her. She met his looks firmly, and with an air of becoming dignity, and it was evident, although he endeavored to disguise it, that something of more importance than usual occupied his thoughts.

He stood for a second or two in the doorway, and seemed anxious to address her, yet at a loss how to begin. Then he seemed abashed at the calm dignity of Inez's manner, and at the same time lost in admiration of her extreme beauty, which, although much impaired by the ravages of care, was still most superlative.

Notwithstanding the firmness which she assumed, Inez felt a trembling apprehension of the interview; and had much difficulty in conquering her feelings.

At length Blodget advanced nearer to our heroine, closing the door after him, and after several ineffectual attempts to speak, he observed, in as insinuating tone as he could assume—

'Beauteous Inez, after a temporary absence from your presence, which has appeared an age to me, I again come to bask in the sunshine of your beauty— again to solicit a return of that passion which I so ardently feel for you.'

'Villain!' ejaculated Inez, 'receive my answer in the utter contempt, disgust, abhorrence I feel for you; and rest assured that no other feeling can ever inhabit my breast towards a wretch who has proved himself destitute of every feeling of humanity.'

'This violence is useless,' returned Blodget; 'I have given you plenty of time to consider: this day I come hither to decide: I have waited patiently long enough.'

'Monster!' cried the distracted lady, and her eyes at the same time beamed an expression which seemed as if it would penetrate to his soul; 'where is my poor father, from whom you have so mercilessly torn me? Can you recollect the unparalleled act of cruelty you have been guilty of, and yet stand there and talk to me, the affianced bride of another, about love?'

'To all these passionate expressions I pay little or no attention; for they affect me not,' returned the hardened villain. 'It is enough that I have fixed my mind on you; I have labored hard, and risked much, to get possession of you—you are now in my power, and mine, in spite of all entreaties and tears, shall be!'

'Oh, heartless miscreant.'

'Nay, think not that I would willingly resort to violence,' observed Blodget, in a milder tone of voice; 'no, I would win you by my actions; by my love;— I would be to you the most ardent and affectionate companion that woman desire; I—'

'Cease!' interrupted Inez, in a commanding tone of voice, which seemed to enforce immediate obedience; 'I will not listen to your guilty language, it disgusts me. Your presence makes me feel as if a fiend, instead of a human being, were standing before me; begone! and leave me again to the solitude of my unjust confinement.'

'Not yet, fair Inez,' returned Blodget, with a supercilious smile; 'you and I must not part until we understand each other.'

'I perfectly understand you, sir,' said Inez, 'and depend upon it, all that you can say will but add to the utter abhorrence which I bear towards you.'

'But you must yield!'

'Never!'

'How can you save yourself? Are you not in my power?'

'True; but I have a friend in Providence who will not suffer me to fall a victim to the nefarious designs of a diabolical villain like you.'

'Upon my word you are very liberal with your compliments;' said Blodget, with a half-sneering laugh, although it was very plain to be seen that he was very much chagrined at the manner in which our heroine addressed him.

'Is there any epithet strong enough that I can apply to a man like you?' demanded Inez. 'Has not your conduct proved you to be a miscreant, too—'

'Come, come,' interrupted Blodget, and a slight scowl passed over his brows, 'I do not mind a little flattery, but when it proceeds to extremes, I must acknowledge that I have not a stomach to take it. Any epithet that you may apply to me, you must be aware cannot have any other effect than that of exasperating me to that which I might afterwards be sorry for. But how can you be so foolish as to remain thus obstinately opposed to the wishes of a man who would make it his unceasing study to render you happy?'

'Happy!' exclaimed Inez, 'and dare you talk to me of happiness, when I am torn from all that renders life desirable? Wretch, unnatural monster you must think me, to be capable of listening to the licentious vows of a man who has been the author of all my miseries! Talk to me of happiness, and keep me confined in this awful house, surrounded only by the votaries of guilt, who would not hesitate to dye their hands in my blood.'

'They dare not; they act alone by my orders,' answered Blodget. 'But why thus delay the time in conversing on matters of no immediate interest? Again, Inez, I solicit your love. Say that you will be mine, all but that which the idle ceremony of wedlock can make you, and there is not a pleasure which gold can purchase, or this world supply, which you shall not have at your command. We will hasten far from hence, and in a place where we are unknown, forget that there are others than ourselves in existence.'

Inez shuddered with horror at the coolness and effrontery with which the libertine uttered these expressions, and she could scarcely believe that she was standing in the presence of a human being.

'Oh, no,' replied Blodget, 'think not that I can be induced to leave you so soon this day, at any rate. Upon your determined answer your fate depends.'

'You have already had my answer,' returned Inez.

'Will nothing persuade you to alter it?'

'Nothing, by Heaven!'

'Beware! take not an oath!'

'I can with safety, for nothing would induce me to swerve from it.'

'You had better bethink yourself.'

'I have thought sufficiently, and I am decided.'

'Recollect that, if you refuse, I shall be compelled to resort to force.'

'I will die first.'

'You will not have the means.'

'Almighty God surely, will never suffer so black a deed.'

'Bah!—that is all idle cant. Think, too, that if you refuse, you will still be kept here a prisoner, deprived of every comfort, and yet subservient to my wishes.'

'Oh, horror! You cannot surely be the monster!'

'I would not willingly, but you would drive me to it.'

'Oh, repent, repent!'

'Pshaw! Will that gratify my desires?'

'It will afford me a far greater gratification.'

'I shall not try it.'

'Alas! you are indeed a guilty miscreant.'

'Thank you, again, for your compliment; I have pointed out to you the horrors that will attend your refusal; say, shall I point out to you the happiness that will attend you, if you comply with my request?'

'I want not to hear them, they cannot make any alteration in my determination,' answered our heroine, covering her face with her handkerchief, and sobbing aloud with her disgusted and wounded feelings.

'Still must I think that you will change your mind;' returned Blodget with the same guilty expression of countenance in which his features were almost constantly clad—'remember the sweets of liberty will then be yours.'

'And of what use would liberty be to me, when it would be purchased by a life of infamy?' demanded Inez; 'could anything ever reconcile it to my conscience, to become the base paramour of a guilty being like you? The bare thought fills me with a sensation of the utmost dread, and death in its most horrible form would be preferable to such a course of life.'

'But is there nothing that could prevail upon you?'

'Nothing;' answered Inez, with a look of the greatest disgust and horror.

'Think again!'

'I have nothing more to say upon the detested subject.'

'If, by so doing, you could purchase the life of Monteagle—'

'Ah!' grasped forth Inez, turning deadly pale, and clutching the arm of Blodget, and with distended eye-lids;—'what mean you? Speak! speak!—I know you have something of a particular nature to impart to me! Reveal it! I beseech you, and keep me not in suspense!—Oh, Blodget if you have indeed any regard for my feelings, tell me, what of Monteagle?'

'Calm your feelings!'

'You rack me!'

'Compose yourself!'

'Talk not to me of composure!' shrieked Inez.

'He is in my power.'

Poor Inez tried hard to speak, but she could not; she was transfixed to the spot, and gazed upon Blodget with a look in which the greatest astonishment and horror were depicted. The announcement of Blodget came like a thunderbolt upon her, and her faculties seemed to be all bound up in the suddenness and unexpectedness of the circumstance.

'If you are not a monster of the blackest dye,' exclaimed Inez at length, 'you will not delight in thus harrowing my feelings! but tell me have you spoken the truth? Do not keep me in suspense! Oh, do not! Have you indeed said that which is true?'

'I have,' answered Blodget;—'Monteagle is now in my power.'

'Are you bent to drive me mad?' exclaimed the frenzied Inez, as, with clasped hands, she gazed vehemently and supplicatingly in the countenance of her oppressor.

'No, no! I would restore you to happiness,' replied Blodget.

'Happiness!' groaned Inez; 'oh, cruel mockery to talk to me thus; and to continue to keep me in this state of agony and suspense.'

'Compose yourself,' again remonstrated Blodget, in a gentler tone, than he had before spoken, and at the same time venturing to approach her closer; 'compose yourself. Consent to my wishes, and Monteagle shall at once be free.—Refuse he dies!'

'Never, miscreant!' cried Inez, and fell powerless to the floor.

Blodget was alarmed,—so still and marble-like did the fair girl lie. No motion of her white bosom gave the slightest evidence that she breathed.

The villain trembled, and for an instant remorse touched his heart. But no sooner did a slight convulsive shudder show that she still lived, than he turned and left the apartment.

Blodget sent the old woman to Inez, who succeeded in restoring her to consciousness.

The next morning Jenkins returned. He seemed in haste.

Sending for several members of his gang he was soon engaged in earnest conversation.

'Gordon, say not a word to Blodget,' said Jenkins.

'Should he try to escape?' said Gordon.

'Shoot him, as you would a mad coyote,' said Jenkins.

'Had we not best confine him?'

'No,—wait my return. He will probably send for Kay, Maretzo, and others of his old cronies. If he tries to bribe one of you to take a message for him to them affect to be won over by his gold, carry the message for him, and then hasten to me at the Mission.'

'But where are you to be found, captain?'

'Joaquin will inform you of my whereabouts.'

'But, captain, why do you wish Kay and the rest of them to be engaged in this affair?'

'In order that they may be captured in the actual commission of a daring crime—as they will doubtless hasten to assist Blodget to carry off the lady.'

Jenkins then visited Blodget.

To the great surprise of Blodget, Jenkins instead of greeting him with friendly warmth, rejected his proffered hand, and addressing him sternly, said: 'I am about to leave this place for a few days, if during my absence you insult Miss Inez by word or look, or ever approach the rooms she occupies, you shall as surely die as my name is Jenkins!' Then turning to a young girl, who had accompanied him to the house, the robber-captain addressed her thus: 'Alice, you will I know do all you can to make this poor young lady as happy as possible while I am away. I do not promise you any reward, for I know your own goodness of heart has induced you to volunteer to be her friend and companion.'

Jenkins then gave the old woman instructions to obey Alice on every point, and whispering a few words to Gordon, Jenkins left the apartment, and soon after the house.

Blodget was astounded at this change in the behavior of Jenkins, and concluded that he had informed upon him, and thus made his own peace with the authorities. He was confirmed in this, when he went to step from the house, for Gordon stepped up to him, and placing a revolver at his breast, threatened to shoot him if he crossed the threshold. Finding an attempt to escape would only lead to his instant death, Blodget determined during Jenkins' absence to consummate his intentions on Inez, and then devise some mode of gaining Gordon to allow him to escape.

The girl whom Jenkins had addressed as Alice, had seen some seventeen springs, the apple-blossoms of which were not more beautifully tinted than her fair cheeks; nor their skies a deeper blue than her love-lit eyes. Her form was perfect—her step light and springy as an antelope's. Her name was Alice Hewlett, and she was known in the neighborhood as 'the Squatter's Daughter.' She had heard of a lady's being confined in Gordon's house, and readily availed herself of the request of Jenkins to be the fair captive's companion, until she could be restored to her friends.

Alice immediately went to Inez.

'My dear young lady, I come to stay with you.'

Inez gazed inquiringly upon her fair, ingenuous face.

'You may safely trust me, Miss.'

'I do—I do—dear girl. Vice never wore so fair a front.'

'Lady, I will not leave you, but at your request.'

'Oh, thanks, thanks. You know not what a load you've taken from my sad heart.'

Jenkins went to the old crone, and gave her some directions, adding sternly, 'Mind and do as I have told you!'

The old woman muttered an obedience to his orders, and he immediately quitted the room.

He had not been gone many minutes, when she retired to her own little closet, where she always had a bottle or two of 'the best,' and was soon in a fair way to enjoy herself, and to become entirely unconscious of all that was taking place; and Blodget hailing the so long-looked for opportunity with pleasure, he ascended the stairs on tiptoe, and having reached the rooms appropriated to the use of Inez, he knocked.

Alice, probably thinking it was the woman, quickly opened the door, but started back with no little amazement, when she beheld the villain Blodget.— He instantly stepped into the room, and Inez hearing the exclamation which Alice had given utterance to came from her room, but on seeing Blodget, she turned very pale, and trembled so violently that she could scarcely prevent herself from sinking on the floor.

The forbidding features of Blodget relaxed into a smile, which he meant to be one of kindness, but he could not conceal his exultation, and the guilty passions that raged like a tempest within his bosom, and turning to Alice, he said, in an authoritative tone—

'Leave the room.'

Alice hesitated, and looked at our heroine.

'Do you hear?' demanded Blodget, in a louder tone;—'begone, I've something to say to this lady, which must not meet your ear.'

'You should have nothing to say to me, sir, which should be kept a secret from a second person. Alice, I desire you to remain where you are; Mr. Blodget can have no authority for obtruding his hateful presence upon one whom he has already so deeply, so irreparably injured. Do not depart, Alice!—I desire you!'

'These mandates are of no avail,' cried Blodget; 'I have long sought this interview, and I will not now be foiled. Begone, I say!'

'I'll remain where I am, sir, while it is the wish of the lady,' returned Alice, in a firm tone.

'Ah!' exclaimed Blodget; his eyes expressive of fierce anger, 'dare you?— Then you must go by force.'

Immediately seizing Alice, as he spoke, by the shoulders, he pushed her violently from the room, and closing the door, locked it, preventing her return. He advanced towards Inez, who, upon the impulse of the moment, was in the act of retreating to her chamber, and fastening herself in, when the villain sprang quickly forward, and seizing her vehemently by the arm, he drew her back.

'Unmanly ruffian!' cried Inez, 'unhand me, or my cries shall reach the ears of those who will punish you for your boldness and cruelty! What is the meaning of this savage outrage?'

'It means, fair Inez,' replied Blodget, forcibly throwing his arm around her waist, and drawing her towards him, 'that, finding I have too long been a forbearing fool, when I had you in my power, I am determined that I will no longer wait for the gratification of my wishes. I have condescended to sue to you, where I might long since have enforced your compliance; I have made you every reasonable proposal, and have submitted patiently to your scorn, and contemptuous rejection of my suit, but I am now roused to a full sense of my folly, and am determined at all hazards, that you shall be mine!'

'Brutal monster!' exclaimed Inez, violently struggling; for the expressions of Blodget, and his determined demeanor, filled her with the utmost terror— 'are you not satisfied with probably having murdered my unfortunate father, and inflicted upon me a series of miseries almost unparalleled in the annals of inhumanity, but that you would now add to your barbarity by so atrocious a crime as you threaten? Oh, help! help!—Holy Virgin, I call upon thee for thy protection!—Oh, save me! save me!'

As the distracted and terrified lady thus screamed, she struggled violently to extricate herself from the embraces of the ruffian Blodget, but her efforts were for some time entirely ineffectual, and with every endeavor she made, the passions of Blodget increased, and his cheeks glowed and his eyes flashed with the guilty desires that raged within his breast. He sought, however, to stifle her cries, but in vain.

'Nay,' he cried, 'you scream for help in vain; there is no one at hand to interpose to save you! The triumph so long protracted, now is mine! This hour; this very moment gives you to my arms!'

'Almighty God! protect me! save me!' again shrieked our heroine, in the most frantic accents, and, with a desperate effort she released herself from Blodget's hold, and retreated to the farther end of the apartment, where, on a table, was a knife. Scarcely knowing what she did, she snatched it up, and, as Blodget approached towards her, she flourished it menacingly, and exclaimed:

'Villain! advance but an inch towards me, and this knife shall stretch me a bleeding corpse at your feet!'

Blodget was completely staggered by the determined air which Inez assumed, and he was transfixed to the spot whereon he stood, not knowing what course to pursue.

Our heroine still flourished the knife menacingly, and kept the villain at bay.

'You see I am resolute,' she cried; 'and, by Heaven, sooner than I will be dishonored, I will put my threat into execution! Death is preferable to the dreadful, the disgusting fate which you have threatened me. Nay, nothing can move me from my purpose! Quit the room, miscreant; unless you would have my death to answer for, in addition to your other numerous crimes!'

'Inez,' ejaculated Blodget, offering to approach her; 'hear me!'

'Not a word,' firmly replied Inez; 'nothing whatever can shake my resolution; begone!'

At that moment a loud noise was heard at the chamber door, and immediately afterwards the voices of several persons.

Blodget turned pale and trembled.

'Ah!' he ejaculated.

'Open the door, or it will be worse for you,' now demanded the voice of Gordon.

'Never!' cried Blodget, desperately, and placing his back against it as he spoke.

'Then we must use force,' returned Gordon; 'now, lads, your aid.'

In an instant the door was burst open, and Gordon, followed by three rough-looking men, entered the room.

'Seize him, my lads; and bear him hence!' cried Gordon, and in a moment the men rushed upon Blodget, who made a desperate resistance, but was quickly overpowered, and was conveyed, struggling, swearing, and foaming at the mouth, from the room, and being dragged to one of the dark vaults underground, was, by the orders of Gordon, locked in, and left to his own reflections, the nature of which may be readily conjectured, but cannot be properly described.

Alice, immediately on being thrust out of the room by Blodget, had hastened below, where, ascertaining that Gordon was from home, although it was very reluctantly that the old woman furnished her with the information, she made the best of her way to the cabaret, where she fortunately found him, in company with the men before mentioned, and having informed him of the perilous situation of our heroine, he left the place, and, as has been shown, arrived just at the critical juncture, to save her from destruction.

Blodget had no sooner been forced away from the room, than our heroine, overpowered by her feelings, and the unusual excitement she had undergone, fainted, and Alice Hewlett was once more left alone with her, and immediately set about the means of restoring her sensibility.

It would be impossible to portray correctly the disappointment and ungovernable rage of Blodget, when he found himself not only foiled in his diabolical attempt, but made a prisoner in that gloomy vault. He raved; he stormed; he cursed and swore, and breathed the most fearful maledictions against Alice, Gordon, and Jenkins. Then he made the place re-echo again with his cries to be released, but the hollow reverberations of that subterranean place, were the only answers he received, and he traversed the limited space in which he was confined, in a state bordering upon madness. He now at once saw that he was caught, trepanned, defeated, and all his well laid schemes rendered abortive, and himself left entirely at the mercy of Jenkins and his associates, and when he recollected the threats which the former had held out to him, if he should make any attempt against the peace of Inez, during his absence, he felt that he had every reason to apprehend the most terrible consequences through his mad impetuosity. All the horrors of an ignominious death rushed upon his mind, and his anguish was so great, that he completely sunk under it. He crouched down in one corner of his cell, and became the image of despair. It appeared as though his career of guilt was fast drawing to a close, and, that fate had destined, that every attempt he should in future make should be frustrated.

In this state he remained for more than two hours, without any one appearing to interrupt him, when he heard some one unbolting the door of his cell, and immediately afterwards it was thrown back on its hinges, and Gordon, accompanied by one of the men who had been his companions in the seizure, entered.

He brought with him a stone pitcher, containing water and a loaf, which he placed on the ground, and then eyed Blodget with a look of the most malignant exultation.

Blodget sprang to his feet; fury gleaming in his eyes, and advancing towards Gordon, he cried, in a hoarse voice:—

'Dastard!—why am I thus seized and made a prisoner in this dismal place?'

'Recollect your recent conduct,' said Gordon coolly, 'and you are answered.'

'And what authority has either he or you for detaining me?' demanded Blodget.

'Upon that point I dare say you will be satisfied at a future time,' returned Gordon, in the same deliberate and careless tones.

'But you will not dare detain me?'

'That has to be proved.'

'Villain! you will have to answer dearly for this,' said Blodget.

'Previous to which,' retorted Gordon, ironically, 'you will probably be called to a slight account for the abduction and unlawful detention of the lady, also for a certain crime since, and—'

'Confusion!' interrupted Blodget;—'am I then placed in the power of every wretch? Oh, Jenkins! Jenkins! for this, my heaviest malediction light upon your head.'

'Trusting that you may soon feel at home in your new apartment,' said Gordon, with a most provoking grin, 'I will now leave you to the enjoyment of it. Come on.'

And thus saying, before Blodget could give utterance to another syllable, although his looks evinced the torturing feelings of chagrin, disappointment, and resentment he was undergoing, Gordon and his companion quitted the cell, and slammed and bolted the door after them, leaving Blodget involved in utter darkness, for they had not supplied him with a lamp.

Blodget threw himself on the hard ground, and he groaned aloud with the agony of his feelings, but his present suffering was nothing compared with the horrors of anticipation, and he dreaded the return of Jenkins, fearing that the terrible result would be that which he promised him.

Three days and nights passed away in this manner, and Blodget was still kept a prisoner in the subterranean vault, and was daily visited by Gordon, who came to bring him his scanty allowance of provisions, and to taunt him with his degraded and altered situation. The unhappy wretch was at length completely subdued in spirit, and was incapable of answering the ruffian, and he was at last so humbled as to entreat Gordon's mercy, and to pray that he would release him from his present place of confinement to one less dismal. This request, however, Gordon only treated with scorn and derision; so true it is that none feel greater pleasure than the guilty in torturing one another. Although Blodget had never given the ruffian the least cause for offence, but, on the contrary, according to his own admission, had liberally rewarded him for the nefarious actions in which he had employed him, he now felt the most savage delight in adding to his misery as much as possible; and the more he saw him suffer, and the more humbled he was, the greater did he exult. He had no doubt he should receive great praise, and something far more substantial from Jenkins for the manner in which he had acted, and he anticipated his return with much impatience. He was not made thoroughly acquainted with Jenkins' intention as regarded Inez, but he had not the least doubt it was to restore her to her friends, and he imagined he would ensure from them a rich reward, in which he also expected to become a sharer to no small amount for the services he had rendered. How far his expectations were realized, will be seen anon.

When our heroine had quite recovered from the shock which she received from the behavior of the villain Blodget, she returned her most heartfelt thanks to the Almighty for her preservation, and for the fortitude with which she had been imbued to resist him. She then expressed her warmest acknowledgments to Alice, to whose presence of mind in hastening for the aid of Gordon, she might, in a great measure, attribute her preservation. The conduct of Gordon, who, there could not be the least doubt, acted entirely by the orders of Jenkins, left her no longer any room to doubt but that the latter was really the friend and protector he had told her was, and now that Blodget was thrust into confinement, from which they were assured he would not be released until the return of the captain, our heroine felt that she was safe.

'What ready means guilt often unthinkingly takes to defeat its own designs:' observed Alice; 'Blodget thrusting me out of the room, was the very cause of bringing about his own confusion, and frustrating his evil intentions; for, had he placed me in another room, and confined me therein, he might easily have silenced the old woman, had she been inclined to oppose him, and thus he would have been almost certain to have obtained his object.'

'Oh, no,' returned Inez, 'my mind was made up; never did I feel more determined, and he perceived it; I would have plunged the knife to my heart, sooner than he would have triumphed in his disgusting and diabolical purpose!'

'Oh, Miss,' said Alice, 'the idea of that makes me shudder with horror! Heaven be praised, that preserved you from such a dreadful and untimely end. But the wretch will no doubt be amply punished for his crimes, and for all the sufferings that he has inflicted upon you.'

'And how think you that Jenkins will dispose of him?' interrogated Inez.

'Deliver him up to the Vigilance Committee,' replied Alice.

'How can he do so without getting himself into trouble?'

'Oh, there is no doubt but that he will readily hit upon a plan,' said Alice; 'I dare say that he has already arranged that, without knowing anything of the late circumstance. Clear up, Miss, for depend upon it, your troubles are fast drawing to a close, and not many days will elapse ere you will be again restored to your friends.'

'Alas,' ejaculated Inez, tears gushing to her eyes, 'perhaps I have no dear friends to receive me! Oh, how my poor heart chills at the thought.'

'Pray, Miss,' said Alice, 'do not encourage fears which, after all, may prove unfounded. Great, no doubt, as has been the sufferings of Monteagle and your father, I firmly believe that they are still living, or Jenkins and the others would have heard of it.'

'My unhappy lover may have been able to withstand the severity of his accumulated and unparalleled calamities,' observed Inez, 'but, my poor father; oh, well am I convinced that his mind must have now become a wreck, in which case, it would be a mercy if the Almighty should be pleased to take him to Himself. Poor grey-haired old man, fondest of parents, best of human beings, shall I ever again be enfolded to thy paternal bosom, with the conviction that thou art conscious it is thy poor persecuted daughter thou dost embrace?—Alas! I fear never!'

'Oh, yes, Miss, you will,' ejaculated Alice, energetically, 'Heaven in its infinite mercy will not deny you such a blessing after the many afflictions you have so undeservedly undergone. Have you not every reason to place the firmest reliance upon its goodness, after the manner in which you have ever been preserved in the moment of the most imminent danger?'

'Yes, my good girl,' replied our heroine, drying her tears, 'indeed I have, and it is ungrateful in me thus to give way to despair. But my mind is so continually tormented, that I scarcely know what I am saying.'

'At any rate,' observed her companion, 'now that Blodget is made a prisoner you may rest yourself secure, and Jenkins, I dare say, will not be long before he returns; when you will speedily be made acquainted with intentions, which, as I have all along predicted, depend upon it, will be all in your favor.'

The ideas of Alice were too reasonable to be rejected by Inez, and she looked forward to the return of Jenkins with the greatest anxiety.

A fortnight had now waned away, and still Jenkins and his companions did not return, and Gordon, who did not expect that they would be gone so long, was fearful lest some accident should have befallen them. He still kept the wretched Blodget confined in the same place, and he now became the complete victim of despair. His form had wasted away, and his countenance betrayed the deep, the intense agony which perpetually tortured his mind. How dreary were the days and nights passed in that dark cell, where he had nothing to commune but his own dreadful thoughts, and where the horrors of his own guilty conscience constantly brought to his imagination the many crimes he had committed. Conjecture cannot form but a weak picture of the mental sufferings of that man of crime. Oh, who would be guilty, did they but think upon the horrors that must sooner or later overtake them?—For the gratification of some moment of sensual pleasure; for the transitory indulgence of some ambitious wish, the unhappy wretch falls into crime, to pay for it by years of mental suffering, and ignominious death, and an eternity of torment!—Oh, how fearful the price, would but erring mortals pause and think!

It was on a stormy midnight, when nearly three weeks had elapsed since Jenkins had left, when a party who were in company with Gordon in the little back room, smoking, were suddenly aroused by hearing a shrill whistle. The cigars were removed from their lips in an instant, and they jumped hastily to their feet.

'Jenkins's signal, by all that's fortunate;' exclaimed Gordon, advancing towards the door, 'they have come back at last, and all safe, I hope!'

'This has, indeed, been a long trip captain,' said Gordon, 'and I had began to fear that you were never going to return.'

'Better late than never,' answered Jenkins; 'but how is all at the house?'

'Quite safe, captain,' replied Gordon, with a peculiar grin, 'the lady is in her own apartments with her companion, Alice, and that arrant scoundrel Blodget, confined in one of the vaults underneath, where he has been since two or three days after your departure.'

'Ah!' exclaimed Jenkins, 'has he then dared to scorn the warning that I gave him?'

Gordon briefly related what had taken place between Blodget and our heroine.

'Why, the damned villain!' cried Jenkins, passionately; 'after the strict injunctions which I laid upon him, and knowing that he was placed entirely at my mercy. But he shall pay dearly for it; his doom is sealed.'

'I did not know whether you would approve of the lodging I had given the fellow,' answered Gordon.

'You have acted perfectly right,' said Jenkins; 'and I commend you for what you have done. Blodget shall quickly have another berth, and his career he may reckon at an end. And is the lady quite well?'

Gordon answered in the affirmative.

'I am happy to hear that,' said Jenkins; 'she shall not much longer remain in the position she is now placed in.—Poor lady, I shall for ever regret having been instrumental in any way towards her unhappiness; but I knew not who she was, or the villain Blodget should not have retained possession of her.

However, his time of shame is fast approaching, and bitterly will he have to pay for all.'

'It is, then, your intention to restore the lady to liberty?' asked Gordon.

'Certainly,' answered Jenkins, 'and to her friends.'

'But you will run a great risk in so doing, will you not?'

'No; leave me alone for that; I have arranged everything in my own mind,' said Jenkins.

'But how do you propose to dispose of Blodget?' inquired Gordon.

'I have not exactly made up my mind, although I did threaten him with death,' answered Jenkins. 'To-morrow night, or the next, I shall convey the scoundrel far away from hence.'

'You would not deprive him of life?'

'No,' replied Jenkins, 'not by my own hands; besides it would be a pity to deprive the hangman of a job.'

Gordon did not return any answer to this, for when he recollected the crimes of which he had himself been guilty, he thought that it was not all unlikely that he should himself afford employment for that functionary, sooner or later.

In the morning early, the robber captain was traversing his way along the vaulted passages, and at length stopped at the door of the vault in which Blodget was confined. There he paused and listened, for he could not help feeling that he was only justly punished for the part he had played towards the unfortunate Inez and her friends.

At length he withdrew the bolts, and entered the cell. The dim light which was emitted by the lamp which Jenkins carried, could but faintly penetrate the gloom of the miserable place, so that Blodget did not at first perceive who it was that had entered, and no doubt, did not think that it was any one else than Gordon; and the robber stood contemplating him for a minute or two in silence, but resentment was strongly portrayed in his countenance.

'So, villain,' he at length said, 'you have dared to brave my threats, to disobey my injunctions, and have again offered to—'

He was interrupted by a loud exclamation from Blodget, who, upon recognizing his voice, sprang forward, and in the most abject manner knelt at Jenkins's feet, and looked up in his face with the most earnest supplication.

'Oh, Jenkins,' he cried, in the most impressive tones; 'spare me;—pity me;—pardon me!—I will own my guilt;—I will acknowledge I was wrong; but let the agony I have for the last fortnight endured in this place satisfy you, and do not, oh, do not proceed to extremities.'

Jenkins fixed upon him a look of the utmost contempt, as he replied:

'And have you, then, the effrontery to crave pardon, after setting all my injunctions at defiance? I gave you sufficient warning of what the consequences would be, did you not obey me; you have scorned it, and those consequences you must abide by.'

'No, no;' groaned the poor terrified wretch, still remaining on his knees, and looking the very picture of death, with the excess of his fears; 'you will not surely do as you say?—You will not deliver me up to justice?—Consign me to an ignominious and violent death! Pause ere you do so!—My death will avail you nothing. Suffer me therefore to live to repent, and I promise you that neither Inez or her friends shall receive any further annoyance from me!'

'I will take especial care that they do not;' returned Jenkins with a sarcastic grin.'

'My life will at any time be in your hands,' added the poor, trembling coward; 'should I again break my word, Jenkins, I beg of you, I supplicate to you, in the most humble manner do not doom me yet to death!'

'Despicable scoundrel!' ejaculated Jenkins; 'so dead to the sufferings of others; and yet so fearful of suffering himself. Wretch! you deserve to die the death of a dog, and you will do so.'

Blodget groaned and covered his face with his hands.

'Prepare yourself to depart from here in my custody to-morrow night,' said Jenkins, as he moved towards the door of the cell.

'Whither, Jenkins, and for what purpose? Oh, tell me! tell me!' entreated Blodget, his whole frame violently convulsed with the power of his emotions. Jenkins looked at him for a moment in silence, and then replied,—

'You will know soon; at present I shall leave you to form your own conjectures, and to ask your conscience what ought to be your destiny.'

'Stay, Jenkins, I beseech you!' cried the unfortunate prisoner, in delirious accents; but Jenkins had immediately quitted the cell, and securing the door was quickly far out of hearing.

'inquire whether Miss Inez will do me the favor to grant me an interview,' said Jenkins, addressing himself to Gordon, soon after he had entered the parlor, after he quitted the place in which Blodget was confined.

Gordon, without offering any observation, hastened to do as he was bid, and quickly returned with an answer in the affirmative. Jenkins then hurried up stairs, and knocking at the door, was ushered into the presence of Inez.

He paused at the door, and bowed to our heroine with an air of the utmost respect, and he was altogether lost in the admiration of Inez's beauty. Her cheeks had become flushed immediately on her hearing the message from Jenkins, and her heart palpitated violently against her side with rekindled hopes.

'Miss,' at last observed Jenkins, in a respectful tone of voice; 'I have no doubt suffered much in your opinion, from the part which I at first unfortunately enacted in the plot against you by your enemy, Blodget.'

Our heroine attempted to reply, but she was too much confused to do so, and Jenkins continued,

'I am now, however, anxious to make all the reparation in my power, by restoring you to liberty and your friends!'

Inez uttered an exclamation of mingled delight and gratitude, and instantly sunk at the feet of Jenkins, and while the tears gushed from her eyes, she sobbed:

'Oh, thanks! thanks! kind sir, for this—'

Jenkins interrupted her, and gently raised her from her knees.

'Nay, my dear lady,' he said, 'I merit not your thanks; for, probably, had it not been for a certain discovery I by accident made, I might still have taken no interest in your fate.'

'A discovery!' repeated Inez, with a look of astonishment.

'Ay,' answered the captain; 'that you are the daughter of one who once befriended me.'

'Know you then my dear father?'

'Lady,' answered Jenkins, in peculiar accents, 'I have reason to know him, to be unceasing in my gratitude towards him.'

'Oh, say, does he still live?'

'He does!'

'Heaven receive my thanks!' cried our heroine, fervently, clasping her hands, and raising her eyes.

'Miss de Castro, I will at once inform you the nature of the kindness your father did me, and you will then see why from being the accomplice and abetter of Blodget, I have become his enemy and your friend. Some three years since, I crossed the plains from Missouri. By the time we had crossed the mountains our teams had given out—our provisions were exhausted—and many of our people dead. It was at this time that your father, with a party, met with us, and not only aided us with mules and provisions, but remained several days attending my children who were prostrated by fever. It was only during my last visit to the Mission that I met your father and learned that his name was de Castro, and that you were his child. I managed to have word conveyed to him that his daughter was safe, and would soon be restored to his arms. I have now hastened here to carry you back, and devise means to give Blodget up to Justice. This cannot be done so speedily or easily as I could wish, for the villain is master of too many secrets involving perhaps the lives of members of my band, for me to proceed rashly in the matter. Meanwhile be cheerful, Alice will remain with you, and in a few days you will be with your father.'

Inez fervently thanked Jenkins, and throwing herself on her knees poured out her fervent thanks to that power that had shielded her from outrage worse than death.

---

# CHAPTER VIII

The scene we are now about to describe was in a room of a hotel; the time, five o'clock in the morning—the persons present were Belcher Kay, Maretzo, and two or three other noisy and dissipated revellers, whose flushed countenances, blood-shot eyes, and other equally striking symptoms, showed plainly enough that they had been 'making a night of it.'

Kay and the Italian appeared to be the most sober of the company, not that their potations had been less deep or frequent than their companions, but that constant practice had so inured them to the wine cup, that it was long ere they showed any ill-effects from it.

They certainly were particularly noisy and merry, and their companions lent their aid to the conviviality, by knocking down everything the aforesaid said or did, in the most tumultuous manner.

One individual, in the classic language of the drunkard, was 'quite done up,' and was stretched at full length upon the floor, under one of the tables, with his hat for a pillow, and a portion of the carpet for a coverlid; and every now and then he added to the general tumult by a loud snore of the most hoggish description.

The proprietor of the hotel had several times requested the party to *break up*, but as the said party threatened to *break his head* instead, if he interfered with them, he thought it was best to desist from his importunities, and after supplying them with enough wine for the night, he retired to his own chamber, and left them, very reluctantly, to the indulgence of their noisy revels.

At the time we have thought proper to open this scene, it was, as we have before stated, about five o'clock in the morning, and the landlord of the hotel had arisen, and his servants also, and the usual bustle in such places prevailed, but still the debauchees continued their riotous mirth, and it appeared as if they had fully made up their minds to make another day of it, at least.

'The song, Kay, the song, the song; we will have no excuses;' shouted Maretzo.

'Ay, ay, the song, the song, we will have no excuses;' chorused three or four voices, and the man under the table gave a loud snore.

'Oh, the song, ah! well I don't mind trying one, just to keep up the conviviality;' said Kay, who was seated on rather a high chair, with his legs negligently deposited on one end of the table, and twiddling a fine-flavoured cigar in his finger and thumb. 'The song—let me see—ah, what shall it be? Oh, I have it—very good I think you will admit.'

And then without any further ceremony, Kay, who had an excellent voice commenced singing.

The demonstrations of applause that greeted this bacchanalian display, were of the most uproarious kind, and by the time the companions of Maretzo and Kay had given full scope to the exuberance of their delight and approbation, they were one and all 'done up,' and one by one dropped off to sleep, leaving the two above-named gentlemen to the uninterrupted enjoyment of their own society.

'Ha! ha! ha!' laughed Maretzo; 'they are regularly floored, poor devils!'

'Completely finished and done up,' coincided Kay;—'ha! ha! ha!'

'They are not half fellows to be done up with one night's carouse, poor devils ha! ha! ha!' observed Maretzo.

'Poor weak creatures to be knocked down with a dozen or two of wine; ha! ha! ha!' again laughed Kay.

'Not like you and I, Kay;' added Maretzo.

'Not a bit of it.'

'No comparison.'

'A loco-foco to the moon.'

'Half a pint of beer to a pipe of wine.'

'They cannot stand anything!'

'Positively nothing!'

'They're twaddlers!'

'Drivellers!'

'Noodles!'

'Boobies!'

'Nincompoops!'

'Humbugs!'

It may be as well to observe here that these compliments were bestowed upon the party at large, who had been liberally carousing Maretzo and Kay, without expecting the latter to pay a cent of the reckoning, and consequently they may be considered fully entitled to the elegant epithets that were lavishly bestowed upon them.

'You and I are the fellows to do it, Maretzo,' said Kay.

'Positively the very fellows,' coincided his friend.

'We are no skulkers while there is plenty of good wine before us,' added Kay.

'Never think of such a thing.'

'It would ruin our reputation, if we were known to do such a thing.'

'And that would be a most melancholy thing.'

'Positively awful!'

'We will never let the enemy beat us.'

'No, d—n!' returned Spangle;—'but down with it, down with it, and at it again.'

'At it again! Hah! ha! ha!'

'We are wine proof!'

'Full proof?'

'Above proof, by —'

'But talking about women,' observed Kay, 'That Blodget was a devilish fortunate fellow.'

'Cunning rogue!' replied Maretzo; 'he managed his business famously, and has contrived admirably to elude the vigilance of Monteagle and the lady's friends.'

'They have not heard anything of them yet, I believe?'

'Nothing!'

'Poor Monteagle! Ha! ha!'

'Ah! poor fool!'

'I wonder what has become of Monteagle?'

'Oh, he is doubtless still making every inquiry after the lady.'

'And it is my firm belief that Inez will never live to see her father, her lover, or her friends again.'

'I am of the same opinion; a sensitive, high-minded woman like her, will never be able to survive long the misery and degradation which Blodget has heaped upon her.'

'He positively must be a smart scoundrel.'

'I never heard of one equal to him.'

'Such a systematic way as he went to work to accomplish his villainy.'

'The ingenious and complicated plot he devised to bring about the gratification of his wishes.'

'The artful manner in which he contrived to make the simpleton, Jenkins, his dupe, too; the ready tool to further his deep-laid stratagem.'

'He must have had his education in the school of art and vice, certainly.'

'Yes, and been a ready pupil, too.'

'But is it not strange that every stratagem has failed to find the slightest clue to the place of retreat?'

'Wonderful!'

'And then the attempt upon Monteagle's life.'

'Doubtless by some ruffian employed by him.'

'There cannot be a doubt of it.'

'To be sure. Revenge has incited him to it.'

'He is a dangerous fellow to offend.'

'A very devil.'

'At any rate, he does not fail to play the very devil with those who excite his enmity.'

'True.'

'But he must be defeated at last.'

'Certainly there is not much prospect of it at present.'

'Oh, no doubt he will be caught in some of his own snares by and bye.'

'But do you think he has ruined the girl?'

'He is villain enough for anything.'

'He must be a monster, indeed, if he could perpetrate such a crime as that. I must have another glass of wine.'

'Do you think that he who did not hesitate to attempt the life of the father, and the violation of the daughter, would shrink from any thing.'

'But, then, her youth—her innocence.'

'Psha!—he is a stranger to such feelings as they ought to inspire.'

'Why, to be sure, from his general conduct, we have an undoubted right to suppose that he is.'

'And yet I think that he has had some other motive for getting the girl in his power; that he has found her necessary to advance his base schemes.'

There was a pause.

'But that Blodget is really a most terrible fellow,' said Kay.

'Every stratagem, every scheme of rascality, I do believe, that that rascal of rascals is up to.'

'Positively every scheme,' said Maretzo, 'but this is a dry subject, and I must have another glass of wine.'

'I feel to want one myself, too,' observed Kay, filling his glass from the decanter: 'Well, here's wishing that Blodget may soon be here.'

'And Inez restored to her lover and friends,' exclaimed Maretzo.

'Quite safe.'

'Quite safe,' repeated Kay.

'And yet I am afraid there is not much chance of that.'

'Nor I.'

'Leave that consummate scoundrel, Blodget, alone for that.'

'Ay, ay.'

'He would not fail to enforce his wishes.'

'To be sure he would not.'

'And what resistance could she make?'

'None at all.'

'She is so completely in his power.'

'Completely.'

'Without a friend at hand to fly to her rescue.'

'Not a friend; and besides no one knows, or can form the least conjecture whither he has taken her.'

'Not the least shadow of an idea,' said Kay.

'Any person would positively imagine that the fellow had some dealings with the devil,' added Maretzo, 'and that she was conveyed away by magic.'

'That they certainly would,' observed Kay.

'I would not mind a hundred dollars to know where the fellow is.'

'Why, that would be rather awkward, I imagine, Maretzo,' returned Kay, with an expressive grin.

'Ha! ha!' laughed Maretzo, clapping his hand significantly to his pocket; 'finances rather queer, you think? Ha! ha! ha! I understand!'

'Funds low.'

'Ha! ha! ha!'

'It is not a very laughable matter though.'

'Very unpleasant.'

'To be straightened for a few hundreds.'

'Very disagreeable.'

'And people have no faith in the word and honor of gentlemen, now-a-days.'

'But we must do something to raise the wind.'

'That is very evident.'

'Quite certain.'

'Quite.'

'We must make good use of these boobies,' said Kay.

'To be sure. Leave us alone for that,' replied Maretzo.

'Oh, yes, I am certain of that.'

'They are very easy.'

'Poor devils.'

'Fit sport for us.'

'Just the sort of game we like to hunt,' returned Maretzo.

'They have got a few thousands, which they seem bent upon wasting.'

'And we might as well reap the benefit as any other persons.'

'To be sure.'

'And we will too.'

'Oh, there is not the least doubt of that; ha! ha! ha!'

'By the by, we ought not to feel much obliged to Blodget for that affair—'

'No, that was a d—d bore.'

'Remarkably unpleasant.'

'A few hundreds out of our way.'

'Yes.'

'We have mingled in some strange scenes together.'

'You may say that.'

'We have been in luck together.'

'In debt together.'

'In prison together.'

'Damme! we have shared all the smiles and frowns of fortune, and may we soon be on more friendly terms with her than ever.'

'Bravo!'

The two friends quaffed off glass after glass, with as much gusto as if they had only just commenced a night's carouse; and then each crossing their legs in an indolent and careless manner, remained silent for a short time. The sleepers were snoring in concert, and did not seem likely to awake for some time, but to monopolize the coffee-room for a chamber, for that day at least.

After the lapse of a short interval, Maretzo looked up with an expression of countenance, half solemn, and half humorous, and, addressing himself to Kay, says:

'Kay, my boy!'

'Well, my dear fellow,' said Kay.

'I have been thinking, Kay.'

'And what have you been thinking?' interrogated his dissipated companion.

'Why, that we have been a pair of d—d scoundrels!'

'Ha! ha! ha! what a discovery!—why, I have known and felt that long ago, Maretzo,' returned Kay.

'We have taken that which did not belong to us,' added Maretzo, 'and borrowed that which we never repaid.'

'And never meant to repay;' observed Kay, with a laugh.

'We have diddled our tailor; broken the fortunes, and the hearts of innumerable bootmakers, hatters, frizzeurs, laundresses, and other creditors.'

'Very true,' remarked Kay, 'and we are likely enough to break the hearts of a great many more, if they are silly enough to trust us.'

'Ah!' ejaculated Maretzo, and he fetched a very deep sigh, reflectively.

'Ah!' mimicked Kay; 'why, confound me, if you are not getting melancholy.'

'I am becoming penitent,' replied Maretzo, in a tone still half serious, 'I am becoming penitent, Kay.'

'Penitent!'

'Yes, downright compunctious.'

'Ha! ha! ha!'

'Don't laugh, I feel a touch of the serious,' remarked Maretzo, 'I think it is high time that we began to think about a reformation, Kay.'

'Well, positively.'

'Ah! it may be well, positively,' repeated Maretzo, 'and, positively, I wish it to be well.'

'And what is your plan of reformation?' inquired Kay.

'Why, matrimony.'

'Matrimony?'

'Ay, sober wedlock,' answered Maretzo, 'it would be advisable for us to do the steady and the amiable for some time, until we can meet with a favorable match; a handsome sum in the shape of a wedding dowry, and a handsome wife, and then we may settle down into two worthy gentlemen, very patterns of domesticated virtue.'

'Not a bad plan,' said Kay, smiling, 'but it is almost too soon to think about that, yet.'

'Not at all.'

'That is only your opinion.'

'And I have no doubt, as we have hitherto generally agreed, that it will be your opinion also.'

'I cannot make up my mind to be shackled just yet, my dear fellow,' replied Kay.

'Nonsense, you may let the opportunity go by, and then you would repent it, take my word for it.'

'Probably, I might,' said Kay, 'but I shall e'en trust fortune a little while longer.'

'But fortune will not trust you—we owe her too large an account already,' observed Maretzo.

'But I am determined to jilt the jade still further, yet.'

'Mind you do not deceive yourself.'

'Leave me alone for that.'

'After all, if a pretty girl, with a handsome portion is thrown in your way, I do not fear but that I shall be able to make you a convert.'

'Well, we'll leave that till the opportunity offers itself.'

'Be it so.'

'But you are really serious?'

'Cursed serious.'

'Ha, ha, ha! we must have another glass of wine after that,' laughed Kay, 'here's fortune and matrimony.'

'Fortune and matrimony,' responded Maretzo, raising the glass to his lips; and then another pause of a few minutes took place.

'I have been thinking, Kay,' at length Maretzo broke silence, 'that, after all, the whereabouts of Blodget, and Inez may not be so difficult for Monteagle to trace out as hitherto it has proved.'

At this, the door opened, and the landlord entered, saying that a man wished to speak to Kay.

'Tell him to come in. Who the deuce can it be?' said Kay.

'Doubtless one of our fellows,' said Maretzo.

The man now entered.

'Well,' said Kay. 'I'm the person you asked for.'

The visitor went to the door, and turned the key. He then said, in a low tone, 'Is your companion to be trusted?'

'True as steel,' said Kay.

'Blodget is in trouble and needs your assistance. He is at Gordon's house.— Jenkins has informed on him, and he can't leave the house without almost certain death. He wishes you and a person he called Maretzo, to be there to-night. With your aid he can get off, carrying the lady with him. He says he won't mind a couple of thousand, if you can get him out of this scrape.'

'Now, my good fellow, how do we know that this isn't all gas. A trap, may be?' said Kay.

'He told me to tell you, if you doubted me, to remember *the old man in the old house!*'

Kay started, but quickly recovering himself said, 'All right, we'll be on hand.'

The man left the house, and mounting his horse rode to the Mission. At a small house near the church he found Joaquin, by whom he was conducted to Jenkins, who was in company with Monteagle and some Californians, friends of Inez and her family.

The party speedily set off across the country towards the house where Inez was confined. But speedy as they were, they found they had been anticipated by Kay and Maretzo, who had set off to aid Blodget the instant the man had left. On arriving at the house they knocked boldly at the door. Gordon opened it, but upon seeing who the visitors were he attempted to slam it in their faces, but ere he succeeded a long Spanish knife was driven to his heart by Maretzo, and the wretch fell a bleeding corpse on the floor. Blodget was soon released.

'Bear a-hand,' cried Kay. 'We must be out of this d—d quick. If Jenkins or any of his gang arrive, we're gone chickens.'

'One moment,' cried Blodget. 'I'll have this d—d stubborn Spanish b—h if I have to carry her corpse across my saddle!' as he spoke he sprang up stairs.

Alice had overheard what passed for she was sitting by Inez's bedside watching her slumbers.

The brave girl instantly determined to save Inez, even at peril of her own life.

She extinguished the light, and throwing the veil of Inez over her head, and her mantle over her shoulders, she stood with beating heart, as she heard the villain Blodget's steps upon the stairs.

'Inez!' cried the ruffian, as he opened the door of the chamber.

'Who calls me?' said Alice, imitating the voice of Inez.

The ruffian made no reply, but seizing her shrinking form in his arms, he bore her to the front of the ranch, where Kay and Maretzo stood ready to mount, holding a spare horse that they had brought to facilitate Blodget's escape. The ruffian sprang to his horse's back, dragging Alice up before, and dashing the rowels into his horse's flanks, flew off at full speed, followed by Kay and Maretzo.

They had not been gone many moments, ere Jenkins, Monteagle, and their friends arrived. The bloody body of Gordon, which first arrested their attention at the threshold, filled them with dreadful forebodings.

Lights were procured, and Monteagle sought the chamber in which he was told he would find Inez. He burst into the room. A lady lay on the bed. 'Inez!' he shouted.

The lady turned her head, and his eyes fell upon her countenance!

'Gracious Heaven!' he almost shrieked; 'is this some beauteous vision got up to torture me to madness? Inez!—My Inez!'

A wild shriek answered him!—It was no delusion! He sprang forward with delirious speed, just time enough to clasp the fainting form of his long-lost betrothed in his arms!

How shall our weak pen essay the task to describe the scene which followed this strange, this unexpected meeting?

Insensible, Inez was conveyed to an apartment in the cabaret, whither Monteagle followed, and could not be persuaded to leave her sight for an instant.

Again and again he enfolded her in his arms; pressed warm kisses on her lips, her cheeks, her temples, and laughed and wept like a child, by turns!—Then he threw himself upon his knees, clasps his hands vehemently together, and poured forth an eloquent prayer to the most High!

Joaquin began to entertain a fear that the sudden surprise, and so powerful a shock as it must be to his feelings, would have a fatal effect upon his senses; and he did all that he possibly could to calm his emotions.

His efforts were, however, for some time unavailing, but at length he became more tranquilized, and resigning Inez to the care of the persons who had been called in to attend her, he sank into a chair, and covering his face with his hands, gave full vent to the emotions that overflowed his heart, in a copious flood of tears.

Joaquin in this did not attempt to interrupt him, for he well knew what a relief it would be to him, and he turned his eyes from Monteagle to watch the progress which was being made towards the recovery of Inez.

His joy was scarcely less than that of Monteagle, although it did not exhibit itself in so violent a manner, and his heart teemed with gratitude to the Almighty, who had brought about their restoration to each other in so miraculous a manner.

It was not long before Inez was restored to animation; and, looking eagerly around her, she exclaimed:—

'Where is he?—Was it a dream?—Oh, where is Monteagle?'

'He is here, my love, my long lost one!—My only hope!' cried Monteagle, and again they were enfolded to each other's hearts, while further utterance was denied them by the power of their emotions!

We must hastily draw a veil over that scene which the imagination of our readers can depicture far better than any language of ours, however powerful, we could describe it!

Those moments were a foretaste of Heaven, succeeding the torment of purgatory! Their extacy was so great, that they could scarcely believe the evidence of their senses. It was some time ere they could satisfy themselves that they spoke, they breathed, or that they were still inhabitants of this sublunary scene!

But when, by the joint efforts of Joaquin and others, they became more tranquilized, the scene which followed was affecting in the extreme. They rested for a few hours, as they were not sufficiently composed to resume their journey to that home in which they had not together met for so long a period, and where they had never expected to meet again; and their friends, after a short time, left them to themselves, to enter into that mutual explanation, they were each so anxious to obtain.

With what feelings of horror, disgust, and indignation, did Monteagle listen to the recital of his love, but how did his heart overflow with gratitude, when he heard of the manner in which Inez had been enabled to resist the diabolical attempts and importunities of the villain Blodget; and as he pressed her to his heart, he again poured forth his thanks to the Almighty for her preservation from such accumulated and fearful dangers.

'The monster! the fiend!—for he cannot be anything human, although he bears the form of man,' cried Monteagle, speaking of Blodget; 'oh, how I regret that he has been suffered to escape my vengeance!'

'But he will not that of Heaven, dearest,' ejaculated Inez; 'oh, most assuredly that will ere long overtake him in its most terrible form, for the many, the almost unequalled crimes of which he has been guilty!'

'True, my love,' returned Monteagle, and his eyes sparkled with rapture as he gazed upon that dear countenance he had never expected to behold again; 'and oh, if ever atrocity deserved punishment, dreadful will be his doom. To concoct so infernal a plot, by which he tore you from my arms.'

Inez smiled beautifully through her tears, and throwing her fair arms around the neck of Monteagle, the kisses she so fervently pressed upon his lips, convinced him powerfully of her affection.

'Say no more upon that painful subject, my dearest,' she ejaculated; 'let it from this joyful moment be for ever buried in oblivion.'

'It shall, it shall, my sweetest,' replied Monteagle; 'but oh, what a debt of gratitude do I owe to your generous preserver, Jenkins. Would that I could see him, that I might to himself express the power of my feelings. Nothing can ever sufficiently reward that man for the inestimable service he has rendered me.'

'I need not assure you,' rejoined Inez, 'that I most warmly concur in your feelings; and I trust that at some future period, Jenkins may be able to visit us, and receive the demonstrations of our mutual gratitude, and, moreover, be persuaded to quit the life he is at present leading.'

'Pity it is that he should, by some cursed fatality urging him on to crime, be driven from it,' observed Monteagle; 'but I dare say that his offences have never been so heinous as to exclude him from all hope of earthly pardon.'

'No, I cannot believe that they have,' replied Inez; 'but he is so much attached to his present wild life of freedom, and his reckless associates, that I am doubtful whether he will ever be induced to abandon them.'

'My influence and exertions to induce him to do so, shall not be wanting,' said Monteagle. 'Still I am sorry that he should have changed his first determination, namely, to deliver the wretch Blodget into the hands of justice. While I know that villain to be living and still at large, my mind cannot be entirely at rest, for, however watchful and vigilant we may be, after what we have experienced from his villainous artifices, have we not reason to fear that he will devise some means of further annoying us, and gratifying his demonical revenge?'

'Do not, I beg of you, my love,' said our heroine, 'harass your mind by apprehensions.'

'Heaven grant that your surmises may prove correct, Inez,' observed Monteagle; 'but I candidly own that I cannot entirely divest my mind of the fears which I have described; and should anything happen again to you, my love, all my manly fortitude would entirely forsake me, and I should never be able to survive the shock!'

'Pray, Monteagle,' urged Inez, 'if you would not make me miserable, endeavor, struggle to banish such gloomy imaginings from your bosom, and trust to the goodness of Providence which has hitherto so mercifully preserved us, when the darkest snares of villainy sought to ruin and destroy us.'

'For your sake, my own love,' replied Monteagle, once more affectionately and passionately kissing her cheek, 'I will endeavor to do so; still you surely will not blame me for not placing too much confidence in our security, which might prevent me from being watchful and wary to defeat any base plans that might be devised against our future peace?'

'Oh, no, in that you will only act with prudence and wisdom, although, I must repeat that I sincerely trust there will not be found to be any necessity for that precaution. But my poor father—what of him?'

'He is well in body.'

'But how has he supported my absence?'

'Oh, he suffered terribly.'

'Did he give himself up to grief?'

'At first he did—he was as one struck to the earth by a sudden, violent blow. Joaquin, however, roused him from his despondency, by urging the absolute necessity of pursuing the abductors. Thus urged, your father shook off his despondency, and appearing to forget his years, joined in the search for your abductors with all the ardor of youth. Indeed it became almost necessary forcibly to restrain him, lest he should become totally deranged.'

'*Totally* deranged! Then his mind was affected by my loss?'

'Oh, my love,' ejaculated Monteagle, 'Would that heaven had spared me that painful task; but pray be calm and bear the melancholy intelligence with fortitude and resignation.'

'Speak on, speak on; I'm prepared for the worst,' ejaculated our heroine—'Tell me of my poor father.'

'When I left your home the physicians hoped he might recover, as at intervals reason seemed returning, when he would call for his daughter Inez, and then relapse into unconsciousness.'

'Oh, let us hasten to my poor dear father.'

They were soon in their saddles, and on road to the Mission.

# CHAPTER XIX

## The Seducer's Terrible End.

A few nights after Blodget's escape found him walking the streets of San Francisco, but disguised as he thought too effectually to be recognized by any eye, however sharp.

There was a cloud upon Blodget's brow as he emerged from the court into the semi-obscurity of Montgomery street, and his mind was evidently ill at ease. He tried to hum a fashionable opera air when he had walked a little distance, but there seemed something in his throat which choked him, and the sounds died upon his lips. Then he quickened his pace, when a young female emerged from a street which he was passing, and laid her hand upon his arm. He turned his head, and beheld Carlotta.

She was thinner than when he had seen her last, and looked as if she had recently been ill; but her dark eyes were as lustrous as then, and there was the same gloss upon her raven hair. At the moment that she emerged from the shade of the court, and laid her hand upon his, there was a strange and almost indescribable expression upon her dark countenance, but it passed away as quickly as a flight of birds over a stream, and when Blodget's eyes met hers, they read nothing therein but pleasure at meeting him again.

'Ah, my little wild rose of the islands!' said he, 'what are you doing at this hour of the night, when all such pretty wild birds should be in their nests.'

'Well, I can't say I was looking for you,' returned Carlotta, 'but I am glad that I have met you, nevertheless. But I should ask you where you have been wandering, you naughty man?'

'Oh, I have been to the theatre, and then walked this way with a friend,' returned Blodget. 'But where are you staying—can you take me home with you?'

'Fie!' said Carlotta, playfully.

'I really cannot part with you, my charmer,' said Blodget. 'If you cannot take me to your quarters, wherever they may be, you must come somewhere with me.'

'You must not think of going where my people are,' observed the Chilean girl, 'remember how near the detection of our amour was costing our lives.'

'Then come with me, my beauty,' said Blodget. 'There is a house not far from here which will suit our purpose, and I shall not part with you until daylight.'

'Then I go with you, Blodget,' said Carlotta. 'Promise me that you will not seek to detain me more than an hour, and I will not refuse you the happiness you covet.'

Blodget promised, and the Chilean girl accompanied him to an accommodation-house in the neighborhood, where they were conducted to a neatly furnished bedchamber on the first floor.

'We shall have time to drink a bottle of champagne in the hour that you have promised to remain with me,' observed Blodget, and he gave the girl, who had preceded them with a light, some silver to procure it.

They sat down, and Blodget threw his arm round the waist of his dark-eyed companion, and drawing her towards him, impressed a kiss upon her lips. She smiled upon him, but her lips did not give back the kiss, and there was a glitter in her night dark eyes at the moment which was not the radiance which springs from happiness or love. Blodget, however, failed to detect anything unusual or peculiar in the expression of that glance. The wine was brought, and placed upon a small round table convenient to Blodget's hand, and he filled the glasses, handing one to Carlotta and taking one himself.

'The sparkling juice will bring back to your dark cheeks a glow that seems wanting there,' said he, as he sat down the glasses and immediately refilled them.

'Come, drink,' he cried.

'It will be the last time we'll drink together.'

'Why, what the deuce makes you think so?' said Blodget.

'I don't know,' replied the girl, 'but I have said it, and you'll see if it don't come to pass.'

'D—d nonsense,' cried Blodget, laughing, and then he drew his companion on his knee, and kissed her repeatedly and eagerly.

Carlotta was silent, but she reclined her dark cheek against her seducer's, and quietly and adroitly drew from her pocket a little phial containing some liquid. Concealing the phial in her hand, she then threw her arm over Blodget's shoulder, and noiselessly drawing the tiny cork, poured the contents of the phial into his glass.

'Another glass of champagne, my glow-worm,' said Blodget, 'and the soft delights of love, the thrilling joys of warm and impassioned nature are ours.'

Carlotta removed her arm from his shoulder as he turned slightly to reach his wine, and while she kept her eyes upon the glasses to observe that he gave her the one that she had drank from before, she returned the empty phial to her pocket.

'I suppose nothing unpleasant came of our dalliance?' said Blodget, in a half interrogative tone, as he handed the girl her glass.

'Why do you suppose so? Ought you not rather to suppose just the reverse? Was not something unpleasant naturally to be expected?'

'Well, perhaps I might have supposed so,' returned Blodget, deprecatingly, and a little disconcerted by the girl's reply.

There was a moment's pause, and both sat with their glasses in their hands, Blodget's eyes fixed upon the floor, the girl surveying the countenance of her seducer, as if she were trying to read his thoughts.

'Well, what was it?' Blodget at length inquired.

'A boy,' returned Carlotta. 'It died, and I was glad of it, for if it had lived it might have been as faithless as his father.'

'Do you want to quarrel?'

'No.'

'For heaven's sake cease,' exclaimed Blodget, suddenly raising the wineglass to his lips, and emptying it at a draught.

Carlotta drank her wine quickly as he spoke, and rose from his knee, where she had contrived to sit while upbraiding him with his inconstancy and duplicity. Her dark eyes were fixed upon his countenance, which changed the moment he had swallowed the wine, his lips becoming white, and the expression of his features becoming ghastly and cadaverous.

'You are a dead man and I am avenged!' exclaimed the girl in a hissing whisper; and then she glided towards the door, and turned the key in the lock.

A faint groan which seemed to struggle feebly and faintly upwards, was the only sign of vitality which Blodget gave, and then his head fell upon his breast and his arms fell powerless at his side.

Quickly and silently Carlotta drew the sheets from the bed, knotted them together, and then fastened one end securely to the bedpost nearest the window; this done, she noiselessly raised the sash, and looked out. The night was dark and foggy, but she could see that there was a small yard below, with a door in the wall, which opened into a court at the rear of the house. Dropping one end of the sheets from the window, she immediately got out upon the sill, and grasping the sheet firmly with both hands, descended in safety into the yard. She could hear laughter and the tinkling of glasses in the back parlor, but the shutters were closed, and noiselessly unbolting the door in the yard fence, she hurried swiftly out, and in a few minutes was far away.

---

# CHAPTER XX

## The Return to the Mission.

Let us now rejoin Inez and Monteagle whom we left on their road to the Mission.

What powerful sensations of unspeakable delight rushed through the veins of Inez, and monopolized every feeling of her heart, when those scenes which she had never expected to behold again, once more burst upon her vision. The tumult of rapturous and conflicting ideas that darted to her brain, were almost overwhelming, and, although her tongue was eager to give expression to her sentiments, the strength of her emotions would not permit her to give utterance to a single syllable. She looked in the countenance of her lover with an expression of the most unbounded affection and delight, and she fully perceived that he reciprocated her feelings. Tears filled his eyes, and taking her hand he pressed it to his lips with eloquent silence.

Not the slightest change appeared to have taken place in everything upon which the eyes of our heroine rested, since last she had gazed upon those well known scenes. The bright beams of a silvery moon were shining serenely upon every thing around, and a melancholy silence, so consonant with her own state of mind, prevailed. But, alas, she reflected, what a change had taken place in the home of her childhood! That home which had once abounded in every happiness that the human mind could wish for, was now the abode of sorrow; that fond parent, whose every joy and hope were centered in her, was a maniac and would be insensible to the felicity of her restoration to his arms.

This last thought was too afflicting for endurance, and overcome by her emotion she leant her head upon the bosom of Monteagle, and burst into an hysterical flood of tears.

In vain did Monteagle endeavor to tranquilize her feelings, he felt how powerful was the cause she had for sorrow, and the anguish he endured was scarcely less than her own.

Joaquin exerted himself to the utmost to calm the feelings of them both, and he at length succeeded.

Monteagle, we should have mentioned before, had taken the precaution to send forward a person to the Mission, with a letter, making them briefly acquainted with the fortunate meeting which had taken place between him and our heroine, and of their coming, so that the surprise might not be too sudden for them; and they were, therefore, fully aware that they would exert themselves to the utmost to meet the unexpected pleasure which awaited them; the more especially as the precarious and lamentable situation of Senor de Castro rendered the greatest care necessary.

At length the elegant, but unostentatious, mansion, burst upon their vision, and Providence imbued the mind of Inez with a calm feeling of joy, which she had never experienced before. Everything seemed to dance before her eyes to welcome her return to that once happy home, and the horses appeared to move with the most tedious slowness, as they cantered along the road which led to the garden gates.

They reached those gates; they were already open, and standing to receive them were beings endeared to them by every affectionate and grateful feeling.

Let not the too presumptuous pen attempt to describe the scene which followed, language is by far too weak to convey any idea of it. Tears, sobs, and broken sentences of unbounded transport, burst from the overcharged bosoms of each individual; and then Inez felt herself led along the avenue which conducted to the hall.

Although her eyes were dimmed by tears, and her thoughts were so fully occupied, our heroine could yet behold several of the old domestics standing in the path, who, as she passed, raised their hands and eyes towards Heaven, and gave utterance to their simple, but forcible, exclamations of gratitude to the Most High for the restoration of their 'dear young lady' to her home and friends.

Another moment and Inez found herself in the well known parlor, endeared to her by so many fond remembrances and associations; and sinking on her knees, she clasped her hands fervently towards Heaven, and gave full vent to the expression of her ardent and spontaneous ejaculations of thanksgiving to the Almighty disposer of all events for her deliverance.

No one offered to interrupt her, they were also too much occupied with the feelings of astonishment and unspeakable delight that filled their bosoms. But at length, Inez having ended her solemn prayer, suddenly arose from her knees, and looking eagerly around the room, she said:

'But where is he? He is not here! Where is the poor old man—that he is not present to snatch his unfortunate daughter once more to his heart, and weep his tears of joy upon her bosom! My father—my poor, dear father; where is he?'

'My dear Inez,' replied the Padre; 'I can fully appreciate the anxiety of your feelings; but pray endeavor to restrain them. Your father has retired to his chamber and sleeps—do not disturb him lest—'

'And think you,' interrupted our heroine, with the most violent emotion depicted in her countenance; 'think you that I can rest calmly one moment without beholding that unfortunate, that doting parent from whom I have been so long and so cruelly separated? No—no—no—I will go to him; not an instant—'

Quickly up the stairs which led to the well known chamber of her father, our heroine bounded, but when she arrived at the door, she paused; a deathlike faintness came over her, she breathed short, and she was unable to move a step further.

Monteagle and others entreated her to return to the parlor, and to defer the trying scene till the morning, but she answered them by a look which fully convinced them of her determination, and they therefore desisted.

In a few moments she partially recovered herself, but still she had not sufficient courage or resolution to enter the chamber.

She stood and listened, supported by the arm of her lover, and her ears caught the sound of the breathing of the patient, every respiration going to her heart like a stream of fire.

In a moment the breathing sounds ceased, and all was still as death.

'He sleeps, he sleeps, and probably dreams of her who—'

'Hark! hark!' hastily interrupted our heroine; 'those sounds—do listen;—those words—those words—my heart will burst!'

They listened with breathless attention, and Monteagle supported the form of Inez, in a state of agony too powerful for description. In low and plaintive tones, sufficient to draw tears from the eyes of the most insensible individual, the unfortunate de Castro was singing, apparently in his sleep, the words of a song Inez had so often sung to please him, and which brought to the memory many powerful and agonizing recollections.

'God! God! support me!' gasped forth Inez, clinging to the arm of her lover, and her whole frame convulsed with anguish.

'Father! father! dear, dear father! I can bear no more,' cried Inez; and tearing herself from the hold of Monteagle, she rushed into the chamber, and darted to the side of the bed.

Senor de Castro was sitting up in the bed when Inez entered the room, and was staring vacantly around him. His countenance had undergone little or no perceptible change; the ruddy glow of health was on his cheeks, and so calm and serene was its expression, that it seemed almost impossible that his mind could be in the deplorable condition in which it was.

On beholding Inez and the others enter, he exhibited emotion, but when his eyes rested upon the former, a sweet smile irradiated his features, and laughing with all the joyousness of a child, he exclaimed:—

'Beautiful!—oh, how beautiful!—what a bright and lovely vision!—Her very self!—So like her!—But 'tis only fancy—only fancy—ha! ha! ha!—How beautiful!'

'Father! father!—dear, dear father! Do you not know me? Oh, God! what a bitter trial is this!' frantically sobbed forth the distracted Inez, as she threw her arms around the poor old man's neck, and pressed warm and delirious kisses upon his lips.

In a few moments Senor de Castro began to regain his scattered senses, and gazed round him like one slowly awaking from a fearful dream.

He at length fully recognized his child. Then followed a scene too affecting for pen or pencil to describe.

But one subject remained to cloud their happiness. It was the absence of Alice Hewlett, of whose abduction, by Blodget, they learned from the old woman at the ranch. Bitterly did Inez deplore the sad fate which had befallen the lovely 'Squatter's Daughter.'

Brown fled upon hearing of the arrest of the gang.

Monteagle was of course cleared of all complicity in the robbery of the store, by this confession, and Mr. Vandewater gave him a share in his business as some recompense for his unjust dismissal.

The little church at the Mission was soon after gaily decorated, and before its humble altar the hands of Inez and Monteagle were united. Their hearts had been so from the day our hero bore the fainting maiden in safety from the flames.

THE END.